Snowbound "grabbed me from the first page and kept me on the edge of my seat until nearly the end. I love the British feel of it and enjoyed the writer's style tremendously. So if you're looking for a very well written, fast paced, lesbian romance—heavy on the action and blood and light on the romance—this is one for your ereader or bookshelf."
—*C-Spot Reviews*

Desolation Point

Desolation Point "is the second of Cari Hunter's novels and is another great example of a romance action adventure. A real page turner from beginning to end. Ms. Hunter is a master at an adventure plot and comes up with more twists and turns than the mountain trails they are hiking. Well written, edited and crafted, this is an excellent book and I can't wait to read the sequel."—*Lesbian Reading Room*

"Cari Hunter provides thrills galore in her adventure/romance *Desolation Point*. In the hands of a lesser writer and scenarist, this could be pretty rote and by-the-book, but Cari Hunter breathes a great deal of life into the characters and the situation. Her descriptions of the scenery are sumptuous, and she has a keen sense of pacing. The action sequences never drag, and she takes full advantage of the valleys between the peaks by deepening her characters, working their relationship, and setting up the next hurdle."—*Out In Print*

Tumbledown

"Once again Ms. Hunter outdoes herself in the tension and pace of the plot. We literally know from the first two pages that the evil is hunting them, but we are held on the edge of our seats for the whole book to see what will unfold, how they will cope, whether they will survive—and at what cost this time. I literally couldn't put it down. *Tumbledown* is a wonderful read."—*Lesbian Reading Room*

"Even though this is a continuation of the *Desolation Point* plot, this is an entirely different sort of thriller with elements of a police procedural. Other thriller authors (yes, I'm looking at you, Patterson and Grisham) could take lessons from Hunter when it comes to writing these babies. Twists and turns and forgotten or unconventional weaponry along with pluck and spirit keep me breathless and reading way past my bedtime."—*Out In Print*

Reviewers Love The Dark Peak Series

No Good Reason

"Truly terrible things, as well as truly lovely things, abound in the mystery-thriller *No Good Reason*. The plot takes off immediately as a captive woman makes her bloody escape and the— Well, this is not a romance, dear reader, so brace yourself…After visiting America for her last two books, *Desolation Point* and *Tumbledown*, Hunter returns to the land of hot tea and the bacon butty in her latest novel. Our heroines are Detective Sanne Jensen and Dr. Meg Fielding, best mates forever and sometimes something more. Their relationship is indefinable and complicated, but not in a hot mess of drama way. Rather, they share unspoken depths, comfortably silly moments, rock-solid friendship, and an intimacy that will make your heart ache just a wee bit."—*C-Spot Reviews*

"Cari Hunter is a master of crime suspense stories. *No Good Reason* brings tension and drama to strong medical and police procedural knowledge. The plot keeps us on the edge of our metaphorical seat, turning the pages long into the night. The setting of the English Peak District adds ambiance and a drama of its own without excluding anybody. And through it all a glimmer of humour and a large dose of humanity keep us engaged and enthralled."—*Curve Magazine*

"This novel is dark and brooding and brilliantly written. Hunter transports you right into the world she creates and keeps you firmly in the grip of the icy weather, craggy rocks and oppressive atmosphere."—*The Lesbian Review*

Cold to the Touch

"Right from the beginning I was hooked. Hunter never gives the reader a chance to get bored. This book is intelligently written, and gives you an action packed adventure, with great characters."
—*The Romantic Reader Blog*

"Cari Hunter writes decidedly good stories. She combines excellent plot lines, which twist and turn, with crime drama and just the right amount of thriller to keep us on the edge of our seats. Each book feels distinctive, enjoyably new and refreshingly different to standard crime dramas. *Cold to the Touch* is a sequel to the excellent *No Good Reason*, and fans of Sanne and Meg will love where she takes them this time. *Cold to the Touch* is more than strong enough to stand alone, but why miss an excellent series?"
—*Lesbian Reading Room*

"The mystery was well told and the gradual build-up of tension was ideal. Interweaving it with Meg's story was a brilliant touch. I felt scared for her and hoped Sanne would be able to help before it was too late.The romantic side story was subtle but just right. The murder case took precedence as it should in a police procedural."
—*Inked Rainbow Reads*

A Quiet Death

"This cracking good mystery also has a thorough respect for the various ethnic subcultures it explores. I learned things, which is never bad for a reader. Moreover, it has a distinctly British flavour, not pandering to American tastes. Of the three of Hunter's books I've read and reviewed for this blog, this has got to be my favorite. Interesting plot, great characters, muscular prose—I'm more than chuffed. I'm potty about it. And that's no bollocks."—*Out in Print*

"Cari Hunter is my go-to author for lesbian fiction's mystery/thriller category. Each and every one of her books is engaging, fast-paced, well thought out, and well written. *A Quiet Death*, the third in the Dark Peak series, is no different. Hunter has not only a talent for bringing her characters to life and dropping the reader into the scene but also for balancing dark, deadly serious story lines with levity and humor so the reader doesn't get lost in despair over the heartbreaking cases."—*C-Spot Reviews*

By the Author

Snowbound

Desolation Point

Tumbledown

Alias

The Dark Peak Series:

No Good Reason

Cold to the Touch

A Quiet Death

Visit us at www.boldstrokesbooks.com

ALIAS

by
Cari Hunter

2018

This Trade Paperback Original Is Published By
Bold Strokes Books, Inc.
P.O. Box 249
Valley Falls, NY 12185

First Edition: June 2018

Credits
Editor: Cindy Cresap
Production Design: Stacia Seaman
Cover Design by Sheri (hindsightgraphics@gmail.com)

Acknowledgments

Thanks and a Raspberry Ruffle bar to the BSB gang, especially Sandy for dealing with all the behind the scenes stuff, and my editor, Cindy, for her feedback, support, and cookery discussions in the margins. To Sheri for getting the cover absolutely spot-on. To Kel and Col for fielding last minute police procedural enquiries at stupid o'clock. To all the folks who read my books, send feedback, write reviews, and happily chat about daft stuff online. To the wonderful Nicki Vincent for giving my characters not just a voice but a heart and a soul on audio. And to Cat, for the hours she spends unwinding my sleep-deprived prose, but mostly for making me feel so loved.

Acknowledgments

For Cat

Always

CHAPTER ONE

I know she's dead. I know it without feeling for a pulse, but I go through the motions anyway, pressing on her cold wrist and counting silently to ten. When I let go, her arm hangs limp, its blood-sticky fingers grazing my cheek every time the wind rocks the car. She was breathing at first, three or four desperate gurgles a minute, her staved-in chest moving all to shit and her head bobbing with the effort, but she gave in before I was able to get my hand free, before I could try to help her or touch her or let her know she wasn't on her own. Before I could remember her name. Her seat belt is stopping her from falling onto me, her body contorted around it like a puppet with its strings cut. And I still can't remember her name.

I can't actually remember a fucking thing, but I realise after a few seconds of blind panic that I'm going to die here too unless I move.

Moving hurts. It hurts so much I start whimpering, the sound fading in and out along with the scream of the storm and the ballistic rattle of rain on the passenger side. Details come to me in fragments, logical pieces of information disrupted by the pain and the sheer terror of being stuck in the dark with a woman I probably killed. I must have been driving, because my legs are folded beneath the steering wheel, and at some point my left arm has snapped. I can't see much, but I can feel the grind of broken bones, and there's an open wound where they've poked through the skin. Blinking blood from my eyes, I unfasten my seat belt with the hand that still works. Gravity immediately kicks in, and I slip sideways in the seat, smacking the grounded window hard enough to force a yelp from me. I spend an untold amount of time struggling to stay conscious, blackness creeping over my vision and then relenting to provide another glimpse of the ghost-white arm dangling above me.

A flash of lightning shows that the car is tucked on its side between two tall trees, as if I'd meant to park it there. Branches creak and bow, firing down the occasional pinecone, and the unpredictable bangs on the bodywork fuck up my nerves as I shift onto my knees.

"Phone," I mumble through thick lips and a couple of chipped teeth. I'm sure I have a mobile, but I don't know where I usually keep it. My pocket? A bag? Or chucked in the glove compartment, out of reach in front of the dead woman? I pat my jeans and coat, finding nothing but a wallet. A stabbing sensation beneath my breast tells me I have broken ribs, and with no warning whatsoever, I retch and vomit onto my lap.

"Fucking hell."

The car seems to spin, and my chin hits my chest as my head lolls. I cough through a mouthful of bile and blood, grimacing; the taste is foul enough to jerk me awake like smelling salts. There's a half-empty bottle of water jammed by the handbrake, and I use it to swill my mouth out. With the bitterness and some of the fog cleared, I restart the search for my mobile, managing to drag my legs free until I'm curled in an uncomfortable ball on the driver's door. I spot my phone wedged in the crack of the seat, still connected to its in-car charging lead, and I tug it loose, my fingers clumsy and slow. A spider's web of splintered glass covers its screen, but it comes to life when I tap it, displaying a factory-set wallpaper and a signal strength that reads "Emergency Calls Only." I dial 999, my hand shaking so hard as I put the phone to my ear that I'm scared I'll lose my hold on it. I hear a faint tone, then nothing.

"Hello?" No one answers, and terror pitches my voice up a notch. "Hello? Is anyone there?"

Again I catch the slightest whisper of sound, but it vanishes at once, buried in a buzz that overwhelms everything. The solution is so simple it almost eludes me. I switch the phone to my other ear, the one that's not leaking fluid down my cheek, and interrupt a woman asking which service I require.

"Ambulance," I say and then clear my throat and repeat myself with more conviction. "Ambulance and police." I peer out the cracked windscreen as if all the answers lie beyond it. "But I don't know where I am."

"It's all right, just stay on the line. Can you tell me what's happened?"

I nod, calmed by her assurance. "The car crashed. It's rolled, and I can't see the road."

"Are you injured?"

"Yes."

"Are you trapped in the vehicle?"

I have two ways out: the windscreen, or up and over the dead woman.

"No, I'm not trapped," I say, although the thought of climbing over the body or shoving through the glass drenches me in cold sweat.

She asks me about my breathing and chest pains, and warns me against moving. It's probably good advice, but I doubt anyone will find me unless I get back to the road.

"Are you on your own?" she asks after a pause to let me pant through a spasm ripping across my ribs.

"No, but she's dead." A sob chokes me. I can't tell whether it's grief or self-pity, and I wipe snot from my nose while the woman holds an urgent conference with a third party. She's all business when she comes back on the line.

"The police are attempting to trace your mobile signal, so you need to leave your phone switched on. It'll take longer than it does on the telly, but they should be able to narrow your location down to a few hundred yards. Is your phone fully charged?"

I check the screen, straining to read the figure by the battery signal. "It's at forty-one percent."

"That's not too bad." She sounds as if she wants to come out here herself to wrap me in blankets and ply me with hot chocolate. "It might be a while before they get to you, so I'd better not keep you on the line, but I'll call you every fifteen minutes to see how you are. Is that all right?"

"Yes, thank you," I lie instinctively, loath to upset her. I don't want her to go. I don't want her to leave me with the corpse and the horror film soundtrack outside the car. I'm so scared. I'm struggling to pull enough air into my battered lungs, and she must hear some of my hysterics, because she starts up a soothing recitation of words that I can't really distinguish but that stop me hyperventilating.

"What's your name?" she asks, as I steady myself by leaning against the steering wheel.

The question bewilders me. I haven't got a fucking clue. I trap the phone between my ear and shoulder while I fumble the wallet from my pocket. According to a bus pass marked "GMPTE," my name is Rebecca Elliott, but nothing about it feels familiar, and I stutter when I read it out to her.

"I'm Margy," she tells me. "Margy Lloyd. Are you okay for me to hang up now?"

"Yes, that's okay," I say, and Margy tells me to sit tight an instant before the line goes dead.

I can't sit tight. I'm calmer, but it's getting harder for me to breathe, and the right side of my chest doesn't seem to be moving properly. I can't manage the climb one-handed, so I wait for the moon to peek out between the dispersing storm clouds, and then I eye the windscreen, spotting a bulls-eyed section that might give if I put the boot in. And I am wearing boots: sensible hiking-type boots that don't appear to have seen much action.

Getting into a position where I can set my feet against the glass leaves me lightheaded and limp as a wrung-out dishcloth. I almost miss Margy's first check-in call, dropping the phone when it starts to ring and then able only to grunt at intervals during her overly cheerful but noncommittal "They're making good progress" update. I gasp an acknowledgement and—before common sense can intervene—aim a kick at the windscreen as soon as she hangs up. The glass doesn't break, but a good-sized portion peels forward, encouraging me to inch over the dashboard. There's nothing to hold on to as I push outside. The crash has torn the car bonnet into jagged pieces, and I slide across them, my clothing protecting me from the worst of the sharp edges, though it does nothing to soften my landing. My knees buckle as my feet hit pine needles and rocks, and I pitch forward, sobbing through the agony while sleet soaks my face and hair, and the smell of damp earth gradually overpowers that of blood.

Margy phones me again as I lie there, her voice animated and far too loud, telling me that the police and an ambulance have been dispatched and that they should be close by in no more than thirty minutes.

"Where am I?" I ask her.

"You're just off the A5. Not far from Capel Curig." She speaks slowly, sounding out the syllables.

"Capel Curig," I repeat, and she must detect my incomprehension because she tries to clarify.

"The Snowdonia National Park, near the Glyders mountains." She pauses and then pares things down to the absolute basics. "You're in Wales, love."

"Right." The information means nothing to me. My head aches, and I start shivering as she disconnects. The temptation to stay on the ground and hope someone finds me is almost overwhelming. Instead I use a tree for leverage to haul myself upright.

"Aw, Christ."

My backside hits the tree, and I bend double, grabbing my bad arm and waiting for the pain to settle to something halfway manageable. It doesn't even get close, though, so I opt for distraction instead, unwinding the woollen scarf from my neck to fashion into a sling. I shudder as I use my teeth to pull the knot taut, the sensation of biting down on wool a more mundane sort of unpleasant.

Supported by the full width of the scarf, the shattered bones stop shifting, and my queasiness eases a fraction. The blood covering my forearm is tacky enough to stick the fabric in place, and I take advantage of the adhesive effect, hoping I'll be suitably sedated when it has to be peeled away again. I straighten in increments, breathing through my nose and gripping the tree trunk so fiercely that I drive wedges of bark beneath my fingernails. Still crooked and swaying like a landlubber on high seas, I wait again for the moon and then trace the route the car took down the embankment. I can't accurately gauge the distance, so I count the trees we bounced off—seven or eight—and wonder how the hell I survived. Debris glints in the silver light: the bumper, impaled and standing proud in the forest floor, dozens of multicoloured shards of glass, and a small holdall that has ripped open and scattered its contents. The trees crowd together, blocking my view of the road, but it must be up there somewhere. The car is a Ford Focus, built for commuting, not wilderness expeditions.

Following the trenches carved through the undergrowth should point me in the right direction. The wide swath of destruction meanders somewhat, but that won't add much to the overall distance. I nod as I formulate my plan. It sounds straightforward and feasible in my head: walk up the hill and wait on the road until help arrives, but flaws become apparent when I take my first few steps. My legs are wobblier than watered-down jelly, and I can't seem to pull in enough air through my nose or my mouth. I manage to stagger about fifty yards before I stub my toes on a rock. The sheer insult pushes me over the edge, and I sit on the rock's mossy surface and cry. I can't do this. I don't even know whether I want to, because surviving will mean facing consequences; it will mean people pointing their fingers at me and telling me this was my fault. They won't believe the gaps in my memory. Why would they? They're so damn convenient that I doubt them myself.

My breathing calms the longer I sit here. If I tilt my head a certain way, I can hear birds heralding the as-yet invisible dawn with melodic call and response. Things rustle in the leaf litter, making up for lost time now that the wind has dropped and the sleet has given way to occasional flurries of proper snowflakes. I don't feel cold or frightened anymore, just tired and a bit woozy. I ignore my phone when it rings. The shrill peal sends some small creature scuttling for cover, and I whisper an apology for invading its turf and fucking everything up.

The ringing cuts off and then starts again. I jab a finger on "Accept," succeeding only in smearing claret across the screen. The noise stops, replaced shortly afterward by a thready voice, and I raise the phone, surprised that I managed to answer it.

"Hello?"

Silence. I adjust the phone, but I've remembered to use the ear that's not humming and pulsing along to my heartbeat, and it makes no difference.

"Hello?" I repeat. The name of the every-fifteen-minutes woman escapes me. "Is anyone there?"

I concede defeat, and the phone bounces off my lap and comes to rest against a pinecone that may as well be a mile beyond my reach.

"Fuck it," I whisper, content to sit and quietly expire, surrounded by birdsong and snowflakes and a sense of peace—a peace that's obliterated as someone yells, "Rebecca!"

I react more to the disturbance than the name, lifting my hand as a child might in class.

"Here," I mutter half-heartedly, before remembering that people have gone to a lot of trouble to find me. I try harder. "Here! Over here!"

Standing would demand more strength than I have. I stay put and watch torch beams slash across the forest floor, until sheer bloody-mindedness gets me to my feet. It can't keep me there, though, and the rock grazes my back as I crumple. The movement turns a light toward me, the thud of approaching boots scattering the last of the nocturnal critters.

"Rebecca? Hey, can you open your eyes for me?" The woman's voice is gentle but insistent, a pleasant lilt rolling her words up and down. "I've got her," she says in a more authoritative tone. "About two-fifty yards from the reg plate. No sign of the car. Get the paramedics here ASAP." Her hands cup my face as she finishes her update. She's wearing leather gloves, and I flinch, shoving back against the rock, unable to see anything in the glare of her torch. "No, no, stay still," she says. "The paramedics will be here in a few minutes."

I try to ask her name, but the question gets lost in a wet gargle and a mouthful of blood.

"Jesus," she hisses. She uses a tissue to clean my chin. I don't tell her that I've already been sick on my knees.

"Thanks," I say, managing to keep the splatter to a minimum this time.

"My name is Bronwen Pryce," she says, answering my question more by luck than judgment, folding the tissue to an untainted side and dabbing again. "Detective Sergeant Bronwen Pryce. Are you a 'Rebecca' or a 'Becky'?"

I have no idea. "Rebecca," I hazard, hoping that family or friends will set me right on that one. Guessing makes me nervous, and I want to be forthright with this complete stranger who's wiping gore off my face. "The car's about fifty, maybe sixty yards that way, on its side."

Pryce's gaze follows my pointed finger. I can't see her clearly, just a lot of dark clothing with curls of dark hair slipping out from beneath a dark woolly hat.

"We'll find it, don't worry," she tells me. "Is the woman you were with still in the car?"

I nod, intensifying the dizziness that accompanies even the mildest of movements. Spots dance on my eyeballs, and I clamp my teeth together, determined not to vomit on the detective sergeant.

"Can you tell me her name?" she asks.

I shake my head, recognising my mistake too late to prevent the wave of nausea. I gag, groaning at the wrench in my chest, and slip sideward onto cool, wet leaves. Pryce shouts something incomprehensible, and several voices reply, reinforcements closing in on our position. I'm terrified of fainting, but I feel as if I'm being smothered. A hand curls around mine, its skin warm and soft. Pryce. She's taken her glove off.

CHAPTER TWO

N o. Don't, please. I need…"
　　　　I need to sit up, but they're laying me flat and strangling me with a hard collar. Hands hold me down and fasten straps across my torso and limbs. Air blasts onto my face, and the babble of voices ceases as padded blocks are set against my ears. A face appears in my periphery, an unfamiliar blond-haired bloke wearing a high-vis jacket. He says something to me, punctuating it with a strained smile before shuffling out of view again.

I can't see Pryce either, but I hear her say, "English, lads," and the man reappears, looking sheepish.

"Sorry, love." He enunciates each word as if I'm daft, not deaf. "We're going to carry you up to the ambulance now, where we can take a better look at you. How's the pain?"

"Better," I tell him. Whatever they've given me has dulled things to a tolerable level and taken the sickness with it. The cradle I'm secured in rises and sways on his command, with Pryce lifting one side of the head end. Her brow creases with effort as the embankment becomes steeper, and she breathes through her mouth in little pants. The journey seems to take hours as the team slide and struggle with the awkward weight, and I'm on the verge of insisting they lower me and let me walk when Pryce catches my eye.

"Almost there," she says, and seconds later, blue and red strobes illuminate her face. She's sweating despite the cold, and she heaves a relieved sigh when her boots hit the tarmac.

The stretcher teeters on the guard rail while everyone swaps positions, and I glimpse forensic markers highlighting a four-wheeled skid that terminates at a missing section of the crash barrier. The road is narrow and unlit but straight, and my traumatised brain draws one conclusion: too fast, you fucking idiot.

Bright overhead lights and warmer air welcome us into the ambulance. The paramedics begin to cut off my clothes, and I close my eyes gratefully as Pryce covers me with a thick blanket. She speaks to the men in Welsh, taking my clothing from them and folding it into paper evidence bags. They're all preoccupied with their respective tasks, and no one is telling me anything. I feel the cold metal of a stethoscope on my chest and watch the blond man frown as he moves the disc around and presses with growing insistence. I stare at the fluid draining from a bag above my head and ignore the cuff squeezing my good arm. I'm trembling and nauseous again, and the lurch of the vehicle pulling away sends bile into the back of my mouth. I swallow, my throat working convulsively, and Pryce shouts a warning an instant before the ambulance stops and my cradle is flipped onto its side. A tube is forced between my lips, sucking out a stream of red and yellow. I watch the colours swirl together until my vision blurs. Then I close my eyes and let it all disappear.

There's no gentle awakening like you see on the telly. No private room with a remote-controlled bed and a kindly nurse to bathe my forehead. Instead I'm pinned by the glare of a surgical spotlight, and someone seems to be shoving a drill bit into my chest. I quickly establish that flight isn't possible, so I fight, lashing out with my arm and landing a weak punch on a woman's breast. She steps aside, preventing my second attempt by catching my wrist in a loose grip. Her surgical gloves are slick with fresh blood.

"It's all right, Rebecca, you're in the hospital," she says. Then, over her shoulder, "Bron, could you?" She offers my hand, and Pryce comes across to take it, raising it to clear the field for whatever the doctor is doing.

"Hey," Pryce says, somehow managing to cut through the ruckus and focus my attention on her. "The doc's trying to push a hosepipe into your lung, so no sudden moves, okay?"

The doctor sticks her tongue out briefly at Pryce's creative interpretation of medical procedure. "It's a chest drain into the pleural cavity to reinflate your lung, Rebecca," she says. "You'll feel a lot better after this, I promise." She bows her head again, and the tugging and pushing restarts. I grip Pryce's hand, sweating through the discomfort, until I hear the doctor mutter in approval.

"All done," she announces. "How're her sats?"

"Ninety-three," someone calls, and the doctor beams as if she's just won a long-odds bet.

"Any easier to breathe?" she asks me.

"Much, thank you," I say, enjoying the novelty of two cooperating lungs.

The doctor snaps off her gloves. "You're doing great. You're going to need an operation to fix your arm, but we'll have you back on your feet in no time."

"Mmm." Someone's given me more morphine, and it's hit me like a sledgehammer. It reminds me of the time I broke my leg as a child and my dad sang to keep me calm in the anaesthetic room. My eyes fill with tears; I'm overjoyed to have that memory back.

Pryce leans low, curiosity brightening her tired face. "What's that you're humming?"

"'Alice the Camel,'" I tell her, and carry on in a loop until it lulls me back to sleep.

❖

I don't dream. I wake disorientated, my muscles tensed against the expectation of pain, but I'm muzzy-headed and warm and comfortable. I've been moved to a different cubicle, this one dimly lit by banks of monitors and drip stands, and silent except for the whisper of oxygen through the tubing below my nose.

Both visitors' chairs are empty, but there's a white mug balanced on the arm of the closest one and a jacket draped around it. Relieved to have privacy, I pull my sheets and gown loose, swearing as multiple IVs hamper my efforts. A kinked line sets off an alarm, and I flick the tube to fix it before anyone comes to investigate. I'm black and blue beneath the gown, my torso a patchwork of cuts and bruises complemented by the mass of orange sticky tape holding a length of tubing in place. A soft splint encases my left arm from just below my elbow to where my fingers poke out as fat as unpopped sausages. I pat a spot on my head that feels weird and draughty, finding wiry stitches and a bald patch the size of my palm. Rendered quiescent by the drugs, I debate the merits of shaving all my hair off when I get discharged, and get a brief, vivid flash of having been there and done that and quite liked the result.

The curtains around my bed part just as I'm trying to get my gown to sit fully under my bum. It's undignified enough that I've been catheterised while unconscious; I don't need my arse exposing as well. The nurse smiles when he sees I'm awake, and he easily fathoms what I'm up to.

"Do you want me to call a chaperone?" he asks, half turning to leave.

"No," I say. If he's my nurse then I'm sure he's seen it all already. It's the owner of the coffee cup that I'm worried about. "I can't…I can't get it right on my own."

"Roll to your left." He puts a hand on my shoulder to help things along, and his voice dulls as he speaks into my damaged ear. "Good. Hold there for a sec." He rearranges the gown and reties a knot. "You're all done. My name's Hanif, by the way."

I hit the pillows again, clammy and reeling. "What time is it?"

"Nine thirty-seven a.m. You came onto the high-dependency unit about four hours ago. I heard you had a rough night."

"Yeah." I blink to clear an unwanted image of the dead woman's arm swinging like a lazy pendulum. "I think I came off lightly, considering."

"I know, I heard that too." Hanif tidies the bedding and hands me a small device. "This is the control for your morphine pump. It'll allow you to administer a dose every hour and a half. Don't try to be brave and manage without it. Go by the timer on the pump. You're due in about forty minutes."

"I won't be brave," I promise him. The relentless ache in my arm is setting my teeth on edge. I shuffle around, trying to alleviate the throbbing, and end up staring at the abandoned chairs. They presumably answer the question I've been avoiding, but I steel myself and ask it anyway. "Did anyone manage to contact my family?"

He snatches up the mug as if annoyed that its presence has fed me false hope. "I'm not sure what's going on with that. There's a police officer still in the department, so I'll see if she'll come in and speak to you."

He closes the curtains behind him, leaving me with the useless pump and a sense of dread that's so all-encompassing it skyrockets my pulse and sets off multiple alarms. The doctor from the A&E hurries into the cubicle and rests a hand on my shoulder.

"Rebecca? Easy, you're okay. Settle down."

I'm not okay. I'm on my own and in bits in a strange hospital in fucking Wales of all places, and the only reason I have a name is because I read it off a bus pass. I want my mum and dad to hold my hand and fill in the massive blanks in my head, but I don't know whether they're even alive or whether I still talk to them. If they were, and if I did, they would have come here, wouldn't they?

The doctor is watching me closely, and I focus on her as she coaches my breathing. She's tall, slender, and blond, with a pixie cut that flatters her face. She must be hours late off her shift by now, and her makeup isn't quite covering the shadows beneath her eyes. Her nose crinkles as she assesses my pupils with a thin light and tells me to track her finger. It's only when she stoops to listen to my chest that I see Pryce standing by the chairs.

"You remember DS Pryce?" the doctor asks, and seems pleased when I nod. "Good. Do you remember my name?"

"No." I frown at the croak in my voice. My mouth is as dry as sand.

"Here," she says, offering me water through a straw. "Shall we start from the top, then?"

I nod again, savouring the water and unwilling to release the straw. The doctor keeps the glass steady and speaks slowly enough that her well-disguised Scouse accent becomes apparent.

"I'm Esther Lewis, one of the trauma specialists at Bangor General. I took care of you in A&E, and I'll be keeping an eye on you while you're an inpatient here. Once you'd stabilised last night, you had an operation to fix the break in your arm. You fractured both of the bones in your lower arm, and you have a couple of plates in there now to hold everything together. You'll get a proper cast on that once the swelling has reduced." She touches the right side of my chest. "Two of your ribs here are broken, and one of them collapsed your lung. Your right eardrum ruptured, which is why you're having trouble hearing, and we think this"—her fingers graze my new bald spot—"is the reason your memory isn't quite up to speed."

I arc an eyebrow at the understatement and untangle my tongue from the straw. "Will it come back?"

"Dr. Chander, your neurologist, is optimistic. The CT scan showed a subdural haematoma—essentially a gathering of blood—that's pressing on your brain. It's small and doesn't seem to be actively bleeding, so we're managing it conservatively for now, which is a fancy way of saying we're leaving it to sort itself out."

I don't like the idea of neurosurgery, but I'd prefer my brain to be unsquashed. "What if it starts bleeding again?"

Lewis puts my glass down and jots a note on my chart. "Then Dr. Chander gets a chance to play with his drill, and believe me, nothing makes him happier."

This surprises a laugh out of me. She squeezes my hand, obviously pleased to have brightened my outlook somewhat.

"It won't come to that," she says. "The clot is tiny, and we have you on lots of good drugs. You might never get clarity for those minutes just prior to the car crash—that's common in traumatic brain injuries— but you should get everything else back, so don't be worrying." She looks over to Pryce and back to me. "Do you feel up to answering a few questions?"

It seems like the least I could do. "I'll try."

"Atta girl. Don't tire her out," she warns Pryce. "She should be pressing this little button in twenty-seven minutes."

"Yes, Doctor." Pryce keeps her face straight, but there's an easy intimacy to their exchange, and even half-cut on morphine I can tell their relationship goes beyond the purely professional.

After switching on a small lamp, Lewis leaves us alone. Pryce waits for the curtain to close and then pulls up the chair with her coat on it. She looks exhausted.

"Have you been here all night?" I ask. It's the first time I've seen her clearly. Like Lewis, she's a few inches taller than me, with an athletic build, and the hair that seemed so dark by the crash site is actually shot through with auburn lowlights, her haphazard ponytail coming apart at the seams. She's not wearing makeup, and her Celtic knot earrings seem little more than an afterthought.

"Yes," she answers without inflection, sinking into the chair.

It takes me a few seconds to think back to my question. I wince. "Sorry."

She waves away my apology and retrieves a notepad from her bag. "We're having difficulty tracing your family," she says by way of an opener. "Or your friends. Well, anyone, really."

I watch her find a blank page and ready her pen. "Are they not in my phone?" I hadn't thought to look last night, but it seems an obvious place to find contacts.

"You'd think so, wouldn't you?" She taps her teeth with her pen. "But your phone was new, brand new in fact. The box and receipt were in the car."

"Shit," I say. "The woman I was with, do you know who she is? I mean, who she was?"

"Not as yet, no. She had no ID on her." Pryce eyeballs me. "I don't suppose you've had any flashes of inspiration where she's concerned, have you?"

I shake my head, my mouth parched again. Pryce refills my water glass and hands it to me.

"What about the crash?" she asks as I drink. "Can you tell me what happened there?"

"No," I say, hating the weakness of my voice and repeating my answer with more emphasis. "No, I don't know who she was or why we crashed. I don't even know what we were doing in Wales. I don't think I'm Welsh, am I?"

An almost-smile tweaks the corners of Pryce's lips. "You're definitely not Welsh. From your accent, I'd say Manchester, which would fit in with your bus pass."

"Manchester, eh?" It's elating to have actual information. A possible hometown, or at least a geographical area.

"We ran your prints and those of the decedent through the PNC," she continues, "but nothing came up. Using Manchester as a starting point for yourself, I've issued requests to the electoral register and the DVLA, the driving licence agency, but Rebecca Elliott is a common enough name that any hits I get will take time to follow up and eliminate."

I bend my legs to lessen the persistent stabbing of my ribs. "Could you do an appeal? Maybe take some photos?"

She tucks a length of hair behind her ear. She's not a fidgeter—she has the classic stoicism of a seasoned detective—and the gesture betrays her unease. "Photos might not help us much right now."

I catch on immediately and run my fingers across my face. "Have you got a mirror?"

She glances at the curtain, as if willing someone to interrupt us. "That's probably not a good idea."

"Please?" I can't get to the bathroom, but I'm not averse to launching an attempt. I'm about to wiggle out a foot to prove I mean business when Pryce sighs and relents, fishing out not a mirror but her mobile. With her fingers on my chin, she turns me into the light and takes a few shots. She deletes a couple and shows me the rest.

They're not pretty. I stare at the face on the screen, at its distorted jaw and puffy eyes and the sutured laceration that splits its right eyebrow. It doesn't seem like me. I've no connection to this young woman with the blue-black hair and the small silver ring in her nose.

I touch the piercing, making sure it's really there, and peer beneath my gown to check my belly button. It's unadorned, but there's an intricate tattoo of roses and thorns curling around my right biceps. At some point in my life, I appear to have embraced the stereotype of anti-establishment rebel. I rub my forehead with the heel of my hand. There are five minutes left on the pump.

"Did you run the tattoo?" I ask.

"Yes. No luck." Pryce closes her notebook and secures it with an elastic band. "I think my time's about up. I'll be back to see you later."

She doesn't specify when. I watch her go, and I count the last thirty seconds on the pump, hitting the button on zero. Nothing happens at first, but then I get the slow-release high that smoothes the edges off everything. I drift and doze, mellow enough not to be worried when I realise that even if I don't have a record, I've obviously been in trouble with the police before, because I knew to ask about the tattoo and I knew what a PNC check was without Pryce having to explain it.

CHAPTER THREE

They don't muck about at Bangor General. I spend the rest of the morning sleeping, self-medicating, and sleeping some more, and finally open my eyes to a cheery note on the cubicle's whiteboard informing me that it's sunny with occasional showers outside and that I have an appointment with the physiotherapist at one thirty p.m. I'm tempted to get myself good and stupefied in advance, but I've been hiding away in a drug fog for hours and it seems like cheating somehow.

The physio is a punctual and perennially cheerful sort who runs me through a series of breathing exercises to prevent pneumonia and then tells me that there's nothing wrong with my legs and I really should try getting out of bed. I stare at her, unsure whether she's taking the piss or merely bonkers.

"I have all this stuff," I say when she fails to acknowledge my concerns and readies a high-backed armchair.

"Oh, don't worry, it's all portable. I'll get Hanif to give us a lift."

Minutes later, supported by Hanif and with the physio manoeuvring my attachments, I shuffle eight steps to the chair and lower myself into it.

"Excellent, that's enough for today," she says. "Keep going with those exercises, and I'll see you tomorrow."

She bustles out, and I sag back, drained by her enthusiasm and the unexpected exertion.

"Cup of tea?" Hanif says, draping a blanket over my knees, his voice and expression deadpan.

"Coffee?" I counter instinctively.

"Not a problem. Milk and sugar?" He notices my indecision. "How about I bring both and let you experiment?"

"That would be great. Thanks."

I fold my arms across my chest, hugging the blanket close. I don't really get how this works. My personal life—who I am, where I'm from, what I do for a living, my likes and dislikes—are a blank, but I was able to work a mobile phone, and I knew to call 999 for the emergency services. I can function in the everyday, operate its gadgets, and interact. It's only when it comes to myself that I feel as if a section of my brain has been scooped out. Perhaps that's what the blood clot is nudging against, and as the clot recedes it'll release all the parts it's trapping. I cross my eyes at my rubbish grasp of neurophysiology. Whatever I do as a career, I'm pretty sure I'm not a brain surgeon.

Trial and error tells me I prefer my coffee white with two sugars. Or maybe I don't, but this new post-brain-injury me does. I'm dunking a ginger nut when there's a tap on the cubicle wall and Pryce pokes her head through the curtain.

"Didn't waste any time getting you on your feet, did they?" She sits next to me. "How are you?"

I suck my ginger nut—chewing won't be happening for a while yet—and make a "so-so" gesture as she removes her notebook from her bag. She looks refreshed, as if she's snatched a couple of hours' sleep and a shower. Her hair is neat, knotted back and clipped in place, and she's changed into a smart shirt and dress trousers. Her air of official efficiency makes me wary.

"What department do you work in?" I ask. Anyone who's ever watched reality TV knows that it's uniformed officers, not detectives, who respond to car crashes.

She crosses her legs, her notebook open and balanced. "Major Crimes. I was on my way home from a conference last night when our techs fixed your location, so I volunteered to help with the search. Given the circumstances, I'm working your case until told otherwise."

I place my half-eaten biscuit back on the plate. It seems too frivolous to eat during this conversation. "Have you identified her yet?" I ask.

"No." Pryce glances at her book. I can see neat handwriting and bullet points but can't read it from here. "Shall I tell you what we've been able to establish so far?" The question is rhetorical; she's already barrelling onward. "Your car was in excellent condition. The report from the vehicle examiner states there was no mechanical fault that might have contributed to the crash. Although the debris is still being gathered for reconstruction, there is no evidence yet to indicate the involvement of another vehicle. There were no animal carcasses in the road or on the verges to suggest you might have swerved to avoid one or been in collision with one. Scene analysis undertaken by the RPSIO—that's the Road Policing Senior Investigating Officer—estimates you were travelling at speeds between fifty and sixty miles an hour, so inside the statutory limit—"

"But too fast for the conditions," I murmur. It's not an admission of guilt, just a rudimentary conclusion based on the stretch of road I saw from the barrier last night: ink-black and slick with rain and snow.

"It would seem so," she says. "Your bloods were negative for alcohol or drugs. We've traced the car to a rental agency in Ardwick, Manchester. You appear to have signed the agreement, and CCTV shows the decedent with you in the agency at four thirty-eight yesterday afternoon."

The latter detail jerks my head up, but Pryce is already shaking hers.

"The quality of the recording is too poor for us to release it to the public. We can see it's the two of you, but little else. Number plate recognition cameras place you on the M60 twenty-five minutes later, and then the M56, so we're assuming you left for Wales directly from Ardwick."

"I'm not sure I understand," I say, which is a very mild way of putting it. "The woman last night on the 999 call, she said we were in Snowdonia. Why the hell would we have been there? Do you think we were going on holiday?" I sit up straighter, buoyed by a sudden recollection. "Oh! Did you find the holdall and the clothes?"

"We found one bag at the scene," Pryce confirms. She angles her head, evaluating me. "You're what? An eight? Maybe a ten, at a push? And about five foot five?"

I shrug, taking her word on that.

"The clothes were all fourteen to sixteen. The post mortem measurements imply they belonged to your companion."

"So I was taking her somewhere, possibly giving her a lift?"

"All the way to Wales," Pryce says, and I hear the scepticism in her voice. She takes out a small plastic evidence bag and hands it to me. "We found these lodged in the passenger footwell. Do you recognise them?"

"No," I say, rubbing my finger over the larger key. It's a typical Chubb door key, and the other is a smaller, flatter one for a Yale lock.

"Any idea what they open?" she asks.

"At a guess, a front door."

"But that's just a guess?"

The edge to her voice makes me bristle. If I could provide her with an answer, I would. Then she wouldn't have to keep watching the monitors for telltale physiological signs of subterfuge. If my heart rate is spiking, it's because she's pissing me off.

"Yes, that's just a guess," I snap.

She holds up her hands, implying she meant no offence, and then delves into her bag again. I shrink into my chair when I see "North West Wales Coroner's Office" stamped across a large brown envelope. It wouldn't take a genius to decipher my body language, and she turns the envelope plain side up, obviously ruing her error.

"I need you to look at these," she says, her voice low and soft, "but not necessarily today. Not if you're not ready."

A monitor sounds a steady warning, bringing Hanif into the cubicle. He mutes the alarm and checks my blood pressure.

"Are you all right?" he asks, too experienced to go by data alone.

"I'm fine," I say and reiterate it for Pryce's sake. "I'm fine. I want to do this."

Hanif examines my morphine pump. "Stop skipping doses. You'll need the next one to get yourself back into bed." Then, to Pryce, "Twenty minutes, no longer."

She nods without equivocating. He has his own air of authority, and she's a guest on his patch. He leaves the curtains ajar, and she slides a set of photographs out of the envelope before he can change his mind and terminate the interview.

"Ready?" she asks me.

I hold my hand out in lieu of answering, and she passes me the first photograph. The woman at the centre of the colour image looks far more peaceful than she did in the car. Supine on the mortuary's metal table, she has her eyes closed, and her body is covered by a white sheet. Her face is clean and unmarred, apart from the jagged laceration cleaving her left forehead, and someone has brushed the blood from her hair. She's a brunette, and I know her hair reaches halfway down her back, although I can't see that in the shot. Her laugh is loud and infectious, and she loves eighties music and Raspberry Ruffle bars. I used to buy them for her from the corner shop, a handful at a time.

I hear a faint rustle, and Pryce offers me a tissue as a tear drops off my nose and splashes onto the photograph. I blot it dry and wipe my face. There are other images: a cheap costume jewellery ring on the woman's left index finger, a matching bracelet, and a purple hummingbird tattoo low on the right side of her abdomen. I trace the shape of the tattoo, unease creeping over me. This isn't the first time I've seen it.

"Were you friends? Or maybe a couple?" Pryce asks quietly. The latter question doesn't offend me. It's an obvious one to ask, given my reaction, and if the woman and I were closeted, that might explain the clandestine nature of our trip to Wales. Amongst all the grey areas and supposition, one thing I am certain of is my sexuality. Until now, I've been too spaced out to really consider it, but it must be something too deep-rooted to be altered or masked by a whack to the head, because I know that I'm gay. Perhaps that explains the empty chairs at my bedside.

"I'm not sure," I say. "We were friends, I think. At least."

The answer seems to satisfy Pryce for the moment. She starts to pack her things, getting ready to leave, though I've no doubt I'll be seeing her again.

I sniff and swallow, and my ear pops, blanking out the noises of the hospital. In their place I hear a burst of cheesy pop music and laughter, a woman—*this* woman?—imploring me to dance with her. The air is rich with the scent of smoked meats, tomatoes, herbs, and red wine. I'm not convinced by the addition of sauerkraut, but she reassures me and offers me a taste from a wooden spoon. She cups her hand beneath the spoon, catching errant drips, and licks her palm, her eyes wide with delight. The sauce tastes amazing. I swallow again, my tongue poking out to touch the spoon, but the pressure in my ear equalizes and the woman disappears.

"What's a biggos?" I ask Pryce, the question past my lips before it's engaged with my brain.

Looking as bemused as I feel, she retakes her seat and rests her hands on her bag. "I haven't the foggiest. Where did that come from?"

"Just popped into my head. Can you google it?"

"How are we spelling it?"

"B-i-g…" I falter. I've only ever heard it spoken. "Maybe double g?"

"'Bigos.' One g," Pryce tells me, reading from her phone. "It's a hunter's stew. A traditional speciality of—"

"Poland," I say. "She was Polish." I think back to her tattoo, rendered in shades of purple. "May I?"

Pryce proffers the phone without question, and I search first for "purple in Polish," which brings up a word I fail to pronounce. I scowl at it for being so damn literal and try "Polish girls' names" instead, hitting the first link that promises meaning and etymology. I get as far as "J" on the alphabetical list, and butterflies swirl in my belly as I click on one of the names.

"Jolanta," I say out loud, the way she used to emphasise each of its syllables, her accent curling around the sounds. "Her name is Jolanta. It means 'violet' in Polish. She told me it was her favourite colour."

CHAPTER FOUR

It's not one specific trigger but a slow-growing accumulation that brings my mum back to me: the hospital's sponge pudding, the skin on its custard thick enough to repel an axe; the impersonal hands of an agency nurse rolling me to check for pressure sores, and her faint look of distaste as she empties my catheter; the monotonous cycle of observations being taken; the feeling of helplessness as a succession of strangers prod and probe my body and congregate at the foot of the bed to discuss my "case" in incomprehensible jargon.

One of the doctors is awkwardly patting my arm when I first start to see my mum. He's young, with acne still pocking his face, and his beard needs scrubbing out and starting again. He participated for ten minutes in an animated discussion moderated by my neurologist, Dr. Chander, but interacting with an actual patient seems to fall beyond his comfort zone.

"I think I scared him," I hear my mum say. Her accent is far milder than mine, and her voice is so clear she could be sitting beside me. Instead she's in her own hospital bed, swaddled beneath a crocheted blanket that my gran made for her. She tracks the doctor's rapid egress from the ward.

"I wonder if his parents know he's out so late," she murmurs.

I stroke her hand. The skin covering her fingers is paper-thin, and her grip is feeble. Her hair has never grown back, and I've shaved mine again in solidarity. She insists on wearing a woolly hat, because even in the stifling heat of Ward 3, Bay 4, she's always cold.

"I want to go home," she says. "Please don't let me die in here."

And I hug her and kiss her and promise her that I won't.

"Are you finished with this, love?" The twilight shift nurse slides my abandoned supper tray toward her. The doctors have left, and we're alone in the room. My mum is gone.

I manage to say, "Yes, thank you," though I'm still punch-drunk with sorrow. My mum's scent—her face cream and the peppermints she sucked to ease the burning in her throat—overwhelms that of the meal I've hardly touched.

"Didn't fancy the stroganoff, then? Can't say as I blame you." The nurse wrinkles her nose at the lumps of grey meat congealing on a bed of wet rice. "You poor dab. How about I make you some toast instead? You really need to eat something."

She means well, but I don't need toast. I need my mum, who would read Enid Blyton to me when I was poorly and melt cheese into Heinz tomato soup. She died in her own bed, her brain riddled with metastases and her lungs full of fluid.

"Toast would be lovely," I say.

I push my hand under the sheets, digging my nails into my palm to stop myself from falling apart. The instant the nurse leaves, I stuff my fist into my mouth, muffling the sobs that tear through me as I mourn my mum for the second time.

Curling onto my side, I pull my knees up and hide my face with my bandaged arm. The pillow beneath my cheek is soaked, and I'm wracked by that weird open-mouthed juddering that children do when they've cried themselves out. The supper tray has displaced my box of tissues, so I dry my face on the bedding instead and stare at the monitors until the colours become too bright.

Eventually, a yawn catches me off guard. I smother it and start to read the yellow drug labels stuck to all my IVs, sounding the words out and guessing what the medicines might be for. I'm absolutely knackered, but I don't want to sleep. I'm terrified of closing my eyes and finding somebody else I've already lost.

Deemed healthy enough for a regular ward, I'm transferred from HDU before the sun is up, shunted along deserted corridors and into my new single room on the trauma ward, T6. I've swapped the bank of monitors for a window overlooking a car park and a sign that reads *Ysbyty GWYNEDD*. Mesmerised by the sight of people going about their everyday lives, I watch the car park fill up with staff arriving for the early shift, their heads bowed against the persistent rain and a wind strong enough to turn their brollies inside out. Grey clouds mass as day breaks, and the window lets in a draught that smells of petrol fumes and seaweed.

A few minutes after handover, a student nurse comes to introduce herself. She writes her name on the whiteboard in block capitals— CEINWEN—and tells me not to worry about getting it right, because the southerners always say it wrong anyway.

"You have physio at ten, and you're getting a cast put on your arm at eleven," she says, creating a multicoloured schedule punctuated with smiley faces. "And we're going to pop that catheter out as well." She decides against adding that to the day's events. "Shall we do that before breakfast?"

I'd rather she didn't "pop" anything out of me, but I nod my consent, which prompts her to scurry from the room in search of equipment and, hopefully, supervision.

I only have two tubes remaining—an IV and the chest drain— as I eat my porridge and hobble into the bathroom, where Ceinwen expertly directs the shower hose, avoiding my stitches and sticky tape and various other parts too tender to touch. Taking pity on me, she tosses my arse-revealing gown into the laundry and smuggles in a set of scrubs she's pinched from the staff stores.

"There," she says as she combs my damp hair in front of the mirror. "I love this colour. What do you use?" She bites her lip as she hits the question mark, but I smile at her.

"Your guess is as good." I tease out a strand, examining the hint of deep blue along its length. "It's probably called something ridiculous."

"Brazen Blueberry," she suggests, and starts to giggle.

"Exactly." I wipe the mirror clear of steam and peer at my reflection. The swelling around my eyes is less pronounced now, and I can see they're a nondescript hazel. Purple bruises mottle my cheeks and jaw, and my hair has settled loosely around my ears. It's not long enough to tie back, and I seem to have a fringe, though its style is something of a conundrum.

"How about this?" Ceinwen doesn't wait for an answer, and within seconds she's feathered and tousled and swept my fringe across to the right, where it seems to sit naturally. She beams at me. "That looks well tidy. It really suits you."

"It's very fetching," I say, genuinely tickled by my new do. She's even managed to cover my bald spot, but it's the sense of normalcy she's brought in with her that I value the most.

"Oh, before I forget," she says, collecting my wash things, "the ward sister said Detective Pryce will be in to see you at half one."

And as easy as that, my cheerful little bubble bursts.

Pryce phones to say she's running late, allowing me time to adjust to the weight of my new plaster cast and recover from the conniption fit I have when a lifelike sketch of Jolanta appears on the one o'clock news.

"The North Wales Police are appealing for witnesses after a car crash left one woman dead and a second in a serious but stable condition in Bangor General Infirmary. The navy blue Ford Focus veered off the A5 late on Friday evening, leading to a large-scale search and rescue operation after the injured woman managed to alert the emergency services."

I mute the report, but the room's last resident has set the subtitles going, and I don't know how to turn them off. My name is given in full, as well as a brief summary of my amnesia-induced predicament, and Jolanta's image is used again to close out the piece. A hotline number scrolls along the bottom of the screen, and then they're back to discussing whatever the Tories have fucked up this week.

I gulp a glass of lukewarm water, part of me hopeful that someone will come forward to claim me, and the rest knocked for six by the artist's impression of Jolanta. I haven't been able to provide her surname. I think I mostly followed her lead and called her "Jo."

I've just managed to compose myself when Pryce strides in after a cursory knock, her hair wet and rain-scented.

"Not much of a view, is it?" she says, shaking off her coat and hanging it over the bathroom door. She pauses on her way back to the chairs, her head at a slight angle as she regards me.

"Student nurse," I say, helping her out. "She got a bit giddy with the comb earlier."

"Ah." A faint blush colours Pryce's cheeks. "She did a good job."

"Yeah?" I shrug, unwilling to lower my guard. "It'll do for now."

Pryce gets herself comfortable, following her usual routine: bag propped by the chair, notebook open on her lap. She taps her teeth with her pen, signalling a return to business.

"We found your cottage," she says. "It's about eight miles from where you crashed. That's what the keys are for."

"My cottage?" I'm damn sure I don't own a cottage in Snowdonia. My only connection to Wales is a hazy memory of a daytrip to Rhyl when I was young enough to find the Sun Centre exciting. I came out with a pink and white ice cream and a verruca.

"Sorry, no, you don't own it," she says, because apparently, my actual drip feed isn't enough, and she has to provide her information in another. "It's a rental. The owner went round yesterday to check everything was all right and realised you'd never arrived. She'd heard about the crash and put two and two together."

I rub my left temple. I've had a nagging headache all day, and Pryce is making it worse. "How long had I rented it for?"

She consults her notes. "A week. You booked it last minute through an agency and collected the keys at their office in Conwy."

"Why didn't I have a bag in the car, then?" I ask. None of this makes any fucking sense. Pryce throws up her hands, obviously sharing my exasperation. Logical explanations don't seem to be forthcoming, so I go for outlandish. "Could someone have stolen it after the accident?"

Folding her arms, she gives an exaggerated sigh, as if she's willing to let this play out but wants me to understand it's under duress. "Did you see or hear anyone in the vicinity?"

"No." I squeeze my eyes shut and attempt to reconstruct a clear narrative of that night. I can't do it. All I get are snapshots of disconnected visuals that don't come close to forming a whole. I decide to hedge my bets. "I don't think so. But I'd been unconscious for a while."

"Do you think it's plausible that someone followed your car down the embankment on foot, purely to take your luggage?"

"Plausible? No," I mumble, feeling like a chastised schoolgirl. "But I suppose it's not impossible."

She scoots forward, bridging the gap between chair and bed. "Any idea what you might have been carrying that would be worth all that effort?"

"No." I curse myself for gifting her this new angle of attack. I really should think these things through before I open my mouth. My head's pounding, and I can feel tears clogging my throat. "I'm just trying to help," I whisper.

Pryce nods in a distracted way, busy scribbling a note that she encircles and marks with a bold star. I can guess what she's just highlighted (drugs? proceeds of a robbery? incriminating documents used for blackmail? cybercrime gadgets?) because I'm running through the list myself to see whether any of it provokes a response. That nothing prompts so much as a twitch does little to console me.

She shuts her book. "I think that's enough for today. I'm going to speak to Dr. Lewis about taking a formal statement from you. It'll be taken under caution. Do you know what that means?"

"Yes: 'I do not have to say anything. But it may harm my defence…' et cetera, et cetera." That uneasy sensation swirls around in my stomach again. I wait until she's fastening her coat before I say, "I saw the news."

"Ah." Her hand freezes with half the buttons done, and her expression softens into one of concern. "I forgot to warn you about that. I should have, I really meant to, but it just slipped my mind." She seems so sincere that I regret sending her on a guilt trip.

"Hey, I know what it's like to have stuff slip your mind."

A smile brightens her face, giving me a split-second glimpse of Bronwen Pryce rather than the DS. She rests her hand on my arm. "We'll get to the bottom of all this, Rebecca. I know it's a lot to take in, but we'll sort it out."

"One way or another," I say.

Her hand slips away. "Yes. One way or another."

The car rocks, pitching me left to right, and I feel someone grab a handful of my hair and jerk my head up. The violence shocks a moan from me, and the hand lets go as if scalded.

"They're still alive," a man says. The buzz of my bad ear warps his voice, but he sounds frantic, a quaver rattling his speech. He pushes my face away, his gloved fingers exerting enough force to bruise. The smell of his sweat fills the car, and I hear a metallic jangle every time he moves.

"Stop fuckin' bellyaching," a second man says from behind me. "Look at the state of 'em. Problem solved. Come on."

I'm held in place until he's inched well beyond my eyeline. The car boot slams shut, locking out the worst of the storm, and I turn toward the woman's sodden breaths. She's unconscious and bleeding. I open my mouth to speak to her, but I don't know what to call her.

"Jo? *Jo?* Aw, Jesus *fuck!*"

I wake in a twist of sheets and IV tubing, a pillow clutched in front of me like a shield. Blood is trickling along my wrist where I've yanked the line loose, and the dream is receding too quickly for me to catch its details. Panting hard, I stretch out and get a grip on the whiteboard's marker pen. I don't have any paper, so I bring my left arm across my chest and use its new plaster cast as a notepad: *Two men. My accent. Leather glove? Metal.*

I snarl in frustration, unable to lock anything else down and unsure whether what I've written even took place. The timing of the nightmare, hot on the heels of my theorising about the presence of a third party, is too much of a coincidence. This is what happens when my subconscious is allowed to run riot. I can imagine Pryce's face if I suddenly reveal two mystery men who might have caused the crash but managed to leave no evidence of their involvement. She would pin me with that look of hers, the one she reserves for moments when I've yet again denied all knowledge of a fact she deems incontrovertible. Her right eyebrow arches, and her teeth pull on her top lip a little—not enough to be obvious, more like the tell of a poker player aware of the game's foregone conclusion.

Regardless of her scepticism, I'm still unnerved by the dream, and the sound of approaching footsteps makes me push down in the bed, acutely aware of how vulnerable I am now that an appeal has been made and Jolanta's image has gone out on national television. "The female survivor," the news called me, and then blabbed my current location and condition to all and sundry.

The nurse who enters has already been in to check my observations a couple of times. She tucks the pillow behind my head and straightens my sheets.

"Nightmare?" she asks, wrapping a dressing around my leaking vein.

"Yeah," I whisper. I keep my cast pressed close to my body as she resites the IV.

"Can I get you anything, love? Coffee? I can do you some warm milk if you're having trouble sleeping."

"No, thank you. I'm fine."

She drapes the emergency cord over my pillow. "Buzz if you change your mind."

"I will, I promise."

I wait a full minute and then inch my legs out of the covers, letting my bare feet dangle until I'm accustomed to sitting unaided. I slide to the floor before I lose my nerve, gripping the bed rail and my IV pole for balance. Carrying the drain low and loose like a bag of shopping, I limp to the bathroom. No one comes to investigate when I switch the light on, so I turn the left side of my face to the mirror, inspecting the arch of my cheekbone. Set within a broad area of blue-green bruising are two deeper circles of purple. I press my fingertips against them and feel the corresponding sting where the man dug in with his own.

"Shit," I whisper.

Mindful of how often my obs are taken, I turn out the light and hobble back to bed. The nurse has left my door ajar, and I lie wide-awake and jittery, listening to an elderly woman call for help every thirty seconds. I peek at the underside of my cast, murmuring the words there in an effort to make sense of them, but there's no light bulb revelation, no eureka moment where everything falls into place and I find out exactly why I'm in Wales or why two men would leave me and my friend for dead in a smashed-up car.

CHAPTER FIVE

Monday and Tuesday pass by on the whiteboard. Ceinwen takes to drawing little weather symbols based on each morning's forecast, and I compare her predictions to the permanent layer of gloom that sits over the car park. The sun breaks through on Wednesday, and she adds the requisite smiley face and an ice cream cone to her sketch.

"Deep breath in," Dr. Lewis tells me, her steth poised over the brittle side of my chest. "Good. Hold it. Okay, let it out." Satisfied, she drapes her steth around her neck. She removed the drain an hour ago, and Ceinwen has promised to celebrate my new tube-free status with a trip around the grounds if the day stays fine.

Lewis perches on my bed and offers me an Everton Mint. We suck them in comfortable contemplation while she writes on my chart.

"Your CT showed a moderate reduction in the subdural haematoma," she says, after she's crunched her mint. "You don't have any signs of infection, and your post-drain chest X-ray looks fine. How are the headaches?"

"Manageable." On average, they hit me every twelve hours or so, but I've stopped asking for painkillers in case Pryce arrives unannounced and I'm too stoned to deal with her. I haven't said a word about the men to anyone. The bruises have merged into one, and I've been studiously ignoring the scribbles on my cast.

"All on that left side?" Lewis checks my pupils with her penlight.

"Yes," I say. Then, pre-empting her follow-up questions, "But there's no weakness or loss of function or other funny stuff, and the tinnitus isn't as loud."

She chuckles. "You know me too well."

I don't really know her at all, but I can see that something's troubling her, and I have an inkling what it may be. I sit straighter on the bed, ignoring the stitch that immediately pulls on my ribs.

"When do I get to go home, Doc?" I ask, in as cheerful a voice as I can muster.

She folds her arms, seeing through my ruse in a heartbeat. "How does the end of the week sound?"

It sounds bloody scary, given that I don't actually have a home to go to.

"Okay," I venture, and the recently reattached sats probe registers a pulse rate of one-oh-eight.

"Yeah, that's what I thought." She reaches over and silences the alarm. "When did you last speak to Detective Pryce?"

"Sunday afternoon. I think I've had a couple of days off for good behaviour."

Lewis lets out a short laugh. "She's all heart, that one."

Though her reply matches the wryness of mine, she catches herself and her smile fades. She takes a breath as if she's about to retract her comment or add a qualification, but then she seems to think better of it and signs my chart instead. Whatever her history with Pryce, she's not going to share it with a patient, and curious as I am, I appreciate her discretion.

"I know Detective Pryce is doing her best to trace your family and friends," she says quietly.

"What if she doesn't find anyone?" I say, finally finding the balls to ask one of the questions that have been keeping me awake at night. "That could happen, couldn't it? I'll have nowhere to go, no money, no job. I'll end up in one of those hostels for drunks and smackheads. *Shit.*" I release the sheet I've wound into a knot.

"We'll sort something out for you, I promise," Lewis says, but she can barely look me in the eye, and she shouldn't be making promises that she won't be able to keep.

❖

I manage without a wheelchair, linking Ceinwen's arm instead for a slow and steady plod toward the main entrance.

"I bet you go to the gym a lot," she says, as we join the throng of IV-trailing patients on their way outside for a fag.

I perform an awkward sidestep to avoid a doctor jaywalking with his phone. "What makes you think that?"

Ceinwen squeezes my biceps and laughs when I tense. "This puppy," she says, and I realise her hand is wrapped around a healthy bulge of muscle.

"Hmm, you might be on to something."

I'm no power lifter, but I've obviously done regular training with weights. Intrigued, I toe up one leg of my scrubs trousers and find a well-toned calf that's probably pounded more than a few laps on the track.

"Maybe I'm a runner." That feels close but not quite right. Enlightenment comes in the form of a toddler who overtakes us wearing a full Cardiff City kit. "No, it's not running. I play footy. I scored a hat-trick once and got to keep the ball."

"Oh!" Ceinwen does an excited little hop. "This is perfect! We just need to find the team that's missing a player."

I shake my head, hating to be the fly in the ointment. "I'm not sure. I think I was on a team"—our strip was white with navy socks, and the year that we managed to win something, a cup or maybe the league, we got so drunk we couldn't find the team bus when it was time to go home—"but I don't...I dropped out for some reason."

Ceinwen utters a stream of furious Welsh, which must contain at least one swear word because a middle-aged man in a tweed jacket tuts as he hurries past us.

"I thought we had it," she says, releasing her stranglehold on my arm and smoothing the sleeve of the sweater she's loaned me. "I thought we'd be able to find you."

"Well, it's something, which is more than we had five minutes ago."

"True." She goes into the newsagents and comes out with two ice lollies, apparently undeterred by the weather report predicting a high of four degrees.

A frigid blast of air hits us when we step outside. We look at our ice lollies and shrug, nibbling on the shell of strawberry sorbet as we wander past Outpatients and find a bench near A&E. The sky is cloudless and brilliant blue, and pockets of frost are lingering in shaded spots. Stretching my legs, I lift my face to the sun.

"You should make a list," Ceinwen says, flicking a piece of pink ice at an optimistic seagull. It squawks its disgust at her and steals a discarded chip as recompense. "A list of all the stuff you're figuring out, because even the tiniest scrap might turn out to be really important."

I nod, glad that her sweater covers the notes I've already made on my cast. "Okay, well, I'm right-handed, probably sporty, and I don't speak Welsh."

She's found a pen in her bag and is scribbling dutifully. "You prefer marmalade to Marmite."

I give her a moment to jot that down while I steel my nerve. "I think I'm gay," I tell her quietly.

"Hmm," she says, and starts a new bullet point. "You do have a distinct vibe."

"What bloody vibe?" I nudge her with my elbow, relieved that she's still sitting there. "Explain."

She laughs. "It's nothing you can explain. You just have a way about you."

"A gay way."

"Yes, exactly. A gay way."

I ponder that for a few seconds. "Is it the hair?"

"Among other things." She raises a finger. "Moving on, you also swear quite a lot, and you sound like the love child of Liam Gallagher and Lena Headey."

"In short, I'm a lesbian northern scrubber."

She snorts. "I'm writing that down."

Something cold drips onto my fingers, and a sharp shake of my shoulder tears me away from a memory of a lad with a dark mop of hair and an infectious laugh.

"Rebecca?" Ceinwen rests her palm on my forehead as if checking for a fever.

"I have a brother," I murmur as she eases my ice lolly from my grip and swaps it for a napkin. "Older than me, and he doesn't live in Manchester. Bleedin' hell, this is proper fucking weird."

"Did you see someone who looked like him?" She cranes her neck and scans the ambulance bay. Seeing no one of note, she wipes my fingers to stop me shredding the tissue.

"No, it was what we were just talking about. When I moved away, he used to joke about it, about me turning into an inner-city scrubber." I lick a splodge of vanilla from my thumb. "Crap. This could throw the whole Manchester theory through a loop."

"Perhaps you weren't born there, you just live there now."

"Perhaps." I can only picture my brother as a child, ruddy-cheeked and racing barefoot across a rough field. He squirts me with water that smells of Fairy liquid, and I squeal, returning fire with my own homemade cannon. Our rope swing hangs from the oak near the river.

Falling off it caused the break to my leg, but my dad didn't cut it down, he just told us to be more careful.

"I grew up in the countryside," I say, and I can see our cottage now, nestled at the top of the field. My bedroom was at the back, overlooking the yard where the ducks and hens would torment the dog. It seems idyllic, but the images bring disquiet with them, and I'm sure I left this place as soon as I was old enough. I feel the tickle of goose pimples as they rise along my right arm. The cast on my left prevents me from rubbing them away, so I pull the sweater over my hand and watch the seagull strutting in front of a pigeon until my urge to shiver has passed.

"Right, come on, or you'll catch a chill." Ceinwen is about to tug me up when her stance stiffens and she mutters, "Uh-oh."

I catch sight of Pryce making a beeline for our bench, before Ceinwen assumes a defensive position and blocks my view. "Was she on today's guest list?" she mutters.

"No." I stand up beside her. It's the first time I've been able to meet Pryce on her level, and I'm still a few inches too short. She nods a curt greeting, her eyes hidden behind dark glasses.

"I need to speak to you," she says, and then raises her shades as if surprised to find Ceinwen hasn't taken the hint and made herself scarce. "About a private matter."

Ceinwen folds her arms and juts out her chin. I doubt she's much older than eighteen, but she's got the protective instincts of a newly whelped bulldog.

"We were going back inside, Detective," she says.

"It's okay," I tell her. "You head off. I'm sure we won't be far behind you."

Her brow furrows, but she relents, with a final caveat aimed at Pryce. "Will you see her to the ward when you're done?"

"Absolutely," Pryce says. I can't tell whether she's taking the piss, but her guarantee is sufficient to placate Ceinwen.

"Here." Ceinwen wraps her jacket around my shoulders. "Don't be too long. I'll have a brew ready for you."

She hurries off, using A&E as a shortcut, and I lose sight of her in the ambulance bay as a vehicle reverses in with its blues flashing. My right palm, still hidden in my sweater, is clammy, and I feel dizzy enough to sit down without waiting on ceremony.

"What have you found?" I ask. Pryce has never been one for exchanging pleasantries or small talk, but her body language is even more guarded than usual, and she's yet to look me in the eye. Whatever is going on, this isn't a routine visit.

She sits next to me, leaving her bag unopened for once.

"I had a phone call this morning from Detective Inspector Tahir Ansari at Manchester Metropolitan Police," she says. "He oversees their Major Crime Team."

I nod, unable to reply. Major Crime. The words whip around my head as briskly as the wind is agitating the litter. Not piddling misdemeanour, not a slapped wrist and a suspended sentence, but *Major Crime*. Jesus Christ. What the fuck have I done?

If Pryce notices my nervous breakdown, she pays it no heed, continuing her monologue in the same formal tone.

"Yesterday afternoon one of the MCT saw a news bulletin that featured an update on your case. DI Ansari was alerted first thing this morning, and I've been back and forth on the phone and email with MMP since then."

"For fuck's sake!" I blurt out before common sense can rein me in. "Stop stringing me along. If you're going to arrest me, then fucking arrest me." My burst of defiance is short-lived, and it shatters along with my voice. "*Please*," I whisper. "Just tell me what I did and get it over with."

"I'm not here to arrest you." She meets and holds my gaze, her eyes narrowing even though the sun is behind her and half-blinding me. If her manner is meant to be reassuring, it's falling well short. "Your name isn't Rebecca Elliott. It's Alis Clarke, and you work for MMP's Major Crime Team."

"What the fuck?" I mumble. I have to clutch the arm of the bench, because I think I might pass out.

"Put your head between your knees," she instructs me.

"No, I fucking won't." I bat at the hand she presses to my neck. "You're talking shit." But even as I spit out the denial, I know she's telling the truth. The name feels right in a way that "Rebecca" never did, and my familiarity with police protocols and terminology suddenly makes sense. I should be relieved, but I feel as if the ground is opening up, ready to swallow me whole. Too bewildered to process the ramifications, I grasp at a simple fact: if the police have ID'd me, they have contact details for my next of kin. I chew on my lip, splitting the skin with a ragged tooth. "My dad. Did someone call my dad? And my brother? I have a brother."

"I spoke to your brother an hour ago," Pryce says. Then, quietly, "Do you want me to start from the beginning?"

"Yes." I answer automatically, the tang of blood mixing with strawberry ice as I swallow.

She shifts on the bench, as if she's getting comfortable before telling a bedtime story, and hands me a sheet of paper copied from my MMP personnel file. The photograph attached to the copy is tiny, but I can see that it's me, and apparently I spell my name A-l-i-s, not A-l-i-c-e.

"You've been with MMP for nine years and worked Major Crimes as a detective constable for the past four," Pryce says. "Thirteen months ago, you volunteered for an undercover operation and were given the alias Rebecca Elliott." She holds up a hand to prevent any interruptions. "I only have the basics. Your DI was less than forthcoming about the nature of your assignment. I know that it involved a full-time job in a factory called Hamer & Sons, and that on Friday afternoon, for reasons that are still unclear, you managed to dupe your handler and head out here. Neither he nor DI Ansari could offer any explanation for your actions or why you were with Jolanta. In fact, neither was aware of any connection or relationship you may have had with her, but employment records show she worked your shift pattern at the factory."

It's so subtle I almost miss it, the barest change of emphasis when Pryce says "relationship," but it offers a succinct explanation for her stony demeanour. For the first time, we're talking as one police officer to another, and she's evidently convinced that I had dishonourable reasons for abandoning my assignment to abscond with a potential witness. My instincts, blunted by a thunderclap migraine, warn me to say nothing in my defence, and I defer to them even as alarm bells start to clamour in my head and the rhythmic throbbing behind my left temple provides an accompanying drumbeat.

"DI Ansari and Detective Constable Keith Wallace will be here to interview you later this afternoon," she says. "I've updated them with regard to the road collision investigation, but I imagine they'll take everything else off my hands."

"Everything else," I repeat, still stupefied.

"Your identity and background, whatever Jolanta's role was in all of this, any potential charges that MMP may want to bring." She ticks off the items in the manner of one reading from a shopping list.

"All right, I get it," I snap. "And you need a statement, and I might be facing charges of death by dangerous driving. Did I miss anything?"

"It could be driving without due care," she says, as if that would make things easier to bear. She hands me a card with her details. "Use this if you need me before I next contact you."

"Cheers." I give her a jaunty thumbs up. I suspect Alis might be sarkier than Rebecca. "Are we done?"

She unfolds her sunglasses but doesn't put them on. "Your brother is driving over first thing tomorrow. Your dad's abroad at the moment, and I've not been able to get in touch with him."

"Thank you," I say with sincerity this time. Pryce doesn't answer, and there's a conspicuous pause in the conversation. She hasn't mentioned my mum, and I don't want to force her to break the news to me. "I think my mum died," I add.

"She did," she says softly. "I'm sorry."

"Yeah, me too." I push to my feet, weaving slightly until she steadies me. "Am I okay to go back now?"

"Yes." She hesitates. "Do you want me to walk you over there? I said I would."

"No, I'll be fine."

Her sunglasses go back on, masking her reaction, but some of the rigidity has left her posture. "I'll be in touch," she says.

"Right." I let her walk a yard or so and then I call out, "DS Pryce?"

She stops immediately, raising her glasses again as she turns, and I see the concern that flashes across her face. "Alis?"

I close the gap. I'd rather not shout this. "What's my brother's name?"

"Martin," she says. "His name is Martin."

Disorientated by the headache, I get lost somewhere between Rheumatology and Stoma Care. I stagger into the public toilets and kneel on the floor of the farthest cubicle, where I cling to the bowl and throw up my Strawberry Split. Someone taps on the door as I'm using a handful of tissue to clean my face.

"Are you all right in there, love?"

"Yes, thank you," I say.

I lean my cheek against the wall, avoiding its red-pen declaration "Caryl Jones luvs cock," and listen to the blast of the hand dryer and the fading click of high heels. The toilet stinks even after I flush it, but I don't move. Locked in where no one can find me, I feel safe enough to dissect the bombshell Pryce just dropped. I soon realise there's not much for me to work with, though. The revelation of my real name hasn't miraculously restored my memory, and I seem to have more in common with Rebecca Elliott, factory worker, than with Detective Constable Alis Clarke.

Another wave of nausea hits me as I whisper the names aloud, because whichever of them I go by, I'm in deep shit. I retch, flush, and reclaim my spot on the floor. An infant wails in the next cubicle, its mum too harassed to enquire after my well-being. I'm cold but sweating in Ceinwen's jacket, and every scenario I conjure up ends with me facing disciplinary hearings and dismissal at best, a custodial sentence or a second attempt on my life at worst. I feel like a child abandoned in a crowd, scared stiff and surrounded by strangers whose lives are far better mapped out than mine. Sickly and miserable, I shove my hands into the pockets of the jacket and feel the edge of Pryce's card dig into my fingers. I know it will list three ways to contact her: mobile, direct office line, and email, and for a moment, the urge to confide in her is so strong that I raid all of Ceinwen's other pockets in the hope of finding loose change for a pay phone, but even with thirty pence sitting on the palm of my hand, I stay where I am.

It's not that I don't trust Pryce. I do, implicitly. I'm sure she would listen to everything I had to say and take meticulous notes of my claims regarding the two men at the crash. She would examine my bruises for fingerprints, even though they've vanished and she doesn't really believe me anyway, and then she would type a report and send it off to Major Crimes at Manchester Metropolitan Police, because that's how inter-force investigations are supposed to operate, and she plays by the rules.

I, on the other hand, seem to have broken a number of them, and the more I think about it, the more convinced I become that I must have had a bloody good reason for doing so. I don't believe that Jolanta and I were slipping off to a cosy cottage to indulge in a forbidden sexual liaison. For a start, I would have packed a bag, and we definitely wouldn't have invited a couple of thugs to tag along. Which leaves only one possible explanation: we were trying to get away from someone, and we failed. Or, more specifically, I failed her. I'm the police officer, the one employed to protect the vulnerable and keep them from harm. Instead, my actions and the decisions I made got Jo killed.

My eyes fix on the flimsy door lock, my fingers twitching around

Pryce's card. I'm certain now that I can't call her. The less she knows—the less involved she is—the safer it will be for her, and I can't risk her telling anyone at MMP that I remember the men being in the car. I might be able to trust her, but if I didn't say a word to my colleagues before I fled with Jolanta, I obviously don't trust them.

CHAPTER SIX

Dusk drops the temperature below freezing, and I sit by my open window as the sky over the car park turns pink. In anticipation of my visitors, I've changed into scrubs with a top that matches the bottoms, and muffled the worst of my headache with ibuprofen. My arm is resting in a complicated Velcro-strapped sling, not to alleviate the painful shoulder I fabricated, but because I'm ever more paranoid that someone will see the writing on its cast.

The knock on the door comes far too soon. Pinpricks of stars are just beginning to appear, and the cold air is free of the medicalised stench that clings to everything in the hospital.

"Alis?"

I put a name to the voice even before I've turned to check it's really him. Keith Wallace drops a plastic bag on the overbed table and crosses the floor in four big strides. He stands in front of me for a moment and then smothers me in a hug.

"Hey," I murmur into his chest. His heart is booming beneath my ear, and he smells of stale tobacco and the gum he chews after every fag. Pushing sixty, he's unhappily married, with two kids who refuse to leave home, and he's been a detective with MMP for longer than I've been alive.

All of this hits me so quickly I feel as if I'm compiling a speed-dating profile. Likes: growing dahlias on his allotment, real ale, and fishing. Dislikes: Man United, slugs, and "all that social media shite."

"You recognise me, then?" he asks as he releases me.

"Naw, I just let any old bugger come in here and cop a feel."

He hacks out a laugh, and I perch on my bed, leaving him a choice of chairs.

"Are you on your own?" I ask.

"No, the DI is chatting to your doc. You know you're in the shit, don't you?"

"Aye," I say, lapsing into his accent, which is broader than mine.

His chubby face flushes as red as a post box. He's on a shitload of blood pressure and cholesterol meds, none of which seem to be working at the moment.

"What the hell were you thinking?" he says, his voice rising along with his colour. "Fucking off like that? You made me look a right twat. God, Al. Driving over here, I didn't know whether to kiss you or throttle you, and now to see you all beaten up—"

"I'm sorry," I whisper, and I truly am, because I think he's a good bloke who was probably easy to hoodwink. "I'm so sorry. Have I got you in trouble?"

"No." He slumps in the chair and rests his hands atop his belly. It's rounded and firm enough to support a pint pot without spilling a drop. "Not after the stunt you pulled with your mobile."

That draws a complete blank. "Dare I ask?"

He raises an eyebrow but then seems to realise I'm not having him on. "You really don't have the foggiest, do you?"

When I shake my head, he glances at the door. It's still closed, and there's no sign of Ansari lurking outside, so he pulls his chair closer to the bed and explains in a rapid undertone. "You used an app to send a text like clockwork every time you were scheduled to check in. Each message was slightly different, and I had no reason to think you weren't writing them. We weren't due a face-to-face until tomorrow." He picks at a greasy splotch of yellow on his tie, reminding me that he also likes a good fry-up. "I caught the tail end of yesterday's lunchtime news. I wasn't really listening to it until they mentioned the accident and your alias, and even then I didn't think anything of it. I mean, what are the odds that it was you, right? But it nagged at me for the rest of the day, so eventually I drove out to your Gorton flat. There was a load of junk mail behind your door, and I found your phone lying by your bed."

I nod, avoiding his eyes. I don't want him to see how troubled I am by the lengths I went to.

"Was she worth it?" he asks. "Was she worth sending your bloody career up the Swanee?"

The door opens again, saving me from having to answer, and a smartly dressed Pakistani man walks in. Instinct compels me to scramble to my feet, but he waves off my attempt before my heels have hit the tiles.

"Evening, sir." I keep my greeting formal, not daring to downgrade to "boss." Ansari is far younger than Wallace—mid forties, perhaps?—and he's giving me that sweaty-armpit, butterflies-in-the-belly feeling that superiors provoke in underlings they rarely encounter.

"DC Clarke." He shakes my hand, his grip firm and cool against the damp heat of mine. "How are you feeling?"

"Better than I was, sir." I touch my head, drawing his attention to my Frankenstein sutures. "Still muddled up here, but I'm getting some things back."

"I was just speaking to Dr. Lewis. She tells me it's a gradual and rather unpredictable process."

"Yes, it's very frustrating." I raise my head, ensuring I make good eye contact. "Obviously, I want to help you as much as I can."

"I appreciate that," he says. "Dr. Lewis asked that we keep this brief, given the amount of information you've had to process today, and I've already spoken at length to DS Pryce, so I just have the one question."

He takes a small Dictaphone from his pocket and sets it running. I'm sure there are rules about recording interviews, but I'm too rattled to object.

"What exactly was the nature of your relationship with Jolanta Starek?" he asks.

I don't need to exaggerate the effect this enquiry has on me. I sway on the spot and grab the rail on my bed. Wallace lurches forward, but Ansari's hand on his arm stops him. I was naive enough to believe I was prepared for this, but as I look at Ansari's face, at the challenge and barely contained fury bright in his eyes, doubt begins to pepper holes in everything I've rehearsed. What if I'm closeted at work? I would guess that I'm out, but to what extent? Immediate colleagues or all the way up to the brass?

"We...uh..." Tears start to cloud my vision. I'm not only outing myself here, I'm outing Jolanta, and I don't even think she was gay. Her parents have just lost their daughter; they shouldn't be forced to read sordid lies in the tabloids as they grieve.

I wipe my face on a tissue and blow my nose. Ansari makes a point of checking his watch, as if he has somewhere far more important to be than slumming in a hospital room with a detective he can't wait to scrape from the bottom of his team. I screw up the tissue and shove it into my sling. Fuck him. Someone murdered Jolanta and almost killed me, and it's possible one of his precious team is involved. If he wants an angle of attack, I have to make sure it's the wrong one.

"We were lovers," I tell him. I bow my head in contrition and improvise slightly. "I didn't mean for it to happen, sir, any of it. We must have been coming here so we could be together without worrying about being seen. I probably thought no one would miss me if I set my phone to send automatic texts."

I can hear the scratch of his pen as he takes notes. He doesn't write much, and he stops the recorder once he's sure I've finished speaking.

"I'll be handing this over to the Serious Misconduct Investigation Unit," he says. "I strongly suggest you contact your Federation rep."

"Yes, sir." Under normal circumstances, the prospect of a SMIU hearing would be an officer's worst nightmare, but it's the least of my current concerns.

I push off the bed as Ansari stands to leave. Wallace doesn't dare hug me again, but he knuckles my chin behind Ansari's back.

"See you soon, Al," he says.

"Yeah, I hope so, mate."

I want to go with them, to get home and start searching through my case notes. I can't do anything while I'm stuck in here, and if the SMIU suspend me, they'll demand my files. I let five minutes pass and then dodder barefooted to the nurses' station.

"Hey, is Dr. Lewis still around?" I ask its lone occupant.

"Nope. She went home." The nurse continues to leaf through a medical formulary. "Anything I can do for you?"

Discharge me, steal me some clothes, and smuggle me to Manchester, I think. "No," I say. "Thanks, though."

Back in my room, I have an impotent, wall-thumping paddy, and plot to sign myself out first thing in the morning, whether or not Lewis approves. My bravado lasts for all of forty seconds before it's replaced by an exhaustion so complete I barely make it to my bed. As I drag my legs under the covers, I spot the plastic bag Wallace brought and pull it toward me. He must have made another trip to my flat prior to coming here, because the bag is full of clothes—my clothes. Jeans, T-shirts, a jacket, pyjamas, even underwear. One of the socks jangles, and I empty out a couple of keys that presumably belong to my alias. There's no mobile, though. He hasn't gone so far as to return that to me. He's slipped a raisin and biscuit Yorkie into the middle of everything and stuck a Post-it Note on its wrapper: "These are your favourite."

With my head pillowed on my jacket, I open the chocolate bar and stuff a chunk into my mouth, letting it melt and then crunching the biscuit pieces. Despite everything that's happened today, I fall asleep smiling.

❖

I'm awake with the larks the next morning, which is fortunate, because getting washed and dressed one-handed takes forever. The fingers on my bad hand are less swollen than they were, but they're not very dextrous, making even simple tasks such as squirting toothpaste assume immeasurable layers of complexity. When I root through my bag of clothing, I'm relieved to discover that I favour crop-top bras without hooks and eyes. I need to show Lewis I can cope, so I muss and feather my fringe until it resembles Ceinwen's style, and use my teeth to help me tie the laces on my trainers.

Lewis sticks her head around the door before the breakfast trolley has started to rattle along the corridor.

"Morning," she says with the pep of someone who can put her knickers on in less than fifteen minutes. "Ceinwen said you wanted to speak to me."

"Yeah." I drag the word out as she notes my neatly folded scrubs and the toiletries I've repacked in their plastic wallet.

"Ah. Planning the great escape, are we?"

I nod, but it's hard to maintain a façade of steely determination when I'm fidgety with impatience. "I think someone might need this room more than I do."

"You do, huh?" She sits on my bed. "I thought we'd pencilled in your discharge for the end of the week."

"We did, but I have a place to live now, and family, so I'm sure I'll be all right."

"Do you live on your own?" she asks.

That's a good question. Wallace implied that Rebecca rented her own flat, but I'm not Rebecca anymore. Alis Clarke will have an entirely different address.

"Fucking hell," I mutter. I was so sure I had this figured out, but I haven't even grasped the basics. I forgot to ask where I live, I don't have the door keys to my place, and if there's an alarm to deactivate, then I really am fucked.

To her credit, Lewis doesn't jump on my insecurities and use them to her advantage, and when she does speak, she sounds less like a doctor talking to a patient than a professional chatting informally with another.

"Look, I'm not going to muck you around, Alis. You probably are fit for discharge. I just want to make sure you're safe."

I nod, careful not to react to her choice of phrasing. "I'll be okay. I have a few things to sort out, but I can manage."

"You've made up your mind, haven't you?"

"Yes," I say, drawing a line beneath the discussion. "I appreciate everything you've done for me, Doc."

"You did most of the hard work yourself. I'll discharge you into the care of a colleague of mine at Manchester Royal, and I'm sure Dr. Chander will do likewise. Were you hoping your brother would give you a lift home?"

"Aye, that was the plan."

She could drive a truck through the holes in my plan, but she chooses not to. "I'll get your papers and your meds sorted," she says. "Don't go anywhere without those."

I attempt a demure look and cross my heart.

She rolls her eyes. "You coppers are all the bloody same. Stubborn as mules and twice as daft."

I can't argue with that.

An hour later, a paper bag of take-home meds sits beside my empty porridge bowl. My appetite has improved day by day, and I'm spreading marmalade on a second slice of toast when someone knocks on my door. Expecting Martin, I freeze, the knife poised mid-smear, but it's Pryce who walks in.

"Hey." She stops a couple of steps beyond the threshold. "Sorry, I know it's early. Are you busy? I can come back."

"No, you're fine." I wave the knife at her, casting blobs of marmalade willy-nilly. She's brought coffee—two takeaway cups in a holder—and she seems so unsure of herself that I discount how much of a shit she was yesterday and attempt to put her at ease by offering my plate. "Toast?"

The gesture earns me a smile. She accepts a piece and places it on a napkin before putting one of the cups and a handful of sugar sachets in front of me.

After almost a week of tepid, insipid hospital brews, the scent of freshly ground coffee and full-fat milk rising from the gap in the lid sets my mouth watering. My only problem is getting the damn sugar into it without throwing it all over the floor.

"Here." She lifts the lid from the cup. "How many do you have?"

"Two, please."

I watch her shake the sugar onto the foam and stir it in, and then she sits back to watch me take my first joyful sip. I can't help myself; I moan with pleasure and let my eyes close. "Aw, Christ on a crutch, that's good."

Despite Pryce's chuckle, her face is sober when I peek over the brim of the cup, and I start to worry about why she's here, bearing gifts, at stupid o'clock in the morning. Still cradling my coffee with my right hand, I'm working up the nerve to ask her when she pre-empts me.

"I was just on my way into work, and Esther sent me a text." She picks up her drink but puts it down again without tasting it and corrects herself in a murmur. "Dr. Lewis. Dr. Lewis sent me a text to say you were going home."

"Aye." I gulp a hot mouthful, killing time while I endeavour to formulate a more intellectual response. I'm accustomed to the DS version of Pryce, the official one with sharp edges and suspicious eyes, not this strange fallible woman picking at the rim of her cup as her hair falls from its tie and curls around her face.

"I might be able to cadge a lift with my brother," I say.

She nods, but I doubt she's really listening. She pushes her cup away and brushes the scraps of paper into a neat pile.

"I should've handled things better," she says so softly that I have to lean closer. "Yesterday, I mean. I didn't have any right to speak to you the way I did, and I wanted to apologise for that."

"Oh." I'm gobsmacked. I'd guessed at a few motives for her visit, but an apology wasn't one of them. Flustered, I fall back on magnanimity. "It's okay. No harm done."

She shakes her head. "It's not okay. My conduct was far from okay. I don't have all the facts, and I had no right to judge your actions."

I have more of the facts than she does, and guilt creeps over me as I look at her reddened cheeks and the puffiness beneath her eyes. I bet she's been awake for most of the night worrying. She seems the type to let something like this chew a hole right through her conscience.

"It's my fuck-up, not yours," I tell her. "You were only the messenger."

"Still, under the circumstances," she sighs and opens her hands, "I wish I'd broken the news with more discretion."

"Hey, hindsight is a wonderful thing." I manoeuvre the cup in front of her. "Come on, it'll get cold."

She relents and drops three sugars in it. By the time she's screwed up the packets and added them to the mound of debris, she's relaxed enough to suck the foam from the stirrer. I catch myself staring as her lips purse around the wooden stick, and I quickly avert my eyes.

"Are you based here in Bangor?" I ask, for want of anything else to say.

"No, Colwyn Bay. That's where our headquarters are." She stretches out her legs, holding her cup loosely with both hands. "But I live near Betws-y-Coed, so I was sort of passing by."

Her wry expression tells me that's a fib. "Betws-y-Coed," I say, mimicking the singsong lilt she wrapped around the name. "That sounds so much prettier than Ardwick or Beswick."

"It's lovely." Her voice is wistful. "I don't have any neighbours, just mountains, lakes, and rivers."

The description strikes a chord. "I think I ran away from somewhere like that. Not recently," I add, spotting her confusion. "When I was eighteen or so. I have this image of a farmhouse and a field where we'd play, but every time I think about it, it's all scratchy and wrong."

Her brow knits. "Scratchy and wrong?"

"Yeah, like ants under my skin." Right on cue, the wrist encased by the cast begins to itch. I snarl and grab the knitting needle Ceinwen sneaked in from her gran's, digging it in until the irritation is soothed. As metaphors go, it's bang on.

"That's a tidy trick," Pryce says, but her head is tilted, and she's obviously dwelling on what I said. "Any idea why you left?"

I pause, the knitting needle still buried. "At a guess, it was possibly a gay thing."

"Right." Pryce takes a moment to sip her coffee, and her voice is solemn when she continues. "Not easy, is it? Being the only queer kid in the village."

"No, I don't think it was." It's a relief just to voice this, even if I can't pinpoint what actually happened. "I hope I haven't spent my adult life in hiding as well."

She has no difficulty following my train of thought. "You mean with the UC assignment?"

"Aye. New name, new job, new role to play." I touch the ring in my nose. "I want this to be Alis, not Rebecca."

She shrugs, a hint of amusement in her eyes. "Either way, it suits you." She checks her watch. "Hell, I should get a move on."

I nod, reluctant to see her go. We're not friends by any stretch, but I've enjoyed chatting to her. Given my current run of luck, she'll probably arrest me the next time she sees me.

"Have a safe trip home," she says.

I raise my cup in salute. "Wherever home may be."

"Oh, I might be able to help with that." She pats her pockets and then rummages through her bag, eventually pulling out a wallet—*my* wallet—and a piece of paper. "This was logged into evidence. And these are the addresses for you and your alias. I thought DC Wallace would have given them to you."

"Must've slipped his mind. He brought me a Yorkie instead."

She laughs. "Got his priorities straight, then. We didn't find any keys, other than the ones for the rental cottage. I can only assume they were thrown out in the crash."

I focus on the paper and decide not to challenge that assumption. Wallace must have given me his own set of keys for Rebecca's flat. The addresses mean nothing to me. Apparently, I live in Chorlton and my alias lived in Gorton, and both areas have Manchester postcodes.

"At least you have somewhere to aim for now," Pryce says.

I open the wallet. "And seventy quid."

"Don't spend it all at once." She stands to leave, and I slip off the bed to walk her to the door. She opens the door a crack but doesn't go through. "I'll keep you updated."

"Thank you." The polite exchange is our standard method of parting, yet it feels different this time, cut through with something I can't put my finger on. I shake the hand she offers. Her grip is strong and solid, and I have to bite my tongue to stop myself shutting the door again and telling her all my secrets.

I don't wave her off or watch her walk down the corridor. I go back to sitting on my bed, waiting for something else to happen.

CHAPTER SEVEN

My brother never arrives. Ceinwen comes in to deliver his apologies; it would seem another family emergency has trumped this lesser family emergency, and he will phone me at a later, unspecified time. Undeterred, I gather my meagre belongings and persuade her to arrange a taxi. She hugs me at the ward entrance, and I exchange the chocolates I've bought at the newsagents for Wallace's battered plastic bag.

"Good luck," she says. She feathers her fingers through my fringe and nods her approval. "You'll be fine, Alis. Go on, now. You don't want some old dear stealing your taxi."

I kiss her cheek, too choked up to do anything but clutch my bag and walk away. This small ward has been my sole place of safety. I know its layout, its routines, and its staff, and everything that lies beyond its entrance seems dense with threat and unpredictability—with the possible exception of Muhammad, that is, who beams at me as I approach his taxi, and then ushers me into its back seat.

"Train station," he says. "You in a rush, no?"

"No, no rush." I don't have a timetable, and I'm too busy fighting off the minor panic attack induced by fastening my seat belt to worry about missing the next train.

He peers into his rearview mirror as he pulls from the bay. "You all fixed now?" he asks. His eyes stray to the ridge of sutures splitting my hair.

"Yes," I gasp between heaving breaths, obviously far from fixed. My fingers start to tingle and then contort like claws, and I shut my mouth, sucking air in through my nose until my chest is burning, but I'm no longer panting as if sprinting for a photo finish.

Tempting though it is to cower on the seat and ask Muhammad to just drive around in circles for the rest of the day, I find that the more I do independently, the more confident I become. I tip Muhammad and manage to spend thirty-odd quid on a ticket to Manchester Piccadilly without stumbling over which banknote is which. The 9:22 is running late. I buy a Manchester A-Z in WHSmith and stand alone on the platform like a knock-off Paddington Bear for whom no one packed a lunch or supplied a proper suitcase.

Prominent wounds and an accompanying whiff of institutional shampoo guarantee me a seat on my own. I settle by the window and look out at deserted, wind-lashed beaches and seaside towns battened down and dormant for the winter. As the train rattles through Colwyn Bay, I picture Pryce at her desk, diligently at work on another case now that she's handed mine off to MMP. I see her laughing and cheerful, because she's probably less taciturn with her colleagues. Besides which, she has a really pretty smile.

We leave the sea views and then Wales behind and head back into England. A change at Crewe hurtles us into the northern towns. We cross Stockport's huge redbrick viaduct, and I crane my neck to spot the stupid blue pyramid that marks Junction 1 on the M60. The outskirts of Manchester slow the train to a crawl, and that skin-prickling sensation I described to Pryce afflicts me again as we enter beaten-down neighbourhoods with their tightly pressed terraced streets. I catch glimpses of the A6—the bottleneck road connecting Stockport to Manchester—and I remember weaving around the taxis and buses, blues on and sirens blaring, and cursing at the pedestrians who'd wander out regardless. Ardwick, where I rented our car, sits five minutes away, off a parallel feeder road, while Gorton is farther to the east. I plot my route to Rebecca's address using the A-Z and then tuck it out of sight again, unwilling to look like a guest in my hometown. Jo and I would catch the bus to work together. We'd sit on the top deck to reduce the impact of the potholes, and get stoned on the second-hand smoke from the schoolkids' joints.

Station Approach at Piccadilly is a heaving melee of besuited business types avoiding the no-fixed-abodes scavving on the floor for fag ends, and the students eating bacon butties. The occasional lost tourist adds an extra obstacle to the slalom, their wheeled trolleys clattering over the paving flags and getting in everyone's way. I lurk at the periphery, holding my bag close to my chest while I gather my bearings. From this vantage point, I can see the main bus stops: number 192 from the front stand, and 200-205 from the middle and rear. Any of the 200s would take me to Rebecca's, and I still have her pass in my wallet. A free ride beats wasting another tenner on a taxi, so I wander slowly down to the stop. Even with my bruises and the chunk missing from my hair, it's easy to blend in with a crowd entirely taken up with its own business, and I join a loose queue, willing the driver of the 201 to get off his phone and open the door.

Sticky heat envelops me when we're finally allowed to board, the windows streaming with the condensation generated by commuters herded in and trapped together for the hour-long slog into the city. I show the driver my pass, and he waves me on, unaware that I'm no longer the woman grinning at him from its photo. Huddled on one of the elevated seats, I tick off the journey's landmarks, my eyes peeled for the Tesco superstore and Mabs, the decades-old, recession-resistant lighting shop. I ping the bell at Tesco and help a teenaged mum extricate a double buggy and a chickenpox-covered child.

"Ta, chuck," she says, and I smile at her accent and the general hubbub that surrounds me as I step off into Gorton.

Standing aside to let the girl steer her brood past, I count two streets up from Mabs, realising as I do so that I needn't have bothered: the bright yellow awning of Louella's Caribbean Cafe is like a beacon amid the second-hand furniture shops and cheap takeaways, and it sits right on the corner of the street I need. Chivvied by the automated peep of a pedestrian crossing, I hurry over the main road. Gorton's back streets are not a good place to hang around looking indecisive, and my keys are in my hand before I reach Louella's. I take a right and then the second left onto Turing Avenue, striding along as if I'm not using the painted numbers on the wheelie bins to gauge my progress. Elevated above the street, the three-storey terraced houses might once have been sought after, but the area has gone to shit around them, and most are divided into bedsits or used as hostels. Number sixteen looks much like the others, but subtle distinguishing features—the pattern of missing flagstones on its narrow path, and the flower pots optimistically arranged by the entrance, lush with weeds—click something in my memory and confirm I'm in the right place.

The front door swings open when I push it, and I have a vivid recollection of a running battle with the landlord to get the lock fixed. Soft jazz drifts from the ground floor flat, bringing with it the scent of dope and home baking. I once accepted a piece of carrot cake from Bernie and spent the rest of the afternoon lying on my bed giving names to all the mould patches on the ceiling.

Climbing the two flights of stairs knocks the wind out of me.

It's already been a long day, and I feel like a nowty toddler, achy and hungry and overdue a nap. Too weary to be apprehensive, I unlock Flat C and drop my bag, splaying my palm against the wall of the narrow hallway until my head stops spinning. When I slap the light switch, a low-energy bulb gradually brightens the magnolia wallpaper and picks out the tatty but cheerful runner that covers most of the bargain basement laminate flooring.

The layout is simple: bedroom and living room to the right, bathroom and kitchen to the left. I use the loo and then wash hours of travelling from my face, luxuriating in soap that smells of honey and vanilla, and a towel that doesn't grate the top layer from my skin. It's weird to be home but not home, because everything here is in keeping with Rebecca's budget rather than that of a detective constable, so the toiletries are supermarket own brand, and when my rumbling stomach directs me to the kitchen, the first cupboard I open is full of Aldi baked beans and soups. I came here to find my case files and my laptop, but I can't think beyond emptying a tin of beef and chunky veg broth into a saucepan and stuffing my face with a handful of stale imitation Ritz. Half a packet of crackers later, I leave the soup to simmer and go to explore the remaining rooms.

The first of two closed doors leads to the bedroom. I stop dead on its threshold, a cracker poised between my teeth.

"Fuck."

The room has been ransacked, every drawer emptied and tossed. The bedding and mattress lie gutted, hacked open with something serrated, and the lava lamp that entertained me for hours the day Bernie got me stoned is bleeding fluid and green gel onto the carpet.

"Shit, shit, shit!"

I drop to my knees and lay my hand on the wet patch. It's still soaking and spreading, and I scramble backward like a crippled crab, my eyes darting to the wardrobe, the bed frame, anywhere an intruder with a knife might hide.

I cringe as I hit the doorjamb, the thud of bone on wood reverberating through the tiny flat. I haven't been quiet since I got here, though. I've flushed the toilet, banged cupboards, and rooted through the cutlery for a tin opener, and no one's pounced on me or attempted to make a run for it.

A determined mantra of "It's probably just a burglary" gets me off the floor. I bring the remnants of the lava lamp with me, leading with the sharp end as I check the room for bogeymen and then head back into the hallway. I don't tiptoe or creep. If someone is lying in wait for me, I want them to think I'm blundering obliviously toward my fate, not armed with broken glass and fully prepared to use it.

The destruction of the living room has obviously been interrupted by my arrival. The bookshelves on the far side of the room are upended, their contents strewn about. The near side is as yet untouched. I can't see the perpetrator, but I only have an instant to brace myself before a man barrels out from behind the sofa and launches me into the hallway. I manage a couple of wild slashes as I slump against the wall, earning a splatter of blood that's rewarded with a kick in my guts.

"Stupid fucking slag!" he snarls, and lands another kick.

I vomit crackers onto his laces and slip from his grasp, my efforts with the glass now limited to stabbing at his ankles. He curses again, his voice disappearing beneath the roar of my ear going to shit, and he belts me with a weighted rucksack as he shakes his leg free. I'm too far off balance to grab the bag, so I settle for making myself as small a target as possible and not provoking him further. He steps over me, his boot landing an inch from my nose, and seconds later the front door slams behind him.

I close my eyes, quite happy to stay put for a while, secure in a ball, with Ella Fitzgerald crooning faintly in my good ear and my knees drawn up to lessen the throbbing in my belly.

The smell of burning soup eventually forces me to my feet. I groan as pain twists through my abdomen, but everything's relative, and I've had worse over the last week. Using the wall as a prop, I limp into the kitchen and extinguish the gas. Thick smoke is rising from the pan, and it rushes out of the window I open. Three storeys below, Gorton is carrying on as if nothing has happened. A crappy car with an overloud exhaust roars over the speed bumps, and something races along Hyde Road with its sirens blaring.

The sound of someone else's emergency goads me into action. I'll have to report the break-in. A normal person, one who doesn't suspect that the violent invasion of her home may have been an inside job, would report it immediately, and I have to be seen to be acting normally. Allowing myself twenty minutes' grace, the time it might take Ms. Normality to recover her equilibrium, I use it to process the raided rooms. My laptop is missing, and the hard copies of files I presume are related to my UC assignment are strewn across the small dining table. The man has been clever, not making it obvious that the files were his target. They're disturbed but appear intact, their pages still neatly bound and numbered. He could easily have used his mobile to photograph the salient details, though, and most of it's probably duplicated on the laptop, should he manage to crack my password.

I don't have an inventory of my possessions, but a suspicious gap beneath the telly suggests he's taken a DVD player or similar, and when I check the drawers in the bedroom I find a jar of small change almost emptied. Sitting on the shredded mattress, I take stock of the carnage and begin to question whether this was the handiwork of anyone other than a smack rat hitting an easy target. It's as if I'm caught in a grotesque game, where one side is covering up a crime within a crime and I go along with it because their tactic happens to work to my advantage. But then perhaps I'm just being paranoid. Perhaps I timed my homecoming to unfortunate and shitty perfection.

The uncertainty sets my head pounding and kicks up my tinnitus. I dry-swallow a couple of ibuprofen and limp across to the phone on my bedside table. I'm debating which number to call—999? 101? Wallace's?—when I spot the boots upended and tossed beneath my desk. They're work boots, my size, steel-toed and sturdy. A stamp on their inner lining marks them as "Property of Hamer & Sons," and they're an exact match to the pair that just gave my belly button a deep purple halo.

"Bollocks," I mutter.

So much for my smack rat theory.

CHAPTER EIGHT

The paramedic stands in front of me, her hands on her hips. She is not amused. Neither am I, but I'm not budging from my seat in the kitchen, no matter how many times she taps her foot. Apparently, I "lack capacity" to refuse a trip to the hospital, and try as I might, I can't convince her that this is due to my pre-existing head injury and not the result of being booted in the abdomen.

"You're disorientated." She points to the first item on her paperwork. "You couldn't tell me the date."

She's splitting hairs—my guess was one day out—and she's starting to piss me off. I'm about to suggest exactly where she can stick her clipboard when Wallace walks in.

"Bloody Nora." He tips my chin, examining me for fresh damage. "You've not been home five minutes."

"Yeah, hell of a welcoming committee." I lower his hand, squeezing his pudgy fingers. "I'm okay."

"She's not okay," the paramedic pipes up. "She needs regular neuro obs at the hospital."

"She'd fail 'em," Wallace says. Then, to me, "Didn't you explain all of this?"

I shrug. "Several times, but she has a checklist."

"How's about I run you to A&E after we're finished here?" he says, before turning to the paramedic for her approval. "Any problems in the meantime, I'll drop the nines again."

The paramedic huffs and deliberates and then writes a long postscript absolving her of any responsibility should my grey matter suddenly leak from my nose. I accept a copy and promise to take it with me on the trip to A&E that Wallace and I will absolutely not be making.

He waits until the front door closes behind her and then he nods to the hallway.

"SOCO are on their way. Did you get a good look at him?"

I shake my head. "Taller than me. White, heavyset, wearing a navy or black jacket and black gloves. He had his hood up, so I couldn't see his face properly. He knocked me to the floor within seconds."

"He hurt you?"

"No." I fold the ambulance report in two and slip it in my pocket. "No, I'm fine."

Wallace scratches his jaw but doesn't push the issue. "How'd he get in?"

Oh shit. In all the excitement, I'd not even considered this. *Used the key I've not seen since the crash* is the most plausible explanation. It wasn't as if the door was hanging from its hinges when I arrived.

"I'm not sure," I say, and as we go to have a look, I actually cross my fingers in the hope that the bloke's been smart enough to leave a mark, no matter how subtle.

"Any idiot with a hairclip and a bit of knowhow could've picked this," Wallace says. He puts a grubby pair of glasses on and peers at the Yale lock. "See these scratches?"

I lean closer and nod at the faint gouges. They'll do nicely.

"Crafty bastard," he continues. "I'll have words with your landlord. The main door is knackered as well."

"Yeah, I noticed." I lead him back to the living room, where we survey the mess.

"Jesus. Did he take much?"

"He got my laptop and whatever I had under the telly—possibly a DVD?" I don't mention the files. I've left them as they were, scattered at random in the same manner as the magazines and newspapers I'd kept on the coffee table. "The bedroom is worse than this. I think there's a bit of cheap jewellery and some money missing, but he trashed everything he set his mucky little paws on."

"Fucker was probably high as a kite," Wallace says, and I murmur my accord, keen to encourage this conclusion. He doesn't spot the incongruity of a perp being dextrous enough to lock pick while smacked off his tits. "Good thing you don't live here anymore, eh?"

"Aye, there is that." I lean on the wall as he walks to my bedroom and gives a low whistle. I should be suffering more of a reaction to this, to the shock of being assaulted and of having a stranger violate my privacy, but the day's traumas have simply slotted beside the accumulated trauma of the past six, and I can't risk separating them and focusing on any one thing. Not yet.

"Priti called me on the way over," he says. "She's been pecking my damn head since yesterday. Did you listen to these messages?"

He shows me the landline phone with its flashing answer-machine icon. I take the handset into the kitchen, and the sound of Priti's voice, steeped in concern, is like a salve on my frazzled nerves.

"Phone her," he tells me. "You've got thirteen months to catch up on."

Getting up close and personal with some bloke's size fourteens doesn't seem to have exacerbated the issues with my memory. If anything, being in the flat, surrounded by my belongings, is akin to having a dedicated prompter, someone standing in the wings and gently reminding me of the time I bought those socks with the sheep on them, or of the evening Jo and I almost blew up the microwave making popcorn to go with an *Alien* double bill. I don't have any memories of Priti being here, but I find her photograph hidden in my bedside cabinet, and it's less of a subtle nudge and more of a sledgehammer.

"She transferred to DV about eight months back," Wallace says, looking at the photo over my shoulder. Priti and I are arm in arm, wearing matching kits and grubby from a football match. "And she ditched that bellend she was seeing—James?"

"Josh," I say and then frown as if second-guessing myself. Wallace is obviously well tuned in to the MMP grapevine, and the last thing I need is him spreading the word that I'm on the mend. "Or it could've been James."

"Either way, he was a twerp." He taps the photo. "Your hair looks miles better now. When was this taken?"

I turn the image to check the date, though I could easily reel off the specifics. Priti and I met at Sedgely Park on the first day of our training course, class of 2009. We worked out of Longsight for five years, until we decided we'd done our time in uniform and applied for positions on the MCT. I'm not surprised by her move to Domestic Violence; she'd never really settled on Major Crimes.

"Seven...wait, no, eight years," I tell Wallace. "Did we play hockey or something?"

"Football," he says in the undertone I'm coming to think of as his "no sudden moves or revelations" voice. "You had a cracking left foot."

I've probably still got one, but he seems content to write me off, so I continue to nudge him in that direction. He's on the verge of either patting my head or hugging me when I'm rescued by a knock on the door.

"Hello? Al? You there?" Priti calls out from the hallway, and I meet her halfway, stumbling into her arms like an overwrought drunk as my carefully constructed defences collapse en masse.

"Hey, hey, it's okay, you're all right."

She continues to murmur while I sob against her neck, a week's worth of hurt and confusion and fear coming out in wet blasts of snot and saliva. She's smaller than I am, and we resort to sitting on the floor, shoulder to shoulder, our fingers entwined. She pulls her sleeve over her free hand and uses it to clean my face.

"Alis Clarke," she says, "what have you been doing to yourself?" Her accent is far more Bolton than Kerala, and there's no suggestion of rebuke or censure in her question. She probably doesn't want an answer, not right now at any rate.

"I fucked everything up," I whisper.

"Mmhm." She sets her palm on my cheek, bringing our faces close together. "I know you, my darling, and I'm sure there was more to it than that. Now come and pack a bag. I'm taking you home."

I nod but don't move until she tugs my hand. Then I kiss her forehead, overwhelmed by the simple trust she's just shown in me. I can't tell her how right she is, that there's a hell of a lot more behind what's happened, but I love her for not thinking the worst of me.

❖

When Priti said "home" she meant mine: a ground-floor, one-bedroom flat in a large detached Edwardian.

"Bloody hell. How much rent do I pay?" I ask. The street is quiet and tree-lined, and I know from googling on Ceinwen's phone that property in Chorlton doesn't come cheap.

"You don't rent this, darling. You own it." Priti laughs as my jaw actually drops. "It was a complete shithole when you bought it. You charmed the pants off the vendor and got it for a song. And I do mean that literally."

I follow her into a sunny entrance hall with a hardwood floor. "Which part?"

"Both parts." She laughs again and drops the front door key into my hand. She's always had a spare. "Did you find yours?"

"No." Wallace and I searched everywhere, but none of my keys were in the Gorton flat. Changing the locks to this property will be number one on the to-do list I'm yet to write.

"Are you hungry?" she asks. "I'm starving. Fortunately I brought provisions." She hoists two large bags aloft and bustles past me, making a beeline for the kitchen.

"Need any help?" I call above the clang of pots.

"No, thanks! You can't cook for shit."

"Oh." This revelation deflates me. After seven days of hospital food, I'd been looking forward to meals that weren't mass-produced and pre-packaged. With hindsight, burning the soup was probably an omen, but there were extenuating circumstances at the time. For a moment, listening to her vigorous chopping, I entertain the possibility that my skill set might be different now, like those people who wake from comas speaking fluent German, but I can't conjure up a single recipe idea, nor the inclination to remedy that, so I reconcile myself to a future of microwave dinners and salad, and go to find my bedroom.

My first attempt takes me into a cubbyhole cluttered with a shoe rack and cleaning bits and bobs. My bedroom is the next door along, a south-facing room with a bay window whose sill is so wide you could curl up on it and read a book. Several of the multicoloured cushions scattered along the ledge have distinct backside-shaped dips in them. I seem to have furnished the rest of the room with a job lot from IKEA. An oversized double bed dominates the space, its pale wooden frame a close match to the freestanding wardrobe and a bookshelf that's straining at the seams. Three of the walls are a soft sage green, with the fourth papered in a swirling floral pattern. I peer closer at the design, sure that my choice of forget-me-nots wasn't intended to be ironic.

I haven't brought much from the other flat, just enough clothes to cover the work boots I stuffed into the corner of the bag, plus all of the case files. Wallace was on the phone when I told him I was taking those. He made a "be my guest" gesture and continued to argue with his wife. I should have time to read through them before the SMIU come sniffing around, but for the moment I shove the holdall under the bed and grab a pair of pyjamas.

The scent of onions and garlic is wafting down the hallway as I run a bath hot enough to fill the bathroom with steam. Keeping my casted arm elevated, I sink beneath a layer of bubbles so thick they cascade over the side. The warmth soothes the spasms in my ribs and the newer, more intense pain around my midriff. My head bobs, too heavy for my neck. I let my chin drop onto my chest and doze, until Priti wakes me by building a tower of froth on my nose.

"Hey." I blink and go cross-eyed looking at the bubbles. She blows them away and taps my forehead with a sponge.

"Tea's nearly done." She dips the sponge and eases it around the bruising on my face. "Do you need help with anything?"

I deliberate and then raise one hairy leg from the depths. "How good a friend are you?"

"The best you've ever had," she says, and flips the top off the shaving gel.

❖

Our early dinner is the antithesis of mass-produced and pre-packaged. Lapsing into an easy routine, Priti and I sit together on the sofa, our lap-trays laden with plates of biryani and warm parathas. I shovel in forkfuls of chicken and rice, trying at first to isolate flavours and then giving up and simply enjoying the mix. Half a bottle of wine sends my head into a pleasant whirl, and once the plates are cleared, I snuggle beneath the blanket Priti throws over us and watch her thumbing through an old photo album.

"Here we go," she says, setting the open album on my knee. "That's your mum and dad, with Martin."

I slip the picture from its sleeve and hold it closer. It's a summer picnic shot, with the green swell of the moors in the background and everyone barefoot from paddling in the river. The Clarke family traits have divided along gender lines: Martin is a trimmer, blonder version of my dad, while I've inherited my mum's darker colouring and the way her nose ruffles when she smiles. I took this photo myself, fumbling with the focus and getting nowty at Martin for pulling stupid faces.

"How long ago did she die?" I ask.

"It was before I met you," Priti says. "Twelve years, maybe? You were temping, factory work mostly, but you took a lot of time off to care for her."

"Twelve years? Jesus." My mum's death feels so recent that the sorrow of it follows me around like a tangible thing, yet I'm probably at the stage where I only visit her grave at Christmas and birthdays.

I flick through the rest of the album, tracking the passage of 1997: snow thick on the ground in February; an awkward teenage birthday party where only two people appear to have turned up; my dad beaming in the straw by a new calf, his hands and forearms covered with gore; prize-giving at Hawdale Secondary School. From annotations on the backs of the Polaroids, I learn that my mum and dad are called Lisa and Harry and that we lived on Hawclough Farm, nestled in the Saddleworth moors. I look hollow-eyed and miserable in many of the shots, as if I'm already aware I'm a square peg in a round hole.

In 1999, another girl starts to appear in the photos with me. We're about the same age, and I obviously adore her. We sit side by side at a pub lunch, two baby dykes clasping hands beneath the table, surrounded by an oblivious family.

"That's Shelley," Priti says, nudging closer to rest her chin on my shoulder. "Your first love."

For the next few pages the sullen teenage me disappears, replaced by a girl with sparkling eyes, bright purple hair, and a mischievous grin. The album stops abruptly midway through October, leaving Halloween, my sixteenth birthday, and Christmas undocumented.

Priti uncurls my fingers from the empty pages and closes the album.

"Your dad caught you at it in one of the barns," she says, an instant before the memory hits me. "He dragged Shelley back to her parents and wouldn't let you out of the house for weeks. You missed a load of school."

I'd missed even more when I started bunking off, too ashamed and too fucked up to want to sit in a classroom full of whispered gossip and snide glances. I scraped grades good enough for sixth form and picked a college in Stalybridge, two bus rides away.

"You hated your mum and dad for ages," Priti tells me quietly. "You moved to a shared dosshouse in Manchester, and you only went back to Hawclough when your mum was diagnosed."

"What are we like now? Me and dad and Martin?" It's an honest enquiry. I have faint impressions of them but little that I can class as reliable.

"Better. Martin was too busy on the farm to really get involved, and your dad stopped behaving like such a twat once he realised there were worse things in life than having a gay daughter."

I nod. I'd suspected as much, but I'm relieved to have it confirmed. "Did he remarry?"

"No. He signed the farm over to Martin and went to live in Tenerife. He bought an apartment there after your mum died. Martin's married with three kids. You have a few photos of them on your phone."

"Three? God." I lean my head back on the sofa, resigned to my role as the absent aunt, thirteen months undercover having severed my already brittle family ties. I bet I'm the copper who volunteers to work Christmas and New Year.

The album lands with a thud as Priti drops it out of sight by the side of the sofa.

"Do you want to talk about it?" she asks, and I know she's not referring to my trip down Half-Memory Lane. "*Any* of it?"

"Worst-case scenario, I might get done for death by dangerous," I say. "There's a DS at Colwyn Bay who's dealing with that side of it." I want to tell her more about Pryce, about how much I trust Pryce to do the right thing in terms of the investigation and any charges she may bring, but Priti cuts in.

"Have you spoken to a lawyer?"

"No."

"Been questioned under caution?"

"No." I squeeze her fingers. "Not yet."

"Well, you get a bloody good lawyer first. You hear me?"

I look her in the eye, glad to have someone fighting my corner. "I hear you."

"Did you take your case files from the flat?" she asks, and then gives me a serene smile. "What? You going to 'no comment' me?"

"No comment."

"Yeah, yeah. Fuck off." She mimics my position: head back, feet on the coffee table, legs crossed at the ankles. "Copy what you can and then volunteer them to the SMIU. That'll keep them occupied for a while, and it's the first thing they'll ask for now that your laptop's done a bunk."

"Aye." I keep my response noncommittal, unsure what she might have worked out, and silently starting to panic.

"I mean it, Al." She doesn't shout, not with our faces almost touching, but her voice rises. "These arseholes don't muck around, and you can't hope to defend yourself if you don't have a clue what your assignment was."

"Oh," I say. "No, no, of course not."

"This isn't without precedent," she says. She's on a roll now and doesn't notice when I gulp her glass of juice to regulate my breathing. "Look at that bloke from the Met, the one who went UC for years and had all those affairs. If you and this Jolanta lady really were in a relationship, perhaps it was a part of your assignment."

"Perhaps." I put the glass down, happy to explore this tangent with her. "It's certainly worth looking into."

"It'd be bloody typical of our lot as well: set something like this up and then leave you high and dry when it all goes to shit." She huffs, her eyes narrowing. "You won't find it in those files, either. They wouldn't be able to make it official or anything."

This grabs my attention for a completely different reason, and she hits the jackpot on my behalf as she continues.

"You'll have kept a copy, though," she says. "You're not stupid. You'll have everything on a disc or a memory stick somewhere. If I were you, that's the first thing I'd be looking for."

CHAPTER NINE

Have you got everything you need?" Priti asks. Like a mother hen on overdrive, she's doled out painkillers and tucked me into bed by nine.

"Yes, thanks. I think I'm sorted." I pat the empty half of the mattress. "You sure you don't want to sleep in here? We can top and tail."

She helps herself to another pillow and heads for the door. "The sofa is fine. I have to be up at six, and you're a wriggler."

"Right." I study her in the lamplight, the eco-friendly bulb casting shadows across her dark skin.

"We kissed once," she says, adding "mind reader" to her impressive list of talents. "We were drunk, and I'd never kissed a girl, so you volunteered for the purposes of"—she bends her fingers into air quotes—"expanding my painfully narrow horizons."

I snort a laugh. I would give my eyeteeth to remember that night. "And how did that work out?"

"Not too shabby. The lack of stubble rash was a real bonus. Unfortunately, it would seem that I lack even the slightest inclination towards bisexuality."

"Priti Dewan." I clamp my hand to my heart. "You wound me."

She comes over to plant a kiss on my forehead. "Go to sleep, you daft sod. I'm in the next room if you need anything."

"Thank you."

"You'd do the same for me," she says. "Light on or off?"

"On for a while, I think."

She narrows her eyes and passes me the pile of case files I've set on my bedside table. "Don't stay up too late."

"I won't. I'll be good."

Withholding comment, she closes my door behind her. A few seconds later I hear the murmur of the television, and I wait until the creak of the sofa tells me she's settled down. I check the obvious places first, tiptoeing from the bed to remove the clothes from my drawers. I unfold and refold everything, shaking out knickers, bras, and socks over the mattress, and then run my fingers around each empty space, testing the wood for loose panels or hidey-holes. One-handed and still tipsy, I take almost an hour to search the first cabinet, and I discover nothing but a penchant for novelty socks and mismatched underwear.

"Bugger it all to damnation!"

I fling the last pair of socks over my shoulder and slump on the bed, scowling at my next target, a wardrobe with a rail full of smart shirts for office days and a lower level devoted to casual. Mustering the energy to crack on, I try to think like the pre-crash me, the one who hopefully had the gumption to store incriminating evidence on some device other than her MMP-issue laptop. Would I really have been stupid enough to hide it here, when any police officer with a contact in human resources could find out my address? Lateral thinking reintroduces the issue of my missing house keys, and I walk slowly around the room, scrutinising its surfaces and shelves for signs of disturbance. Thirteen months' worth of dust works as well as any of SOCO's fancy science, and I confidently conclude no one's been in my bedroom.

Having thrown doubt on the necessity of searching my wardrobe, I decide to postpone the task until morning. Too hyper to sleep, I wriggle beneath the quilt and pull the uppermost case file onto my lap.

The optimistic and possibly geeky side of me is hoping to unearth a convenient précis summarising the basics, alongside a dramatis personae and a well-inked map. Instead, a handful of grainy surveillance shots flutter onto the bedding, while the remainder of the file comprises pages of alphabetised expenses. I arrange the photos in no particular order, creating a montage of men getting into and out of vehicles, most of them taken in the same car park beside a large mill bearing "Hamer & Sons" signage. The men are all white, sted-head types who look like they eat bricks for breakfast, and I'm not surprised when the names on the reverse reveal four of them to be members of the Hamer dynasty.

A brief flick through the second file provides copies of their criminal records. These are extensive and varied, but none of the men have clocked any major prison time, and a disproportionate number of cases against them have collapsed before reaching trial. Donald Hamer, the eldest of those photographed and the founder of Hamer & Sons, has no record at all. A Manchester-born-and-bred father of five, his home shopping company has flourished despite the recession and Brexit and stiff competition from the online giants. He employs more than eleven hundred staff at his main distribution centre in Ardwick, and I was one of them.

According to file #M342, I started working at the Ardwick branch just after New Year. Months of tedious, diary-like entries record order picking for ten-hour shifts—household goods, DIY, home entertainment, and clothing. I've noted the names of team leaders and colleagues, shift patterns and departments, but the most exciting incident I come across in fifty-plus pages is an ambulance being called for a lass with bellyache. Most of the employees appear to be Eastern Europeans, and I usually work on DIY alongside Jolanta and a lad called Krzysztof Janicki.

Stifling a yawn, I hold up a colour photo of Jolanta and Krzys. It looks like we've gone out for a few drinks after a shift, and Jo and Krzys are laughing for the camera, pints in hand. I find his background check a few pages later. It's unremarkable, but there's a mobile number listed for him, and his home address is just down the road in Longsight. I copy everything onto a notepad and clip the photo to it. Finding his face among all these strangers is like a shot of caffeine, and I continue to skim read the day-by-day reports, scanning for anomalies or breaks in the routine. Nothing untoward happens until eleven months into the assignment, and then two events occur almost simultaneously: Jolanta begins a new shift pattern, and Krzys and I are transferred to a different team, a transfer that apparently comes with a two-hundred-pound-a-month pay rise.

The file ends there on December 12, and I grab the final three, but my efforts to arrange them chronologically are hampered by my abandonment of the journal format. In its place are notes of companies and individuals, their names set against a series of numbers and letters, all rendered in a variety of colours. At no point have I included a key to my inscrutable coding system. I must never have imagined needing one.

"For fuck's sake!"

I launch the third file from my knee and kick it to the floor for good measure. It's only as the room starts to blur that I realise my fit of pique will have consequences. The ceiling spins and dips as I smack my head back onto the pillow, and I close my eyes, waiting out the spike in my blood pressure and the pounding at my right temple. A sudden deafness on that side is gradually replaced by my usual tinnitus, and I scrub tears from my cheeks, alarmed by how fragile my recovery seems to be. Scared of moving, I stare at the lampshade above me and try to make sense of the information in the files.

I start with the basics. MMP clearly suspect the company of being a front, which means that the Hamers are probably distributing more than cordless drills and smoothie makers.

"Oh shit!" Gritting my teeth against the pain in my head, I grab my notepad and bedside phone and dial Krzys's mobile number. It starts to ring. "Come on, mate," I mutter. "Come on, please pick up."

Krzys changed shifts when I did, moving onto the team that prompted me to collate a mass of incomprehensible rainbow-themed data. His name, image, and contact details may have been seen by the man who broke into my other flat and assaulted me, and it's obvious from my journal that Krzys and I were friends.

The phone clicks to an answering service, but I don't leave a message. What the fuck would I say?

I lie awake for most of the night, snatching the odd few minutes of restless sleep between long, sweat-soaked hours spent fretting. I don't phone Krzys again. I can't risk my home number making multiple appearances on his call register. At four a.m., too antsy to stay in bed, I photocopy the colour-coded pages using my printer. I make notes of anything that strikes me as significant, half-filling my pad before I hear Priti's alarm go off next door. She starts the shower, and I tidy my room while the hum of the boiler provides cover. I'm back in bed, impersonating the newly woken, when she peeks round the door.

"That time already?" I ask, adding a yawn for extra effect.

"Yep." She sits on the bed and rests her hand on my thigh. "You look like hell warmed over. Stay put and I'll fetch you a brew."

I don't argue. I feel as awful as I apparently look, and I have to use both hands to steady the mug of coffee she brings me.

"Bad night?" she asks.

"Mmm." The coffee is too hot to gulp, but I do my best. She's made it strong enough to wake the dead. "Everything's a bit cockeyed. I mean, this is my actual bed, but I feel like a guest here."

"That'll change once you've got your bearings." Her keys jangle as she tugs them from her pocket. "I'd best get a wriggle on. I've left you all my phone numbers, and there should be enough food to tide you over. We can do a proper shop tonight if you want."

"Priti?"

She looks at me, chewing through the gloss on her lower lip. "What?"

"I'm fine."

She kisses my cheek and then rubs away the smear of makeup. "You're not fine. Don't give me that crap. You're pale, and you're shaking like an alky. You need to stay in bed and…well, just stay in bed. Watch *Jeremy Kyle* and *Cash in the Attic* and eat chocolate. You've lost far too much weight."

I've taken her hand halfway through her outburst, and I use it to pull her into a hug. "Okay, so I'm not fine just yet, but I will be," I tell her. "Please don't worry."

She sniffles into my neck but eventually releases me. "Feet up. Telly. Chocolate," she reminds me. "I'll be home about seven."

I plump my pillows and make a show of getting comfy. "I promise not to have your tea ready or anything."

"That's the spirit."

I track her footsteps down the hall, followed by the click of her key in the lock. Her car starts first time, and she leaves the engine running while she scrapes the frost from her windscreen. As the pebbles on the driveway crunch beneath her tyres, I'm already on the phone, ordering a taxi to Longsight, and shimmying out of my pyjamas.

The pip of the taxi's horn sends me pelting to the front door, a shower-damp Pavlov's dog with my shirt half-buttoned and my trainers unlaced. The taxi driver, bloodshot and bleary at the end of his shift, doesn't bat an eyelid at my state of undress. He drops me outside the address I give him—five doors down from where I actually need to be—and pockets my tenner without offering change.

There's a light on at Krzys's house, but the terrace has been split into flats, and I'm not sure which window is his. I press the buzzer marked "K. Janicki." If he's still working the same shift pattern, he's on an early today, so he'll probably be getting ready to catch the bus. I wait two minutes and buzz again, stepping away from the door to watch the front windows for signs of life. When I buzz for the third time, a face appears at the ground floor bay, the curtains parting properly to reveal a black woman who glowers at me as she ties a cord around her dressing gown.

"I'm looking for Krzys," I mouth, exaggerating each syllable and pointing to the relevant buzzer like an imbecilic mime. Still shooting daggers at me, the woman swipes her curtains shut. Her silhouette stoops and then disappears, and I kick the step, debating my next move. I'm about to head back to the telephone box I'd spotted on the main road when I hear the front door open. The woman doesn't look any friendlier in the flesh. She folds her arms, her ample form filling the doorway.

"You family?"

"Uh. No." I'm too sleep-deprived to concoct a cover story that would factor in my obvious injuries, an unpredictable timeframe, and a choice of identities. Conscious of the slippered foot tapping a beat on the step, I default to the simplest option and hope she doesn't recognise me from the news. "I'm a friend of his. I work with him at Hamer's. We usually get the bus together, but he's not been answering his phone."

Her stance relaxes a fraction. "Shouldn't you be off sick?"

"Yeah," I say, cradling my casted arm. I left in such a hurry that I've forgotten my sling. "But this is my third strike."

The woman nods her understanding, sympathy replacing the hostility in her expression. "That bunch of louts wouldn't know an honest day's work if it bit them on the arse." She ushers me into a foyer littered with junk mail, where the smell of fried food is thick enough to make my skin feel greasy.

"I haven't seen Krzysztof for at least a week." Her gaze strays to a door off the first-floor landing, and she pulls a key from the pocket of her gown. "I keep this for him, but I been too scared to let myself in."

"That's understandable," I say, pondering the legalities of searching his flat under less than bona fide circumstances. My concern for him quickly overrides any procedural heebie-jeebies, however, and I take the plunge. "Would you like me to come in with you?"

She hands over the key and follows a couple of steps behind me as I walk up the stairs.

"I knocked on a few times," she says. "I got duff knees, so I don't get out much, and he used to do odds and sods for me: pick up my shopping, pay my gas and leccy." She bends double at the top, panting for breath. "I couldn't smell nothing when I knocked. I had a neighbour go that way one time, and you never forget the stink."

"I can imagine." I pause with the key poised in the lock, my fingers slippery around the metal. I can't smell anything other than congealed fat, but still I brace myself for that putrid hit of decomposition.

"Krzys?" I call as I push the door wide. No swarm of bluebottles assails me, and my first cautious breath detects only a faint floral trace from a plug-in air freshener. The flat is silent and secured, its windows shut and its curtains drawn. Walking through each of its four rooms in sequence, I start to spot gaps here and there: toiletries missing from a shelf above the bath, a space in a row of shoes, a hook where a winter coat may have hung. As his neighbour sinks onto the sofa, I cover my hand with my sleeve and check his bedroom for his wallet, keys, passport, and mobile. I can't find any of them, and the half-empty drawers suggest he packed a bag before he left. There's no sign of a struggle or of haste. His bed is made, and the flat is tidy. Whatever prompted his departure, it doesn't seem to have thrown him into a blind panic.

"Perhaps he went to visit his family," the woman says, fanning her face with a copy of the *Manchester Evening News*. "Why wouldn't he have told me, though? He knows I'd worry."

I'm wondering that as well, but it's easier to sidestep the question and store it for later.

"Do you have a number for his parents?" I ask. I haven't seen an address book, and there's no landline handset with a convenient directory.

"No, I think he kept everything on his mobile. No one writes nothing down these days." The movement of the newspaper halts midswing, and I catch the date on the front page as her hand slows: it's ten days old. "Should we report him missing to the police?"

I pretend to consider this for a few beats and then shake my head. "I'm not sure what we'd tell them. That we're worried about a grown man who looks to have taken off on his own accord? I mean, there's no sign of a struggle, and he doesn't have any mental health problems, does he?"

"Not that I know of. He was always cheerful."

I sit on the edge of the coffee table, facing her. "I think he'd be very low priority for the police, then."

She nods, her cheeks puffing out as she exhales.

"What's your name?" I ask.

"Deirdre."

"I'm Rebecca." I shake her hand and gesture to my cast. "I smashed my mobile when I did this, and I'm still waiting for the insurance to pay out. Do you have a number I can reach you on?"

She scribbles her home number on a corner of the *MEN* and tears off the scrap.

"Do you really think he's okay?" she asks as she closes his front door.

I don't know what to think, and I'm tired of lying. "I'll phone you the minute I hear anything," I say.

Her face falls, and her bottom lip begins to quiver. I probably should have lied.

I never did make a to-do list, so I start one on the bus home, and phone a locksmith en route. He arrives bang on his appointment time. I provide the requisite brew and make myself scarce, firing up my personal laptop and then staring baffled at the logon screen for my online banking account. Convinced I will have written my account number and password down somewhere, I combine two outstanding tasks and scour the rest of my bedroom for them.

My MMP warrant card and ID badge are my first notable discoveries. I hold the badge in front of the mirror, comparing its photo to the current me. The nose ring is noticeably absent from the photo, as are the blue highlights, and my right eyebrow lacks its current scabbed-over split. Otherwise, nothing much has altered. I'm a few years older now, and I have a bald spot to grow out, but I doubt that my role as Rebecca deviated wildly from my norm. Priti told me I've had the piercing for years; Shelley and I made a drunken pact to get them done in a two-for-one deal.

To his credit, the locksmith withholds comment when he finds me sitting cross-legged beneath my desk, tapping its underside. I write him a cheque from the account I can't access and do my best not to look like a shifty chancer as I hand it over.

Distracted by thoughts of a coffee break, I'm mooching through the Fs on my alphabetically arranged CD shelf when a slip of paper flutters from a lyrics insert. Written on it are email addresses, various website logins, and all the necessaries to access two bank accounts. The latter information sends a sudden lurch of self-doubt through me—why would I need two accounts?—but one turns out to be a current account for my wages and bills, and the other an online saver offering a better rate of interest. I log on to the first as my blood pressure settles and my ear stops shrieking. Thirteen months of almost untouched wages have left me with a healthy balance, and I do a spot of transferring between the two accounts before going to the *Auto Trader* website.

I sold my car prior to embarking on my UC assignment, a decision Priti attributed to my fondness for method acting, though I suspect it had more to do with a clapped-out engine that wouldn't have survived a year of stasis. Relying on public transport might have been fine for Rebecca, but for me it's an impractical pain in the arse.

The Pakistani chap flogging an eight-year-old automatic VW Polo in Longsight can scarcely believe his luck. I don't question the rattle it makes whenever I turn right, and he doesn't question whether I should be driving with one arm in a cast. His grin shows all his teeth as he shakes my hand, and then he seems to have a fit of conscience and knocks off three hundred for cash. I arrange collection for the next day, once I've sorted out insurance and persuaded my bank to part with a couple of thousand.

My stamina waves the white flag on the way home, so I doze in the taxi and reward myself with a proper nap after lunch. The phone wakes me as I turn over, three new messages on the answer machine indicating I've been sleeping with my deafer ear uppermost.

"SMIU want your files," Wallace tells me. "And they want to arrange a meeting with you ASAP. Can you bring the files in this afternoon? That might keep them sweet."

They can have the files, but I'm buggered if I'll make things easy for them. "Send a taxi on their account and I'll come in. I want my mobile as well. If they're not finished picking it apart, tough shit."

"They're finished," he says. "There wasn't much on it."

I can't dispute that, but there's a principle at work here, and I refuse to simply roll over and play dead.

"I'll pass on the message about the cab," he continues. "I'm sure they won't quibble, so be ready within the hour."

The taxi driver beeps his horn twenty-three minutes later. After telling him to leave his meter running, I continue to double-check the files for anything I might have missed and rack up a bill for thirty-five quid.

The MCT are based at Belle Vue police station, a recently rebuilt four-storey with standardised royal blue trimming. Wallace meets me at the entrance, visitor's pass in hand, but I've brought my warrant card and ID, and the chap on security waves me through. The station is a warren of starkly lit, fusty corridors. Some of the doors are pass-card protected, others bear the warning "Graphic material is viewed within this unit," but most are propped open to provide glimpses of standard office life, except that these offices come with incident boards and mug shots and employees whose families sometimes forget what they look like.

The MMP grapevine has apparently been working overtime, and I get a mixed response from the people we pass. A scant few of them offer supportive nods, the ones on the fence avert their eyes, and there's outright hostility from those who have already made up their minds about me. For the most part I keep my head down, walking quickly and focusing on the fake leather peeling off Wallace's shoes. MMP are a family; that's one aspect of the job I've always loved. I just never expected to be the reckless young daughter who's shamed their good name.

"Hey, Al? Al!"

I turn at the rapid pound of footsteps, and I'm immediately gathered into a boisterous hug. Unprepared for the contact, I stiffen, and the man releases me, babbling apologies. Wallace steps in to introduce us, but I decide it's okay for me to recognise my ex-response partner, and I smile at him as he grins and punches me on the shoulder.

"Still a knob, eh, Jez?" I say and hug him properly this time, happy to find someone I can still consider a friend.

"Aye, so my missus tells me."

"Sweet Jesus." I grab his shirtsleeve and examine his wedding band. "Congratulations."

He extricates his fingers from mine. "It's been six years, Al."

"Oh. Shit." I'm not sure what else to say. I've grown so accustomed to exaggerating the amnesia that it's galling to find myself genuinely caught out.

"She's called Paula," he says. "Two kids, one dog, and a rabbit that hates me."

I nod, remembering the rabbit, if nothing else. "Are you on the MCT?"

"No, TPU. Trafficking and Prostitution Unit," he says, expanding for my benefit. "Busiest team in the Met. Speaking of which, I'd best get on. I'm late for a briefing. Here"—he presses his card into my hand—"meet me for a brew? For old time's sake?"

"Yeah, I'd love to."

I worked with Jez Stephens for four years. My big brother in blue, who would supply all the sweets for our night shifts and laugh at his own farts. We've saved each other's arses more times than I can count. He's older and greyer than my last fuzzy impression of him, but I suppose shift work and a psychotic rabbit will do that to a person.

Wallace clears his throat, uncomfortable at being cast as a third wheel. "We should make a move as well," he says, and breaks up the impromptu reunion by heading off in the opposite direction to Jez.

I trot behind, catching him up as he enters the MCT office. The open-plan room is quiet, with most of the desks deserted and the computers on standby.

"Gang-related shooting in Levenshulme last night," Wallace tells me. "One critical, and one young kid caught in the crossfire. He died early this morning."

"Arseholes," I mutter.

"Jersey and O'Shea copped for it, but the boss wanted everyone on the door-to-door."

I make an affirmative-type noise, feeling like a spare part. My desk has been allocated to someone else—we were always fighting for space—and I only recognise one of the team members still in the office: Phil Trent, who doesn't look up from whatever he's typing, his stubby fingers battering the keys into submission. He and I used to restock the team's biccie cache, collecting a couple of quid from petty cash and nipping out to the corner shop in our lunch break. We'd argue over which sort to buy, debating the advantages a Garibaldi might have over a ginger nut, but he'd always defer to my final selection. I don't attempt to greet him as I follow Wallace past his desk. It's easier to pretend he's a stranger than admit how much his contempt hurts me, and Wallace makes no attempt to play intermediary. Instead he leads me to an interview room at the rear of the office. I should probably be grateful it's not the one used to interview suspects, but it's not the softly furnished one designed to comfort victims, either.

A woman's voice answers his knock, and he ushers me inside, careful to remain well back from the threshold, and then closes the door on me with an ominous clink. Ansari and another detective are seated in a neat arc behind the room's central table, their chairs positioned with such precision that I'm tempted to check the floor for guide markers. They've helped themselves to coffee from a cafetière, the clunky institutional cups and saucers set out like a tea party they've been obliged to bring in under budget. I stand there like the proverbial deer in headlights, one that was lured into the middle of the road by its mate and then abandoned in front of a speeding truck. I'm not in any way prepared for an official meeting. I haven't even taken my fucking nose ring out.

The woman to Ansari's left—early forties, blond bob, tasteful pearl earrings—is the first to acknowledge me.

"DC Clarke?" She rises and offers her hand. "I'm Detective Sergeant Granger, SMIU."

I nod in response, biting my tongue and refusing to break the awkward silence. They must have homes to go to, so sooner or later one of them will relent and tell me why we're here. I suspect it's not simply to exchange files for a mobile phone.

Ansari cracks within the minute. "Take a seat," he says.

The lone available chair is on the opposite side of the table. I pull it farther back, propping my bag against its leg as Pryce would have done. Unlike her, I opt for a non-confrontational pose, my hand in my lap and my legs crossed at the ankles. I still don't volunteer to speak, though. My brain might be temperamental at the moment, but I'm not stupid.

"Thank you for coming in, Alis. Are you feeling any better?" Granger asks. Her accent, all proper vowels and devoid of glottal stops, screams "privately educated in Cheshire."

I stare at her, convinced she's taking the piss, until she raises an eyebrow in expectation.

"Just terrific," I say before I can help myself. "This is very therapeutic."

Her chair creaks as she leans forward, and the draught she creates tells me she's a smoker who overcompensates with perfume.

"Did you bring the files?" she asks.

"Yes, I did." I turn to Ansari. Since the organ grinder is present, it seems redundant to deal with the monkey. "Do you have my mobile phone?"

Anger pinkens Ansari's cheeks, but he's the one who blinks first, removing a clear evidence bag from his briefcase and sliding it across to me. Almost disappointed by his capitulation, I pocket the phone and heft the files onto the table. It wasn't as if I could have left the room without relinquishing them.

"We'll need time to review those," Granger says. "Am I to understand that there are considerable gaps in your memory with regard to your assignment?"

"Yes, ma'am." I push the files closer to her. "I could hazard a few guesses based on the content of these, but I would prefer to be as well-informed as possible. For obvious reasons."

"Of course. I'll ask DC Wallace to liaise with you. I would ask that you refrain from discussing this matter with anyone. Our intention is to keep the details out of the media for as long as practicable, in an effort to salvage whatever we can of the case against Hamer's. As far as they are concerned, two of their employees were involved in a car accident, and the severity of Rebecca Elliott's injuries mean she will be unable to return to work. There will be no mention made of any sexual relationship."

"Yes, ma'am," I repeat, because that's a safe, standard response that doesn't reveal the major flaw in her plan: that Hamer's already know about me, and we're caught in a game of bluff and double bluff that's so convoluted it's making my head spin.

She clicks her pen and sets it at an angle across the pristine page of her notepad. There's something unsettling about the gesture, as if she's signalling an end to the preliminary niceties. She takes a sip of her coffee and then recites a speech she's clearly made before. "Given the serious nature of this investigation and the weight of the potential charges that could be brought against you, it is our intention to suspend you with pay, effective immediately."

I slide my hand out of view and clutch the chair. Everything goes grey for a few seconds, Granger's figure turning monochromatic and indistinct around the edges. Her earrings flash too bright against the shadows, and I squint until I'm sure I won't topple sideward. She's still talking, telling me what to do with my warrant card and who to contact at HR and when my next meeting is likely to be scheduled for, but most of the details are swallowed by a cresting wave of tinnitus, and none of them sink in. I sit motionless, wretched and humiliated, watching her lips move as she politely confirms that they're throwing me to the wolves.

❖

Wallace is waiting outside the interview room. One look at my face and he backs against the wall, his hands raised in supplication.

"Don't shoot the messenger, Al," he says, as Ansari and Granger stride out of earshot. "Ansari told me to phone you."

"Yeah? Was he listening in on the fucking call? Is that why you didn't warn me, you fucking arsehole?"

"I didn't know anyone from SMIU was going to be there, I swear." I don't believe him. He probably saw it as payback for the automated text trick. I can't blame him, really, and acknowledging that is enough to sap all the fight from me.

"I've been suspended," I tell him. "I think you're my escort off the premises."

He nods, confirming he'd been forewarned of that as well, and gives me an A4 envelope.

"Your assignment briefing, all of my notes, and a few forms from HR," he says. "I didn't think you'd want to be dealing with them today."

"No, I don't. Thank you." I pull out my ID and warrant. "Are you to take these?"

He studies the floor like a kid being put on detention. "Aye. Sorry, Al."

"Not your fault, mate. Like you said, you're only the messenger."

When we set off down the corridor, he adjusts his pace to mine as if afraid I might bolt and wreak havoc just to spite him. I pause at the entrance to the ladies' loo.

"Am I okay to nip in? I'm busting."

"Sure, no probs."

The only woman in there leaves as I enter. I bypass the toilets and head for the bank of lockers that divides the changing area, the key to mine already in my hand. According to the files, I've been back to the station three times during the UC work, for a high-level debrief and two six-monthly welfare reviews, so it's not inconceivable I may have stashed something here.

Like many of my colleagues, I never got around to putting my name on my locker, which might explain why it hasn't been jemmied open. A pattern of rainbow stickers in the top right corner marks mine out from a crowd of similarly anonymous façades, and inside it's full of the crap you'd expect to see in any shift worker's emergency supplies: tins of soup and beans, toothbrush and toothpaste, tampons, spare uniform, Biros, and a pile of pigeonhole memoranda. The top shelf yields nothing but dust and an out-of-date Kit Kat. Mindful of Wallace watching the clock, I tug shirts and a high-vis jacket from their hangers, kneeling to fumble in their pockets as I rummage through the bottom shelf with my recalcitrant left hand. I'm cramming everything back inside when a grey scribble catches my eye: "2311," shining in pencil on the inner wall. It reads like a date, November 23rd, the most obvious way to remember a pin number or perhaps an MMP system logon. The numbers don't ring a bell and neither does the date, but I transfer the four digits to my cast for posterity. If nothing else, I'll need to withdraw cash at some point.

"Sorry, mate," I say to Wallace, shoving down a tampon I've left sticking out of my bag, as if I'm mortified by the whole business of menstruation.

He scratches the back of his neck, his embarrassment far more authentic than mine. "I called a taxi for you," he says. "It should be here about now."

"Thanks."

I'd rush ahead of him if I could remember the way out. Less than twenty minutes have elapsed since I surrendered my warrant card, but the corridors are full of murmuring colleagues, and I no longer feel I belong here.

Chapter Ten

The taxi driver is happy to make a detour to Asda. When I reappear with a full trolley, he helps me unload and turns a blind eye to the bag that clinks and is far heavier than the rest. Back home and beset by good intentions, I pile an assortment of toppings onto a cheese and tomato pizza, the laborious one-handed slicing made bearable by a bottle of fruity cider that tastes like pop. I prop a second bottle on the side of the bath, slurping it through a straw as I wash off the afternoon's fear-sweat. The alcohol takes care of the rest, dulling the shame and the stress to a tolerable level, and I'm drowsing on the sofa by the time Priti comes home.

"Hey." She moves an empty bottle—my fourth—and sits on the edge of the coffee table. "I heard."

"Grapevine or Wallace?" I say, past caring either way.

"Bit of both. I'm not going to ask whether you're okay."

"I'm drunk," I tell her, somewhat unnecessarily. "And I made pizza."

Scepticism crinkles her nose. "You *made* it?"

"Well, I added extra stuff to it. Does that count?"

"Absolutely." She takes my hand and splays it against hers. "What you doin'?" I ask.

"Checking you've still got all your fingers, if you've been drunk-dicing."

"Oh. I was sober back then." I wiggle each one for her in turn. "See?"

Midway through the pizza, I start to cry. Priti passes me a piece of kitchen roll and waits out my subdued burst of misery.

"I love being a police officer," I whisper. I fold in on myself, the pizza forgotten. "Even the shitty parts, the parts we all moan about. I love it, and I don't want to do anything else."

"It might not come to that," she says, though there's little conviction in her tone. She must know that everything will be different even if the SMIU exonerate me; that people will have formed their own opinions, no matter the official verdict. The worst part, the part she can't know, is that I'll only be able to clear my name by pointing the finger at another officer, and I don't think there'll be a way back from that. Whatever the outcome, my career with MMP probably ended late this afternoon.

"Come on," she says, stretching out her hand.

"Huh?" I blink at her. "Come on, what?"

"You need a change of scenery. Sugar and Spice at Silk. My treat."

Canal Street, the pedestrianised heart of Manchester's Gay Village, is heaving. I cling to Priti's arm, daunted by the sheer number of people tottering along the frosty cobbles, every member of the rainbow coalition present and correct, as well as the usual gaggle of tourists and hen parties. I watch a gang of raucous queers posing by one of the locks and taking Snapchat selfies. They're all young, about the age I was when I first started coming here. I virtually lived in the Village when I moved to Manchester, volunteering on the crisis helpline, marching in Pride, and racking up one-night stands that seldom progressed beyond the closest toilet cubicle. Everything I needed to know about oral sex, I learned from a woman called Maya in the loo at Vanilla.

There's a popular local singer headlining at Silk, and the club is standing room only. Priti elbows her way to the bar, returning with something sweet and fizzy and definitely not alcoholic.

"You'll thank me for it in the morning," she says when I pull my face.

I kiss her cheek. "In case I forget in the morning," I tell her.

We listen to the set, swaying with the rest of the crowd and singing along to the songs we recognise. The lights are dim, the mood mellow and increasingly sultry, and before the encore rolls around, I'm being pressed into a dingy nook by a woman with long plaits and dimpled cheeks. She grazes a finger across the scar splitting my eyebrow and then touches her lips to it. I close my eyes, not resisting but not really in the mood either. Her tongue stud clacks against my teeth when she kisses me, the taste of second-hand beer and dope hot and stale in her mouth. I inch back, catching hold of fingers that have already unfastened my jeans.

"Sorry, no," I say. "I didn't mean…I just don't…"

She flicks up her hands—no harm done—her expression bemused rather than offended. The crowd swallows her up as she walks away, and I struggle to button my trousers, still drunk enough for dexterity to be an issue.

I find Priti by the bar, holding a shouted conversation with a ChapStick lesbian who's far too young to be wearing a flat cap.

"I'm going to go home," I say. "You stay. I'll get a taxi."

The lass glowers at me for interrupting, but Priti ignores her. She downs her drink in one, takes my hand, and leads me out into the cold air.

❖

My head hurts. Not the jackhammer pain of a clot pressing on my brain, but a common or garden hangover that comes with a foul, cottony mouth and an urge to throttle the chirpy chorus of birds trilling outside my window. Switching on a lamp sends needles through my eyeballs. I groan and cover my face with both hands, adding insult to injury by bashing myself with my cast.

"Oww…"

The sound squeaks out, prolonged and pitiful, and it's about then that I decide to man the fuck up and open my eyes.

A pint of water is sitting on my bedside table, propping up a box of aspirin and a note from Priti saying one of her cases has gone to shit, the vic is drain-circling in the ITU, and she has no idea when she'll be home. I take two of the tablets, drink the whole glass of water, and stagger into the shower with an Aldi bag wrapped around my arm and my toothbrush sticking out of my mouth. Once clean and dressed, I almost feel human again, and a mountain of toast washed down by strong coffee kicks the last of my headache in the arse.

I'm spreading out Wallace's notes when the phone rings. Expecting telesales, I answer with half an eye still on the pages in front of me.

"Hello? Alis?" A man's voice, the rich tenor of his tone doing little to disguise the concern undercutting his greeting.

"Martin?" I'm ninety percent certain it's him. Even with the distortion of age and the phone line, he sounds like the lad who hurtled barefoot over the fields with me. I hear him close a door, muffling the babble of a child and a dog's persistent bark.

"Yes, it's me," he says. "I've kept meaning to call, but it's been bedlam here. Did you get my message?"

"I got it, don't worry. How's Karen?" (Karen fell off a horse and broke her leg hours after he'd arranged to visit me in the hospital. I think she's his wife rather than one of his children, but I'm not confident enough to be more specific.)

"Better, thanks. She's coming home this afternoon, but it's left me running the farm and juggling the kids single-handed."

"Give her my best," I say. "And don't worry about me. I'm home as well, and Priti's babysitting."

"Good, that's good. You seem…" He hesitates and scratches something within earshot. "Well, more like *you* than I expected."

"Yeah, I'm getting there. My doc is really pleased with my progress." It's difficult to maintain my false cheer, but I want Martin safely out of the way on his farm with his family, content that his little sister is recuperating without need of further assistance.

"Great." He doesn't ask the obvious questions—the whys or wherefores or what happens next—and I realise this is likely to be the first conversation we've had in months, that our lives are entirely separate entities, and that we don't have a thing in common. He does a weird, choked cough, a habit from childhood, used to underscore decisions he knew I'd oppose. "Look, I spoke to Dad and told him to stay put. You know how he is with the winter weather. It'd set his rheumatism off if he came over."

"That's fine, I understand," I say, getting the gist from his terse summary. If my dad and I were at all close, he'd have been here a week ago.

"He sends his love," Martin adds as an afterthought, and then slaps his hand against a hard surface. "Right, I'd best go before Oliver feeds his breakfast to the dog."

"No worries. Thanks for calling."

He bypasses the signing-off conventions, the empty pledges to keep in touch, in favour of telling me to take care and hanging up. I listen to the dial tone for a moment, as if he might come back on and fit properly into my rose-tinted image of him. Then I sit the phone back on its base and pick up the first page of Wallace's notes.

❖

The baked beans I've added to my cheese toastie escape from a crack in its corner and make a splatter pattern on my notepad. Licking tomato sauce from the heel of my hand, I reposition my plate to catch the worst of it and dab at the errant splodges. They haven't hidden much of any importance. Wallace has taken the easy option in his case updates, using my reports as the basis for his and copying chunks of text verbatim when he couldn't be bothered paraphrasing. The initial assignment briefing confirms what I'd already figured out: that Hamer's is suspected of supplying drugs on an industrial scale, and that I was to somehow finagle my way onto one of the relevant distribution teams. My shift transfer is documented toward the end of the reports, with a concurrent reduction in official contact to allow me to bed in. None of my multicoloured handiwork has made it into the file, so its translation remains a mystery. All things considered, the toastie is the definite high point of my morning.

I'm scrubbing cheddar from the Breville when Mr. Akhtar calls to postpone my car pickup. I agree to a new time with him and take the opportunity to examine every nook and cranny on my mobile. I enter "2311" as a possible passcode and then scowl at the tech department label I find stuck to the back: "Code reset to 1111." That sets the theme for the next half hour, as MMP's willingness to return the phone is immediately explained by an empty call log and contacts folder. I've wiped all of my texts and WhatsApp and Facebook messages, and the sole surviving app is the one I used to contact Wallace. Any photos I might have taken are gone, those of family undoubtedly removed prior to the assignment, and subsequent ones deleted at some later, unspecified point. The realistic part of me applauds my decisions as sensible precautions, but that doesn't stop the desperate and impulsive part from lobbing the phone across the table. It bounces once and lands in the fruit bowl with a satisfying clunk, where it starts to vibrate beneath a banana.

"For fuck's sake," I mutter, fishing it out again. The text is from Priti: *All well there?*

No, it's not. I stab my fingers on the screen, daring the autocorrect to interfere. *This thing's bloody useless, Wallace's notes are crap, and I don't know what to do next. I think someone tried to kill me, and if I put one foot wrong they'll try again.*

I pace to the door, the phone in my hand, the text poised on the screen. It feels good, just for a moment, to pretend I can confide in someone. Back at the table, I delete the message and write another: *Yep, all well. Hope things are okay with you too.* I add a smiley face and hit "send."

❖

The early shift at Hamer's runs from seven till three, and everyone who gets the bus home walks to the stops via Dunstan Street. At two forty-five, I turn onto Dunstan and squeeze my newly purchased, nondescript silver Polo between a souped-up Corsa and a white Tranny van. I pull a cap low over my hair, obscuring my face with its peak, and pretend to be absorbed in my mobile. I'm more interested in the file photo of Jolanta and Krzys that rests on my knee, though, and I compare Krzys's image to the first employees who hurry past the car. Without warning, the sky darkens and a heavy shower of sleet prompts a rush to open brollies and raise hoods. I swear beneath my breath as faces disappear from view, and I narrow my focus to the men, straining to compare their profiles. The mass exodus soon thins to a trickle and then stops altogether. I drum on the steering wheel, loath to admit defeat when I've barely even started, but the late shift will already be entrenched, a half-hour crossover ensuring that the wheels of Hamer's grind twenty-four seven. Nothing more will happen until the night shift swaps in, and there's no point returning for that, when I can see little enough in the daylight.

"Damn it!"

I clout the wheel, beeping the horn and sending an alley cat skittering for cover. From my position, I can see the main gate of Hamer's: an ornate, wrought iron contraption controlled on a remote and only ever opened for management. Squinting at it through the sleet, I remember that we lesser employees had to use a side entrance, with a security pat-down mandatory on the way out and scheduled to take place off the clock. That extra fifteen minutes tagged onto the end of every shift dropped the pay below minimum wage, but the unions seemed disinclined to raise the issue.

Under cover of dusk, I take off my cap and hold my head in my hand, my fingers seeking out the ragged line of sutures. I push on the ridge as if that might somehow reorganise the priorities up there, exchanging useless snippets about workers' rights for the reason I rented a car and took Jolanta to Wales, or for the identity of the men who were out there with us that night. Nothing happens beyond the development of a slight itch left of centre. I start the car, fiddling with its levers and dials until the headlights and windscreen wipers cooperate, and then merge onto the A6, one in a long line of commuters heading for home.

A lamp is glowing in the corner of my living room, courtesy of a timer set to give the illusion of occupation. Priti replied to my earlier text to confirm she'll be out till morning at the earliest. I haven't been alone overnight since the accident, and I'm grateful for the low hum of my neighbour's telly and the clatter of pots as the couple above prepare their tea. Sitting on the sofa, the TV remote loose in my hand, I stare at the blank screen and contemplate my next move. Half an hour later, the six o'clock news starts next door, and I'm still none the wiser. Krzys is missing, my factory stakeout was a dead loss and a stupid idea, and I'm no closer to finding the mythical flash drive that may hold the answers. My suspension means I can't access any of MMP's resources, and the loss of my ID stymies any unauthorised investigation.

The remote drops to the floor as I bring my knees under my chin and wrap my arms around them. Weary to the bone, I close my eyes, the temptation to follow Krzys's lead and simply disappear becoming more attractive by the second. I don't think I can do this on my own. I'm tying myself in knots, and sooner or later, I'm going to drop a bollock in front of the wrong person. I know I can't run. Running would be as good as an admission of guilt, and the people who really are responsible for Jolanta's death would get off scot-free. For a moment, wallowing at rock bottom, I consider calling Pryce and telling her everything. As a sergeant, she outranks me, so I could lay it all in her lap and let her decide what to do next. If she agreed to pursue the case as a murder enquiry, wouldn't she have jurisdiction? Isn't that how it works?

I can't answer those questions with any degree of certainty, though, and I don't come close to picking up the phone. Unwilling to vegetate in front of the television, I lump the Yellow Pages onto my lap and begin to leaf through it, paying particular attention to adverts for gyms, safety deposit boxes, private mailboxes: anywhere a combination number might access secure storage. I compile a list of companies to contact during office hours, my eyes growing heavy with two-thirds of the directory still to go. I fall asleep without much warning these days, like a narcoleptic kitten, and I scarcely have time to pull a blanket from the back of the sofa before the room starts to fade out. I hear a thump as the Yellow Pages slides off my lap, and then nothing.

❖

I'm not sure what wakes me. I scrabble to sit upright, thrashing my feet to untangle them from the blanket. The living room is pitch-black, the lamp timed to go out at eleven, and it's silent apart from the rhythmic tick of the mantelpiece clock. My pulse is slamming along with it, two beats for every tick. Nightmare, I decide, just as I hear the scratch at my front door.

"Fuck…"

I roll off the sofa, landing hard on my knees, and crouch on all fours.

"Priti?" I whisper, but it's not her. She'd be in by now, not rattling at the lock. Whoever has my keys has obviously used them to get through the shared entrance and then fallen foul of my new locks.

The noise stops abruptly as I dart into the kitchen and pull a rolling pin from the closest drawer. I creep to the door and peek through the letterbox. The foyer is deserted, the main door secured. I set the pin on the hall carpet, every action slow and deliberate as I fight to regain my composure. Seconds later, an ominous rustling from my bedroom sends me hurtling back to square one.

"Oh no, no, no!" The words scrape from my dry mouth, more a plea than any threat of resistance. I've left one of the windows on a security latch, fastened in place but opened a crack, and the right tools would force the lock in no time. The sound of splitting plastic spurs me to move, and I kick open my bedroom door as a keen breeze billows the curtains inward, revealing the outline of a figure with one boot on the sill, a knee nudging the cloth. He's not completely inside yet, but he's too committed to give up.

I run at the window, slamming both hands on the frame and bashing it into his leg. He yelps and kicks, but his boot comes nowhere near me, and I shove harder on the uPVC, trapping his ankle as he tries to yank it free. Anger annihilates my terror, and I pull the frame inward so I can smash it out again.

"Fuck you!" I scream at him, and he throws himself backward, using his entire body weight to drag himself free. I can't see his face as he gets to his feet, only a black balaclava and a white flash of skin and teeth. He limps across to a waiting car, a dark SUV that someone else is driving. The angle is all wrong for me to catch its reg number, and I'm not brave or stupid enough to chase after it.

I shut the window, fumbling with its lock and being careful not to touch the smear of fresh blood on the frame. The man must have cut his hand when he forced the mechanism. With no intention of calling the police this time, I do SOCO's job for them, wiping the blood onto a clean tissue and sealing the evidence in a sandwich bag. There was blood at the scene of the first break-in as well, though whether a sample was actually sent to the lab is anyone's guess. Regardless, a comparison might be useful at some point.

I'm calm while I do this, methodical and precise. As soon as I run out of tasks, I turn every light on in the flat and crawl fully dressed beneath my quilt with my rolling pin and my mobile. I've made a flask of coffee strong enough to keep me awake till next week, and I sip my first cup as I unlock my phone to see why it's blinking at me. The text is from an unknown number, my empty directory registering every text beside those from Priti as anonymous.

I need to speak to you regarding your case. When would you be available for interview in Colwyn Bay? DS Pryce.

She sent the message at about the time I was attempting to hobble the balaclava bloke. Someone at MMP has obviously given her my number.

I could come over tomorrow, I type. Tomorrow's Sunday, so I'm probably being optimistic, but I don't want to be here on my own. Aware that she might have a life outside her job, I add some wriggle room for her: *Or whenever's best for you.*

Not expecting a reply before morning, I don't fret over sending the text, and I jump sky high when my phone buzzes almost immediately: *Tomorrow's fine. Can you get here for 10 o'clock?*

I'm about to respond in the affirmative when an addendum arrives: *I'll meet you at the Delfryn Cafe by Llyn Ogwen, a few miles outside Capel Curig.*

It's the village closest to the car crash. Does she think I won't recognise the name? She must intend to drive the route with me, perhaps shock me into providing an honest account. The underhand tactic puts my back up, but at least I've figured it out in advance.

Ten at the Delfryn Cafe, I type. *I'll see you tomorrow.*

She doesn't reply.

CHAPTER ELEVEN

I don't expect to sleep, but I wake at five thirty-two with my cheek stuck to the pillow and the rolling pin still clutched in my fist. Rain is pattering against the window, and the room is cold enough to make my nose run. Sniffling into a tissue, I stand in front of my wardrobe and consider my options. Pryce has only ever seen me in scrubs or casual castoffs, and for once I'd like to meet her on a more equal footing. I flick through the hangers for an outfit that's smart without being too rigid, something that gives an air of professionalism, but not professionalism with a rod up my arse like her. I settle on a pale blue shirt with sleeves that will cover my cast, paired with navy jeans. Having ample experience of police interviews, I decide to pack a change of clothing and spare underwear in case things overrun. I can always stay at a B&B and travel back in the morning; it might be my best chance of a peaceful night.

The shirt looks the part, but it's a bugger to button and it knocks my schedule to shit. I'm still filling the kettle when my taxi arrives. Sacrificing coffee for punctuality, I grab my bag and coat and then run back for my toothbrush and toothpaste. One advantage of deciding not to drive to Wales—aside from not having to control a car single-handed for a couple of hours—is the opportunity to finish dressing on the train, and I step onto the platform at Bangor looking every inch the professional who's managed two and a half hours' sleep wrapped around a rolling pin. I hail another taxi and sit in the front at the driver's suggestion, showing him Pryce's text in lieu of embarrassing myself with dodgy pronunciation. He grunts an affirmative, and I tighten my seat belt as he accelerates from the rank.

"You hiking?" he asks, cutting up an Audi before taking a roundabout on two wheels.

"What?"

He brakes hard for a red light and looks at me as if I'm simple.

"Hiking, in Snowdonia. A lot of great routes start near that cafe."

"Oh, no. I'm meeting someone." I peer out the window as the road begins to twist and climb. "We'll probably go for a drive."

The morning mist starts to thin, revealing snow-capped peaks, their faces bristly with jagged rocks and scree. This could be the first time I've seen the area in daylight, and it's so beautiful that it distracts me from the white-knuckle ride and the nagging, sickening sense of déjà vu evoked by the route.

"That's Tryfan," the driver says, following my gaze to an isolated beast of a mountain. Snow is lying thick in the gullies on its flank, creating an undulating concertina effect and accentuating its irregular fin-like shape. There must be dozens of paths to its summit, but it stands aloof as if daring anyone to stake a claim.

"It means 'three rocks,' " he continues. "Those on top, there."

I watch mist eddy around the distinctive triad. I've heard the name before, spoken in an eager estate agent's pitch: "Stunning view of Tryfan. Really, you won't find a better one."

"Have you ever been up there?" I ask, more to mute the voice in my head than out of any genuine interest.

"A few times. Broke my ankle on the North Ridge ten years back." He grins at me. He's missing two of his front teeth. "I'm too fagged out for that now, but a young un like you, you'd have no trouble if you picked the right weather for it."

"Best wait till I get rid of this, eh?" I hitch up my coat sleeve, revealing my cast, and he laughs his agreement.

Despite his laissez-faire attitude to road regulations, he's about the best taxi driver I could have hoped for, providing an unobtrusive commentary about the area while avoiding personal questions. I only start to feel anxious once he pulls into a rough lay-by and parks behind a Land Rover Discovery that's seen plenty of off-roading.

"Delfryn Cafe." He points to a white-clad lakeside cottage. "They do the best fry-up around here."

"Cheers, mate." I over-tip him and swap the warmth of the cab for a biting wind and sharp pellets of snow, my sense of abandonment growing as he spins the car and skids back onto the road. I watch his brake lights disappear around a bend and then place my hand on the Disco's bonnet. I'd hoped to get here first, get the lay of the land, and perhaps eat something to settle my stomach, but the metal is warm, and it's the only vehicle in the lay-by.

Keen to get out of the cold if nothing else, I pick a route around ice-crisp puddles and enter the cafe through its side door, stepping into a wall of heat and steam generated by an open fire and a kitchen on full pelt. Temporarily blinded, I stay on the threshold, struggling to pick Pryce out from an unanticipated party of middle-aged hikers who seem to have invaded the small room en masse. A waitress bustles past me, swooping three plates between a chap taking off his coat and a nowty-faced woman who misjudges an attempt to grab the waitress's arm. As the dust settles in her wake, I spot Pryce in the corner window seat. Sensible enough to have checked the weather prior to setting out, she's dressed far more appropriately than I am, her fleece pullover and the rucksack by her chair allowing her to blend in with the Snowdonia crowd. No one is paying her any mind, which seems to suit her just fine.

As if alerted by a sixth sense, she turns from the window as I approach and stands to offer her hand. We shake in an awkward greeting, and I don't sit until she gestures to the seat opposite her.

"I appreciate you coming out here," she says after I've dragged my chair across the granite floor. "I didn't think you'd get my text last night."

I fiddle with the menu, craving caffeine and calories. I'm going to let her order first. I bet she's the one bobby who goes into a greasy spoon and requests muesli with yoghurt.

"My sleep patterns are a bit buggered up," I say, omitting the part about sharing my bed with a kitchen utensil. "I'm staying awake late and needing a nap by mid-afternoon."

The fleet-footed waitress politely interrupts to place a cafe latte in front of me. "Can I get you anything to eat?" she asks.

"I recommend the full Welsh," Pryce says, as my preconceptions make an about-turn and march out the door. "It'll set you up for the day."

"I'm game if you are." I'm starving but unwilling to be the only one smearing myself with egg yolk and lard. I catch her eye over the rim of the menu, and she nods, accepting the challenge.

"Okay, then," the waitress says, sounding a little dubious, as if Pryce and I fail to fit her stereotype of cheerful, bourgeois, outdoorsy types and she's now questioning what we're doing dining out in the middle of nowhere on a Sunday morning. I sympathise entirely, but she undermines our comradeship by confiscating my menu before scuttling off. Needing something to do with my hands, I cradle my mug of coffee and turn back to Pryce.

"Either she's very good at her job, or I have you to thank for this." Pryce slides two sachets of brown sugar across the table. "I'm sure she's competent, but no, she's not psychic."

"Thank you, then." I sprinkle sugar onto the froth, letting it sit and sweeten my first sip. I want to ask why she chose this as our meeting place, but at some unseen signal, the gang of hikers mobilises toward the exit, forcing me to wait out the general ballyhoo and squeal of metal chairs on stone. I steal surreptitious glances at her, trying to read her body language. My only conclusion is that she seems more at ease here than she ever did in the hospital, and that the low winter sunlight is catching her eyes and the auburn strands in her hair and making her look rather lovely. I take too deep a gulp of coffee and burn my mouth, which at least gives me something else to focus upon. She's looking beyond me at the last of the group as he shoulders his rucksack and disentangles his hiking poles.

"Snowdon," she says, as if she's been assessing their potential and has reached a decision. "Walk up and get the train down. Either that, or a gentle stroll around Llyn Idwal."

"Llyn." I roll the unfamiliar word around on my tongue, mimicking her inflection. "Is that lake?"

"Yes. This is Llyn Ogwen. Idwal is a kilometre or so from the Ranger Base car park. I go swimming there after work sometimes. It's got a great beach, and once the crowds have gone home, I get the water, the sky, and the mountains to myself."

I picture her marching up there alone and launching herself into the frigid water, a masochistic test of endurance she's devised to build character, but the affection in her tone tells me I'm doing her a disservice.

"It must be a bloody chilly spot to take a dip," I say, making amends by being nice. "Do you wear a wetsuit?"

"No, a regular costume." She sips her coffee. "Unless it's really late. Then I don't even bother with that."

I splutter into my drink, shooting a shower of foam up my nose. I can, and have, imagined her doing a lot of things: arresting grannies, putting the fear of God into miscreants, confiscating sweets from infants, but skinny dipping was never one of them. I'm rescued by the fortuitous arrival of heaped plates of sausage, bacon, eggs, shellfish of indeterminate species, and what I initially mistake for slices of black pudding until I detect a conspicuous whiff of the seaside.

"Why does my breakfast smell like seaweed?" I ask.

She chuckles and cuts into a piece of her not-black-pudding. "They're laver bread cakes. Seaweed paste mixed with oatmeal and fried in bacon fat. Feel free to pass them over if you don't like them."

I've never been a fussy eater, and being best mates with Priti has further broadened my horizons. I shrug and take a generous bite, chewing slowly as if I'm a connoisseur of fine fried breakfasts. The taste is reminiscent of standing on a beach in a bracing wind with sea spray hitting my face, only crunchier and wrapped in a hint of bacon. Pryce certainly won't be getting any leftovers. She nods her approval as I tuck in, and we eat in silence for a while. There's safety to be found in a plate of good food. It's hard to conduct official business when you're cramming bacon, cockles, and sausage onto your fork.

"My dad used to make these for Friday supper," Pryce says, dipping her cake in egg yolk. "He split with my mam when I was seven, and I'd stay with him every other weekend. Laver bread cakes on the griddle were his way of showing an effort before he went out to the club for the night."

I stop eating and look at her, but she's preoccupied cutting the rind from her bacon, and she doesn't seem to be angling for sympathy.

"Does he still live local?" I ask.

She slices through the last of the fat and arranges the bacon on a piece of toast. "He's in Rhyl, about half a mile from my mam. She remarried and decided she liked her new kids better, and he phones me when he's run out of fags."

"Oh." I'm about to put down my fork when she shrugs and bites into her butty. My lazy profiling had assigned her a traditional middle-class upbringing, not this mess of indifferent, chain-smoking, club-dwelling parents.

"Did you speak to your brother?" she asks, reminding me that my family is nothing to shout about either.

"Aye, he phoned yesterday. His wife broke her leg, so he's stuck minding three children and a farm. Reading between the lines, we're not very close. And my dad lives in Tenerife."

She licks ketchup from her thumb and wipes her fingers on a napkin. "I suppose you'd have to be a bit of a loner to accept a long-term UC case."

"I suppose," I mutter, but I don't want her to see me as a social misfit whose life was so crap I sought another. I was settled in my flat, I had friends and a coveted role on the MCT, and I played on the footy team, none of which fits the profile of alienated malcontent. It's more plausible that I viewed the assignment as a challenge, something I could do that might actually make a difference. I leave her to believe what she wants, though. I doubt I can sway her opinion, when she holds me responsible for Jolanta's death.

We finish our breakfast without speaking. I can't think of a neutral topic to steer conversation onto, and she seems to have hammered the shutters back in place. Her eye contact falls away, and her posture stiffens. I calculate the bites of food remaining on her plate, as if the last scrap of bacon is all that prevents her from opening her rucksack and pulling out a file full of damnation.

She's mopping her plate with toast when a second group of hikers tromps through the door, ushered into seats by a braying gobshite decked out in the latest high-spec clobber.

"Snowdon Horseshoe," Pryce says, swirling her bread through a puddle of yolk. "He'll probably end up cragfast on Crib Goch."

I nod, liking the sound of that, whatever it means. The volume in the small room increases exponentially, and she requests our bill from the waitress in a series of charade-like hand signals. Ignoring my protests, she pays the full amount and hauls her bag onto her lap.

"Come for a drive with me," she says.

We walk out into bright sunshine, the breeze chivvying the clouds along to leave large patches of blue sky. The sudden switch from humidity to brittle cold sets off an ache deep in the mending bones of my bad arm and plays havoc with my heat-swollen fingers. Oblivious to the grinding of my teeth, Pryce dons sunglasses, and I follow her across to the Discovery. I clamber into the passenger seat, nosing around the cab while she stashes our bags in the boot.

You can tell a lot about a car's owner from its interior, and this one is no exception. Spartan and devoid of personal knickknacks, detritus, or fuzzy dice, it's a closed book, which matches Pryce to a tee. She climbs in as I'm attempting to fasten my seat belt and guides my hand to the catch, ensuring the buckle clicks into place before she starts the engine. She puts the Disco into gear but doesn't move off.

"There's Brufen in the glove box. Take a couple if it's bothering you," she says, watching me try to reposition my arm without drawing attention to it. What I really want to do is hold the damn thing in the air until the blood drains from my fingers.

"It's just the weather. It'll settle in a minute." My smile feels like I've dragged my lips through barbed wire.

"I broke mine a few years ago. Right radius and ulna." She checks her mirror and rejoins the main road, accelerating with care so that we don't get bounced around. "Bloke called Taff smacked me with a fire extinguisher as I tried to arrest him."

"Arsehole," I murmur, finding solidarity in our shattered bones.

"Yes, he was." She shrugs, her eyes fixed on the road. "I headbutted him and gave him a concussion."

A laugh rattles out of me before I can stop it, and the corner of her lip curls upward as she smiles.

"He deserved it," she says. "He was lucky my mate didn't bean him with the extinguisher."

She slows for a bend, passing a lorry on a curve that forces the Disco toward the rocky verge. The violent motion raises the hairs on the back of my neck, and I lunge for the passenger armrest, mashing my sore fingers through its handle and clinging to the plastic. Tryfan is looming on the horizon, and the closer we get to it, the less air there seems to be in the car.

"Alis?"

I shake my head, closing my eyes tight.

"*Alis!*"

The snap of my name acts like a plunge into ice water. I look at her, my teeth chattering.

"It's okay," she says. "It's okay, we're not going that far."

I don't know how far "that far" is. I don't even know which direction I was travelling in that night, but her assurance loosens my grip on the door. Another hundred yards, and she indicates right, nosing into a turning that most people would drive past without noticing. She follows a rutted track until it tapers out by a small brook, and then she nudges the car into a space between two boulders and switches off the engine. This spot seems to be an unofficial refuge rather than the start of any obvious trails, and there's not a soul in sight.

"That's more like it," Pryce murmurs, eyeing the deserted landscape with satisfaction. "We were searching for a drunk, suicidal lad a few years ago and used this as a rendezvous point. I don't think he expected it to be so cold in late May, and it sobered him somewhat. When we found him, he was trying to light a pile of wet leaves by whacking two pieces of slate together."

"Yeah? How did that work out for him?" I keep my tone jovial, because it's the only thing that stops me from shaking her and yelling "Why the fuck have you brought me here?"

"Minor lacs to his fingers, and hypothermia," she says, but instead of elaborating, she lets the anecdote die a sudden death and pulls a folded piece of paper from her pocket. She rests it on her knee, still folded. I can see printed type: random letters and the odd number, but nothing I can properly decipher. She toys with it for a few seconds, turning it and straightening it again. If I didn't know better, I'd think she was nervous.

"I worked overtime yesterday," she says, her fingers still busy with their adjusting. "The CPS have been pushing us hard on a nightclub stabbing, and I'd arranged a second interview with the vic's best friend." She pauses and frowns as if unsure why she's telling me this. She's not usually a scene setter, tending to favour the direct approach. "Anyway, I was on my own in the office, so they put the call through to me."

A bird lands on one of the boulders. I watch it preen and open its beak in a song that's buried beneath my tinnitus.

"Pryce?" I say once it becomes apparent that her pause is more of a full stop. "What the hell is going on? What call?"

"Sorry, I don't mean to be all cloak and dagger, I just…" She shakes her head and rips a little chunk off the paper. "I shouldn't be doing this."

I set my hand on hers, leaving it there until the movement of her fingers ceases, and then withdrawing. "I'm pretty sure we're on our own," I say quietly. "And that bird's not for telling. So what was the call?"

She looks straight at me, daring me to blink. "Two possible witnesses. A woman and her husband who saw your car that night."

"Oh." I manage to form the sound while my battered brain screams profanities. "And?"

She hands me the paper, but I can't focus well enough to read it, so she paraphrases. "They remember your car passing at speed, approximately half a mile from the scene of the crash. You drew their attention because it was pouring down and foggy and you were going far too fast."

I nod, starting to relax slightly. The witnesses have only confirmed what she suspected.

"There was something else," she continues. "The woman described a second vehicle, a dark-coloured SUV, possibly an Audi, almost sitting on your rear bumper. She thought you were racing each other. You were swerving all over the road."

If practicality allowed, I'd have knotted myself into a foetal position right here on the passenger seat, my legs up by the time she said "second vehicle" and gently rocking before she got to "bumper." As it is, I stare at the sheet of paper, picking out the words most likely to drop me in the crap: "SUV," "racing," "swerving."

"Wh—why did it take them so long to come forward?" I ask, stalling for time. I don't have the faintest idea how to play this, and every option I claw at threatens to unleash the mother of all shitstorms.

"They have a caravan in Capel Curig. They were on their way home that night and only saw the witness appeal sign when they drove up again yesterday." She rests her hands in her lap: okay, your turn.

I mimic her position, covering the paper and concealing its text. "Did they get a reg?" I ask, with remarkable calm.

"The plate might have started with a J, but the woman wasn't certain." Pryce slides the sheet from my grip and refolds it. "Any of this ringing a bell?"

"No. None of it."

This earns a sceptical arc of her eyebrow. "*None* of it?"

"No," I repeat with more emphasis. "He sounds like a typical arsehole Audi driver. I mean, there was no impact debris on the road, so it's not like he ran us off it. At that speed, the car they saw might not even have been ours." I'm sweating beneath my shirt, cold beads of it slithering down my back to gather by the elastic of my knickers. I'm getting this all wrong. I should be keen to pass on the blame to a third party, relieved to learn that someone else might have caused the crash, and I can practically hear the cogs whirring as she processes my reaction. Condensation is steaming the windscreen, obscuring the view and hemming us in. Nothing happens when I flick the switch for the window, so I open the door and kick it wide.

"Alis?"

I bolt like a starter from the blocks, lurching toward the brook as if I might find some kind of haven on its opposite bank, but she grabs my arm before I can get my toes wet, and I can't shake her off. I'm not even sure that I want to.

"Hey, it's all right," she says. "It's all right. I haven't told anyone." I stop struggling and bend forward, my hands on my knees, cold air burning my lungs. "There's nothing to tell," I gasp between frigid breaths. "I don't know anything."

"I can help you." There's an odd strain to her voice, not quite a plea but close. If this is an act, she'll be shortlisted come Oscar night. "But you have to trust me."

That word again, dangled just out of reach like a carrot on a stick. Instinct bellows at me to grab the opportunity with both hands, reminding me that I do need help, that I need someone like Pryce with her insider access and her integrity.

"I can't remember," I whisper. I can't drag her into this, *down* with this. "I can't remember what happened."

She takes my hand and slowly encourages me to stand upright. "Come over here," she says and leads me across to a low rock. We sit facing the amphitheatre formed by Tryfan, a wide expanse of scrub and scree dotted with weather-beaten trees and snowdrifts. The brook and the birds provide the orchestra, their combined melody rising and falling with the breeze.

"Shall I tell you what I think?" she asks. She's released my hand, but the rock is small, and we're sitting shoulder to shoulder. "I think you're scared," she says into the silence of my non-answer. "I don't think you know exactly what went on that night, but you know more than you've told me, and you're scared to death of whatever you're hiding."

Like me, she's looking directly ahead, not seeking a reaction, simply laying out the facts as she understands them. It's comforting, somehow, to hear her assemble the jigsaw puzzle.

"Maybe I'm one of the bad guys," I whisper, barely managing to voice a fear that still chews away at me in my darkest moments. I hang my head, ashamed by the mere possibility. I don't feel like a bad person, I really don't, but I was working on my own for months, and I have a hefty mortgage to pay. If someone had named a price, would I have been tempted?

"Maybe you are," she says, which doesn't exactly boost my confidence. "That'll come out in the wash, one way or another. At a guess—and this is only a guess, mind—there are two plausible scenarios that put you and Jolanta in that car." She raises her index finger. "One, you were both on the take, something went pear-shaped, and you had to get out of Dodge. Two, for whatever reason, you were trying to find a safe place for Jolanta, and the driver of that Audi made sure you never got there. What troubles me is that you didn't choose to alert anyone in MMP. Now, that would be understandable if you'd gone rogue, but if either of you were in danger and needed help, then the obvious place to turn for that would be your own force." She doesn't need to spell the rest out, and the implications settle all around us. Our shoulders slump, and the deepening of our breathing sends out heavy puffs of white.

"How did I do?" she asks, angling her head until she can see my face.

"A little too well," I admit, but there's no point refastening the gate when the horse is halfway to Llandudno.

"Determined to solve the whole damn mystery on your own, aren't you?"

I shrug, and she shakes her head in despair.

"Despite having been suspended," she says.

"Yeah," I say. "That's proving to be a bit of a ball ache." Before I can second-guess myself, I take off my coat and unbutton my shirtsleeve, rolling it up past my cast. I tilt my wrist to display its scribbled clues: *Two men. My accent. Leather glove? Metal*, and, off to one side, *2311.*

"Where did those come from?" she asks. Somewhat understandably, she doesn't seem impressed by my sterling detective work.

I shuffle my bottom like the idiot newbie who's just arrested an innocent bystander. "I had a nightmare my third night in the hospital, and I wrote what I remembered as soon as I woke up. Two men got into the car after we'd crashed. They took the keys to my flat in Gorton, and they left us to die." I touch the ridge of my cheekbone. "I found bruises here where one of them gripped me."

Her eyes flick to the spot I indicate, searching for evidence long since faded. "It's not much to go on," she says with admirable tact. "Could you identify either of the men?"

"No."

"And you have no idea why they wanted you dead?"

"No."

"What about MMP? Do you think someone there might be involved?"

I nod miserably, and she kicks at a pebble, sending it spiralling into the water.

"You and Jolanta weren't lovers, were you?"

"No, we weren't." The words crack on their way out of my throat, and I don't say anything else. I've already overplayed my hand. She doesn't budge, though. She doesn't caution me and march me to the car.

"These last three days," she says, "I'm assuming you've not been recuperating like a model patient. So what have you been up to?"

I tick my adventures off an imaginary list: foiling a couple of break-ins, getting kicked in the guts, chasing Krzys's shadow, staking out the factory, searching high and low for a flash drive that may not exist, pondering the significance of 2311.

"It's a long story," I hedge.

She picks up my coat and drapes it around my shoulders. "Tell it to me."

CHAPTER TWELVE

Pryce's fingertips are cold, their tentative pressure raising a chain reaction of goose pimples across my abdomen. I'm already shivering, the heightened adrenaline of the morning ebbing away now that I've laid everything in the open for her to dissect.

"When did you last see a doctor?" she asks, moving her hand from the ugly stain around my belly button and lowering my shirt.

I tuck myself in, refastening my coat and folding my arms. I can't seem to get warm no matter what I do, and I answer through clattering teeth. "I'm fine. A paramedic checked me out."

"Mmhm." She doesn't even bother to articulate her incredulity, and I pity every perp who's ever had the misfortune to sit opposite her in an interrogation. She must have innumerable counter-theories and arguments to debunk what I've just told her, but she hasn't yet launched her opening salvo.

"Is that bag of yours an overnight bag?" she asks.

Keeping my arms locked across my chest prevents me from scratching my head in cartoon-like confusion. "Uh…yeah."

She stands and brushes grit from her backside. "Good. I'll interview you under caution tomorrow. In the meantime we've got quite a bit of work to do."

I'm still processing the *interview under caution* part as she makes a beeline for the car.

"What the fuck?" I mutter, swaying onto my feet, unbalanced by numb toes and a damp arse. "Hey!" I raise my voice, forcing her to backtrack a few steps. "Hang on a minute! Where are we going?"

"My place," she says, and elaborates as I gape at her. "Look, the cafe will be overrun by now, and we can't do this in the office, not without setting off all the bells and whistles. I'll book you into a B&B on the way, but I guarantee I'll have better coffee."

"Hmm. I might need something stronger."

She smiles. "Let's stick with coffee for now."

Punch-drunk with relief and worry, I let her lead me to the Disco and fasten my seat belt. The claustrophobic panic of our first trip down the A5 has been beaten into submission by an all-encompassing lethargy that knocks me into a stupor. I doze, rolling awake again as we stop at a cosy-looking bed and breakfast, but I'm not coherent enough to get out and participate in the registration process. The rumble of the wheels on the unpaved driveway compels me to crack open an eye, but she hushes me and tells me to go back to sleep, her voice so soothing that I obey it without question.

I dream of sea salt and a mountain that darts like a shark, the images underscored by a lilting tune with incomprehensible lyrics. I wake properly when the song tapers off and cold air hits my face. I'm alone in the car, with the engine ticking over, and I can see Pryce in the rearview mirror, refastening a wrought iron gate.

"Sorry, I keep meaning to oil the lock," she says as she gets back in and sets off slowly along the narrow lane. She studies me in the shade cast by a line of trees. "You staying with me this time?"

I yawn and scrub sleep from my eyes. "Think so."

Sunlight is dappling the car, highlighting a stream in spate dashing across the stones, and swathes of copper-coloured moorland.

"You weren't kidding about living in the middle of nowhere," I say.

"I never kid," she retorts, deadpan, and reverses into her parking spot in one smooth, done-it-a-thousand-times manoeuvre.

I spot her house then: a pretty stone cottage, elevated above the lane and accessed via a curving set of steps. A wooden table and chairs sit on a small walled patio, a vantage point with a view stretching for miles. Nostalgia sweeps over me in an unwelcome wave, and I smell fresh bread, and bacon frying with golden-yolked eggs. Martin and I would eat breakfast outside in summer, tousle haired and pyjama clad, dipping toast soldiers in the eggs and squabbling over whose turn it was to muck out the chickens.

The slam of the car boot and footsteps crunching on gravel haul me back to Snowdonia. I join Pryce at the side of the car, hurrying along with her as the sun disappears behind a bank of thick cloud and hail begins to fall.

"Careful, they're slippery," she warns me, taking the steps two at a time as I almost go arse over tit on the first.

She's opened the front door and switched on the hallway light by the time I've skidded my way to the top of the flight. I stamp my feet on the mat and revert to old habits, slipping off my boots. She's done likewise, and I initially put mine beside hers before deciding that looks far too domesticated and rearranging them to face the opposite direction. Following the sound of running water, I find her in the kitchen, filling a kettle with one hand and retrieving mugs with the other. An overhead light casts a mellow glow on the traditional farmhouse kitchen: Belfast sink, wooden countertops, and an Aga belting out heat. A single plate and bowl sit on the drainer, one knife and one fork in the cutlery tub. I can picture her sitting alone at her table—I bet she never eats off her knee—perhaps reading a book or a journal, and it makes me sad that she's chosen to isolate herself out here. Then I get annoyed at myself for being so damn patronising. She doesn't live here because there are no other options for her; she lives here because she wants to.

I still haven't moved beyond the doorway. I teeter there on an invisible line, beset by doubts, with second thoughts piling like a train wreck on top of third, fourth, and fifth ones.

"Pryce, I..." I stare at my socks, waiting out the splash of the tap.

She places the kettle on the Aga, and everything is so like Hawclough that it makes me want to bawl. "What?" she asks.

I rub my temple where it's beginning to ache. "Why are you doing this?"

"Honestly?"

"Yeah, honestly."

She dries her hands on a tea towel and then folds it into a neat square and sets it on the counter. "You know when something just doesn't sit right? Like a lid that's not quite snug when you press it down?"

"Itch you can't scratch?" I suggest.

"Exactly." She holds my gaze, steady and resolute. "Your case is the itch I can't scratch, and it has been ever since that night in the wood."

"I don't—"

"You flinched," she says. "When I touched your face. I bet you don't remember, do you?"

I start to shake my head, but I do remember. I remember panicking and pushing away, and the solid barrier of the rock stopping me.

"You were like an animal in a trap," she says. "Nowhere to run, bleeding all over, and yet you still tried. It stuck with me. I wanted to know why you'd do that, and it makes sense now." She gestures at my cast, its multicoloured clues hidden beneath my sleeve. "I was wearing leather gloves."

"You took them off," I whisper.

She nods. "I didn't understand why I needed to, at the time. I sort of put two and two together, but I only got to four this afternoon."

"What are you going to do now, then?" I ask, unable to keep the challenge from my question.

"You mean, who else am I going to tell?"

"Yeah, that."

"No one."

I throw up my hands, exasperated by her sanguinity. She's not stupid; she must have considered the potential consequences.

"You could lose your job," I say. "You know that, don't you?"

"Perhaps. Unless the end justifies the means. Look, the second I make this official, my DI will want to liaise with MMP, and that'll tip off whoever might be on the take there. It seems more logical to get as far as we can on our own."

"Just the two of us," I say.

She nods. "Just the two of us."

The kettle starts to whistle, a shrill, keen siren. For a second, it ramps up the tension, but then she rolls her eyes, and I let out a shaky laugh.

"Couldn't have timed that any better," I say.

"Not even if I'd planned it." She slides the kettle from the stove, muting its shriek, and pours water into the mugs. Outside, the hail has softened to snow, and I watch flakes settle on the bare soil of raised vegetable beds.

"Here." She hands me a mug of coffee and nudges the sugar bowl toward me. She's made tea for herself, proper builder's tea, not one of those perfumed, herbal monstrosities. We sit at the kitchen table, where she tears the cellophane from a new notepad and writes "Alis" on the first page of our unauthorised case file, dotting a bullet point on the next line down.

"You should report the second break-in," she says, holding her pen like a single chopstick and tapping her thumb with it. "Low-key. Just request a FWIN for future reference, and highlight the incident as a potential security concern in the neighbourhood. If someone in MMP has their eye on you and you want your amnesia cover to stick, you need to keep reacting to these events, or they'll smell a rat."

"I will," I say. "I'll go through the non-emergency line so Wallace won't get wind of it."

"Good." She doesn't lecture me on safety or remind me that one slip-up will probably lead to another attempt on my life. I'm grateful she doesn't feel the need to spell it out for me, because I'm shitting bricks as it is.

"Are you able to run the blood sample?" I ask. It's a big ask. A DNA match would give us our first real suspect, but she'd have to falsify the reason for the request, and I'm not sure how far she's willing to stick out her neck.

She jots a note on the second page: "Break-in—blood analysis," which seems to be the first item on a to-do list. More contemplative tapping.

"You wouldn't happen to have it with you?" she says.

I open my hands helplessly. "It's in my fridge."

"Send it via a courier and address it directly to me. The labs will be four to five weeks at best on a routine analysis, so the sooner you can get it here, the better. In the meantime, I can run a nationwide search on John Does to see whether anyone matching your description of this Krzysztof chap has turned up. Email me a copy of his photo when you get back. That might be easier to obtain a positive ID from."

"Right." I want to thank her, but we've fallen into the natural rhythm of a case briefing, the give and take of dealing with outstanding issues, planning future tasks, and deciding what to prioritise, and emotions don't have a place here. Besides which, we might reach a point where all our hard work ultimately exposes me as a criminal mastermind, so I don't think we're supposed to be bonding.

"Have you managed to access your bank accounts?" she asks.

"Yes. I've got two current accounts and one on PayPal." I shake my head in anticipation of her follow-up question. "There were no unusual transactions. No deposits other than my wages. I spent over a year living in a shithole, eating Aldi baked beans and soups. I wasn't exactly living the high life."

"Nothing wrong with Aldi," she says, neatly side-stepping the snide "No, not yet," response I expected. "This number, 2311," she continues, moving right along. "Why would you write a vitally important code in a locker you can't access with any regularity?"

I gnaw at a piece of dry skin on my thumb as I mull this over.

Criminal mastermind I may be, but I hadn't spotted that flaw. Three times, three times I'd been to Belle Vue since the start of the UC assignment. Each occasion was listed in Wallace's bloody file. How the hell did I convince myself that 2311 could have any significance? "I wouldn't," I conclude. I fold my arms on the table and drop my head onto them, bouncing off my cast with a hollow thud. "Bollocks."

"Easy, you'll give yourself a concussion." It's hard to tell for sure through my tinnitus, but I think she sounds amused.

"Yeah? Might knock some bleedin' sense in." I peek up at her. "I'm really sorry. I think I'm usually better than this. Christ, I *hope* I am."

"Well, you've had a lot on your plate."

Straightening in my chair, I tidy my hair to cover the fuzz of my not-quite-bald spot. "Yeah. Plus, my brain got bashed."

She smiles, graciously accepting my defence. "It did, but still, I think we can put that particular clue aside."

I turn her notepad toward me, scanning the neat handwriting. She's written more than we've discussed, cramming things down while they're fresh in her mind. I press my finger on a note that reads "route CCTV," smearing the fresh ink onto my skin.

"I'm pretty sure I was planning to come back that night," I say. "My toothbrush and toiletries were still in the Gorton flat, and you never found anything of mine at the scene, did you?"

"No, but the men could've rummaged through the remnants of Jolanta's bag and removed yours in its entirety. The wreckage was spread over a wide enough area for them to have risked taking a bag and hoping no one noticed it was missing. They got the keys to your flat from somewhere."

"My pocket," I say. "I keep my keys in my coat pocket." I conceal a shudder by swallowing a mouthful of hot coffee. This is something I've tried not to dwell upon: the thought of someone touching me, going through my clothing, while I was unconscious. I clutch the mug to my chest, my knuckles turning white as my fingers burn, but within seconds, she's easing the mug from my grip. She wets a tea towel with cold water and presses it to my reddened palm.

"Should we call it a day?" she asks.

"No, I'm all right. Sorry." I squeeze the towel, letting water seep over my skin.

"You don't need to keep apologising," she says. "If this gets to be too much, just tell me."

"It won't. I'm okay." I return the cloth to the sink, as if that proves I'm one hundred percent fixed and not in the least bit traumatised. "Did you check the local CCTV?" I ask, refocusing the timeline to before the crash. I know she used ANPR cameras to track my car into Wales, but these days the councils have stuck cameras onto every other lamppost, and one of them might have caught the Audi.

"Only for your car," she says. "Plate recognition won't work on a partial, and I can't submit a far-reaching request if we're keeping things below the radar."

"What about the footage you already examined? Do you still have access to it?"

"Yes, it's part of the case file." She adds a dash to the original bullet point. "Fancy taking a look?"

"Sign me up," I say, happy to have a task.

"That leaves the flash drive." She heads a fresh page. "Or disc, or whatever it may be that these people are repeatedly breaking into your home to retrieve."

"How do they even *know* about it?" I ask. "*I* don't even know it exists, not for sure, so how the hell do they?"

"They probably don't," she says. "They've probably just reached the same conclusion you have: that you recorded these events at some point, by some means, whether that's a file, a disc, a set of notes, a diary entry, or something incriminating scribbled on the bottom of a shopping list. They'll think they have the luxury of time, given your head injury, and we need to keep them thinking that."

I nod. It makes perfect sense when she explains it. "I made a list of places to try," I say. "PO boxes, safety deposit centres, gyms with combination lockers, although we can possibly scratch that one now."

"You didn't have a car as Rebecca, did you?"

"No."

"Think local, then. Somewhere easily accessible via public transport, or taxi at a push. How close were you living to Manchester?"

"Quarter of an hour on the bus." I pick up her thread. "Big, anonymous city, less chance of being remembered if anyone from MMP started flashing my photo around."

"Precisely. Get as far as you can with those. If you hit a brick wall, I'll drive up and see what my ID shakes loose."

"Thank you," I say, throwing caution to the wind as I sense the end of our brainstorming session. "For all of this. For everything."

"You're welcome." She collects our empty mugs, her movements stiff and uneasy as she stands. "Do you want—"

"I should get going," I say, cutting into whatever her offer might have been. She's done enough today; I can't force her to play the affable hostess as well.

She nods, her expression schooled and unreadable. "I'll give you a lift. You may as well walk as wait for a taxi."

"What happens tomorrow?" I ask. "With the interview?"

"Nine thirty at our HQ in Colwyn Bay. Give my name at the desk." She sighs, acknowledging the inadequacy of her answer. "I've put it off for as long as I can, but my DI isn't renowned for his patience. Do you have a lawyer?"

"No, not yet."

She drops the mugs into the sink, scribbles a name and phone number on her pad, and tears the sheet out for me. "I've spoken to her already and pencilled her in, pending your agreement. If I were in your shoes, I'd want her in my corner."

I slip the paper into my pocket. "Will you be charging me?" I ask quietly.

This time her face is an open book, her forehead furrowed by worry lines. "I don't know, but you need to be prepared for that if we're suppressing evidence that might exonerate you."

"Or dig me into an even deeper hole," I say, ever the optimist.

"There are other options, Alis. Despite what I said earlier, we could pass all of this to my DI and leave it in his hands. It'd be safer. *You'd* be safer."

I'm fastening my coat, but the urgency in her voice makes me stop and give her suggestion proper consideration. I don't deliberate for long.

"I appreciate the offer, but I'd rather take my chances."

"Yeah." She smiles sadly. "Yeah, I thought you might say that."

CHAPTER THIRTEEN

In keeping with police headquarters nationwide, the Colwyn Bay HQ is not a thing of beauty, resembling a multi-storey car park from the seventies in all its grey, breeze-block glory. I'm in no rush to enter, and I stand at the base of its steps as people in civvies come and go. The detectives are easy to spot, especially those who've perfected their game face, a look of humourless intensity that always made me nervous and deferential when I was a beat bobby.

"Alis?"

I turn at the unfamiliar voice, and a woman strides toward me, hand outstretched in greeting.

"Odelia Madaki." She squints at me in the weak sunlight. "It *is* Alis, isn't it? Detective Pryce was quite exact in her description."

"I'll bet she was." I shake her hand. "Let me guess. 'Nose ring, plaster cast, chunk missing from her head'?"

"I couldn't possibly divulge," she says, and I warm to her at once when she lets out a lusty laugh and winks at me.

"I appreciate you finding time for this at such short notice," I say as we walk up the steps. I'd phoned her from the B&B, but Pryce had taken it upon herself to email the pertinent sections of my case file, so there wasn't much for me to add.

"Not a problem." She holds the door for me. "I must admit, I'm quite intrigued. Your case certainly makes a change from the parade of drunken halfwits and recidivist miscreants I usually deal with."

"I can imagine," I say, relieved that she's chatting to me as a colleague rather than a perp. We get the lift to ourselves, and she hits the button for the fourth floor. "I'm not going to no-comment this," I tell her, as the metal box judders and starts its crawl upward. "It'll only piss them off."

Checking her reflection in the mirrored walls, she tucks a plait of hair into a clip and adjusts her skirt. "That shouldn't be a problem. The difficulties you're having with your memory will actually work to your advantage. Keep your responses short and succinct, don't speculate or offer information they haven't asked for, and heed any advice I give you."

I nod, her commonsense composure lessening the antsiness that saw me skip breakfast. "I can't tell them what I don't know," I say with all the sincerity I can muster, omitting to disclose that this is actually all a fucking farce and that Pryce is sitting on a whole load of additional information she won't be bringing to the table. I feel terrible for stringing Odelia along, but not terrible enough to jeopardise the fragile accord that Pryce and I established yesterday.

The officer at the front desk must have given the MCT a heads-up, because Pryce meets us as we exit the lift. She shakes Odelia's hand and sends a perfunctory nod in my direction before ushering us into a typically austere interview room, where a young detective with florid red hair is perched on the table, playing with his phone. He stands, pocketing the phone in a smooth motion, and waits for Pryce to introduce him.

"This is Detective Constable Hughes," she says. "He'll be assisting in the interview today. Can I get either of you a drink? Tea? Coffee?"

"Coffee, if you don't mind," I say, hoping she'll notice the shadows beneath my eyes and make it strong enough to stand the spoon up in. I slept well, perhaps too well, locked in my room and cocooned in an eiderdown quilt, and I woke feeling sluggish, with a thick head.

"Sugar?" she asks, giving me a pointed reminder of how the next few hours need to go.

"Two, please."

"I'll sort it," Hughes says, throwing me a dirty look as if it's my fault he's had to assume the role of Brew Bitch.

We take our seats as he leaves, Pryce and Odelia arranging their paperwork while I wait like a spare part. The room smells of sweat and that indescribable fustiness that comes from a general disregard for personal hygiene. Harsh strip lights bleed the colour from everything, with the exception of Odelia's complexion, which has taken on a healthy glow.

"We'll be recording audio only," Pryce says, ticking a box on a pre-interview pro forma. "If you nod or shake your head, I will state that you have done so. DC Hughes and I will take notes throughout the course of the interview. We won't interrupt you as you answer a question, and I would advise that you fully consider any question to which you respond."

I nod at intervals as she proceeds through the customary rigmarole, allowing the familiar instructions to wash over me while I focus my attention on the eventual goal. I take a sip of the manky coffee that Hughes dumps in front of me and manage to keep my hand steady as Pryce recites the caution:

"You do not have to say anything. But it may harm your defence if you do not mention when questioned something which you later rely on in court…"

How many times have I uttered the same words? Yelled them above the racket while I'm brawling in the street with a raucous scrote? Stated them clearly for the tearful middle-aged family man with a computer full of child pornography? I never imagined I'd be on the receiving end, and the recitation still packs a punch despite the less than legitimate circumstances.

Using the techniques of all good interviewers—encouraging conversation, establishing a rapport, communicating interest—Pryce eases me into the proceedings with a few general, open-ended questions about my role at MMP, my assignment at Hamer's, and the last solid memories I have "prior to the events of February the ninth."

I do my best to paint a picture of working side by side with Jolanta and of a close friendship that developed into a full-blown relationship. I leave gaps in the narrative, and I'm careful not to pin myself down to specific dates, but the overall story is sufficiently convincing that neither detective challenges its veracity.

"I want to concentrate on February the ninth now," Pryce says. "Could you tell us what you remember from that day?"

I shake my head, looking beyond her to the blank wall and doing my damnedest not to remember anything at all. A brutal barrage of images assails me regardless, flashing across the grey paint like a sadistic slideshow.

"Jo's arm," I say too quietly for the tape. I clear my throat and try again. "I remember coming to in the car after the crash and seeing Jo's arm. Her fingers were right here. Close enough to touch."

"Was she alive?"

"No." When I close my eyes, the gore-streaked horror show follows me into the dark. Snapping them open again, I focus on Pryce, who gives me a subtle nod, encouraging me to continue. "No. She was at first. I could hear her breathing. But then she stopped." I can't seem to construct anything beyond the simplest of sentences, the interview equivalent of an infant's first reading book. I don't want to describe the associated terror or the pain or the confusion.

"Do you want to take a break?"

I use one sleeve to wipe at the tiny puddle that's gathered on the desk and then dry my face with the other. "I'm okay, thanks. I'd prefer to get this over with."

"May I just clarify something?" Hughes asks, shuffling through his notes. He has an unprepossessing demeanour, but I've always been wary of the quiet ones. "Would you have us believe that the remainder of that day—hiring the car, arranging to rent the cottage, your reasons for doing both, the reason Ms. Starek packed a bag and you didn't, the brand new mobile phone, the text app set to deceive your MMP handler—that all of those things have been lost to your head injury?"

His petulance splatters crimson blotches across his throat. When he glances at Pryce as if seeking retrospective sanction for his outburst, she pins him with a look that says "nice timing, you dick."

"I'm being as cooperative as I can, DC Hughes," I say. "I've admitted to an illicit affair with Jolanta Starek, and a desire to conceal our relationship would explain the factors you seem to consider loose ends. However, I can't and won't admit to something I have no recollection of, which means I can't tell you how or why the car crashed, or why Jo's was the only bag recovered from the scene. As for my mobile, I'd left it at my flat, set to contact my handler, so I would obviously have needed to buy a new one."

I've kept my tone polite but cool throughout, and he seems to realise I'm no rank amateur likely to crumble beneath the first bit of pressure he applies. He drinks half a glass of water, figuratively waving a white flag and allowing Pryce to reassume the lead.

"Would you describe yourself as an advanced driver?" she asks.

"I drove response as a uniformed officer," I say. "I wasn't trained to pursuit standard, but my training would have been more advanced than that of the average road user."

"Did Ms. Starek drive?"

"No. I don't think she had a licence, and she couldn't afford to run a car."

"Can you recall the weather conditions on the night of February the ninth?"

"It was raining, cold. I think…I think it sleeted at one point."

"There were patches of fog as well," she says. "Had you ever driven that route before?"

"Not to my knowledge."

I sense Odelia stiffen as she sees the trap open, but I don't react. I want Pryce to plant this seed for Hughes. She removes a pair of photographs from her folder and sets them on the table. They're standard post-collision shots: the four-wheel skid mark dotted with numbered forensic plates.

"Can you explain why, given the conditions as described, you might have chosen to drive at speeds between fifty and sixty miles per hour on an unlit mountain road?"

"No." I hang my head. "Unless…"

"Unless what?" Hughes prompts me when I fail to complete the thought. Odelia wraps a peremptory hand around my biceps, but I give him the resolution he's desperate for.

"Unless I was showing off," I whisper. "I might've been trying to impress her."

He can't resist an opening like that. Bristling with outrage, he leans forward and prods the photos like they do on the telly. "Instead you got her killed."

"I know," I say, my grief and my guilt in no way feigned. "I know I did."

Odelia loosens her grip, resting her hand on my cast instead. "I would like to emphasise that this is supposition on the part of my client," she says, "and that, in the absence of witnesses or wholly reliable testimony, supposition is all it will ever be."

"Noted," Pryce says. She retrieves the photographs and closes the file. "I think that about covers everything for the moment. I'm terminating the interview at eleven thirty-eight."

It seems redundant to ask what happens next. Due to the complexity of the case, the evidence will be forwarded to the Crown Prosecution Service. If there are grounds for prosecution, they'll give the go-ahead and determine the appropriate charges. They're busy people, often battling a significant backlog, so I'm going to be in limbo for a while yet.

"Thank you for your time," Pryce says, once we've shuffled into the corridor and we're standing around like the first guests to arrive at an office party. "I'll be in touch." This she directs at me. I nod, and that's that: Odelia and I walk in one direction, and she heads off in the other.

"Are you going straight back to Manchester now?" Odelia asks as we enter the lift.

"That was the plan," I say as if I actually have a plan rather than a set of vague objectives arranged around solving an impossible mystery and not dying.

"Don't expect to hear anything from the CPS for four to six weeks, and that's an optimistic estimate," she says. "In fact, at this stage I can see Pryce holding off on the submission, because they're likely to knock it back."

That depends on how long Pryce can sit on the witness statement, but these things are easy to misplace in an overrun and underfunded department. She might mention it to her DI as he tries to eat his lunch with one hand and answer an email with the other, all the while ignoring the ringing phone on his desk. If our MCT ever needed overtime authorising, we'd watch for Ansari coming through the office with a carton from the canteen.

"Would it be okay to call you when the CPS give their verdict?" I ask.

"Of course." She hands me her card. "And be sure to phone me if you have a light-bulb moment that fills in any of those blank bits."

"I will. Cheers, Odelia."

We part company in the foyer, where the officer on the desk tells me a taxi is already en route. I send up a silent thank-you to Pryce and settle by the window to wait.

❖

The train is ambling away from Chester when a text buzzes my phone. The number shows up as anonymous, but it's Pryce, apparently using her own mobile: *I've emailed the CCTV in a zip file. Let me know if you have any problems opening it.* I'm in the middle of typing a reply when she tags on an addendum: *PS—you did fine today.*

I delete my original, standard acknowledgement and dither over the writing of a new message. Every jolt of the train reminds me I'm heading away from the relative sanctuary of the past thirty or so hours. Hashing things out with Pryce was like taking my first breath of fresh air after days of being smothered. Unable to put any of this into a text, I write an inadequate, *Cheers, keep in touch*, hoping that last part doesn't sound as needy as it actually is, and then distract myself by phoning 101 to report break-in number two.

By the time I get home, I'm lightheaded and tripping over my feet. There's no sign that Priti has been back, and the blood sample is undisturbed in the fridge. The courier arrives within the hour, accepting a sizable tip in exchange for his promise to deliver the package directly into Pryce's hands. As his van pulls out of the driveway, I sink onto the sofa, fully intending to download the CCTV file the moment I can get my eyes to focus. Closing them proves to be a mistake, though. I wake choking on drool and achy from dozing off in an upright position.

"Bloody hell." I dry my chin, straining to see the clock. The room is dark, the slats of the window blinds limned with a faint orange glow from the streetlights. I switch on my laptop and nip to the loo while it loads, dreading coming back to find that Pryce has requested a read receipt. I don't want her to think she's partnered herself with a complete slacker.

A splash of cold water on my face clears the lingering cobwebs, and I install myself at the kitchen table, fortified by strong coffee and a corned beef barm. The zip unspools eight hours of footage onto the desktop: two CCTV cameras, with a four-hour window for each. I settle in to watch the first file, a lamp-post-mounted, council-funded beady eye that focuses on the post office precinct in Bethesda and captures an oblique view of the A5. I experiment with different speeds, settling on one that allows me to eyeball passing cars and study the people who come and go, while skipping past the dead air.

The post office is shut, but Friday night sees the chippy and the Co-Op shop attracting a steady stream of customers. Scrawny teens slouch along the low wall framing the car park, the boldest among them stepping forward every now and again to pester adults into buying booze and fags, any acquired booty shared down the line and back. Most of the people approach on foot, only a handful using the car park, and they depart with laden bags and the single-minded determination of folks intent on spending the night stuffing their faces in front of a gas fire. Some exchange greetings or chat beneath the precinct's shelter, and no one looks out of place. The handful of cars that go by are hatchbacks, and although one of them is likely to be my rental car, it's impossible to distinguish anything other than hazy shapes and sizes. Mist wipes out at least ten full minutes of footage. Three and a half hours in, the precinct is deserted, the wind lashing rain across the pavements and destroying the umbrellas of those foolhardy enough to venture out. Patchy fog doesn't quite obscure the overweight man pissing in a doorway, and the tape stops abruptly with a distinct sense of anticlimax.

Mindful of the time lost to my nap, I brew another mug of coffee and start the second file. An identifying stamp in the top corner marks it as a static camera situated just beyond the junction of the A5 and the A4244. A quick check on Google Maps tells me Jolanta and I must have driven past it, unless we took a ridiculously roundabout route that night. Rush hour has been and gone, thinning the flow of traffic and making it easier for me to track through the tape. Pryce provided a helpful recap of the rental car's specifics in her email—Ford Focus, navy blue, registration KW15 OXP—alongside similar details for the Audi SUV described by the caravanning witnesses. The footage is black and white, but I squint at each of the vehicles, dismissing anything in shades of pale grey and concentrating on the darker ones. My coffee goes cold and something in my lower back starts to twinge, and an hour into the tape, at twelve minutes past seven, our car passes the camera.

"Oh!"

I reel back as I jab the mouse, hitting the wrong bit of it and swapping the video for the desktop. I try again, placing my fingers with precision as if one false move might cause the footage to self-destruct. It doesn't, of course. It's still there when I recover it, paused with a Ford Focus, registration KW-something or other, frozen front and centre. I can see the outline of two people in the front seat: me and Jolanta, minutes away from the crash that will kill her. It's like looking at a ghost, and I can't do a thing to change what's about to happen to her.

Sick with dread, I set the tape going again. Two small cars go past, driven slowly in deference to the storm. The third, less than ninety seconds behind ours, is a large Audi SUV, black as midnight. Somehow I feel calmer for seeing it in the flesh. Up until this moment, I still had doubts about this whole unlikely scenario. With my chair pulled right up to the table, I inch the frames forward to the best possible angle. As with our own car, the registration is unclear. The first letter isn't a J, it's a D, but the rest is lost to the weather. I try every trick in the book to sharpen the image, and when I fail, I swallow past the hatred boiling in my throat and whisper a heartfelt vow to find the two fuckers who murdered my friend.

Full of hyped-up energy, I spend a while grabbing screenshots, intending to email them to Pryce on the off-chance she has a trustworthy tech on her team. I'm creaking my stiff legs toward the kitchen for some form of sustenance and possibly alcohol when Priti lets herself in the front door. I freeze, caught red-handed, and then bolt back to the table, stubbing my toe on a chair in my haste to close the images and hide the file from the desktop.

"Hey!" I call, tapping my foot as the *Manchester Evening News* website loads. I hit a random story and meet her in the hallway, where she sags into my arms like a sack of spuds. "Hey," I say again, more quietly this time, a murmur of comfort into her hair. The tangled strands smell of hospital potpourri: a blend of disinfectant, canteen, and stale cigarettes. I guide her into the living room and sit beside her on the sofa.

"She died," she says, as if we're midway through a conversation. "Late last night. I've just come from the PM."

"Husband or partner?"

"Partner, and he's done a runner with her three-year-old daughter."

"Christ."

"Yeah. He has family in Salford, so we don't think he's gone far." She pushes back a little and fusses with my hair. "Sorry to desert you. Have you been all right?"

"I've been fine," I say, mentally editing the events of the past few days. "I have a new car. Well, new to me, at any rate. Martin phoned on Saturday, and I went to Colwyn Bay this morning for my interview."

"Bloody hell. Was Pryce there?"

"Yep. Read me my caution and everything." I hesitate as Priti pulls her face. I've not told her much about Pryce, but I haven't painted too flattering a portrait either. "She was okay, actually. Fair in her questioning, and she arranged transport for me."

Priti huffs. "Least she could do, when she's dragging you all the way to Wales."

Aware that overt dissent on my part will seem weird, I steer the conversation into less turbulent waters. "Did you have any tea?"

"I don't think I had any lunch." She slumps forward, her head in her hands.

I lean her against the sofa cushions and drag the ottoman toward her, sticking her feet on it. "Stay put and I'll rustle something up."

"Something quick," she mumbles, her eyes closing. "I have to get back to the office."

"It's gone seven. Where the hell did you sleep the last couple of nights?"

"I didn't sleep Saturday. Sunday night one of the docs took pity on me and let me kip in their staffroom." She tugs at the neck of her shirt and sniffs. "Shitting Nora, I need a shower."

"Go and have one," I say. "I'll be a while. Being cack-handed puts a real dent in my culinary prowess."

She heaves herself upright and pats my chest as she passes. "Try not to lop off a finger."

"I will do my very best."

We eat at the table, soup and more corned beef sandwiches, with a side of oven curly fries to make it seem like an actual meal. Priti tucks in with gusto, as if she's been starved as well as sleep-deprived, finishing her bowl and then waving her spoon at my laptop, now closed on the placemat.

"Catching up online?"

"Not really. I was reading the news. It's cheaper than buying a paper."

She gesticulates with a chip, dripping ketchup onto her wrist. "You never were one for social media. You stayed off Facebook and the like. Said they caused more trouble than they were worth."

"Pet pictures, babies, and bitching are all I remember."

"That pretty much sums it up." She smiles, but she's fiddling with her sandwich now, picking off the crust in strips. "Al, have you really been okay on your own?"

I nod, knowing instinctively what she's tiptoeing around and wanting to make it easy for her. "You can go home, love. Work your case without fretting over me."

Her sigh combines her relief and frustration. "It's just, with all the coming and going at stupid hours, and my place being closer to the office, and—"

"And it makes sense," I say, careful not to appear too enthusiastic. While I'm not going to shove her out the door, her absence will keep her out of harm's way and make any further collaborations with Pryce a lot more straightforward. "I love having you here, and my God, I appreciate your cooking, but fending for myself will do me the world of good."

"I don't want you to fend!" she says. "You should be convalescing, not fending. Shit, you're going to sit around in your underwear and eat crap out of tins, aren't you?"

I take a moment to wistfully consider that notion. "Not a chance," I say. "I'll get dressed in real clothes and eat real food and go out and do stuff."

"Sensible stuff," she counters. "Because I know you, Alis Clarke, better than you know yourself, and I know there must be questions you're asking about what happened to you."

"Yes, there are," I admit, because she'll catch a lie. "But I'm not going to do anything daft."

She looks right at me, her brown eyes alert and canny. "Promise me."

I raise my right hand. "I promise," I say. Out of sight, I cross the fingers on my left.

CHAPTER FOURTEEN

Having rescued my prepared list of secure storage companies from the underside of a sofa cushion, I set an early alarm, full of good intentions to trek into Manchester and visit them all in person. The requirements stipulated on the companies' websites suggest I used my own ID instead of Rebecca's bus pass, so I arrange my passport and driving licence atop a change of clothes and take the rolling pin to bed again.

Still feeling industrious after a reasonable night's sleep, I'm eating breakfast in front of the laptop, sending Audi screen grabs to Pryce, when an email from DS Granger arrives to ruin my can-do mood. Her terse missive informs me I've been scheduled to appear before a disciplinary panel a fortnight from today at nine a.m. sharp, and she would like the name of my Federation rep ASAP. I stick two fingers up at her demand and then scurry for my mobile like a well-behaved, penitent junior detective. Pryce can't help me with this one, being out of area, and Wallace would throw in any old name for the sake of a quiet life. Priti, the obvious choice, is up to her eyes in a murder and misper, so I find Jez's card and text the mobile listed on it. I only ask him to recommend a rep, but he replies with an invitation for coffee and gossip, which seems too attractive a proposition to pass up.

A bright, frosty morning tempts us along the road to Debdale Park, where our window seat in the lakeside cafe provides an excellent view of a man sprawled on the grass in a sea of super-strength lager cans. Every so often he fishes in his pocket for a slice of Warburton's and the Canada geese flock around him in adoration.

"To Duck-Bread Daryl," Jez says, raising his coffee mug in salute to one of our favourite regulars. I've arrested Daryl more times than I care to count—drunk and disorderly, drunk and half-naked, drunk and apparently dead—but I frown as if I'm trying to place his face, and Jez smiles in sympathy.

"He's one you're better off forgetting," he says.

I blow on my coffee, steaming the window as Daryl attempts to roll away from the goose pecking his arse. "I dunno, he looks like a pillar of society."

Jez chuckles and tears a chunk off his crumpet. "So how are you doing? In general and"—he taps the side of his head—"up here?"

"Not too shabby. I seem to be getting the hang of living at home again, though the novelty's going to wear off PDQ if I can't get back to work."

He uses a napkin to wipe butter from his fingers. "And the rest?"

"The rest feels like constantly having the rug pulled out from under me," I say, which is as close to putting it into words as I can manage. "I see people and I don't know whether I should greet them as friends or complete strangers. Even the simplest stuff—what I like to eat, how I take my coffee, what brand of bloody toothpaste I prefer—I'm having to relearn from scratch, and I'm probably getting most of it wrong."

"One sugar." He knuckles my chin gently. "In your coffee. If that helps."

"Yeah?" I look at him in disbelief. "I take two now."

"Aw, bollocks." He's trying not to laugh. "You think that's bad? I'm stuck with bloody sweeteners."

I uncrumple the tiny packet he's discarded by his spoon. "Are you dieting?"

"Nope, diabetic. I scored a hat-trick the last time I saw my doc: diabetes, high blood pressure, and cholesterol through the roof."

"Ouch."

He always did have a tendency to bin the sandwiches he'd packed for a night shift in favour of a kebab or pizza, and he drank like a fish and rolled his own fags, but I think he's actually lost weight, and he no longer reeks of stale tobacco. A smattering of five o'clock shadow adds to his debonair new image.

"You look fabulous," I say and stick my tongue out when he lobs a packet of Canderel at my head.

"Anyway," he says, dragging the word out, flustered. "You wanted to talk Fed reps?"

"Yes, please. Who would you choose if you were in my shoes?"

"Rob Reid," he says with certainty. "He's a newish DC on the TPU, but he's a shit-hot rep, and he loves a good scrap with the brass."

"Sounds perfect." I scan the page Jez puts in front of me. It's been torn from the back of the monthly Federation freebie, and Reid's contact details are listed beneath a black-and-white picture of him in dress uniform. He looks about twelve.

"He's older than he seems," Jez says, proving we're still in synch despite my malfunctioning grey matter. "And he's like a dog with a bone when he gets stuck into a case."

"I'll give him a call." I tuck the paper into my wallet. "Okay, then, what's the gossip? Start with the most salacious bit and work your way down."

He folds his arms and puffs out his cheeks, making a show of sorting through a host of possible options. "I think my favourite is the big bag o' cash conspiracy."

"Go on," I say, regretting asking the question.

"Rumour has it that you fled west with your girl and a case full of ill-gotten gains. That you intended to lie low for a while and then head off to sunnier climes."

"Wow." I'm not really shocked. The Manchester Met grapevine is legendary, its capacity for invention boundless. "It's not enough that I had an affair with a witness, I have to be on the take as well? If that's true, where's the money?"

He waggles his eyebrows at me. "That's the question, ain't it?"

"Welsh police nicked it?" I suggest. "Or maybe the paramedics? Because they were the only ones down that embankment with me." The humour has vanished from my voice. I'm sure the single piece of luggage isn't common knowledge, but the accusation has hit too close to home.

"You know what people are like, Al," he says. "Give them an inch and all of a sudden you're Jesse James and Mata Hari rolled into one."

"My fault for asking. I suppose I should be grateful that no one's gone to the press with it yet."

"To small mercies." He makes another toast and drains his mug. "Hell, I have to run. I've got an interview at ten."

I sip my coffee, considering ordering another, and reflect fondly on the days when I had a job to go to and a schedule to keep. He kisses the top of my head, and I smile up at him.

"Hang in there, kid," he says.

"I will. Keep in touch."

The bell above the door jangles as he leaves. I wave to catch the attention of the waitress, and watch Daryl use a crust to wipe goose shit from his forehead. For a moment I almost envy him, drunk by breakfast time and cavorting about in the sunshine without a care in the world. Then he turns to one side and vomits down his coat, and I remember there's a lot to be said for sobriety.

❖

I arrive in Manchester later than I'd intended, but still within that mid-morning lull between rush hour and the offices emptying out for lunch. In the shade of the bus stop, I open an A-Z, the double-page city centre spread adorned with black crosses marking the places I need to visit. In recognition of my unreliable mental acuity, I've also plotted the most efficient route to hit them all. I look around before setting off, studying the faces of those people close by me—a black man in an ill-fitting jacket, an acne-riddled teen smoking a joint, a woman tugging an infant along by his arm. None of them are paying me the slightest bit of attention, but there's no harm in being paranoid when people really are out to get you.

I start on Piccadilly, slipping my woolly hat into my pocket to ensure the sutures criss-crossing my skull add veracity to the story I've concocted.

"Hey," I say to the girl behind the counter of Safe Mail 4 U. "This is going to sound a bit strange, but I'm pretty sure I rented a mailbox somewhere in Manchester, only I can't remember where." I make a vague, embarrassed gesture toward my head. "I wondered whether it might be possible to check using my ID?"

Not adept at multitasking, the girl has slowed her gum chewing and is tilting her head to one side as she stares at the slash of black thread closing my wound. A miasma of dope surrounds her.

"Does it hurt?" she asks.

"Itches, mostly."

"Yikes." She swivels my passport so it's facing her on the counter and starts to type into the computer. "I like your nose ring. I might get my tongue done. Friend of mine did her own with an ice cube and a big sewing needle."

"Bloody hell, I don't think I'd recommend that."

"Yeah, it all went black and she needed a shitload of antibiotics."

She stops clacking keys and shakes her head. "You're not on here. Sorry."

"Damn," I say with feeling. I suppose hitting the jackpot on the first attempt was asking a bit much. "I appreciate you taking the time."

"Oh, no worries. Hey, you should shave your hair. It'd look bazzin' with that scar."

I laugh; I fucking love Manchester. "I'll think about it."

She pops a pink bubble over her nose. "Good luck finding yer box," she says, scraping her chin clean.

The encounter sets the tone for the day. No one quibbles about running my ID through their system, and the safety deposit centre on Shude Hill sticks my finger into their biometric scanner, where a red light indicates I'm not one of theirs, whatever my name.

I eat a very late lunch on the hoof: a lukewarm Gregg's sausage roll, the pastry flaking down my coat and the greasy taste of the cheap meat so steeped in nostalgia that it immediately makes me crave another. The sky dulls as I dust off my clothes, and I shiver, footsore and cranky, with two places left on my list. A sharp shower drenches the Northern Quarter, sending a gang of goths sprinting into Affleck's Palace, their Doc Martens splashing through the flash-flooded gutters. Pulling up my hood, I skulk in a doorway until the worst is over and then dodge a bus on Oldham Street to get to my next address.

The mailbox store is blink-and-you'll-miss-it tiny, squashed between an Oxfam shop and a cafe heralding its all-day breakfasts in gaudy picture ads. I weave through the bus stop queue, earning glares and a few sniggers from the school kids amassed on the pavement. It's warm inside the shop, and the row of the street is silenced by a heavy front door and a radio playing soft rock.

"Can I help you?" a lady asks from behind the counter, and I realise I've been standing there for a while, panic-breathing and dripping rainwater onto her floor.

"Yes, sorry." I move closer, taking off my hood. Banks of trendy overhead spotlights leave me with nowhere to hide, and I deliver my standard speech with her gaze fluttering around my war wounds like a demented butterfly.

"Oh my goodness," she says as I finish my tale of woe. "You're the niece!"

"The niece," I repeat, mystified. "I don't—"

"Your uncle phoned, oh my goodness, when was it? Last Thursday? Might have been Wednesday?" She flicks through a diary, failing to pinpoint a date. "His name escapes me. Oh, but you'll know it anyway, won't you?"

Not bloody likely, I think, as she tinkles a laugh.

"He said that you'd been in a terrible accident, you poor dear, and that you'd asked him to try to keep your little business going while you were in the hospital, only you couldn't tell him where all your mail was being sent." Her nose crinkles with pity, but her forehead has been Botoxed into stasis. "What a shame about your hair, dear."

"Mm," I say, not really listening. "I might shave it all off." I want to duck beneath my hood again, but it's too late; I'm standing in front of a small CCTV camera.

"Your uncle could've saved you a trip out in the rain, couldn't he? I checked your name against our accounts, but you're not on our list. You should be in bed, not wandering the streets. You'll catch your death."

"We must have our wires crossed," I say. "He gave me a list of places he hadn't managed to contact, and yours is on it."

She nods. "Easy mistake. He sounded like a nice man, very polite."

I want to bark out questions—Accent? Inflection? Age? Name?— but a chap in a business suit has approached the desk, and she's already batting her eyelashes at him.

"Thanks anyway," I say, and she raises a dismissive hand.

"Fuck," I whisper, back out on the street, with the rain battering the awning above Cash Converters. Although none of the other store assistants mentioned my "uncle," they might not have been on shift that particular day, or perhaps they simply failed to make the connection. Whoever he was, he must have drawn as big a blank as my own, but the thought of his tactics anticipating mine creeps me the fuck out.

A-Z in hand again, I turn in the direction of Piccadilly, completing my circular route with one shop left to try. The rain stops, but I leave my hood up as I stride alongside commuters on their way to the train station. *Safety in numbers*, I chant in a silent loop. *You're okay, just one of the herd. There's safety in numbers.*

The bus is full, a soggy, drooping line of commuters swaying in its aisle, too accustomed to the overcrowding to raise a fuss. I'm crammed into a window seat beside a bloke playing a fruit-themed game on his phone, the repetitive "blip-blip" on the soundtrack punching further holes in my crumbling equilibrium. The final store on my list went out of business and is being transformed into a gourmet pasty shop by someone with no appreciation of oxymorons. Granted an early reprieve, I dived on the bus as its doors were closing, a move that almost cost me a foot but guaranteed that anyone stalking me would be left at the stop.

My bravado lasts until I enter my empty flat. Spooked by the silence and shadows, I switch on all the lights and return to the hall, ready to bolt for the door at the slightest sound. There's nothing, not even the hum of a neighbour's television. I wait another two minutes, counting the seconds, before I slip off my boots and tiptoe into the bedroom. Wincing at the creak of springs when I sit on the bed, I yank my legs up, curling them beneath me as if there's a monster lying in the dark, poised to grab my ankle. I know it's stupid and irrational, but I can't look. Martin always did the checks. My big brother, with his cricket bat in one hand and his torch in the other. He'd peer under the bed, open my wardrobes, and shake out the curtains.

"All clear, Al," he'd tell me. "You can go to sleep now."

And I would, as soon as he'd given me his word. I'd snuggle into my quilt with the nightlight on and wake to sunshine and the bleating of sheep.

I'm reaching for the rolling pin on my bedside cabinet—not quite a cricket bat but enough to put a dent in someone—when my mobile rings. I jump sky high, knocking the pin and the phone onto the floor.

"Shit!"

Lying prostrate across the bed, I track the phone from its ringtone, my eyes squeezed shut, because everyone knows that the bogeyman can't get you if you can't see him. I accept the call without looking at the ID.

"Hello?" I say, managing to sit up, using the rolling pin in my casted hand like a lever.

"Hello? Alis? Is this a bad time?" Pryce says, and my hand twitches hard enough to thwack the pin into my knee.

"No, no, not at all. What's up?"

I hear soft footsteps in the background of the call, and running water that lessens and then stops as a tap squeaks. I imagine her face damp with steam as she leans over the bath, her hair escaping its neat knot. Of course, she might just be washing her dinner pots, her shirtsleeves up and a pan scourer at the ready.

"I got the images you sent, but Mal, the tech lad, won't be able to do much with them for a few days."

"Okay," I say, not expecting miracles either way. "Still, it's good you found someone."

"I've known him for years. He's very discreet. But that's not why I'm calling."

"Right," I say, confused and curious in equal measure. "Go on."

She starts another tap going and closes a door to muffle the sound. "I wondered whether you were free tomorrow. I've taken a week's leave—well, time owing—and I've booked a hotel in Manchester."

My confusion edges out the curiosity. "Are you interviewing me again?"

"No, nothing like that. I spoke to Jolanta's landlord, and he agreed to give me a key to her house. I want you to come and search it with me."

Her blunt request elicits the desired response. "Where should we meet?" I ask, pushing all of my misgivings aside to be dealt with later.

"Where do you suggest? I'm staying at the Ducie. It's one of those apartment hotels."

Ducie Street is close to Piccadilly, but I'd rather meet somewhere less central, so I give her an address at a retail park that's sure to be crowded.

"Got it," she says. "Can you make it for ten?"

"Yep."

"Good. I'll see you then."

I hang up, smiling at her confidence, her utter disregard for the usual "I'll text you if I get stuck in traffic" conventions. If she says ten, she'll be there for ten. I bet she'd stick her head under my bed if I asked her to.

Feeling braver but not that brave, I stay put and phone Rob Reid. He turns out to be a chipper sort who doesn't seem surprised to hear from me. I agree to read through and complete a stack of forms for him, and he promises to arrange a face-to-face once he's reviewed the paperwork. He ends the call by telling me not to worry, which earns him a place on a long list of people with unrealistic expectations of my psyche.

"Don't be so fucking mard," I tell myself, inching my toes toward the hardwood floor.

Standing unmolested and triumphant, I consider the task-free evening that stretches before me. I could go to the Village for a drink, or to the cinema, or really go nuts and treat myself to a fancy meal, something I won't have done for months on Rebecca's budget. The possibilities are limitless.

I'm towelling my hair dry when the doorbell rings and a delivery lad hands me my slap-up dinner of fish, chips, and gravy. I tip him more than the food's worth, and he doesn't question why I haven't walked two minutes around the corner to collect it. Staying in is the new going out, I decide, pyjama-clad and eating chippy with half an eye on a terrible romcom. My plate squeaks a protest as I stab a chip with more force than necessary.

"Balls to this," I mutter, outraged by my passivity. I might not be able to remember my life, but I want it back.

CHAPTER FIFTEEN

My alarm squawks at seven, giving me plenty of time to catch the 203 into Manchester and meander toward Ancoats. Distracted en route by the rumbles of my belly, I detour into one of the Northern Quarter's artisanal cafes, emerging with coffee, a bag of pastries, and an empty wallet. Juggling bags and cups, I eat a croissant, which silences my gastric percussion and leaves me with a stitch to walk off.

The shops are only just opening when I cross the main road to the retail park, but there's a meltdown sale at one of the computer outlets, and the car park is busy with bargain hunters. I weave through a group of Asian lads who seem hell-bent on being first in the queue, and perch on a low railing outside Toys R Us, my arse dampening as I melt the frost coating the metal. Pryce's Disco noses out of Tariff Street at five to ten. I raise a hand as she nears the roundabout, and she pulls into the space in front of me.

"Morning," I say, attempting to proffer provisions one-handed without nosediving into the passenger seat. "I wasn't sure if you'd managed any breakfast."

She accepts everything I hold out, lifting it well clear of my graceless entrance and waiting until I've stopped shuffling my backside into place. "I had a bite before I set off, but that was hours ago, so thank you for this."

"I think I still owe you a few," I say.

Her seat creaks as she leans back and pops the lid from her cup. As Toys R Us vanishes behind swirls of steam, she takes a delicate little sip, her upper lip forming a pout above the rim.

"I'm not keeping a tab," she murmurs, and I have to bite into a cinnamon swirl to stop my jaw from flapping.

"Pastry?" I say once I've swallowed without choking. She chooses an apple Danish, and we settle into our picnic, tacitly recognising the futility of small talk while wrangling flaky pastry and icing. The car grows warm, and it's so pleasant in this haven of misted windows and cafe scents that I could stay here all day. Another couple of blissful minutes pass before she steers things back toward the business at hand.

"DC Hughes is tearing his hair out over you," she says, dabbing crumbs with a licked finger. She doesn't sound or look too concerned, so I follow her lead, keeping things casual.

"He is?"

She nods. "I signed over the bulk of your case to him after your interview, and left him puzzling the semantics of 'dangerous' and 'without due care.' He'll probably still be at it when I get back."

"Poor lad. Has he asked for the CCTV yet?"

"He's requested it, but he won't know what he's looking for without the witness statement."

I rub my forehead with the heel of my hand, uneasy for her sake. "Pryce…"

"I know. If there was a better way, I would take it. As it is, the longer he agonises over the fine print, the longer we have to sort the rest out." She starts the engine, forestalling any dissent on my part. "Jolanta's address is on the paperwork in the glove box."

I find the details and purloin her A-Z. I could programme her sat nav, but I have a good idea where the street is, and I'd rather give directions than submit to the whims of an automated map.

"How on earth did you get the time off?" I ask, as she turns out of the car park and heads away from the city centre.

"Countless accrued days, an unexpected capitulation on my nightclub stabbing, and a DI who's easily distracted by bara brith."

"Left at the lights," I tell her. "Who the hell is Bara Brith?"

She laughs. "Not a who, a what. It's a sort of fruit bread, flavoured with tea and best eaten spread with butter."

"You bought a fruit bread and used it to bribe your DI? I'm impressed."

"I didn't *buy* it." She gives me a horrified look as she overtakes a moped veering around the potholes on Stockport Road. "I *made* it. I'm not a bloody savage."

I raise my hands in surrender, tickled that I've provoked her into swearing. "If it's any consolation, I'm reliably informed that I burn salad."

She slows for a red light, sliding the Disco into neutral when she's come to a complete stop and applying the handbrake. "I enjoy cooking, but it's a pain sometimes, cooking for one." There's sadness in her voice and more than a hint of regret. The Pryce I first met would have rectified her lapse at once, but she looks at me and shrugs. "I cook for my team whenever I get the chance."

I don't react to the chink I've glimpsed in her armour. "Yeah? They must love you."

"Their waistlines don't."

I reset the conversation by assuming the role of tour guide, pointing out the landmarks of Levenshulme—the Canadian Charcoal Pit, the Antique Village, and the McVitie's factory where they make Jaffa Cakes. If you're a fan of post-industrial squalor, Levenshulme's back streets are a real treat: row upon row of redbrick terraces crammed into a grid, their only outdoor space high-walled concrete yards and alleyways gated to deter burglars. Jo's rented house is in the middle of one such terrace, its green front door an oasis in a wasteland of boarded-up façades and smashed windows.

Broken glass crunches beneath my boot when I get out of the Disco, and a lad walking past blows his cigarette smoke toward us, yanking on the harness of his Staffy as it pisses on a lamp post.

"Welcome to Levenshulme," I say, joining Pryce on the pavement. She has the door key in her hand. "Has the landlord been in since—" I swallow and give the question another go. "Since she died?"

"Once, to read the meters. He seemed like a decent chap, and he's not sure what to do with her things."

Pryce opens the door, and we enter the front living room. It's quiet and dark, the curtains drawn, their heavy material holding the air still. Unseen in the gloom, I clutch the back of the sofa. I can smell Jo's perfume and the herbs she'd use to flavour her cooking. The room has the atmosphere of a shrine, the clock stopped and the traces of her fading day by day.

"I'm going to turn a light on," Pryce warns. Her voice is hushed, respectful.

I shield my eyes as the bulb in the corner lamp stutters and catches, illuminating an eclectic mishmash of furniture. Jo was in constant awe of the local charity shops. She would link my arm and lead me to her latest purchase: "Ten pounds for the chair! I am sewing a nice cover for it. What do you think? This purple or this purple?"

"Her parents," I say, slow to connect the dots around Pryce's earlier comment. "Are they not coming to collect her stuff?"

Pryce steps closer, blocking much of the light and casting us into shadow. At some point she's pulled on a pair of nitrile gloves, but it won't matter if my own prints are found here.

"I've spoken to her father a number of times," she says. "But it's…it's quite complicated."

"Complicated how?" All I can come up with is the expense, because Jo was dirt poor and she sent every extra penny she earned to her parents. "Was her mum ill? I'm sure she mentioned treatment for cancer or something."

"Breast cancer," Pryce confirms. "She's having chemo at the moment, but that's not really the problem. Jolanta's parents are Catholics, staunch Catholics, and I had to feed them the official line."

"The official line," I repeat like an idiot. "I don't—" And then I do. "Fuck. You told them that we were seeing each other, that she was gay. Why the fuck would you do that?"

"Because her father asked," Pryce says, refusing to snap back. "Because the Polish police who delivered the death message said enough to sow the seed, and he demanded that I explain exactly how his daughter came to die. And because the press will get hold of this when MMP finally go public with it, and I'd rather he heard it from me. He won't accept responsibility for her belongings." She shifts a fraction, allowing me to see her, as if she thinks remaining in the dark would be the coward's way out. "He hasn't even made arrangements for her body."

"He what?" I can see she's not lying, but I don't want to believe her. I've always assumed Jo got buried while I was in the hospital and that one day I'll go to Poland and plant violets on her grave. "Where the fuck is she, then? Have you left her in the fucking morgue?"

"We don't have any option for now."

"I'll pay for a funeral." It's not an offer, it's a statement of fact, but my conviction wavers almost at once, and I sit on the sofa, my head bowed. "Shit. I don't know whether she wanted to be cremated or not."

There's a pause and then a rustle of cloth and cushion as Pryce sits beside me. She's close enough for me to feel her warmth, and I want so much to lean into it, but I don't move a muscle.

"When all this is sorted, I'm sure her family will want to take her home," she says.

It's precisely the right thing for her to tell me, and she's blurry around the edges when I look at her.

"Thank you," I say, my gratitude nonspecific and all-encompassing.

She holds out a tissue. "Any time."

We sit for a moment on Jo's tassel-bedecked bargain of a sofa. I skinned all my knuckles trying to fit it through her front door, and she taught me a wealth of Polish swear words. The memory, and the debt I owe to her and her family, gives me a necessary kick up the arse.

"Ready to get started?" I say, standing up and offering my hand. There's practicality behind the gesture, because the cushions suck you in like quicksand and Pryce doesn't have the knack of escaping.

"Christ," she mutters, grabbing on and allowing me to pull her up. "It's like sitting in a bucket."

It feels good to share a smile, and I squeeze her hand before letting it go.

"Upstairs first?" I suggest.

We go through the kitchen to reach the stairs, and I glance around at the countertops, the crammed spice rack and the crock pots Jo favoured for her many varieties of casserole. Nothing seems to have been disturbed, but I feel like an insect approaching the edge of a spider's web.

"They'll have been here already, won't they?" I say, tiptoeing up the stairs as if someone might be lying in wait at the top.

"Most probably. If they took Jolanta's key from her, they could've let themselves in at any time."

I stop on the landing, debating which of the three closed doors to try first. Trusting an instinct I can't quantify, I push the second door on the right and walk into Jo's bedroom.

"If that's the case, why haven't they trashed the place?" I ask. The room is lived in but tidy, the bed made and the dressing table adorned with trinkets and cheap jewellery.

"I suppose they knew Jolanta wasn't coming back here," she says. "So it wouldn't matter if they rearranged things as they searched, whereas there was every chance that you'd notice if things were wrong in your alias's flat."

The implications of that take a minute to sink in, and they give me the creeps. "Does that mean they're not convinced by my amnesia?"

She's quick to reassure me. "Not necessarily. It's more likely they deemed it an unacceptable risk and that staging a burglary was the safer option."

"Hitting both properties in the same manner might've raised a few eyebrows as well," I say.

"Also true. If they had any doubts about your amnesia, I think we'd know about it by now." She goes to the bedside table and slides out its top drawer. "Okay, then. Any clues as to what we might be looking for?"

"Only vague ones," I say. "Notes, diary entries, calendar entries, receipts, bus tickets dated after December twelfth. According to my files, that's when they changed her shift pattern. I don't think I saw her much after that."

"Until she came to you for help?" Pryce pulls out a handful of papers—letters, receipts, bills—and starts to go through them.

"Yes, possibly." I rattle a drawer that's warped shut. "I don't remember. I hoped coming here might prod me in the right direction, but it's the usual shit; I get the day she bought her bloody sofa and none of the stuff that might help us."

Pryce settles into a more comfortable position, resting against the wardrobe and stretching her legs out on the carpet. "What happened the day she bought her sofa?"

"Nothing." I shake the drawer loose, upending most of its contents onto the floor. "Nothing," I repeat, more quietly, looking at the remnants of Jo's life scattered around me. "It doesn't matter."

"Tell me anyway."

I shrug and pick up a chequebook. It's almost full, with a stub for her rental deposit and another for a water bill. I carry on flicking through it, keeping the story at arm's length. "It wouldn't fit through the door, and we knew we couldn't take out the window, so we ended up with it turned every which way, and I lost half the skin from my fingers. I learned how to say 'fuck' in Polish, and when we'd finally done, we went to the Barbakan to celebrate."

"The theatre?"

"No, Bar-*bakan*. It's a Polish deli in Chorlton. It's always heaving but well worth queuing for. We pooled our resources, came up with a few quid, and treated ourselves to poppy bread and this sausage…wiej something or other, it's shaped like a horseshoe. We had a picnic on the sofa and drank a shitload of cheap vodka." I rest the book on my lap and smile at her, grateful that she pushed me and that I'm getting more of the details back. It was one of the best days I spent with Jo.

"Sounds like a good time was had by all."

"Yeah, but I wouldn't recommend the hangover. No amount of aspirin in the world—" I huff, the rest of the thought beaten out by a weird, restless feeling. I paw through the items left in the drawer and then haul out the one beneath it.

"Alis?"

"I don't know, I don't know." I'm almost snarling at her. "It was silver..."

She edges closer, obviously intrigued but wary of disrupting whatever's going on in my head. "What was?"

"This *thing!*" I make a shape with my hand, a deep U, and we recognise it at the same time.

"A horseshoe," she murmurs. "A pendant? Or maybe a charm?"

"Pendant, on a necklace," I say. "For luck, with a little heart."

"From you? Did you buy it?"

"No, not from me." I open the third drawer, to find the handful of underwear that Jo didn't pack. A pile of socks has been shoved to the back, and I spot a small black gift box caught in their midst. There's an address printed on the underside: "Abdella's, 618 Hyde Road, Gorton." Too curious to keep her distance, Pryce peers over my shoulder as I open the box. The necklace inside is simple, inexpensive silver, bearing a solid horseshoe pendant. A slip of paper reads "Forever yours, K."

"That's Krzys's handwriting," I say. "I saw her wearing it, but she wouldn't tell me where she got it from."

"Were they a couple?"

"Looks that way. Maybe it was early days and they wanted to keep it a secret."

"Well, that's worked in our favour in terms of you and Jo supposedly being an item."

"Yeah." I scratch along my sutures. It's becoming a habit when I'm stressed or when things are twisting my knickers into a knot. At this rate I'm surprised there's any thread left to hold my scalp together. "Do you think those men in the car knew?"

She rocks back on her heels. "It's possible. It might explain why Krzys seems to have done a runner as well."

The pendant twirls on its chain as I hold it in the sunshine. It's fixed the right way up, cupped to stop the luck falling out. Perhaps everything would have been different if Jo had remembered to wear it.

"Is it stealing if I keep it?" I ask. "Just for a while?"

"It's probably safer with you." She smiles, watching the horseshoe catch the light. "Just for a while."

❖

Calling Jo's spare room a "bedroom" might fall foul of the Trade Descriptions Act. Pryce claims the desk wedged into its corner, and I head for a bookshelf full of dog-eared paperbacks.

"Someone's been in here," I say, immediately spotting the lazy error. "Jo was a stickler for categorising by author or genre, and these have been tossed back willy-nilly."

She doesn't look up from where she's arranging a series of typed letters on the carpet. "I know our timeline is sketchy at best, but they can't have found what they were after, or they wouldn't have tried to break into your flat the other night."

"Stands to reason. I probably discharged myself from the hospital earlier than they were expecting and caught them on the hop." I swap a Clive Barker for a Stephen King, offended on Jo's behalf by the disarray on the shelf. "I bet they searched here as soon as the initial fuss about the accident died down. I doubt this street has many Neighbourhood Watch members, so they could've come at any time."

"And if they struck gold here, there would've been no need to up the ante and search your flat." She sets down her final letter and reaches for her phone, frowning as she taps keys, consults the paperwork, and taps again. "Jolanta paid more than two thousand pounds to a specialist clinic in Warsaw in January. How on earth did she afford that?"

"*What?*" I scramble over and snatch up one of the letters. "That can't be right. There's no way in hell she had that kind of money."

The bill in my hand is itemised, the total of seven hundred and forty-three pounds helpfully converted from Polish zloty. A scribbled note marks it as paid in full on 6th January.

"That can't be right," I say again, but my spirited denial has ebbed to a whimper. Where the fuck did she get the money from? I pick up another bill, paid on 25th January, the total just shy of four hundred pounds. Do I have a similar windfall stashed someplace I haven't yet discovered? Is this why we ran?

The uncertainty must be written all over my face, because Pryce extricates the bill from my fingers and lays it on top of the others.

"You might not be involved," she says.

I don't react to the insinuation. I don't have the energy. But although I might be naive, I don't believe that Jo was a happily signed-up member of the Hamer criminal empire, either.

"Maybe she was coerced into doing something, or she got in over her head," I say, clutching at straws. Maybe I did as well. At this stage, anything seems possible.

"These invoices are all for chemo and radiotherapy," Pryce says. "Desperation can do terrible things to a person."

I nod, but I'm unstable enough to be rocked sideways by a blast of vertigo and tinnitus. What was *my* excuse? Where's *my* impoverished, ailing relative in dire need of finances?

"Fuck." I shut my eyes against the tilting room. I hear footsteps, then water running. Seconds later, she lays a cool cloth on the back of my neck, keeping it in place with her palm. "Please don't tell me we'll figure it out," I say. "Don't tell me it'll be okay."

"I won't." She tightens her hand, and water trickles down my spine. "It might not be."

I turn my head carefully and look at her, and she doesn't try to shift away, to re-establish a comfortable, more professional gap between us. There's sympathy rather than condemnation in her expression, and she gives me a pained non-smile as she catches a droplet of water with the cloth.

"Do you want a lift home?"

"No, I want to get this finished." If I leave now, I'll never have the balls to come back here.

"All right." She dries my neck as best she can and takes the cloth to the bathroom, returning with a glass of water. "Need any painkillers?"

My ear sorts itself out as I gulp the water, and the floor stops rolling. "I'm fine," I say, picking up a book to prove my point. "Let's keep going."

We resume our positions, and I spend a further hour leafing through Jo's library to check there's nothing hidden in its pages. Pryce is still busy with the desk as I replace the last book, so I go to the kitchen and work my way through the cupboards. I make rapid progress at first, finding nothing of note among the pans or cutlery, but I stall when I get to the first food cupboard. It's full of half-used packets, each clipped shut to preserve the contents: traditional staples of noodles, rice, and pasta, and the pulses Jo would add to bulk out a stew. She loved to cook, and even on her tiny budget she tried to prepare her meals from scratch, favouring cheaper cuts of meat and mince, and making do with natural yoghurt when a recipe called for cream.

My bum grows numb from the tiles as I try to remember the name of the dumplings she'd stuff with all sorts of fillings and fry in oil. My phone and Google come to my rescue, directing me to the BBC recipe page for pierogi and reminding me of a lively discussion about the wisdom of having a Pancake Day but no Pierogi Day.

"Every day should be Pierogi Day!" she'd declared, and then filled in her calendar to reflect her new law.

"For fuck's sake!" I yell, kicking myself for not thinking of the calendar sooner. I scan the walls, sure that it hung in here somewhere. There's no sign of one in any of the obvious spaces, but closer inspection of the plaster by the fridge reveals a small hole suitable for a hook. I'm barging up the stairs two at a time when Pryce appears on the landing.

"Find something?" she asks, leaning over the banister.

"No, not as such." I stop on the middle step. "But her calendar's been nicked, and they took the bloody hook as well, the crafty little shits."

"Yeah?" She opens her hand, flicking a piece of card in her fingers like a magician working up to the big reveal. "Well, they missed this."

She passes the card through the wooden rails and switches on the landing light. I recognise Jo's handwriting, the concise print and careful lettering. "28 Newbury Road, M19 2AP," she's written on the first line, followed by two mobile numbers and a single date and time: "December 14, 9:30 p.m."

"That's two days after we were swapped around at Hamer's," I say. "And none of the shifts started at that time."

"I put it through Route Planner. The address is about ten minutes from here."

"Yeah, it's Gorton. Did you try the numbers?"

"No, it'd be safer doing that from a payphone."

"True." I check my watch. "By the time we're done here, it'll be dark. Did you have plans for the evening, or do you fancy a stakeout?"

She sighs. "I had my heart set on wearing something glamorous and painting the town red, but a stakeout sounds like fun as well."

"I'll shout you supper afterward," I promise.

"Deal," she says before I can renege, and I literally bite my tongue, pinching the edge between my incisors. If she notices, she hides it well, and she disappears into the spare bedroom. I watch her go, the card creasing in my fist, and wonder what the hell we're both playing at.

CHAPTER SIXTEEN

The phone box stinks of stale urine and damp fag ends. Careful not to touch the receiver to her face, Pryce dials the two mobiles on Jo's card, and we listen to identical "this number has been disconnected" messages, ending the endeavour fifty pence poorer and in dire need of a wash.

"If the phones were linked to something illegal, they were probably burners," I say, raising my voice as shop shutters clatter down and a bus rumbles past on the A6.

She sidesteps an Asian bloke dragging a bucket of Day-Glo artificial flowers back into his pound shop. "It's easy enough to get rid of a cheap pay-as-you-go, but it'll be interesting to see whether they've done anything with that address."

"Depends what it was being used for and whether they were aware Jo had made a note of it."

"True." She stops short outside a Tesco Metro. "It's been a long time since we had breakfast, hasn't it?"

"Aye." I'm starving but haven't wanted to mention food. Whenever we meet, I seem to be stuffing my face with something. I'd blame the painkillers, if I were actually taking them.

After stashing our shopping bags in the footwell of the Disco, Pryce follows my directions through the side streets to Gorton. Twenty-eight Newbury Road sits in the middle of a typical residential terrace, with little to distinguish it from its neighbours. Its tiny front garden is litter-strewn and thick with weeds, and one of the panels on its front door has been kicked in and replaced with plywood. The curtains are drawn, but someone is home; there's a light on in the living room, and a black cat washing itself on the windowsill that pauses mid-lick to watch us drive past.

"Looks like a normal house," I say as Pryce makes a U-turn and parks behind the Volvo outside thirty-four. Although the street is sparsely lit, I clamber into the back seat, making sure I'm well out of sight.

"Do you recognise it?" she asks.

I squint through the tinted rear windows, focusing and unfocusing my eyes as I cajole my brain into taking an interest.

"No," I say. "I don't think I've ever been here."

"If it helps any, I don't think you have, either."

"Huh?"

"You used the map all the way," she says. "You didn't need it for parts of the drive to Jolanta's."

It's a smart observation, but I'm not convinced. "That could be down to us avoiding the main roads."

"Could be. It's just…" She shifts until she's side-on against the seat, her nose crinkling as she tries to elaborate. "You're just different when you're on familiar ground, even if you're only picking up on little things."

I think I know what she's getting at, but I'm not sure I can put it into words. "It's like a head rush," I venture. "Like this big surge of hope that I'll be normal again, and it lasts for a few seconds or minutes before I get shit-scared of what that'll mean."

She nods, a slow inclination of her head, her cheek brushing the leather. "You're scared your normal might be worse than what you have now."

"Wouldn't you be?"

"Yes, I would." She answers quickly, as if at some point she's taken the time to imagine herself in my shoes.

"Cross that bridge when we get to it, eh?" I say, grateful for her honesty but keen to keep our stakeout out of the doldrums.

She smiles, as relieved as I am to let the topic go, and reaches for the bags stuffed in the footwell. "Is it too early for tea if we skipped dinner? My mam was a strict six o'clocker."

"Half six at our house." I grab the bags, happy in the role of rebel. "Sod the rules, I'm hungry."

We split sandwiches and salads, balancing lettuce on the carton lids and chasing cherry tomatoes as they make repeated bids for freedom.

"Do you have any other family?" I ask around a mouthful of chicken and stuffing.

"Two sisters. Deryn's the eldest. She found God and…well, safe to say we don't speak much any more. Mali's a couple of years younger than me. She's married, with two girls of her own, and she teaches primary in Bangor."

Despite the sparse detail, fondness has softened her voice, and I know without asking that she's close to her little sister and nieces. She doesn't reach for her phone and show me the photos she undoubtedly has on there—it's not that sort of conversation—but she seems contented as she nibbles on a carrot stick. I wonder what type of aunt she is: the type who doesn't want mucky hands plastered on her upholstery, or the type who's happy to face-paint on the kitchen floor. Less than a week ago, I'd have thought my money safe on Type A. Not that I have any room to talk.

"I can't remember the names of mine," I say, lowering my sandwich, crumbs flying from it as my hand twitches. "My nephews and nieces, I mean. One of them's called Oliver, but the other two—I don't even know if they're lads or girls."

I haven't bothered to find out, either. I didn't ask Martin about them when he phoned, and I've been too preoccupied to find the photos Priti mentioned.

"Hey." Pryce waits until I look up at her. "It's not your fault. You've had a lot going on."

"Even before all this, I can't have been a good aunt to them. I can't have seen them for a year at least."

"Maybe you didn't like them," she says, and laughs as my eyes widen. "What? Kids aren't for everyone. You're not obliged to dote on the little buggers."

"I suppose not," I say, slightly mollified. "I don't think I'm very maternal."

"Me neither. Esther and I talked about having children, she was quite keen, but it never happened, and then—" She breaks off and coughs, clearing her throat. "Anyway, it never happened."

"Sorry," I say, tongue-tied and awkward. "I didn't mean to make...I know this is weird."

The headlight beam of a passing car flits across her face. She looks saddened and confused and tired. "It is," she says. "Because I think you and I would be friends, were the circumstances not quite so—"

"Fucked up?" I suggest.

"Yes, that."

I open a Twix and offer her half. "When in doubt, fall back on chocolate."

"Hear, hear." She toasts the notion with her bottle of water, and the car suddenly seems to have more air in it.

"Should've planned ahead and brought a flask," I say. "Chocolate without a brew is like Mel without Sue."

She nods. "Everything I know about rough puff pastry, I learned from those two."

The buzz of my phone prevents any further lamentations regarding the untimely demise of *The Great British Bake Off*. The caller ID shows Rob Reid, and I hold up an apologetic hand as I answer the call.

"I hope you don't mind, but I came over to yours this morning and pushed that paperwork through," he says after a general exchange of pleasantries. "I actually knocked on, but there was no answer. Did you get it okay?"

"Uh, no." I stumble over my response, not comfortable with the idea of an unannounced visit. "No, I've been out all day."

"You must be an early bird. I was there at eight." He sounds jocular, but there's curiosity simmering beneath the surface, and I push further into the darkness of the back seat as if he might be able to see what I'm up to.

"I had…I had a few things to do," I say and then almost hit the roof when Pryce touches my knee.

"You okay?" she mouths.

I nod in pathetic little jerks, and she mimes taking a deep breath and chilling the fuck out. I follow her example, managing to steady my voice as I continue. "I can complete the paperwork this evening. When do you want to meet?"

"Sooner rather than later. I've got SMIU pecking my head for preliminaries."

"Tomorrow?" I suggest. I don't want him round at my flat again, so I come up with an alternative. "If it's easier for you, we can meet near Belle Vue. There's a sandwich shop on Corby Street with a couple of tables. I can be there for ten."

"Ten it is, then. Any problems with the forms, give me a bell."

"I will. Thanks."

He ends the call, and I slowly unpeel myself from the leather. "Fed rep," I say to Pryce. "He made a surprise house call this morning."

She raises an eyebrow. "And you're meeting him tomorrow?"

"In public. I'm sure it'll be fine."

"Did someone recommend him?"

"Yes. Jez, my old partner." I become more logical as I calm down.

"Rob was probably just being thorough. He would've missed the post by the time we spoke last night, and he wants to move things along."

"Sounds reasonable," she says, but I can tell by her hesitancy that she still harbours reservations, and I want to put her mind at rest.

"How's about I text you when we're done? We could start going through the companies and names I found in my files."

"The colour-coded ones?"

"Yes. I've not had a chance to do anything with them, but I've got all the copies at home. I could bring them—oh, aye up." I nod toward number twenty-eight, where a teenage girl is dancing from foot to foot in the cold as she rings the bell. She's just come out of the house two doors down. Pryce turns the key in the ignition, not enough to start the engine but enough to lower the passenger side window. A minute passes, and the girl rings again and then raps the letter box for good measure. When the door opens, she's all smiles, making a show of admiring the woman's dress, wolf-whistling and demanding a twirl. The woman complies under duress, distracted by the wailing of a child somewhere behind her. She ushers the girl inside, glancing up and down the street before shutting the door.

"Babysitter?" Pryce says.

"Looks like. Either that or she's very dolled up for a night in front of the telly."

Pryce checks her watch. It's almost half seven. "I wonder who her date is."

"I wonder who *she* is," I counter. "I'm pretty sure I don't know her, and Jo only tended to hang around with me and Krzys."

"Colleague? Someone Jo was moved to work alongside?"

"Sounds feasible. Shall we see where she goes and then call it a night?"

Pryce nods and closes her window against the freezing air. Condensation is forming, along with a frost, but we can't clear it without running the engine. My toes and fingers are starting to go numb, and I can see her shivering, puffs of white marking every exhalation.

"Not like this in the films, is it?" I shove my uncasted hand under my bum to try to warm it. "They always have hot drinks and burgers and witty repartee."

She hugs her arms across her chest. "No mention of frostbite, DVTs, or needing a wee."

I laugh. "*Do* you need a wee?"

"I'm getting there."

"Yeah, me too."

She catches my eye in the rearview mirror. "I'm not proud. I'd nip behind a bush if there was one."

I'm not proud either—I grew up running wild on a farm—but there's a distinct lack of suitable vegetation on Newbury Road. "Stakeouts in Snowdonia must be so much simpler," I say.

"Unless I'm with Hughes. He's far too easy to embarrass."

"You need to choose your mate wisely. I worked with Jez for four years, and we didn't have any secrets left by the end."

"That's the best kind of partner. I miss working response sometimes. Things change when you get to DS. People tend to be more on edge around you. They mind their Ps and Qs, y'know?"

I rerun the conversation we've just had and realise my Ps and Qs deserted me some time ago. She's still watching me in the mirror, reading me like a book.

"Technically, I'm off duty," she says.

I smile at her. "And I'm well on the way to being sacked."

"Well, let's see what we can do about that." She settles into her seat again, notching it back so she can stretch out her legs. In the spirit of solidarity, I co-opt the whole of the rear, kicking off my boots and crossing my ankles. We're sitting quietly, losing the feeling in our extremities, when a car pulls up outside twenty-eight. I drop my legs down and lean forward, all thoughts of full bladders and hypothermia abandoned. The woman comes out to meet it before anyone knocks on or beeps the horn. I can't see the driver, but Pryce makes a rapid note of the reg, make, and model as the woman goes round to the passenger side. We start the engine and follow the car at a surreptitious distance, our heated windscreen making short work of the frost.

It's almost eight p.m., so the roads are quiet and it's easy to keep the car in sight. Its driver treats the speed limit as optional, pushing forty down Hyde Road and forcing Pryce to do likewise. I can tell he's pissing her off, and she slams on the brakes, swearing beneath her breath, as he jumps a red light.

"Keep an eye on him," she snarls, showing me why her team mind their manners around her.

"He's turning right after the bus depot," I tell her, but she's already on it, zipping round a Yaris and decelerating in the nick of time as she spots the camera in the bus lane. She makes the turn three cars behind him and visibly relaxes, lowering her speed and paying more attention to such niceties as changing gear without rattling my teeth.

"Straight through these and then left at the next," I say, and she glances sharply at me. I don't understand why at first—the directions come so naturally—but the car we're supposed to be following is still stationary at the red light. "Oh. Shit."

"Do you remember coming here?"

I shake my head. I don't remember. Not consciously, at any rate.

The left turn has taken us off the main road, and we're passing stretches of wasteland cleared for development that's never happened. Warehouses and factories sit alongside the few remaining residential terraces, the oversized buildings darkening the streets and looming over their far smaller neighbours.

"We're taking a right onto Copthorne just past the next warehouse," I say, a second before the car indicates. "But leave a good gap. He'll be stopping."

She does as I advise, creeping around the corner and tucking in behind a van well shy of the houses the car parks outside. We're farther away than we were on Newbury, but a single street lamp illuminates the woman as she walks to the middle house in a row of three. Its front door opens before she can knock, and the car pulls away the instant the door shuts behind her.

"What the hell?" My skin is crawling, and I'm too hot. I tug on the zip of my coat, yanking at it when it catches on the material.

"Hey, easy," Pryce says. Then, sharper, "Alis, you'll break it."

The zip jerks loose, and I tear my arms from the sleeves, shaking my cast free and balling the coat in my lap. She says nothing. She just passes me a fresh bottle of water and waits as I gulp half of it down.

"Now you're really going to need a wee," she says, and I cough a laugh across the lip of the bottle. "Are you all right?"

My ear is whistling like a kettle on the hob, but I nod and manage to tear my gaze from the house.

"Yes. Sort of."

"Definitely a hit on this one, then?"

"Definitely." I shuffle across the seat until I can see the other side of the road. Two warehouses dominate the immediate view, with a third set back down a shared access road. They vary in size, but all look derelict. Most of the visible windows have been smashed or boarded, and signs warning off trespassers are nailed to the brickwork. One of the three houses opposite is similarly secured, but there are lights on in the other two.

"That car wasn't a taxi," I say.

"No, it didn't have any ID plates on it."

"Friend giving her a lift?" I suggest, trying to err on the bright side.

"Do you really believe that?" Pryce asks quietly.

"No," I say as a Range Rover stops in front of the address. The driver gets out, his raised coat collar covering half of his face. The car's indicators flash as he clicks the central locking over his shoulder, and he heads straight for the end house. He raps twice on the door, sparking a flurry of movement behind the curtains of the middle house.

"They've knocked those two through," I say. "One entrance for the goods, one for the customers. If Jolanta came here with this woman, if she worked here, it might explain her being able to pay the medical bills." I stare at the first door, putting myself on its front step. Is this why I've been here before? To do this? To be used like this? "Fucking hell," I whisper.

"Alis, it doesn't necessarily mean—" Pryce chokes off and starts again. "It doesn't have to mean what you're thinking."

I'm not having it, not this time. I don't need my hand patting. I want to storm in there, grab that man by the throat, and slam the answers out of him. I want to make someone pay for what they did to Jolanta and to me, and it may as well be him.

"What else could it fucking mean?" I snap.

Pryce doesn't have a comeback, a safe, sensible explanation to account for my familiarity with this area.

"I'm not sure," she admits, and the sorrow in her reply feels like the worst kind of sucker punch. It also reminds me that none of this is her fault and I've no right to act like a twat.

"I shouldn't have bitten your head off. I'm sorry."

She nods in acknowledgement, but she's distracted and obviously uncomfortable. She sips from her water and takes her time screwing the cap back.

"Just say it," I urge from the safety of the shadows.

A couple more seconds pass, and then she says, "Was there anything in your files to suggest a promotion?"

"What, like moving onto the other shift line? That implies I'd gained their trust, and my wage slips show a couple of hundred quid increase, so yeah, it was a promotion of sorts. Why do you ask?"

The look she gives me holds a distinct element of pleading, as if she's willing me to work it out myself. I shake my head, unable to help her.

"Because there's a chance you came here as management," she says.

"No! I wouldn't do that! There's no way I'd be involved in *running* this shit." I feel the heat in my cheeks as I protest. It was bad enough picturing myself as one of the women in there, but to think I had a role in organising it is even worse. "No, no, definitely not," I say as if that somehow closes the case—not guilty, Your Honour—despite the Swiss cheese holes in my memory and the evidence stacked to the contrary.

Pryce is kind enough or astute enough not to argue. "We might be barking up the wrong tree anyway," she says. "This is all supposition on our part."

She turns away, concentrating her attention on the house, and we sit without speaking, the air cooling around us. The man in the Range Rover leaves forty-five minutes later, his parking space taken by a younger Asian man in a BMW who strides back and forth on the pavement, smoking a cigarette and chattering into his phone. We instinctively shrink down in our seats, but he's oblivious to our presence and unconcerned about his anonymity. A chunk of bling glints in his earlobe every time he changes direction beneath the streetlight, and he has a habit of sticking his hand down the front of his Superdry jogging bottoms. Pryce nudges her window open, but all we can hear is an excitable stream of Urdu peppered with English swearing. He finishes his fag and flicks the glowing butt into the gutter. He's still on his phone as he enters the house, and his silhouette continues to pace at the upstairs window until someone turns out the light.

"I think I get the general idea," I say, bone-weary and heartsick. I want to go home and drink something strong while lying in the hottest bath I can run.

Pryce, as usual, has no problem reading between the lines, but someone has to be the sensible one in this partnership.

"We should stay until they shut up shop. You might see someone you recognise."

"I know," I say, trying not to shiver too noticeably. "That's what I'm afraid of."

❖

We never make it to the supper I'd promised. The fifth and final male to arrive at the Copthorne house doesn't leave until eleven p.m., and our woman and another, younger woman are picked up shortly afterward. The lights in the houses stay on, but we decide to tail the car again to see where the second woman lives. When we get there, I scribble her address into Pryce's notepad and reread our list of "Things Besides Prostitution That Might Be Happening at Copthorne." It's a very short list, and I wasn't really being serious when I suggested the adult colouring book club.

"Anywhere here will do," I tell Pryce, dropping the pad into her bag. We've reached a compromise between my insistence on getting a bus home and her insistence on giving me a lift, by agreeing to a not-quite-doorstep service. If someone is keeping an eye on my flat, I'm not letting them see her car.

"How far is it?" she asks, scanning the empty streets for ne'er-do-wells.

"About two hundred metres around that corner." I brandish my cast. "If anyone tries anything, I'll clock 'em with this."

She smiles, perhaps remembering that I spent four-plus years patrolling areas far less salubrious than Chorlton's leafy suburbs.

"Armed and moderately dangerous," she says. "I'll see you tomorrow."

"Smashing. I should be at yours for about twelve."

She drives away at a snail's pace, monitoring my progress in her wing mirror until she turns in one direction and I head off in the other. I make it home without incident, collecting a large envelope from Reid en route to the loo. After a quick shower, I whack the central heating on full and get into bed, where I arrange the paperwork on a lap tray and scorch my mouth on a red-hot mug of coffee.

Tapping out an irritated beat with my pen, I scowl at Reid's questions. It's far too late to be doing homework, but I won't be able to tell him I spent most of the night on an illicit stakeout with a Welsh DS, so I start with the easy ones: career to date and undercover assignment brief. The rest are less straightforward, delving into the nitty-gritty of my relationship with Jo—"include specific dates and times"—and the events leading to and immediately following the crash. I stick to my pre-established party line, providing a sketchy overview of an unintentional romance, linking my deception of Wallace to my impropriety, and falling back on the amnesia where necessary. It makes for frustrating reading, but it's the best I can do at short notice, and I'm burying my head into the right dip on my pillow when I spot the message light blinking on my home phone.

"Crap."

I drag myself back into the cold and slap a hand on "play." It's Wallace, who's caught the FWIN for the second break-in and wants to know all about it. I text him a rough synopsis, assuring him that I'm fine, it was probably kids, and there was no harm done. Then I lie awake brooding over how he found out about it, because hundreds of FWINs are issued by MMP each day, and I didn't highlight on mine the fact that I worked for them. Common sense tells me that Wallace can't be involved, that I would never have been transferred onto the drug-packaging shift line had anyone at Hamer's known I was undercover there, but I'm so skittish that I can't discount him entirely. *Keep your friends close but your enemies closer.* My brain trots out the cliché unbidden and adds insult by repeating it on a loop as I try to sleep. I squash the pillow over my ears and listen to my tinnitus instead. The warning is bollocks anyway. How the hell am I supposed to heed it when I can't tell which side anyone is on?

CHAPTER SEVENTEEN

If he wasn't sitting in a butty shop, surrounded by blokes in steel-toed wellies and hi-vis vests, and already smelling of bacon and lard, I'd say Rob Reid had the look of a boy band member about him. Not the lead singer, more the rakish one in the background who got a groupie pregnant and sees the kid every other weekend. He's in his mid-twenties, dark haired and self-assured, standing to shake my hand, and winking at the girl behind the counter when he pays for our drinks. She rolls her eyes at him behind his back and winks at me instead. I smile at her. She's a cute baby dyke, and we have matching nose rings.

"Did you get a chance to go through the questions?" he asks, after allowing me a minute to take off my coat.

"Yes, last night." I give him the envelope, and he leafs through the sheets, checking I've completed every part. I half-expect him to whip out a red pen and award me a grade.

"Do you have anyone who can corroborate this?" He indicates the section focusing on my supposed affair with Jo. "SMIU are caught between a rock and a hard place. They don't want to draw attention to your presence at Hamer's, but their investigation is hamstrung for lack of witnesses."

"That's a shame," I murmur into my mug.

He continues without waiting for me to name names. "They pulled this lad's name from your files, a Krzysztof Janicki. He seems to have worked with you and Starek, but they're having problems finding him." He sets a photo of Krzys on the table. It's one I haven't seen before, and I slide it toward me, pretending to study it, while I wait for my heart to stop going like the clappers.

"I recognise his name from the files," I say, hedging my bets. I didn't return the photo of the three of us to the SMIU, and there was nothing else to suggest we were friends. "We worked the same shift pattern. Other than that…" I shrug and pass the photo back, hoping that'll be the end of it, but Reid is like a dog worrying at a bone.

"His last known address was in Longsight. There was no answer when Granger called round, and he's paid his landlord four months' advance rent, which is odd given the wage at Hamer's." He consults his pad. "His neighbour—a Mrs. Deirdre Asante—hasn't seen him for three weeks."

"Right." It's a struggle to say even that much as I wait to see whether Deirdre has grassed me up.

"Weird, huh?" He stirs another sugar into his tea and crumples the empty packet. Everything sounds too loud and too abrasive, and the smell of sweetness is making my mouth water in a bad way.

"Yeah," I say through a throat full of saliva. "He switched lines with me, didn't he? Could Hamer's have sent him on business somewhere?"

"It's possible, but we'll probably never know."

I nod slowly. If that was a test, I have no idea whether I've passed, nor whether he's held anything back. I came here expecting a conversation with an ally, not a cross-examination.

"So you work with Jez?" I say, tired of being the one under the cosh. "On the TPU?"

"Yes, that's right." He turns to a new page, distracted. "I offered my services when I heard about your case."

My ears prick up. I'd been under the impression that Jez had recommended him without prejudice, and he instantly goes onto my list of people to tread carefully around. I let him skim my answers as I sip my coffee. It's a bitter, cheap brand, reminiscent of three-in-the-morning night shift brews when my eyes were burning and my mouth tasted like the bottom of a budgie's cage. It's perfect, and it allows me to look him in the eye when he's finished reading.

"When did you last see a doctor?" he asks.

I count the days on my fingers. It seems like months since Lewis discharged me, and I cancelled a check-up in Manchester scheduled for the day of Pryce's interview.

"A week ago," I tell him. "I've got a neurology appointment in a fortnight."

He frowns as he jots down the date. "That's after the disciplinary panel. Could you bring it forward?"

"I could try." I have no intention of trying. I haven't yet accepted that the panel will even happen, because I've pinned all my hopes on Pryce and me signing, sealing, and solving everything in the next twelve days.

"Push for a CT scan. We need hard, medical evidence that your amnesia isn't just..." He pauses, grappling for the right word. I let him sweat for a moment. I bet he doesn't get flummoxed very often.

"A convenience?" I say. I'm sure he'd be interested to see a new scan as well.

He stops chewing the end of his pen. He's probably a smoker, used to accompanying a brew with a fag. "It may seem harsh, but yes, a convenience. Incontrovertible facts substantiated by a doctor will be a lot harder for the SMIU to dismiss or discredit. Now, I have transcripts of your emergency call and subsequent contact with the dispatcher, and a list of all the personnel who were on the rescue team that night." He shows me the list. Pryce's name and work mobile are at the top. "Can you think of anyone we've missed? Anyone who might have seen you on the road or in a local shop? Anyone at all?"

"No," I say, still fixating on that top line. "I'm sorry."

He finishes his tea and then steers the meeting onto safer ground, explaining the format of the disciplinary proceedings, the work he will do to prepare for it, and the ways in which I can assist him. I nod at appropriate intervals, ask appropriate questions, and make the odd note, and all the while I'm thinking: twelve days. Twelve days. What the hell can we expect to get done with so little to go on?

"Is there anything you've not disclosed that you want to tell me in complete confidence?" he asks, by way of a conclusion.

"No." I don't trust him as far as I could chuck him, and the only information he's getting from me is stuffed into that brown envelope.

"Okay, then." His smile bares perfect lines of whitened teeth. "Keep in touch, and let me know how your appointment goes."

"I will." I remain seated as he stands, making it clear that we won't be leaving together.

After giving him a ten-minute head start, I sit in my car for a further five, texting Pryce to tell her I'm setting off. I take an unorthodox route into the city, going via Cheetham Hill and Shude Hill to approach Piccadilly the back way and shake off any tail. I knock on the door of Pryce's room a little after twelve, right on schedule.

"Good timing," she says, showing me into an airy kitchen-diner with a view over the canal. A bowl of beaten eggs stands ready on the countertop, alongside grated cheese, sliced peppers, and strips of spiced chicken. She picks up a spatula, having apparently figured out that I function best on a full belly. "Omelette okay?"

"Yes, perfect. What can I do?"

Oil sizzles as it hits a hot frying pan. "Choose your filling."

We eat by the window, watching geese glide around the canal basin. It's started to rain, and clouds sit heavy over the high-rises, the inclement weather keeping the drunks and the spice addicts from the towpath benches. I smile at the view, despite the gloom. Manchester feels like home in a way that Saddleworth never could. One day, when all this is over, perhaps Pryce and I will get a chance to go out and paint it red.

"Did your meeting go okay?" she asks, as we warm our hands on fresh mugs of coffee.

"Sort of. I found out Reid actually volunteered to represent me, and I don't know, there was something about him that seemed off. It might be my aversion to cocky little shitheads, but I didn't like him. On the plus side, I didn't tell him anything useful. He'll phone you at some point. You're his prime witness."

"That's fine. I've already made a statement for MMP, so I'll refer him to that." She clears our plates, putting them in the sink and then turning to lean back against it. "Speaking of witnesses, I've been thinking I should interview the girl from Newbury Road in an official capacity."

"No. *No fucking way*," I say. "They'll know you're up here, that you're involved."

"I *am* involved," she counters. "I'm investigating the crash, and substantiating your explanation of it is a part of that process. Speaking to an acquaintance of the deceased is a sensible way to go about that."

"And how the fuck will you explain finding her name? 'Oh, I unofficially searched the decedent's house with the woman accused of killing her'?"

Once again, Pryce avoids my bait. "She'd be one of several on my list, and we're pretty sure she worked with Jolanta in some capacity, so hopefully she wouldn't think it odd."

"But if she does, she'll go straight to Hamer's and tell them a DS from Wales is poking her nose into their business. Then maybe someone will remember seeing your car last night, and then—"

"What exactly are *you* planning to do?" she retorts. "Spend days deciphering your own coded notes? To what end? You don't need to bring Hamer's down, Alis. That's MMP's job. You need to find out who murdered your friend and why, and whether that person was a colleague. We can't rely on a memory stick that you can't locate and might not even exist, so we need to focus on our only solid lead, and that's the women from Copthorne."

"It's too dangerous." I'm on the verge of pleading with her, but she folds her arms and stands taller.

"Is there anything else?"

For a few seconds I can't fathom her meaning, and when I finally get it, it doesn't make me angry or defensive, just tired.

"No, there's nothing else," I say. "I'd never laid eyes on the woman before last night. She might know me as Rebecca, but I can't remember her. I'm not trying to hide anything or stop you from talking to someone who might drop me in the shit." I take a breath. Pryce hasn't moved from the window, and I can't see her properly. I have no way of telling whether or not she believes me. "I don't want you to get hurt because of me. That's all."

I'm not going to spell it out, to describe how Jo's death feels like a concrete block crushing down on my conscience. If she can't grasp that, she should probably reconsider her career options.

She sits opposite me at the table again. Her face is pale, accentuating the shadows under her eyes left by stress and a late night in an unfamiliar city.

"I think we're out of options," she says. "I've spent the morning trying to come up with a way around this, and there isn't one."

I nod, resigned. "When do you want to go?"

She checks her watch. It's mid-afternoon, late enough for the woman to be out of bed, and a good time to catch the baby having a nap.

"Now," she says.

I don't go with her. I stay behind in her hotel room, chewing the skin on my fingers, digging a fork down my cast to alleviate an imaginary itch, making more coffee and not drinking it, and placing bets on which goose will get to the far side of the canal basin first. Forty minutes later and fresh out of spurious distractions, I find a pen and paper and start to work through the photocopies I've brought with me. Google provides addresses for the named companies and a handful of the individuals, and I arrange them by colour and then alphabetically, making separate tables for the codes I've assigned to each, many of which overlap. Thoughts of putting the data into a pie chart make me peckish, and I wander into the kitchen to pinch an apple from a bag near the microwave. I perch on the counter to eat it, imagining what the Northern Quarter looked like before the majority of its warehouses were converted into apartments for trendy urbanites and students with deep-pocketed parents. The theme sticks with me as I return to the sofa, niggling and nagging until I stop what I'm doing. I've learned by now to pay attention to niggles.

Without really thinking about it, I pull up a satellite view of Copthorne Road on my phone and widen the area to include the warehouses. There are four in total, one set too far back from the main road for us to have seen it last night. I change to street view, which goes no farther than the gap between the first two warehouses, and let the image linger there. The access road looked different when Jo and I crept down it on foot. She tripped into a pothole and grazed her hands, her torch swinging around as she fell, the arc of light giving me a split-second flash of how terrified she was.

My phone snaps to black, and the thread of memory vanishes along with the image.

"No, no. Oh fucking, *come on!*" I punch in the security code and centre the access road on the screen, but all I'm left with is that fretful feeling I get after a weird dream I can no longer describe in any detail. I launch the phone onto the floor, where it bounces and lands screen-up, the image jolted farther to the left. Squinting, I tilt my head and toe the phone back toward me. The street view is dated 2008, and daylight clearly shows the company name on the smaller warehouse: "DH Hamer."

"Jesus."

I home in on the sign. The font and lettering are the same as on the warehouse I worked in. Donald Hamer's sons would have been in their early teens in 2008, too young to play a role in the family business, and all of the active premises are now clustered around the Ardwick flagship. I settle on the sofa again, shoving the photocopies off my cushion, as if clearing a margin around me will give me space to think. Now more than ever I miss the access afforded me as a DC: the ability to identify myself over the phone and have people look through records, or to show my badge on the doorstep and see a perfect stranger become instantly attentive. Without MMP's resources I'm limited to the internet, but I do my best, searching for property registries and, when that fails, scrolling through the local estate agents who specialise in commercial sales. I score one hit out of four, finding the name of the company who owned the larger warehouse featured on street view. They supplied kitchen and bathroom fittings, went into liquidation in 2014, and don't seem to be affiliated with Hamer's. The property has been on the market for almost two years.

Using the satellite mapping as a guide, I draw a sketch of the industrial site and add the names of the two buildings I've linked to businesses. The next obvious step is going to the site in person, but that would be a precarious undertaking, given its proximity to the houses on Copthorne Road. I'm mulling over the logistics when Pryce walks in. I've been so engrossed that she actually startles me, and I smile at her, energised by a few productive hours of quasi-police work but mostly just grateful she's back in one piece.

"You've been busy," she says, observing the chaos I've created in her living room.

"I have, but you first. How'd it go?"

"Put the kettle on, and I'll tell you all about it." She kicks off her shoes and heads into the bathroom.

We reconvene over a brew and a plate of biscuits. Pryce is a dunker. Not so hardcore that she has to slurp up soggy crumbs, more of a delicate dip that's quite genteel when you watch her. And I am watching her, until I realise that I'm gawping and switch my focus to my own ginger nut. She flicks to the relevant page in her notepad, the official standard police-issue one rather than the type she's been using with me.

"Our woman at Newbury Road is Shannon Millward, twenty-three years old. One daughter of eighteen months and a son of seven months."

"Crikey." I cringe at the logistics. "Any sign of dad?"

"Dads, plural, and no, she's on her own with the children." Pryce curls her leg beneath her and rubs at her heel. We've come a long way from the DS who sat bolt upright in the plastic hospital chair, her gimlet stare pinning me like a bug under a scope. "I'd like to say I utilised all my skills and experience to prise the information from her, but Ms. Millward wasn't shy when it came to describing"—Pryce stops to get the quote right—"the 'thick as shit, bone idle twats who spawned these two.'"

"Lovely," I say, impressed by her accent. She's hit broad Manc right on the nose. "Did she tell you anything pertinent to the matter at hand?"

"In a roundabout way, yes. She confirmed that she and Jolanta were moved onto a hospitality project external to Hamer's. She tiptoed around specifics, but I didn't get the impression she'd been forced into anything. She claimed to have been cherry-picked for the role."

My eyebrows almost shoot off my forehead. "What, like it was a privilege? *'Hospitality'?* Who the fuck is she trying to kid?"

"Herself?" Pryce suggests gently. "She was raising two children on her own, on minimum wage. If someone flattered her into thinking she had what it took to be a high-end escort and offered to get rid of all her money worries, I can understand how she might twist that into something she could live with."

"And Jo was equally vulnerable." I put my coffee down before I spill it. I want to smash the mug against the wall. "Those fucking arseholes."

"Vulnerable is the perfect word," she says. "I bet the other woman at Copthorne last night has a carbon-copy background: dependent family, debts to pay, habit to fund, some weakness that Hamer's can exploit. You know as well as I do that coercion can take less obvious forms than brute force."

I scrub my face with both hands, grazing my cheek with the cast. I hate to think of Jo doing this, but she'd have been too proud to tell me or to ask me for help.

"What else did Shannon say about Jo?" I ask. "About us?"

Pryce turns to a fresh page of notes. "This is where things got interesting. She'd heard about Jolanta's death and said she wasn't surprised Jolanta had been going on holiday with you—her interpretation, as I hadn't elaborated on the nature of your relationship. According to her, it would've been the perfect time to get away after 'that argument she had with that Polish bloke.'"

"Which bloke? Did she know his name?"

"No. She'd overheard a heated phone call, but she couldn't understand a word, apart from the odd expletive. Jolanta ended it in tears, but she dismissed it as a lover's tiff when Shannon asked."

"Krzys," I say. "If he bought her that necklace, I bet it was him on the phone. When was the argument? Could Shannon remember?"

"She checked her diary and guesstimated the Tuesday before the Friday of the crash."

I do the sums in my head. "The newspaper in his flat was dated the day after that, and it would tally with when the neighbour last saw him."

"She breaks his heart, and he does a moonlight flit?"

"Yeah, maybe." Taken at face value, it seems the most likely explanation for his disappearance: he made a kneejerk decision, packed his essentials, and went off for a while to clear his head. If his wage had seen a similar bump to mine, it might have covered the four months of rent he'd paid, and if he really has dropped off the grid, he probably won't have heard about Jo's death.

"What's bugging you?" Pryce asks.

"I'm not sure." I've wrapped everything up so neatly that all it's lacking is a red bow on top, and yet...I pass her the sketch of the warehouses. "I think this is one of your itches that I can't scratch."

She splutters a laugh at the mangling of her phrase, and I blush to the roots of my hair.

"You know what I mean," I say.

"Fortunately, I do," she says, but the sketch has caught her interest and she doesn't prolong my embarrassment. "'DH Hamer.' The one and the same?"

"Yes. Slightly different company name, same styling." I show her the image on my phone and then flick to a stock media photograph of the Ardwick warehouse. Seeing them juxtaposed spooks me all over again, and I get up and walk across the room, hashing things out in a staggered monologue. "We were there. Me and Jo. One night, I don't know when. I can't—She fell, hurt her hands. Is that why Copthorne was so familiar? Not the houses, but the warehouses?"

"It could be." She's playing with the street view, willing it to show more. "Any thoughts on why you might have gone there?"

I haven't had the chance to get my head around this, but I try now, stopping and starting a couple of times until I've established a coherent narrative.

"What if Jo saw something while she was working at Copthorne? Something dodgy involving that site. Drop-offs, suspicious activity in a supposedly abandoned warehouse? I was her best mate. She might've confided in me and insisted on coming along for moral support when I went to investigate. I wouldn't have been able to say, 'actually, I'm an undercover detective, and I'd prefer to go on my own.'"

Pryce mulls that over, the sketch in one hand, my phone in the other. "And whatever you found there sent you to Wales?"

"It's one possibility."

Her nose twitches. She's not convinced. "Bit of a coincidence," she says.

"I know." My shoulders drop. "I hope I didn't hide the memory stick in the warehouse. We'd never bloody find it."

"Either way, we need to go for a little look-see."

I nod, the hairs rising on the nape of my neck. "Tonight?" I say, my voice sounding distant, hollow.

She sets down my phone. "Would you be okay with that?"

I feel as if I'm about to reignite a chain reaction I'd only just managed to stop. I don't want to go, but more to the point, I absolutely don't want to take her with me.

"It's fine," I say. I haven't got the energy to argue, and I can't bear to see that suspicious look in her eyes again. Once is enough for today.

I collect our cups and take them into the kitchen. Rain is hitting the window as squally gusts push dark clouds across the horizon. The storm has brought about an early dusk, the sort of evening that makes you want to hunker down in front of a fire with a good book.

"Less chance of anyone seeing us in this," she says from somewhere behind me.

"True." I'm gripping the sink so hard that my palm is starting to hurt. I'd give almost anything to close the blinds and lock us in safely for the night, but she's the only one with a key.

CHAPTER EIGHTEEN

In my dream I'm driving blind. There's no road, no lights, and I can't lift my foot from the accelerator. I want to scream but I can't. I can't do anything except drive and wait for the impact. I brace when I feel a nudge on my shoulder, my whole body tensing in anticipation, but instead of the smash of glass and the multiple impacts of the car rolling, I wake to Pryce, who's kneeling by the sofa, shaking my arm.

"It's quarter to one," she says. "If we're going, we should go."

"I'm awake. I'm up." I allow myself a minute before I move. The old pre-brain-injury me could fall asleep in the middle of a debate, enjoy a restorative cat nap, and continue arguing my point on the other side as if I'd never been interrupted, but these days my grey matter isn't so spry. I sit and wait for wheels to turn and cogs to crank, slowly recalling a laborious afternoon spent pondering the meaning of my coloured codes, and a mutual decision to go to the Copthorne industrial site in the wee hours, when the business at the houses is more likely to have concluded.

Dressed in a black hoodie, black jeans, and boots, Pryce looks every inch the breaker and enterer, and she's packing torches into a rucksack as I weave toward the bathroom.

"Where the hell did you get those?" I ask.

She fastens the rucksack and throws me a matching hoodie. "I nipped out to Asda. These were BOGOF in the Cat Burglar aisle."

I snort, unfolding the sweater across my chest to check its size. It's a perfect fit.

"Thank you kindly," I say.

"You're welcome." She flashes me a broad smile, full of the nervous excitement most police officers experience prior to a raid: that tension of not knowing whether you'll come out the other side with a van full of apprehended scrotes or with your head kicked in.

It's stopped raining while I've been asleep, but thick clouds are covering the sky, leaving only the street lamps and kebab shops to light the city. Taxis send water cascading onto the pavements as they zip by, and the only pedestrians we see are shuffling along, heads down, on the hunt for sheltered doorways. Pryce keeps up with the flow of traffic, not flouting the speed limit as blatantly as most, but not driving so fastidiously that a passing patrol unit might suspect she was drunk and pull her over. She parks around the corner from Copthorne Road and passes me a torch before shouldering the rucksack. We raise our hoods in unison, and I rearrange my sleeve until it covers my cast.

Too hyper for small talk, we set off at a nod, crossing onto Copthorne and keeping to the shadows as we watch the houses for any signs of life. All the lights in the terrace are off, and there are no cars parked outside. The small industrial estate is similarly deserted. It's unlit, and the access road has long since fallen into disrepair, with potholes spread the width of it in places, and grass sprouting from cracks in its tarmac. I crouch and train my torch on the uneven surface, making sure to block its light from the houses behind me.

"This might scupper my 'suspicious activity' theory," I say. I'd expected to be paralysed by anxiety or unspeakable terrors, but Pryce's presence makes it easier for me to remain detached and think like a detective.

Her knees crack as she joins me, her torch beam crossing and then aligning itself with mine. "I agree, it's too overgrown to have been used with any regularity," she says, immediately on the same wavelength. "But that's not to say no one's been here." She shifts her torch a little to the left, picking out a flatter area of vegetation. It's springing back to life, but I can see where tyres have churned it up. It's a wide tread, probably from an SUV or a van.

"Jo and I walked. We didn't drive," I murmur. I can feel the fear from that night beginning to settle over me like a sodden blanket, and I push to my feet, determined to shake it off before it overwhelms me. I look to Pryce, who seems to sense my need for moral support and comes to stand by my side. "Do the tracks stop here or carry on? I can't tell."

We walk a few yards, trying to map the path of the vehicle, but the winter weather, the puddles, and the irregularities of the road make it impossible to be sure.

"Shall we start with the obvious one?" she says, and I realise we've meandered onto the parking spaces for the Hamer warehouse. I freeze as if caught on a tripwire, but nothing happens; no alarms sound, and no dogs or security guards come rushing out.

Keeping our hoods low over our faces, we check for CCTV. Once we're confident no one is monitoring the site remotely, we scout around for an easy point of access. Our quest takes us away from the grille-covered, padlocked front door toward the rear of the building, where nettles and brambles rake our legs, and the boards across the ground floor windows show distinct signs of having been tampered with. I stop at one that I can force up and to the side, creating a gap big enough for us to shimmy through, if we think thin.

"Pryce?" I hiss in momentary panic, as I turn from the window and lose her in the darkness.

"I'm right here," she says, from no more than a couple of feet away, and I smile, too relieved to feel daft.

Holding the board with one hand, I direct my torch inward with the other, illuminating what was once a small office. It's been used as a squat at some point; there are filthy blankets strewn across an upended desk, and foil wraps and needles glittering on the carpet tiles.

"Watch your step." I highlight the detritus as she gingerly climbs through. She puts a hand to her nose, and I hear her taking shallow breaths until she acclimatises to the smell. It's the first thing that hits me when I follow her: a cocktail of urine and faeces so potent it's going to claw inside my olfactory system and set up residence there for the next few hours.

"Nobody home?" I ask as she pokes at the blankets with a broken chair leg.

"Not for a while. There's all sorts of muck settled on these."

We quickly examine what's left of the fixtures and fittings, impelled by an unspoken desire to move on. The bottom drawer of a filing cabinet has made a handy fire pit, and the upper two drawers are empty. The only paperwork we find is a receipt for a Pot Noodle and a bottle of Frosty Jack cider, unlikely to have been purchased by an employee. Three neighbouring offices tell a similar story, and while it's obvious no one has utilised the space for anything other than shooting up, shitting, and sleeping, I can feel myself getting impatient for a different, less tangible reason.

"This isn't right," I say as we reconvene on a gangway overlooking the main factory space. Rusted conveyor belts stand at intervals, ready to feed orders from the storage area to the checkers and the packers. It's a scaled-down version of the Ardwick factory, and that's its only familiar aspect. I've never set foot in this building before.

"I'm sure we didn't come in here," I tell her. "Nothing's sticking." I rap my torch on the safety bar in front of us and try again to find the right words, but I can't. I'm too frustrated, too full of unspent adrenaline to be articulate. "It's not right," I say. "He's not here."

I push off the barrier, ready to walk away, but she grabs my arm, her fingers digging in hard enough to hurt.

"What did you just say?" She doesn't ask it so much as demand, her tone and her grip around my biceps harsh enough to shock a response out of me.

"It's not right," I repeat slowly, and frown when she shakes her head.

"No, the rest of it." She sounds as if she wants to rattle the details loose. "*Who's* not here?"

"I don't—" I stop and replay the statement in my head. Both parts of it. Fuck. "I don't know, I don't know," I whisper, but the answer is right there, only just out of reach. All it'll take is the smallest push and I'll have it.

She releases my arm, and I stagger back, colliding with a metal post and sending a pigeon flapping for the rafters in a tumult of feathers and dust. I want to grab her hand and run, to pin this thing down, because we're so close to finding it.

"We need to get back outside," I say.

We exit the same way we came in, retracing our route through the weeds and onto the road. It's raining again, plump droplets bouncing off the tarmac and filling in the potholes. Too hemmed in by my hood, I shove it down, ignoring Pryce's bark of warning as I close my eyes and attempt to summon up something, *anything* that might prove useful. Within seconds, I'm soaked but still clueless, and I feel her yank my hood up and none too gently bustle me toward the opposite warehouse.

"Is it this one?" She clutches my chin in cold fingers and holds me in place as I look at the building. "We don't have long, Alis. *Think*."

"No. Farther back," I say, galvanized by the command. "We couldn't see the street."

"Okay. Good." She drops her hand and tugs one side of my hood, repositioning the material so it's not blinding me. "Come on, then."

We walk together, close but not touching, our footsteps synched and then slightly off beat. Every roll of loose stone beneath my boots makes my breath shorter and my chest tighter, but there's no startling revelation en route, just the ambient sense of déjà vu that's taken to following me around like a personal miasma.

She slows as we approach the third warehouse, her eyebrow rising in silent inquiry, but I lead her past, my pace increasing to a near jog, my torch beam zigzagging ahead of us.

"This one," I gasp, winded, my ribs reminding me they took a battering in the crash. "It's this one."

"Are you sure?" she asks, not half as out of puff as I am.

"Yes." I'm as sure about this as I've been about anything in the last two weeks, and the roil of nervous nausea in my belly adds extra credence. I creep forward, crossing four parking spaces, their dividing lines broken but still visible. I avoid the thin strips like a superstitious idiot dodging cracks in the pavement, a distraction that keeps me moving until my light catches the *DH HAMER* sign hanging askew by the main entrance.

"Jesus. Fuck." I bend low, propping my hands on my knees. I'm panting, but there's not enough air coming in, and I hear her telling me to breathe through my nose or hold my breath or some shit that I'm not capable of doing because there are sparks dancing in my eyes and I think I'm going to faint.

"It's okay," she's saying. "You're okay. You stay here. I can go in on my own."

And that sorts me out faster than a backhand across the face and a dose of smelling salts.

"I'm coming with you," I tell her in my best brooking-no-argument tone, and I see the flicker of a smile, as if that was her intention all along.

Without further discussion, we slog around the building's perimeter, keeping our eyes peeled for a weak spot. It comes in the form of a shattered window, its glass freshly strewn on its sill. A cursory toe through the weeds finds a lone brick, clean on its uppermost side, and the obvious tool for the vandalism.

Pryce gives a stiff nod to acknowledge the discovery and uses her torch to knock a couple of stubborn shards from the window frame. She boosts me through the gap, and then, unhindered by a plaster cast or a sore chest, she scrambles up and over with ease. We pause to get our bearings, which doesn't take long. The building comprises a single large, open space intersected by rows of heavy-duty shelving. Unlike the first warehouse, no one has co-opted it as a den, but there's still a smell, an insidious drift of decay carried on a through-draught that blends methane and ammonia with an underlying and unmistakeable sweetness. Deirdre Asante was right: once you've smelled it, you never forget it.

"Christ," Pryce whispers. "Where's that coming from?"

I walk away from her, following not the smell but the ghost of a route I've already taken, Jo sobbing and sobbing, her hand clasped in mine. Eight rows in, and along to the farthest recess. There's no light, and I'm feeling my way, inching forward with my soles scuffing the floor. I don't switch my torch on. I know what it's going to show me, and I don't want to see it. The smell gets so strong that it's almost as if I'm chewing on it, and the toe of my boot suddenly hits something that flops and gives beneath the slight pressure. There's a release of liquid that drips into the dirt, and I gag, heaving and then vomiting onto a shelf.

I'm sitting on the floor by the time Pryce finds the right aisle. She comes to me first, giving the body a wide, cautious berth and taking a bottle of water from her rucksack.

"Sip it," she tells me, putting a packet of Polo Mints into my free hand. She uses the remainder of the bottle to sluice the shelf clean and dons a pair of nitrile gloves.

"It's Krzys," I say. "Last time it was only a few hours since, and we could see who it was. Not like now. You can't tell now." My voice catches and quavers. "They've just left him to rot like an animal."

Despite the garbled syntax, she seems to get the gist. She bends low, focusing her light on the blackened hole in the centre of his forehead. The abnormal, flattened angle of his skull suggests the back of it is missing.

"They did it in front of Jo," I say, fighting to get it all out now, because I'll only be able to describe it once, and it might be gone the next time I blink. "Executed him and forced her to watch. I think—" I look at the body, at the tongue lolling from its mouth, as swollen and livid as a slab of liver. The skin on his cheek undulates as maggots wriggle beneath its surface. I gag again and suck my mint until I've swallowed the nausea away.

"You think what?" she asks quietly.

I shake my head, tears filling my eyes. I'm not thinking. I can't.

"He tried to stop her from coming here, working here," I say. "He threatened to go to the police."

"She brought you to the body," Pryce says.

"Yes." There's more, there has to be more, but I can't patch it together, and she doesn't try.

"Fucking hell." She stands, paces, and then turns to study her own footprints. We're leaving evidence everywhere, and I can see the sheen of sweat on her face as she starts to consider the consequences. "I should report this. I have to call it in."

I, not *we.* She's factored me out of this equation.

"And say what?" I ask. "How the hell do you explain this?"

"I don't know." For the first time since we met, she appears to be at a loss. "Just…just let me think."

She stares at the body. It's unrecognisable, so bloated that it barely looks human. I crunch another Polo, and the heat of the peppermint helps to clear my head.

"As soon as you make that phone call, we lose every advantage we have," I say. "MMP might not be able to ID him, but they'll have to ask questions at Hamer's, and any officers on Hamer's payroll will instantly go to ground."

She takes off her gloves and wipes her damp hands on her jeans. "What about an anonymous tip? It's not unfeasible that someone might break in here and find him. I'm surprised they haven't already."

I shake my head. "That keeps us out of the loop, but the knock-on effect will be identical."

"So, what? We pretend this never happened and leave him here?"

"Yes," I say, hating myself. "Until we figure something else out."

"And in the meantime, we give the culprits every opportunity to come back and clean house."

"They've had two weeks to do that. If they gave a shit about anyone finding him, they'd have moved him by now. Their witness is dead, to all intents I'm neutralised, and no one has reported Krzys missing."

"He's in *their* warehouse," she says. "It puts them high on the suspect list."

"Their abandoned, easily-accessible-to-smackheads warehouse," I counter. "It almost works in their favour, in a way. 'Your Honour, why would we be stupid enough to leave a body on our own turf? And why on earth would we be involved in a gangland slaying? We sell garden furniture and George Foreman Grills.' Trying to dispose of him would put trace evidence in their vehicles and on their clothing, adding layer upon layer of complications, whereas this allows for a far cleaner getaway."

"Hmm," she says. Calmer now, she's put on a fresh pair of gloves and is running her hand over the wall. "The body doesn't look as if it's been moved."

"No, it doesn't."

There are no drag marks, and the spray of bone fragments and bloody grey matter she's just found on the breeze blocks are definitive proof that Krzys was murdered here.

"How much of a rush do you think they were in?" she asks, still examining the rough concrete. "They had Jolanta to deal with, who was probably hysterical, and they've just killed a lad, so they're likely to have been agitated off the scale as well."

"The bullet," I say, catching on at last. "Shit. Have you got a spare glove?"

Safely clad in nitrile, I join her in a fingertip search, starting with the wall directly behind the body and then branching out to account for a ricochet. It's a painstaking task, made even more arduous by the possibility of someone discovering us, and hamstrung by inadequate light. I'm on my knees, chasing a glimmer of metal that turns out to be an errant bolt, when I hear Pryce exclaim and call my name. There's a blinding flash as she takes a photo on her phone.

"Have you got...aw, hell. I need a knife or something." Her voice is muffled, half her upper body wedged into a tiny gap between a shelf and the wall.

Knifeless, I scout around for alternatives and hand her a thin strip of rebar I find on the floor. "Any good?"

She surfaces to give me a thumbs-up and delves back in. Five minutes of scratching, tapping, and swearing later, she yelps in pain and then in triumph, re-emerging with a bleeding thumb and the mushroomed remains of a small-calibre bullet.

"Bloody hell," I say as she drops the bullet into my gloved palm and sticks her thumb in her mouth. "How on earth did you spot it?"

"I didn't," she says, around her wounded digit. "I spotted the dent it made when it pinged off the opposite shelf, and I took a wild guess."

I pull her thumb free and assess the damage. "I think you'll live. Did you bleed on anything?"

"No, I caught it in time. We need more photos and to get rid of these footprints."

As I use my own phone to document the scene, she seals the bullet into a tiny evidence bag and scuffs away the prints we've made. When she's satisfied we've done as much as we can, she takes one last, troubled look at Krzys's body. "We should go," she says at length. "Before I change my mind."

CHAPTER NINETEEN

We don't speak on the way back to Pryce's hotel room. She concentrates on the roads, and I watch the streets pass by in streaks of rain and sodium orange. We're at the Apollo roundabout when bright flashes of blue suddenly light up the car. She decelerates as a burst of sirens makes us both jump, but the ambulance tears past, heading for Manchester Royal, and we take the right toward Piccadilly instead.

"Come up," she says, once she's parked in the underground car park and turned the engine off, and I nod despite the late hour, because I'd rather have this conversation now than go home and try to sleep on it.

She makes coffee, doctoring it with generous slugs of whiskey and cream, and we sit on the sofa as the gas fire throws shadow puppets onto the ceiling and soothes the cold from our bones.

"Any further thoughts?" she asks, midway through her mug. I assume she's used the journey to bash her own ideas into shape and wants to avoid me tagging along on her coattails. A "you show me yours before I show you mine" sort of thing. So to speak. As it happens, though, I haven't been idle either.

"Could Krzys have known about the drugs?" I say. "It wasn't obvious from the shop floor unless you knew what to look for, but what if he worked it out or saw something he shouldn't have, and he tried to threaten Hamer's with it in exchange for getting Jo out? Killing him just seems too extreme otherwise, especially if Jo wasn't refusing the work at Copthorne."

"Might you have confided in him?" she asks. "You trusted him as a friend. Could you have recruited him unofficially to collect data for you?"

"No, absolutely not. I wouldn't have risked involving him like that. I wouldn't have. We were mates, that's all."

She's watching me in that unique way she has, analysing every twitch of my body language, every nuance of my speech.

"You think we were working together, the three of us, and I got them killed," I say. No matter what, it always comes around to this sooner or later, and it's easier for me to throw it into the mix than wait for her to blindside me with it. She lowers her gaze, but she doesn't refute the accusation.

"I have to consider all possible avenues. I wouldn't be doing my job otherwise."

"I know. I understand." I try for a smile, but my bottom lip trembles. Over the past couple of days we seemed to have forged a truce, however tentative, tiptoeing toward a conclusion where I'd actually been trying to help Jo and hadn't been complicit in her death. The possibility that I fucked up, getting not just one but both of my best friends murdered, hits me all the harder as a result. And because of what? Greed? Stupidity? Naivety?

Even worse is the way Pryce is looking at me now, clearly asking the same questions. She makes me feel ashamed of something I don't even know I've done.

"I want to go home," I tell her. I close my eyes, and tears run down my face. I rub them away but then start to cry in earnest. "I can't keep doing this. I can't live in fucking limbo like this. I want to go home."

She offers me a tissue. "It's gone four, and you probably shouldn't be driving. Not in this state. Stay on the sofa."

"No. Thanks, but no." I grab my mug and lurch into the kitchen, bouncing off a stupidly situated floor-to-ceiling pillar as the alcohol, the late hour, and Krzys—mainly Krzys—steal the strength from my legs. The mug clatters into the sink, its handle breaking as it hits the plug.

"Sorry. I'll pay for it," I tell her. A laugh bubbles up, bordering on hysterical. "Just add it to my tab."

She catches hold of my hand as I try to walk past her. "You're not running a tab, Alis. How many times do I have to tell you? You don't owe me anything." Her fingers tighten on mine. "Sleep on the sofa. Then I'll know you're safe."

We're only inches apart, so close I can feel the flutter of her breath on my cheek. She's flushed from the fire and the whiskey, maybe from our proximity, and she's beautiful, even at stupid o'clock under the harsh kitchen spotlights. Not that this latter detail is news to me, but the booze seems to have loosened the guard I'd set up around it.

"They might be watching my flat," I protest half-heartedly. "They'll wonder why I've not come home."

"Let them wonder." Her eyes are locked on mine, and there's a challenge there, not just to the perps keeping their theoretical vigil, but to me, and that's all the warning she gives me before her lips brush against mine in a tentative question and then press in with knee-buckling intensity when I do nothing to object.

She forces me back against the counter, her hands tangled in my hair and her tongue flicking out to tease mine. I groan at the sensation and the absolute insanity of what's happening, but there's no fucking way I'm calling a stop, not when she's tugging my T-shirt over my head and I've slid my hand between her jeans and the curve of her arse.

"Not here," I gasp, stilling her fingers on my bra clasp, and she acquiesces at once, leading me away from the window and back to the soft firelight of the living room.

She keeps me standing while she unbuttons my jeans and slides my bra down and off. She kisses the arc of my cheekbone, my jaw, the roses on my tattoo, as her hands find my breasts and then my nipples. I smile when her teeth tug gently on my nose ring, the mild sting eased almost immediately by her tongue, and I bring her lips back to mine, tasting sweetness and whiskey and something unfamiliar that must be her.

Lowering her head, she follows the path of her fingers with her mouth, eventually trailing a line south to the sensitive skin of my abdomen.

"Sofa," she says, and I nod, letting her work my jeans and my underwear over my hips. She kneels between my legs as I sit, and she unbuttons her shirt.

"Take it off," I tell her. I don't recognise my own voice; it's hoarse and tremulous and not a little reckless. I'd love to do the honours for her, but with the cast and my luck, I'd probably knock her unconscious.

She shrugs out of her shirt and unfastens her bra, swaying forward so I can remove it completely. I leave it loose and suck at her breasts through the lace, until she moans low in her throat and wrenches it off. Without missing a beat, she nudges my thighs apart and dips her head to kiss just below my belly button. There's a question in her eyes when she looks up at me, and I answer with a soft "please," just before I feel her tongue push inside me.

"Jesus, Pryce!"

I grab the sofa, digging my nails into the leather, as she uses her fingers and her mouth to fuck me, her free hand tucked firmly beneath my backside to keep me in place. Not that I have any intention of escaping. It's all I can do to keep breathing, especially when I feel her smiling against me. She settles in and takes her time, allowing me moments when I can focus enough to watch her, though these are outweighed by glorious periods where my toes curl and I communicate entirely through profanities.

My feet somehow end up propped on the coffee table, and she uses the extra space to thrust into me, soothing the fierce drive of her fingers with the slippery warmth of her mouth. I come in an undignified spectacle of shuddering and convulsing, my heels clouting the table so hard that she turns to check whether I've broken anything. She lowers my stiff legs one by one and leans her head on my thigh, tracing patterns with her fingers, while I wait for the room to stop spinning.

"Come here," I say. I hook my fingers through her belt loops and guide her onto the sofa. Bless the Ducie Hotel management, they've chosen supersized sofas for their guest rooms, and when she's got her jeans off she lies back, naked apart from her white cotton briefs, and beckons me to her.

I straddle her obediently, brushing her sweaty hair from her forehead and then taking my time kissing her. Wound tighter than a spring, she's less inclined to be leisurely, and it's not long before she starts to squirm beneath me. As she murmurs encouragement, I ease my hand under the elastic of her briefs and slide two fingers inside her, a gradual slow glide that's rewarded by a crook of her leg and the sight of her head falling back on the cushions. I pull back just as slowly, and her mouth opens in a soundless "oh."

Curled into the space she's made for me, I rest my head on the curve of her breast and find a rhythm that makes her pant and rise to meet me. I move my head slightly, capturing a nipple between my lips and grazing it with my teeth, and she makes a noise I'd never have dreamed her capable of making as she comes hard and without warning.

"Oh God." She covers her face with a slack arm. "Sorry."

"Sorry? For what?" I twist my fingers inside her, setting off another series of spasms that she rides out with a hedonistic sigh. "For doing this?"

"No. Well, no. It's just that I usually…" She licks her lips. She's blushing to the tips of her ears, but she's smiling. "I usually take longer."

I smile back at her. "I'm going to consider that a compliment."

"Do," she says, all languid and limp, and not caring that we've probably ruined the sofa. "You definitely earned it."

❖

We add more whiskey and a few ill-advised beers to the growing list of ill-advised things we've done while most of the people in the city acted like responsible adults and went to bed. We do go to bed, but only to preserve the sofa's integrity, and we don't sleep until the din of the morning rush hour has subsided to a background drone.

I wake alone, wrapped in sheets that still smell of her, my body aching pleasantly in some places and less pleasantly in others.

"Fuck," I whisper, holding a sticky palm to my sore head. That's as profound a reaction as I can muster right now. I'm naked beneath the bedding, but my clothes from the previous night are in a neat pile on the bedside cabinet, along with a glass of water and two ibuprofen. I take the pills, drink the water, and hobble into the en suite for a shower, making enough noise to give Pryce fair warning that I'm alive and about to put in an appearance.

I find her in the kitchen, nursing a mug of strong tea, her face as pale as the whitewashed walls.

"Hey," I say.

"Hey." She gestures at the counter, where she's arranged milk, sugar, and a mug.

I opt for tea as well, hoping it'll be kinder to my stomach lining, and then I sit opposite her at the table, offsetting my mug so the smell can't reach me. I haven't had tea since my mum died. It was the only thing she could taste at the end, and she drank it by the bucketful.

"I didn't hear you get up," I say.

"You were asleep." The mug wobbles as she raises it, and her eyes are puffy. I'd lay the blame on a hangover and a very late night, if it weren't for the crumpled tissue poking from her sleeve.

"Pryce," I begin, and shake my head. Jesus fucking Christ. I've spent a good part of the last six hours with my fingers buried in her, and I can't even call her by her first name. "Look, what happened—"

She holds up a hand to cut me off. "It was my fault. I started it." She inhales deeply, and I see her fight to correct her posture, to insert the rod into her spine and jut out her chin. "And it should never have happened. I can't—I don't know what the hell I was thinking."

"*Neither* of us was thinking," I say, trying to be reasonable. We were both consenting adults, when all's said and done.

"Are you sure about that?" she asks, in a tone that would curdle milk. The headache pounding behind my eyes puts everything on a two-second delay, and I'm still processing the question when she clarifies it for me. "Or did you fuck me for your 'Get Out of Jail Free' card?"

"Jesus!" I react more to the crudeness of her language than to what she actually said, but the latter hits me like a fist as she glares at me.

"I've compromised everything, even more so than I already had. And you let me," she says quietly.

"No, I didn't mean for that. That's not why—Christ, I won't tell a soul. I promise." The words sound pathetic even to my own ears, and her answering laugh is short and wild.

"It's easy for you to say that now, Alis, but how can you know *what* you'll do if this all goes badly for you?"

"I wouldn't tell anyone," I insist. I'd get down on my knees and beg her to trust me if I thought it would make a difference. "Fucking hell, Pryce, I forgot everything else. I can forget about this."

She's so unravelled that she almost looks hurt, but I can't retract it. Better to let her think last night meant nothing, even if all I want to do is kiss her until she realises I'm lying.

"We'll find out soon enough, won't we?" Her shoulders sag. She's obviously exhausted, and she no longer seems to have the strength to be angry or bitter or anything much at all.

We sit for a while, not talking, not drinking our tea. There's a finality to the silence, as if she's come to a decision and she's waiting to see whether I work out what it is. I swap my tea for a glass of water, and stay by the window once I've drained it.

"What do we do now?" I ask, because apparently, I'm a glutton for punishment and I need her to tell me she's abandoning me and returning to Wales.

"I can't stay here," she says, choosing her words carefully. "It might be better if you come clean about everything: what we've found, what we suspect, Krzys's body. Perhaps the SMIU will be able to keep a lid on it and investigate from their side. Tell them I've been helping you"—her voice cracks and she shakes her head—"or tell them whatever you want. I'm in enough trouble as it is."

"When are you leaving?" I ask. I won't be following her advice, and I'll be damned if I ever mention her name to the SMIU.

"As soon as I've packed. I'll try to run those plates for you, the ones from the Copthorne house, and tie up any outstanding queries, but I can't be involved to this extent. Not now."

"Why don't *you* contact the SMIU? I could be on a plane out of the country in a couple of hours."

"Because I hope you'll make the right decision." She comes over to the window, watching the geese at the lock so she doesn't have to look at me. "Whatever you might have done, whatever part you might have played in all of this, I believe that you believe what you're saying."

I scoff. "Mostly you believe I'll land you in the crap to save my own neck, if I turn out to be a shithead."

She does look at me then, and I'm shocked to see tears in her eyes. "I don't know what *I'd* do in that situation," she says. "I've no right to predict what you'd do."

Her honesty destroys my righteous indignation. I rip off a piece of kitchen roll, handing it to her in lieu of a tissue.

"Thanks," she says.

"You're welcome."

She wipes her eyes, and we go back to watching the geese fight over a handful of chips that a drunk has lobbed into the canal. As feathers fly and the water churns, he tosses the wrapper in after them and walks away.

CHAPTER TWENTY

In no hurry to get home, I drive around the city, hitting Deansgate at lunchtime as office workers clutching Pret A Manger bags dodge between the near-stationary cars. Suits start to give way to self-conscious trendiness the closer I get to the university, and the complicated cycle lanes are full of students toiling against the headwind and the weight of their textbooks.

For old times' sake, I stop at the Barbakan deli to buy a four-piece loaf and kabanosy. The girl behind the counter greets me by name, my other name, clucking her tongue in sympathy and tossing in a black pudding, with her condolences.

"I lit a candle," she says in heavily accented English. "For Jolanta."

"She would have appreciated that," I tell her, and push out through the crowd before I start bawling.

Alternate showers of sleet and hail hit the windscreen as I leave the main road and slow for the first of many speed bumps. The forecast warned of a cold front hitting us from the north, with snow predicted for the Pennines and a slushy covering possible for the city streets. Between the jolts of traffic-calming measures, I daydream about Pryce sitting in front of her open fire, book in hand—something serious and literary, probably a classic—surrounded by sparkling white fields and mountains. She's drinking whiskey from a crystal tumbler, her feet bare and her hair loose. Then I accelerate to hit a bump extra hard, because if she knew I was romanticising her in such a rose-tinted, hackneyed manner, she'd quite rightly slap me about the head.

When I eventually arrive home, there's no one skulking on the street, and the flat itself shows no signs of intrusion. Wallace has left a "just checking in" message, while Rob Reid's is a more pointed enquiry: have I rescheduled my hospital appointment? And do I have an alternative number for Detective Sergeant Pryce, because she's not answering her work mobile and the officers on her team have told him she's on leave?

I defer replying in favour of a long hot bath, during which I phone Priti to arrange a takeaway and cheesy film extravaganza for tonight. From the sound of her voice, it's a date we're both sorely in need of.

Sinking down into the bubbles, I try to formulate a new plan of action, one I can implement without Pryce's assistance or resources. Handing things over to the SMIU isn't an option, nor is dragging her name through the mud. No matter how anxious I am to clear my own name, I won't do it at the expense of hers. Too booze-addled for sagacity, I go back to basics, reminding myself of her earlier advice: "Find out who murdered your friend and why, and whether that person was a colleague."

"*Friends*," I whisper, covering my face with a warm flannel. Pryce and I hadn't known about Krzys at the time.

The heat is making me dopey, so I drag myself from the tub and have a working lunch in the middle of my bed. Logic returns halfway through a kabanos, and I resolve to construct a possible sequence of events that starts with Krzys's murder and concludes in Snowdonia. It's something Pryce and I never got the opportunity to discuss, and I miss having her to play devil's advocate as I hash out the timeline. We made a good team while it lasted, fitting together well in every sense of the phrase.

"Why murder Krzys?" I write as a header. Then, "Threat to Hamer's/to the drugs operation?/Blackmail to get Jo out of Copthorne?"

I suspect the answer might be "all of the above," so I move to the next point: "Who murdered Krzys?" Had Jo recognised his assailant? She'd been forced to watch, so might I have the identity of his killer secreted away somewhere? Where's the gun? Pryce still has the bullet, and there has to be a weapon out there somewhere that matches it.

Chewing and swallowing without tasting, I scribble the questions down and decide on my next point: "Why tell me?" Because we were still best friends, and I was unconnected to Copthorne, is the simplest answer. Surely the more pertinent question is "What would I have done next?" I was an undercover detective whose relatively straightforward drugs case now included a coldblooded execution. If Jo was too scared to go directly to the police, it seems logical that I would have outed myself as an officer and encouraged her to come to Belle Vue and provide a witness statement.

"Of course you did," I mutter, slapping my crust back onto my plate. I would have given her all the usual spiel: we can protect you; you'll be able to testify via a video link; we'll keep your name out of the press. So what the hell did she say that stopped us from doing any of that? I rock back on my chair and then fling the legs forward again, thumping them onto the laminate as the answer hits me: it must have been Jo who knew someone from MMP was working with Hamer's, and this is the point she dropped the bombshell. It's an answer so glaringly obvious that I bow my head, ashamed that I'm only just making the connection.

Although I can't recall the conversation or even prove it took place, it's the most likely trigger for our flight to Snowdonia. Without that revelation, I would have requested an urgent contact and reported the murder regardless of Jo's consent. Instead, not knowing how deeply the rot had set in, I tried to take her to a place of safety, and someone ambushed us.

I shove my papers and lunch aside and curl under the duvet. I should feel elated, having created a plausible timeline that suggests I'm innocent of any crime, but every word I've written is worthless without proof. Pryce would say I've designed a happy ending for myself, and she has an uncanny knack of being right about these things.

"Fuck her," I say and have an unfortunate flash of me doing just that. It makes me damp and hot, and I pull the pillow over my head, groaning and cursing her name. She'll be halfway to the bloody hills by now, and she's still driving me mad.

With case-related inspiration proving elusive, I launch myself into a full-on housework offensive, hoovering, dusting, polishing the bathroom taps, and, saving the best for last, emptying the fridge of food that's on the verge of sprouting legs and escaping of its own accord. The cleaning frenzy works on two levels: it stops me thinking about Pryce, and it'll prove to Priti that I'm managing and don't need her to move back in.

She arrives at seven o'clock sharp, bearing Chinese takeaway and a selection of mindless action blockbusters. There's a reinvigorated bounce to her step, and she's lost the haggard, sleep-deprived look that had pinched her cheeks and reddened her eyes. I know it well, having seen it in the bathroom mirror not ten minutes ago.

She loads a DVD as I load the plates, and we settle on the sofa with lap trays and a bottle of white wine.

"Cheers," she says, clonking her glass against mine. "Here's to wankers getting exactly what they deserve."

"Hear, hear." I sip my wine as she chugs half of hers. "Yesterday morning, wasn't it?" I ask, struggling to recall the details from the news bulletin.

"Yep. Someone spotted the little prick buying fags in a Texaco. He'd been hiding at his cousin's in Eccles and dressing his daughter as a lad. He'd chopped all her hair off, but she stood there, hands on hips, and told our sarge, 'My name's Chelsea and I'm a *girl*.'"

I toast Chelsea's moxie with a prawn cracker. "Who's got custody?"

"Maternal grandma. Nice house in Heaton Chapel, so we're hoping for a happy ending of sorts." Priti tops up her glass and studies me over its rim. "What's going on with you?"

My sweet and sour suddenly becomes the most interesting thing in the room. I push a piece around my plate, gathering up sauce that I don't feel like eating. "What do you mean?" I ask.

She crunches a cracker thoughtfully and waggles the remnant at me. "You seem different, and I'm not sure if it's in a good way. It's like, you still have that death-warmed-over thing going on, but every now and again you're getting this spaced-out sort of smile on your face."

Bollocks. That was probably when I pulled the coffee table closer for our drinks. I smile at her again, hoping it's a more innocent version than the one she caught earlier. "I'm just happy to see you," I say and she lobs a wonton at my head.

"Fuck off. You've been up to something."

I return the wonton to her plate and chew on a bit of chicken. Although I'd dearly love to tell her everything, I have a promise to keep, and letting slip any kind of hint would inevitably lead to her wheedling the entire story out of me. One sympathetic word and I'd spill my guts before her chow mein went cold.

She turns the volume on the telly down, hushing the clatter of gunfire and explosions.

"Do I need to worry?" she asks.

I shake my head, setting off a shockwave of screeching in my ear.

Instead of challenging me, she closes her hand over mine. "Is there anything I can do to help?"

"No." It's all I can manage, but I take a proper hold of her hand

and cling on to her. She brushes her fingers through my fringe, clearing a space for the kiss she presses to my forehead.

"You know you can call me any time, day or night, don't you?"

I squeeze her hand, which must be answer enough because she makes a show of retrieving the bag of prawn crackers and offering me one.

"Thanks," I say.

She adjusts the volume in time for us to sit back and marvel at Melissa McCarthy's absolute mastery of four-letter invective.

"Just be careful, my darling," Priti says as the scene quietens and moves on. "If you won't let me help you, then that's all I ask."

CHAPTER TWENTY-ONE

Manchester welcomes the weekend with overcast skies and the occasional belt of wet snow. My mood as gloomy as the weather, I open the curtains and get back in bed, where I stare at the clouds and fail to muster the enthusiasm to venture out into the cold again. An hour of fitful dozing makes me feel even worse, however, so I give myself a stern talking to and rummage in my bedside table until I find my gym membership card. My gentle reintroduction session turns into ninety minutes of cardio, topped off by a four-mile stint on the treadmill, and I emerge sweating and starving and ready for anything.

A reread of my timeline over toast and cereal doesn't bring forth many possibilities, though, and I finally plump for two borderline-relevant tasks that I can at least attempt solo. Before setting off, I slip Rebecca Elliott's bus pass into my wallet and check my phone for messages and emails, finding nothing except a text from Priti reminding me of her work mobile number. I hover over my last text to Pryce, the empty space below it enticing me to send another, but no amount of cute emoticons or amusing autocorrect fuck-ups would fix things between us, and the more I think about her, the more I want to speak to her. I drop my phone in my pocket and grab my car keys instead.

The threat of snow-induced chaos hasn't kept people off the roads; it's just made them drive like pillocks. I tailgate a Honda Jazz doing seventeen miles an hour on a forty stretch, until it swerves into a bus stop to let me past. I might have felt guilty, had the driver not interrupted his phone call to lower his window and shout "fucking slut!" at me.

Making up for lost time, I give Curry Mile a wide berth and nip through Gorton to Beswick. The second woman from Copthorne lives in a two-up, two-down almost identical to Shannon Millward's. Outside her house, a lad in a thin coat is scraping the meagre layer of snow from the pavement with his bare hands. As I park and turn off the engine, he stuffs a stone into the centre of his missile and launches it at a younger girl, who takes the hit on her shoulder and retaliates by battering him with her Peppa Pig. The shrieks of juvenile warfare bring out an overweight bloke from next door, who hauls both children up by their collars and shakes them like puppies as he drags them inside. He slams the door hard enough to rattle the foundations, but the blinds at his neighbour's window don't so much as twitch.

I slouch in my seat, drumming the steering wheel as I contemplate my next move. It's clear I haven't thought this through. I can't approach the woman as Alis Clarke, and I have little to no reason to approach her as Rebecca. In fact, making any sort of contact with her risks her tipping off Hamer's, who would smell a rat if they found out I was knocking on the door of Jo's escort colleagues. I need Pryce, with her legitimacy and her lack of connections, not to mention her common sense, which would have politely but firmly stopped me coming here in the first place.

"Fuck's sake," I mutter, though I'm too fed up to put any real vehemence into it.

Deciding to quit while I'm moderately behind, I start the car and retrace my route to Gorton. The local supermarket provides me with a handy parking space, and I double-check the address printed on the box Jo's necklace came in. Abdella's is small and tricky to find, its understated black façade swallowed up by the gaudy signage of the far larger Caribbean minimarkets that surround it. I buzz for entry, and a light flashes green as the lock disengages. Opening the door makes a bell tinkle, and I stop and stare at it like a dog mistrained by Pavlov. It seems familiar, but I can't think why.

A Pakistani woman behind the counter lets me gawp for a few seconds and then clears her throat. "May I help you?"

"Yes, sorry." I take out the box and open it to display the necklace.

"No returns without a receipt," she tells me.

"That's okay. I'm not returning it." I snap the box shut, but I'm floundering already, unsure why I've come here. "A friend of mine bought this a few weeks ago, and I was hoping you might be able to tell me the exact date he came in," I say, thinking on my feet. Detectives like exact dates. We like to put things in order and confirm a sequence of events. If there's a whiteboard and photos to go with that sequence, we're as happy as pigs in shit.

The woman puffs out her cheeks, but it's not as if she's rushed off her feet in her empty shop, so she marches to the till to fetch a handwritten ledger.

"Let me see it again," she says.

I give her the box, and she flicks back a few pages in the ledger and starts to cross-reference a three-digit code on the box lid.

"Twenty-third of December, paid in cash," she says, and a chill passes through me. I can imagine Krzys standing where I am now, weighing up the possibilities, deciding which Jo would like the most, which would suit her, and whether he could afford it.

"Did he leave his name?" I ask, because it's only an assumption that it was Krzys.

"Paid in cash," she repeats. "No name."

"Right. Thank you."

She pushes the box toward me, but I hesitate and glance toward the door. "Are you the only person who works here?"

"No," she says. "I have two sisters."

"And you don't remember selling this necklace?"

She shrugs and then shakes her head. "I don't work Tuesday or Wednesday."

"Okay." I pick up the box. "This is going to sound weird, but do you remember *me* ever coming in here?"

She takes her time, putting on a pair of glasses and leaning in close. "Maybe, with more hair," she says at length.

I lean my hand on the cool glass of the counter, steadying myself. "With a man?" I ask.

"No. A lady, I think."

Jo. Jesus. I work the rest out quickly, and it takes all my self-control not to climb over the counter and rip the ledger from the shop assistant's hands. "Can you check your book on February the ninth?" I say, opening my wallet and pulling out the bus pass I hadn't needed to show the unnamed Copthorne woman. "I think I might've rented a safety deposit box from you."

She clicks her fingers as the penny drops. "Ah! Yes, that's right. Here." Her manicured nail tracks to a payment of seventy-five pounds. "Three months. We are very reasonable."

I nod and show her the ID. Reasonable rates apparently don't require a passport or driving licence; she disappears behind the scenes, bangs about a bit, and reappears holding a small metal box into which she inserts a key. She sets the box in front of me, allowing me to do the honours. The lock catches and then gives as I turn the key, and the lid springs open to reveal a Jiffy bag, unmarked and unsealed. The woman watches me slyly as I tip its contents into my hand, but she sniffs in disgust when all I raise into the light is a neon-pink USB stick. "No refunds on deposits," she warns me. I couldn't care less. It's the best seventy-five quid I've ever spent.

I take my time driving back to my flat, neither harrying the car dawdling in front of me nor trying one of the numerous shortcuts. I'm careful on the speed bumps, giving way to people waiting to pull out, and concentrating on the traffic rather than on the tiny pink flash drive that's burning a metaphorical hole in my pocket. Now that I've found the damn thing, I'm scared shitless of what might be on it, and it's hard not to park on an anonymous side street so I can lie foetal on the back seat for a while.

I kick my boots off on the doormat and go to the loo before I start my laptop. Compared to the state I got in during the journey, I'm quite calm now, even managing a smile as I go through the usual "try the USB one way, fail, flip it, fail, try it the other way again and succeed" rigmarole. Nothing I can do will change what's on the device, so I immediately double-click the first of two files that appear on the desktop.

It's a Word file, its text broken down into a series of short, date- and time-stamped paragraphs in typical police notebook format, only without the signatures or coffee stains. A précis identifies me as the author, and I've provided my full name, rank, and collar number, as if I somehow knew I might not be around to retrieve it. The earliest entry is headed 9 February, 1:35 a.m., which is about fifteen hours before I signed the car rental agreement in Ardwick. In terse sentences I've described Jo banging on the door of my alias's flat at ten p.m., and her half-incoherent account of Krzys's murder. She told me that Krzys had become suspicious about her new shifts and the amount of nights she was working, and that he'd tailed her to Copthorne and figured out exactly what her new job involved. And then she had to explain to me what she'd been doing at Copthorne and how Krzys had begged her to stop, even though he couldn't give her the money she needed. He hadn't known about the drugs after all, but he'd gone over her head and spoken to one of the managers at Hamer's, threatening to tell the police about the prostitution and the sexual exploitation. The potential for an investigation snowballing into other areas had apparently been enough to get him killed. Jo and I went to find his body in the warehouse that night. "See photos," I've written in red and underlined.

I follow the instructions now, opening a gallery of clinical, crime scene type images that show Krzys within hours of his death. The flash on my phone has left nothing to the imagination, and I recoil from a close-up of the bullet wound that's collapsed the back of his head like an egg dropped from height, and the halo of clotted blood and bone fragments surrounding it. As horrific as the decomposing version was, at least it hid everything that made him recognisable as my friend.

I close the gallery and return to the Word file. With Jo dosed up on Night Nurse and sleeping in my bedroom, I've continued to detail the events of that night, documenting the exact location of the body— "trace evidence is likely to be present even if the victim is moved"— and transcribing the conversation that took place in the car on the way home.

"My name isn't Rebecca Elliot," I'd told her. "It's Alis Clarke, and I'm a detective with the Manchester Metropolitan Police." My lips move as I read it now, the exchange so close to how I've imagined it that I probably retained the specifics on some level. "I can help you. We can keep you safe. Please don't cry. It'll be okay."

And then her response, in broken English that in no way diminished its impact: "There is police. They come to the house. With Hamer's. Working with them. All together. How can you keep me safe, Alis Clarke?"

I'd challenged her, of course, my outrage unmistakeable in my rapid-fire interrogation: How could she know that? What proof did she have? Names? Descriptions? How could she be so sure?

"They talk after," she'd said. "Big men like to show off."

Post-coital hubris, that's all it had come down to. Careless pillow talk that wasn't careless enough for the men to have entrusted her with their names. Even when I'd pushed her, the only descriptions she could provide were of two white men, one younger—between twenty and thirty years old—and the other perhaps in his mid-forties.

"The light is dull. I don't like to see them," she'd told me. "They talk like you. Your voice."

"My accent?" I'd asked, unwittingly pre-empting what I would later write on my cast. "Local?"

"Yes, local. And the older man, he has a pipe."

"He smokes a pipe? A proper pipe, like this?" I'd sketched one to clarify the word.

"No, no. The new pipes. For when you stop the cigarettes."

"E-cigs? Vaping?" I'd suggested.

"Yes," she'd said, and I've described her reaction in the file: a lack of eye contact and an ashamed shake of her head. "Tutti-frutti, he liked the best. He tasted sweet."

She had no proof, no names, and descriptions that would match approximately seventy percent of MMP's male officers. I could hardly have gone through them to check their preferred vaping flavour.

I'd believed her, though, and spent the rest of the night bullet-pointing everything I deemed pertinent to the case. I added an explanation of the method behind my colour-coded notes, for fear the files might be destroyed or tampered with, and further backed that up by copying across the names of the businesses and individuals supplied via my production line at Hamer's. The simple act of combining those disparate elements made the flash drive an incendiary piece of evidence. Where before I had the names, some coloured patterns, and unsubstantiated suspicion, I now have a confirmed web of distribution which includes specific shipping dates, a complex and largely concealed pricing structure, and details of the receiving parties.

The notebook entries become more personal and diary-like the further I read. I've described the almost paralysing doubts that set in and the extent to which I was second-guessing my actions. I hadn't slept, instead spending a couple of hours searching for a refuge, somewhere I could take Jo while I returned to Manchester and my assignment. I hadn't had a long-term vision. I'd wanted to find the officers Jo had described, and then I'd wanted out.

There's no attempt to sign off or draw conclusions. The file ends abruptly without mentioning the Snowdonia cottage, the app I'd set for Wallace, or my plan to rent a safety deposit box. The paranoia I was obviously experiencing that night bleeds into me now, and I check over my shoulder, listening out for untoward noises, while I add the video and screen grabs from the traffic camera and the more recent photos of Krzys's body to the flash drive and then make copies of everything on a spare in case something happens to the original.

As I close down the laptop, the fact that I've taken a few steps forward and then been booted back again starts to sink in. I stupidly assumed that finding the flash drive would be the end of it, that I'd be able to pass on the evidence and the names of my corrupt colleagues to Ansari, or to the SMIU, or to anyone—quite frankly—who wasn't me. I knuckle my tired eyes as I debate whether or not the file even puts me in the clear. My reaction to Jo's revelation—shock, dismay, disbelief—seems authentic, but someone accustomed to duplicity, to playing a role, would know to react and record it like that, to give a convincing performance and then manufacture a report I could later use to corroborate my innocence. I certainly wasn't one of the officers using Jo at the house, but there's still nothing to prove I wasn't in league with them.

I shut the laptop and rest my head on it. I consider calling Pryce to ask her if she'll take one of the drives for safekeeping, but I'm so tired that the phone in my pocket might as well be a million miles away. For want of a better idea, I push the pink drive into my cast and close my fist around the other. I'll decide what to do with it later, when the room isn't twirling around so badly and I can think straight. Cushioning my head on my arms, I let my eyes close.

A twenty-minute catnap fails to fill me with inspiration, and I wake with a crick in my neck and my cheek stuck to the laptop. My grip on the flash drive has slackened, but I haven't let go, and I can feel where its sharp metal edge has dug into my fingers. Jo died for this. Those men hunted us down and left us for dead, and even now, when my brain's in bits and I'm on the verge of losing everything, the fuckers won't leave me alone.

Getting pissed off works wonders for my motivation, and without thinking, I'm up and pacing, my eyes roving around the room as I consider and discount various hiding places for the second flash drive. Unable to settle on a secure spot, I shove it alongside the first one, nudging it with a pen until it's snugly embedded toward the base of my wrist.

"Right. Now what?" I ask the empty room, because I've become accustomed to discussing these things, and the habit is apparently going to die hard.

No one replies, of course, and the buzz of an incoming text sounds too much like laughter for my liking. It's Rob Reid, chasing an answer to his earlier message. Lying through my teeth, I concoct an elaborate tale about a gallivanting neurologist, his reticent medical secretary, and an appointment that hasn't yet been brought forward. Reid could easily trap me by making his own enquiries at Manchester Royal, but that's not what makes me carefully place the phone down and delete every word of my unsent message: it's the notion of setting a trap of my own instead. The empty text box is filling the screen, its cursor blinking in readiness. I lock the screen and find a pen and a scrap of paper.

"Rob Reid," I write at the top. I chew the pen and then put "Wallace?" on the line below, adding the question mark to make me feel less of an arsehole. I have no qualms about using Reid to test a theory, but Wallace is too perfectly placed within MMP not to include him as a backup.

In the three minutes it takes for my laptop to restart, I talk myself out of the plan and recommit to it several times over. It's reckless and dangerous, and Pryce would definitely not approve, and I'm tempted to give her a call just so she can confirm that.

I log on to my MMP email account and open two new messages, one of which I address to Reid and the other to Wallace. I use the same header for both: "New information—Urgent," and flag them as high priority to ensure they pique the interest of anyone illicitly monitoring my account. I personalise each message slightly, giving Reid's a more panicked, damsel-in-distress tone, and trying to appeal to the reluctant father figure in Wallace. The content is essentially identical, though: I tell them I've found a flash drive pertaining to the Hamer investigation and it has serious implications for a number of MMP personnel. I don't know what to do with it, and I'm scared.

Mindful that email isn't my usual method of contacting them, I text the same information seconds before I hit "send." I tag on an apology for disturbing their Saturday, hoping that will explain why I haven't tried to speak to them in person. With a bit of luck, they'll catch the texts but not the emails. The longer those sit on the MMP server, the likelier my target is to see them.

I haven't even logged out of my account when Reid calls my mobile. I answer at once, as if I've been waiting on tenterhooks for him to respond.

"Hey," I say, letting my voice catch. "Sorry to disturb you. I didn't know who else to contact."

"It's all right, it's not a problem," he says, but there's no warmth there, just a desire to get down to business. "Where did you find this flash drive?"

"In a safety deposit box at a local jeweller's. I'd put it there before the crash. I think"—I take a breath: all or nothing—"I think I was in danger. I think that's why I went to Wales." I don't mention Jo or Krzys. I want to leave as much to his imagination as possible.

He clears his throat, and I hear him swallow liquid and put a glass down. "You said MMP personnel are involved. That's a hell of an accusation, Alis. Do you have names or any proof to substantiate it?"

"I can't talk about it now," I whisper. "What if they're listening?"

"It's not—*What?* You think your phone's bugged? Alis, come on!" To his credit, his scepticism sounds genuine. "Okay, all right. I need to meet you, then, and get this sorted out. Are you free this evening?"

"No, my friend's coming for supper. She's a DC. She'll know something's wrong if I cancel at the last minute." Christ, the last thing I want is him turning up on my doorstep.

"Tomorrow, then. Name a time and place."

"Midday," I say, aiming for a time when plenty of people will be around. "Same cafe as before. They open later on a Sunday."

"That's fine." His tone tells me it's anything but, though, so I try to appease him.

"I really appreciate this, Rob," I say, laying it on thick. "I mean it. Thank you."

"Don't mention it. I'll see you tomorrow."

I end the call and check my messages. Wallace hasn't replied, but his Saturdays are taken up by football and a curry in Wetherspoons, and his Sundays by hair of the dog and a roast dinner. It's a routine that suits my purposes down to the ground. I have one fish on the hook already. All I need to do is wait and see who else takes the bait.

The setting sun drags all my bluff and bluster down with it. It's one thing to lure criminals out into the open in broad daylight, but quite another to sit alone in my darkening flat and wonder whether they'll break in during the night. If Reid is one of the men Jo described, he's unlikely to wait until tomorrow to make his move, and he already knows where I live.

Armed with the rolling pin I've been nursing on my lap, I check the locks on the front door for the nth time, rattling the security chain and peeking through the peephole. The corridor is empty and dark, the lights set to come on when they sense motion, and I avert my eyes almost at once, as if I'm tempting fate by looking.

Back in the living room, I heave my sofa against the door and barricade myself in, until I need a wee and have to venture out into the hallway again. I collect a knife on my return trip, plus a can of deodorant that I set next to a lighter. I'm not averse to fighting dirty if push comes to shove, though my lack of dexterity may well scupper my chances.

With the muted television providing a semblance of companionship, I toy with my mobile phone, flicking between Priti and Pryce on its contacts list. I wanted to handle this on my own, but if the worst does happen tonight and the flash drives are taken, it seems remiss not to have warned someone that I've painted a big bullseye on my forehead. And, much as I love Priti, the obvious person to tell is Pryce.

I call her number, leaving a brief "please ring me back, it's important" message on her voice mail. I send her a text as well, and then collect my duvet and pillow and drag them onto the sofa. Having blocked the door again, I surround myself with weapons. It's going to be a very long night.

❖

It snows during the night. I notice the first flakes falling when I check the street at eleven p.m., and I nestle on the windowsill to watch the gardens, the cars, and finally the roads turn white. It won't last—it rarely does, this close to the city—but it takes my mind off my current predicament and makes me think of Saddleworth and sledging on the moors with Martin. We'd stay out until we were so tired we couldn't even stagger to the top of the run, and Mum would have drop scones and hot chocolate ready for us when we got home, frozen and wet through because the drifts had been up to our waists. Proper seasons were one of the few things I missed on moving to Manchester, with its mild, soggy climate, and the snow now gathering outside lulls me into a doze that somehow sees me through to dawn.

I dismantle my fortress and take a shower before checking my phone for messages. I needn't have worried; there's nothing from Pryce or Wallace. Perhaps Pryce is snowed in, her mobile out of range and her landline severed by the storm. It's easier to make excuses for her than accept she's cut me loose.

Allowing plenty of time to get to Belle Vue, I take a new, circuitous route, passing playing fields crammed with kids racing down slopes that are more mud than snow, and managing not to lose my patience with churchgoers obliged to brave the conditions. I arrive early and park where I can observe the customers coming and going. They look like normal folk, wrapped up against the weather and eager to increase their cholesterol levels. Any of them could be employees of Hamer's, or, given the cafe's proximity to the station and the average copper's affinity for bacon butties, they could all work for MMP.

I go inside at ten to, taking my coffee to the table nearest the door and picking the seat with the best view of the room. No one seems unduly interested in me. I get a couple of "good mornings" and someone borrows the ketchup from my table, but that's it until Reid sits down with a plate of crumpets and what passes for an espresso in these parts.

"Morning," he says, holding out the plate and a napkin. "Here. You look like crap."

I wasn't hungry, but there's real butter on the crumpets, and they smell divine. "Thanks."

He takes the other and lets me eat, grimacing as he chases his last bite with his shot of rocket fuel.

"Jesus wept." He opens the file he's keeping on my case. "And on that note, exactly what the fuck is going on, Alis? What have you found?"

This isn't the "softly softly, earn my confidence" approach I'd expected, and I chew my crumpet for longer than necessary as I dissect his body language and expression. He's maintaining eye contact and, far from looking like someone who's plotting to kidnap me at gunpoint and torture me into revealing all, he looks intrigued, possibly even excited, which means he's not the only one wondering what the fuck is going on.

"I found a USB stick, a drive that I'd hidden," I say.

He nods, his pen still poised. "You told me that much last night. What was on it? Do you have it with you?"

"No. I'm sorry. I couldn't risk bringing it. I think people are watching me, watching my flat."

"What makes you think that? Have you seen someone following you?"

"No," I say and realise it's the truth. I've no proof that anyone's been tailing me, unless I count the two break-ins. The rest is just supposition, combined with a healthy dose of neurosis. My stalkers are either very good or they exist entirely in my imagination.

"But the drive is somewhere safe?"

"Yes."

"And did I read your email correctly? You think someone at MMP is on the payroll at Hamer's?"

"I think so, yes."

He whistles and leans back in his chair. "Fuck me. You know I have to tell Granger about this, don't you? Shit." He writes something and scribbles it out again. "Shit. Who is it?" he asks, but then holds up a hand. "No, no, don't tell me. Unless you think it'd be best if I know?"

For the first time I'm reminded how young he is. He's looking to me for guidance and assurance, because technically I'm his senior, with more years on the force. Far from reeling my first fish in, I'm watching him unhook himself and wriggle free.

"You're probably right," I say. "It'll be easier if the SMIU can't get their claws into you. Ignorance is bliss and all that."

He smiles, relieved. "I'll phone Granger as soon as we're done. I'm sure she'll want to arrange a meeting ASAP." He closes my file, but curiosity gets the better of him. "And I can continue to represent you, if you're okay with that?"

"That's fine," I say, but from his expression he's already checked out of the meeting, no doubt visualising an investigation that will whip up a media frenzy and move him a few rungs up the MMP ladder. He's asked none of the fundamental questions about the cause of the crash, why Jo and I were really in Wales, and whether I've lied about our relationship. He's neglected to connect the ransacking of my alias's flat, Krzys's disappearance, and my come-and-go memory. It's going to get me out of here sooner, though, so I'm not going to complain. Good luck to him. If those really are his priorities, I'm certain he'll go far.

A minor three-vehicle collision has turned the main road into a car park, and ambulances and police are in attendance, corralling people in an attempt to get the queues moving. One of the paramedics is standing aside, sharing a joke with a traffic bobby, and I feel a pang of envy as I watch them laugh. I miss that easy camaraderie, with its junk-food fuelled night shifts and inappropriate humour that would appal anyone outside the uniformed services. The incident is a simple rear-end shunt, the cars hardly damaged, but seeing the dents in the bumpers fills my own car with the sound of tearing metal and smashing glass, and I have to stop at a petrol station for a bottle of water. If this case doesn't end my career, there's every chance the PTSD will.

My mobile buzzes while I'm in my hallway, trying to free my cast from my coat sleeve. The call cuts off, displaying Pryce's home number, but she rings again before I can call her back.

"Hey." I sit on the sofa, pretending this is a casual, catch-up conversation and we're about to exchange anecdotes about the snow. "Did you get my message?" I ask, unsure whether she's had reception on her mobile.

"Yes. What's going on?" She sounds tired and distant, as if she's had even less sleep than I have since Friday and she doesn't want to be dragged back into this saga. I can't say I blame her, but it's good to hear her voice, no matter how withdrawn she is.

"I found the flash drive," I say because she's obviously not in the mood for small talk. "And I want you to have a copy of it."

"What? Alis, no, I can't." She makes a pained noise that's half groan, half gasp. "I can't do that."

"*Please*. I emailed Reid and Wallace and told them about it, and I'm almost sure our perp in MMP will pick those mails up, so I need you to keep the drive safe because I don't think—Pryce, I don't think I'll be here to do it."

"Alis." The way she whispers my name brings tears to my eyes. "What have you done?"

I hug my knees, longing to have her here, even if it's to bollock me. "I just wanted to end this," I say. "I'm so sorry."

"It's okay." She might be crying as well, it's hard to tell. "It's okay." She pauses, coughing and then swallowing as if trying to compose herself. "Don't…don't risk putting it in the post, though. Bring it here, and we'll get everything sorted out. I can report it to my DI. He'll know what to do for the best."

"Yeah?" I grapple for the lifeline, however precarious.

"Yeah," she says, and this time I hear her sob. "Can you come today?"

"I'll set off now," I tell her. "I can be there in a couple of hours."

❖

Further snowfall turns two hours into four as the traffic crawls along the motorway and the coastal road gets clogged by another accident. There's no answer when I call Pryce to tell her I'll be late, and

I worry about the state of the track to her cottage, hatching bold plans to hike through the drifts if necessary.

The A5 into Snowdonia—tricky at the best of times—is slick with fresh snow, and even with my wiper blades on high it's a battle to keep my windscreen clear. My pulse booms in my bad ear, warning me that this is where I crashed, as if I need the reminder. Of all the things I've forgotten, that certainly isn't one. It's almost dark, though sunset is still an hour away, and every corner looks identical: hairpin bends with mountains crowded either side, their summits concealed by masses of clouds. Having slept through my first trip to her cottage, I double-checked the route before setting off, and I decelerate well in advance of her turn-off, my tyres settling neatly into wider tracks that cut a path through the worst of the snow.

Thanking Pryce for her foresight, I make short work of the lane and close the access gate behind me, on my best behaviour. The journey has been so demanding that it's left me little time to think about what I'm going to say to her, and I'm still at a loss as I refasten my seat belt. I resolve to follow her lead, to be cool and professional if that's the way she wants to play it, and to make no mention of Thursday night unless she does. I can do cool and professional, I tell myself, and then I put the car into reverse instead of drive and hurtle backward with an inelegance I can only describe as symbolic.

"Fucking stupid thing." I take my embarrassment out on the gear lever, whacking it into the correct notch and rejoining the tracks I've spun out of. The cottage comes into view around the next bend, with smoke curling from its chimney and deep snow covering its patio. I park beside Pryce's Disco and spend a minute composing myself. Not wanting to appear presumptuous, I decide to leave my overnight bag in the boot. I'll book into the B&B again when we've got everything sorted. At least I'm guaranteed to get some sleep there.

Having negotiated the steps without breaking my neck, I knock on the front door. There's a light on behind the living room curtains, and I hear the lock disengage. The door opens fully, and I stare at the man in front of me. He's broad and tall, mid-thirties, with fair hair, and "MAM" tattooed across his throat. Definitely not Pryce's DI, I realise too late to do anything but stumble as he grabs the collar of my coat and yanks me over the threshold. Momentum sends me into the wall, bouncing my head off the exposed stonework, and I sink to my knees, stunned, my vision grey at the edges.

"You took your fucking time," he says.

"Where's Pryce?" I gasp, unable to think beyond that. "Where is she? Have you hurt her?" I drag myself up, bringing her umbrella with me, but he knocks it away and backhands me across the face.

"Behave yourself," he warns.

I drool crimson-specked saliva onto the tiles. "Where *is* she?"

Instead of answering, he wraps a fist round my collar and pushes me ahead of him. It's only five steps into the living room, not enough time to process what's happening. I can taste copper, and my cheek feels hot and swollen, and then all of that fades away as he stops me and jerks my head up.

"Oh God," I whisper. I stagger back, but he rights me, forcing me to look. I don't know which is worse, the sight of Pryce bound to a chair in the middle of the room, or that of Jez sitting on the edge of her sofa.

"Sorry, Al," he says, as if this is just one of those things and he hasn't got her blood all over his knuckles. "It couldn't be helped."

"You fucking *arsehole!*" I try to lunge for him, only to be anchored in place by the prick still standing behind me. "You're supposed to be a *police officer*, Jez. What the fuck happened to you, you pathetic piece of shit?"

His face loses what little colour it had. He's breathing hard and sweating, and he shifts his right hand to show me the gun in it. I bet he's never fired one in his life, though, and he seems uneasy as he adjusts his grip.

"Like I said, it couldn't be helped."

"Fuck you, *mate*," I spit at him, and turn instead to Pryce, who's stirred and managed to lift her head. "Hey," I say softly.

The tape across her mouth stops her from answering. She closes her eyes, sending tears streaking through the blood on her face, and there's nothing but shame in the gesture.

"This isn't your fault," I tell her, and she chokes a sob behind the tape.

They might have forced her to bring me here, but she hasn't made things easy for them, and she's paid a heavy price for resisting. She's covered in cuts and bruises, and I can see a line of cigarette burns snaking up her right arm.

I turn back to Jez, hoping I'm reading things wrong. "How long have you been here?" I ask.

"Too fucking long," his accomplice snarls.

"Easy, Dee," Jez tells him. He gets off the sofa and closes the gap between us. He's trying to smile, assuming the role of good cop. "We need the flash drive, Al. Where is it?"

I glare at him. "Let her go and I'll tell you."

"Al—"

"No!" I slap at the hand he holds out to me. "Let her go! Let her go, and you can have your fucking drive."

The bang is so loud and sudden that I stagger, unable to identify its source until Jez lowers his gun. The bullet has missed Pryce by a couple of feet, hitting the wall and sending chips of stone flying. I'm instantly deafened on my bad side, but I can see her chest heaving, her nostrils flaring above the tape.

"For fuck's sake, Jez," Dee says. "You couldn't hit a barn door." He laughs, and I sense him step away from me. I barely hear him fire, but the bullet slams into Pryce's left shoulder, the impact throwing her back. She takes the chair with her, crashing sideways onto the floor, and I scream her name, kicking at Jez when he pins my arms behind me.

"Get it done," Dee says, his voice a tinny echo. "I'm going for a piss."

Jez waits for him to leave before he releases me. I dart across to Pryce, kneel by her side, and peel the tape from her lips. She's ashen and clammy, but she's conscious, and she groans when I clamp a hand on the ragged hole the bullet's torn in her back.

"Shh, stay still. Stay still."

"Alis," Jez says. He's right behind me, though I didn't hear him move. "He won't be gone for long."

"I *know*," I say, my teeth gritted. "Fucking help me, then."

"I can't. I need the drive. Where is it?" He crouches and puts the gun against her forehead. "I won't miss from here."

Despite her terror, she focuses on me rather than the metal pressing into her skin. "Alis, don't," she whispers, but I can feel her blood pouring across my fingers, and I know we're out of time.

"It's in my cast," I tell him. I'll tell him anything to get him away from her. "You'll have to cut it off."

He nods and lifts his gun clear. He's shaking, and his breath smells weird: fruity and acidic. "Kitchen," he says. "Come on."

He pulls at my arm, urging me to my feet and keeping a grip on me as he leads me to the kitchen. There's a knife block on the counter, and he selects a serrated blade, positioning my cast at an angle so he can hack into it. Starting at the top, he saws downward in awkward increments. The motion works a small Med Alert bracelet free on his wrist, and I hear a faint chime of metal as the links vibrate. The noise makes me dry-heave, and he stops cutting, confused by my reaction.

"You were there in the car that night, weren't you?" I say, swallowing a mouthful of acid. "How the hell did you end up in the middle of this shit? Did you help them murder Krzys as well?"

He starts at the name, which is answer enough, but there's no confession. He just resumes sawing, tearing the blade into my arm as often as he hits the plaster, and getting nowhere near the drives at my wrist.

"Jesus," I hiss. "Use the bloody scissors."

His lack of coordination is clearly part of a bigger problem, though, and he's slow to exchange the knife for the scissors in the block. They snag when he tries to open them, and he squints at the safety mechanism holding them closed, unable to work out how to release it.

I glance at the door while he's distracted. Dee is nowhere to be seen, and I know I'm not going to get a better chance. Steeling myself, I swing my arm, smashing my cast into his nose and then bringing the knife block down onto his head. He grunts, raising a sluggish hand to his face, and I use the block for an uppercut, splitting his chin and dropping him to the floor. His arms collapse beneath him when he attempts to push back up, and his face slams onto the tiles, knocking him senseless.

"Shit." I double over, gasping. There's no way that Dee won't have heard all of this. "Aw, shit."

I grab the gun and shove the scissors and a pair of tea towels into my belt. I've fucked up my left arm again, and my right is shaking so violently I can't aim the gun straight. I won't be able to take Dee on; I'll just have to wing the bastard and hope for the best. I creep toward the living room, braced for the ambush, the gun leading the way. I don't even know how to fire it. Point and shoot, that's all Jez did. I can do that.

The hinges creak as I push the door, and I hold my breath, toeing it wider and peeking into the room. It's empty, apart from Pryce.

"What the hell?" I mutter. I spin, aiming the gun into the hallway, but there's no sign of Dee, so I run across to Pryce, almost colliding with the chair she's still tethered to as I skid onto my knees and drop my supplies. She's started to hyperventilate at the sound of my footsteps, and her eyes widen as she sees me.

"Where? What…happened?" She pants for air between the words, looking beyond me to the door. There's blood everywhere, soaking into her clothes and the carpet and my jeans.

"I bashed him." I display my ruined cast, with the drives poking from a hole near my thumb, and I swear she manages a fucking smile. "Where's Dee?" I ask.

"Don't know…never came back," she whispers. "Leave me. Better on your own."

"Not a chance. Don't talk bollocks." I cut the tape at her ankles and start on the band they've wound beneath her breasts. "Besides, we've got a gun now."

"Ever fired one?" She gasps as her torso slips, and I wrap my arms around her, kicking the chair away as I guide her to the floor.

"No, but how hard can it be?" I free her wrists and wince in sympathy as I unwind the tape. "Sorry, almost done."

"Can't—can't feel much," she says, and then cries out as I bring her arms forward and turn her onto her uninjured side. "God," she whispers. "Oh God, don't!"

Ignoring her pleas, I knot a towel in the middle and push the knot hard against the exit wound, improvising like hell. A scream rips from her, and she tries to roll away, but I hold her still with my knees as I plug the hole in her back and tie the second towel around the first.

"All done. I'm done," I tell her, but I know I have to get her up because it's already been too long and Dee is going to find us and kill us both. She knows that, too, and she doesn't make a sound as I lift her into a sitting position. She sags against me for a couple of seconds, and I stroke the hair away from her forehead.

"On three," I say. "Ready?"

She's standing by two, swaying yet somehow remaining vertical as I return the scissors to my belt and pick up the gun.

"They took my car keys," she says.

I sling her good arm around my shoulders and pull her close. "I've got mine. Are we better round the back?"

She nods, and we go through the kitchen, stepping over Jez, who hasn't moved an inch. Ink-black skies and a swirl of icy wind greet us when I open the door, and Pryce's teeth start to chatter. She's only wearing a T-shirt and jogging bottoms, and her feet are bare. Her shoes and coat were with her umbrella by the front door.

"*Go*," she says, and I do as she tells me, helping her down the steps into the garden.

Keeping to the line of a hedge, we creep through the snow toward the front of the cottage. The men's car is tucked at the side, a black Audi SUV with DJH 1 on its plate. I stab the scissors into its rear tyre as we duck behind it to survey the drive. The glow of a cigarette marks Dee's location. He's up on the front patio, blowing smoke rings, and to reach my car we'll have to cross twenty feet of open space without him spotting or shooting us.

I put my mouth next to Pryce's ear. "Can you run?"

She looks ready to lie down in the snow and call it a day, but her nod is so bloody obstinate that I smile and kiss her cheek.

"Okay, then."

She squeezes my hand, and we set off, clearing the Audi and the cottage and sprinting into no man's land. Within seconds, a flash of torchlight blinds me and sends Pryce to her knees. I haul her up again and propel her before me, clicking the central locking as I slip and slide and fight to stay on my feet. The first bullet flies wide of us and shatters my car's rear window, the second coming closer but disappearing into the hedge. I open the passenger door, practically launch her inside, and run around to the driver's side. Dee is right on us as I start the engine. I slam the gear lever into reverse and stomp on the accelerator, sending us into a wild turn that forces him to dive for cover.

"Seat belt!" I yell, and Pryce grapples for it with her right hand, managing to secure it as we career down the lane. He's not following us yet, but he won't be long, and I still need to get the gate open.

I brake for it in good time and open it without looking behind me. I think I can hear another engine, one that's deeper and more powerful than mine. Taking a chance, I get out again to slam the gate shut behind us.

"Here." I throw my mobile onto her lap. "Keep an eye on its signal."

"'Kay," she says, her eyes closed.

"Pryce?"

"Mmhm?"

"*Pryce!*"

"What?" She looks at me, bleary-eyed and moderately offended.

"Watch the fucking phone."

She studies it as if it's the first time she's seen one, and from the corner of my eye, I see the colossal effort she makes to shake off the lethargy and take an interest.

"No signal," she says, her voice stronger and more coherent. She glances in her wing mirror. "He's coming."

With the unlit lane demanding all of my attention, I hadn't noticed his headlights. They disappear as the road dips, but he's gaining on us.

"Left at the end," she says. "Head for Bangor."

I barely pause at the junction, and she smothers a groan with a cough as she's jolted into the window.

"Sorry," I mutter. I'm finding it harder to grip the wheel as sweat slicks the plastic and the fingers on my left hand swell and stiffen. I snatch a breath and then another, staring out into a maelstrom of flickering white flakes. We're going to crash. I can't drive this fast in these conditions. I can't see properly, and we're going to crash, and she'll die.

"Alis." She doesn't raise her voice, she's calm and fearless, and she instantly gets my attention. "You're doing fine."

"I'm not. He'll catch us."

She checks his position. "Not yet. Keep going."

The road is deserted, so I utilise both lanes, turning into the skids and neutralising corners like they showed us in blue light training. He's closer than he was, only two hundred yards or so behind us, and he's got his high beams on, the lights dazzling me. I can't tell where we are. All the landmarks have disappeared beneath a thick layer of white, and we haven't passed a road sign since leaving the lane.

"Slow down a bit," Pryce says, holding up the mobile. "There's one bar on it."

Going against every instinct, I do as she asks, fixing my eyes on the road rather than the SUV looming in the rear view.

"I need urgent police assistance," she says, after identifying herself to the operator. "Suspect is armed and in pursuit of our vehicle." She gives our approximate location and another that I don't recognise, and switches to Welsh for the rest of the call. The signal cuts her off mid-sentence, but she seems satisfied she got her message across.

"Change of plan," she tells me.

"There was a plan?" The words squeak out of me, because he's within a hundred yards now, and we're not going to make it to Bangor.

"We've got backup en route," she says softly, as if she's talking me down from a ledge. "On my count, I want you to turn off your lights and take a hard left."

"What?" The road is zipping past too quickly for me to see any junctions, let alone one I'll have to find in the dark. "No! Don't be fucking stupid."

"It's not stupid. Hey? Alis?" She waits until I look at her. "Trust me?"

I nod, my eyes back on the road. I do trust her. I always have.

"Good. We've got about thirty seconds."

It's more like twenty when she shouts, "Now!" I kill the lights and yank the wheel to the left. The back end flies out, kicking up ice and stones, and I wrestle with the steering wheel until she grabs it with me and helps me control it. I accelerate cautiously, expecting to send us flying into oblivion, but the tyres grind into level snow, allowing us to make slow but steady progress as I use what little moonlight there is to keep us on the straight and, at times, very narrow track.

"Perfect." She leans back, exhausted. "Keep going as far as you can. The police know we're down here."

There's nothing behind us. He's missed the turn in the darkness, but he'll double back, and he'll spot it before long. The suspension clatters in the ruts beneath the snow, and Pryce clutches her seat, digging her fingers into the fabric. I need to stop, to get her wrapped up in whatever I have in my rucksack, and find somewhere for us to hide.

"What was all that Welsh?" I ask, prodding her leg as her eyes slide shut. "You order us a Happy Meal or something?"

"Fish and chips," she murmurs. "I got you gravy with yours."

"Spot on. How did you know?"

"I had a hunch." She smiles and adjusts her position, alleviating the pressure on her shoulder. "Told them to keep comms in Welsh. Jez had a police radio with him."

"Right," I say. "Nicely done. Are we where I think we are?"

Despite the snow, Tryfan's shape has become more distinct, and I answer my own query when I stop the car by the two boulders marking the end of the track.

"Things were much simpler then, weren't they?" she says, and I realise that the morning we came here was the start of everything. It was the day she agreed to work with me, to help me on a case that's led to two men invading her home and torturing her.

"Yes, they were." I kick my door open. "Stay put."

I grab my rucksack from the boot and shake it out on the back seat. I've packed for the weather, and I tug woolly socks onto her frozen feet, then a pair of trainers I'd stashed in the footwell. They're too small for her, but they're better than nothing.

"Lean forward and put your good arm in. Come on, come on, that's it." She's limp and far too compliant as I work a sweater over her head. I can see fresh blood glistening on her seat, and I wrap a spare shirt on top of the sodden towels bound to her shoulder, yanking it as tightly as I dare, before I tuck her into my thick coat.

"Can't walk far," she says.

I scan the area for suitable cover. "Can you make it to those trees?"

"Maybe. I'll try."

I chuck the gun and a bottle of water into the rucksack and collect the torch from my glove box, rechecking the lane as I stand. Still nothing. We'll only have five minutes once he finds the turning, and the trees are bucking and bending in the wind two hundred yards away through foot-deep snow. She leans heavily on me as I help her from the car.

"Should we stay here and try to shoot him?" I ask.

She inclines her head. "Think you'd hit him?"

"No, not really."

"Trees, then," she says, and we take our first step.

We don't do badly, considering. Pryce manages to keep pace with me, and fresh snow instantly obliterates our footprints. The track behind us remains deserted. It's pitch-black beneath the trees, so I risk switching on the torch, training it on the ground as I search for a place to hide.

"Okay, okay, this'll do," I say, stopping at a boulder that's big enough to conceal us both and offers some shelter from the elements. I brush the snow from its base and then empty the rucksack and sit her on it, placing the gun within easy reach. The trek has left us both winded, and she huddles into my chest when I put my arm around her. She's shivering, and the rasp of her breath against my neck is the only noise I can hear, apart from the rattle of branches high above us. Minutes tick by as we crouch in the darkness, too scared to speak, until I feel her gentle tug on my arm.

"They followed me home on Friday," she whispers, answering a question I've dreaded asking. "I was careless. Opened the door to them. I think…I was hoping it was you."

I tighten my hold on her, waiting for her to continue.

"They wanted…wanted me to phone you. They didn't even know about the flash drive at first, just that we'd found Krzys and interviewed Shannon." She speaks quickly, as if confessing to an impatient priest. "But someone caught your email, told Jez, and he—they…they'd been to my sister's; they showed me photos of her house, of her taking the girls out." She starts to cry. "And that's when I called you."

I can't bear to see her so distressed, and I can't do a thing to fix it. I want to go back to the cottage and kick the living shit out of Jez, or find Dee and shoot out his kneecaps. I'd undoubtedly miss, but I'd make a mess of him while I tried.

"I'm sorry," she murmurs. She's less agitated now, but her tears are still trickling onto my sweater. "For all of it."

I brush my thumb across her damp cheek. "It doesn't matter. None of this matters."

She shakes her head, determined to finish. "You didn't do anything wrong, Alis. During your assignment. I know you didn't. When I asked Jez about it, he laughed at me. Said you were one of the best on the force."

"You really asked him that?" I whisper. It seems like such a simple solution to something I've agonised over for weeks. Too simple, perhaps. I can't bring myself to rely on his answer. "Did you believe him?"

She shifts to look up at me. "Absolutely. He could've strung me along, but he didn't."

I hug her to me and she wraps a hand in my sweater.

"Thank you," I say, still gobsmacked.

"Seemed the least I could do." She's drowsy, her words slurring, and I suddenly understand why she's insisted on telling me everything now.

"Pryce?" I shake her gently, then with more force. "*Pryce?*"

Her hand has dropped into her lap, and when I switch the torch on, her face is grey, her eyes half-lidded.

"No, no, no!" I hold my palm in front of her mouth. She's still breathing, but the puffs of air brushing my fingers are shallow and rapid. I take off my sweater and lower her onto it, and then prop her feet up on a fallen branch. I'm so preoccupied that I don't even notice the light until a gleam of it catches her face, and for a second I think it's my own torch.

"Fuck!" I scramble in front of her, grapple for the gun, and aim for the light. It's a headlight, and it snaps off almost at once, followed by the slam of a car door and footsteps crashing in our direction. I squint, losing my target, the din ebbing to nothing and then blaring as I swallow. Another light blinds me, and I shield my eyes, my finger twitching toward the trigger. Multiple lights, I realise. Three, four beams, cutting through the trees. I glance back toward the clearing. It's suddenly ablaze with flashes of blue and red, and I hear the beat of an approaching helicopter. Someone is yelling at me, his Welsh accent more apparent as he gets closer. He calls me by name, and I throw the gun down, place my hands behind my head, and let him come to us.

❖

"It might be fractured again." The paramedic pushes more gauze into the remnants of my cast, attempting to cover the lacerations Jez inflicted. "How the hell did this happen?"

"Bloke tried to cut it off, so I smacked him with it," I say. I'm not paying much attention to him, because another team of paramedics is swarming all over Pryce, and I'm watching them like a hawk. "Will she be okay?"

He pauses to study the numbers on the monitor they've attached to her. "I think so. You'd almost stopped the bleeding before we got here. There's no way we can tell what the bullet's hit—she'll need surgery to sort that out—but she's stable at the moment." He tilts my chin. "How are you feeling?"

"Like I knackered my arm and got belted in the face."

"What a coincidence," he says. "Do you want any painkillers?"

I shake my head as another man approaches us. He's dressed the same as everyone else here—thick coat, boots, beanie hat—but the officers practically stand to attention when he passes them. I get to my feet, determined to meet him on the level, and it mostly goes to plan, once I've propped my arse on the rock to steady myself.

"DI Keelan. I work with DS Pryce." He shakes my hand. "I've spoken to DI Ansari. He's on his way, but the weather is a problem."

"Did you get him? The man chasing us, did you get him?" I ask. I don't give a shit about Ansari. I want to know where Dee is.

Keelan acknowledges his oversight with an apologetic nod. I can't blame him for being distracted, given that his DS is lying unconscious on a stretcher at his feet. "We—sorry, yes, we got him. His tyre blew out half a mile up the road, and he hit a wall."

"Fancy that," I say, thinking fondly of my scissors. "How hard did he hit it?"

He chuckles, and I immediately warm to him. "Hard enough to break his pelvis. He was screaming like a banshee when we arrived on scene."

"And Je—DC Stephens?"

"Critical but stable. Did you know he was diabetic?"

I rub my bad arm. There's blood covering the writing on the cast, but I can't tell whose it is. "Yes, he told me."

"Well, his injuries were fairly minor, but his blood sugar was through the roof."

"That explains a lot. Speaking of which…" I dig one of the drives from the split in my cast and hold it out to him. I'd rather someone unconnected to MMP had first dibs on it. "Hopefully, this'll explain the rest."

I glance at Pryce as Keelan tucks the drive into an inside pocket. Her face is mostly hidden by an oxygen mask, but I take heart from the sight of her breath misting the plastic.

"I owe her everything," I tell him. "Just—just read the file."

There's not much else I can say, and this standing-up lark is starting to lose its appeal. We shuffle out of the way as the medics and a Mountain Rescue team carry Pryce carefully past us.

"Are you able to walk out of here?" he asks.

"Can I travel with her?"

"I'm not sure. I'll ask the paramedics."

I take his arm. "Right, then. Let's go."

CHAPTER TWENTY-TWO

Apparently, Pryce isn't the only one who needs surgery, but I'm low on the Ysbyty Gwynedd priority list. I get X-rayed and CT scanned, but I'm still in A&E, gowned and tripping on morphine, when Dr. Lewis enters my cubicle.

"Can't stay away, can you?" she says.

I sit up properly, thrilled to see a friendly face. "It's not for want of trying. Any news?"

She perches on the bed and puts a hand on my leg. She's been crying; her eyes are red and puffy. "If I tell you, will you stop bugging the nurses for updates and behave yourself?"

I cross my heart, and she shakes her head, not believing me for a second. "She's just gone to theatre," she says, relenting. "The bullet shattered her shoulder blade. Bone fragments nicked an artery and partially collapsed her lung. The brachial plexus—the group of nerves supplying the hand and arm—is probably damaged, but we won't know how badly until Neuro have assessed her."

I gape at her. I'd realised it was serious, but not this kind of serious. On the telly, everyone gets shot in the shoulder, and all they get is a sling and some sympathy.

"There's a full team in there with her," she says. "Try not to worry."

"Are *you* worried?" I ask quietly.

She looks down at the sheets and nods. "Three days, Alis. Those men held her there for three days. She must have been petrified."

"I know." I've been trying not to think about it, but whenever I'm alone I start with the "what-ifs?" What if things had gone differently that night in the hotel? What if I'd never sent the email? What if she'd never offered to help in the first place? What if I'd never accepted? I don't want to get my life back, possibly even my career, only to see her lose hers.

"She was asking for you," Lewis says. "I told her you were here and doing fine." She clears her throat as if she has something else to add, but she thinks better of it and gets to her feet instead. She finds my notes and leafs through them. "Did you hit your head again?"

"Yeah, but not hard enough to knock any sense in."

She smiles. "Oh, I don't know. You've got good taste, at least."

"Fuck. Is it that obvious?" This thing, whatever this is with Pryce, it mustn't *be* obvious. Our bosses, the SMIU, the CPS, they can't know about it, or it'll jeopardise every aspect of the case we have against the Hamers and Jez. We might get away with having worked the evidence together and run down leads together, and if we're very lucky they'll overlook the fact that we did all of it in secret, but any hint of a sexual relationship between us would be a gift to a defence lawyer, tainting everything we've managed to achieve.

"No, it wasn't obvious. I just know her very well," Lewis says. She puts my notes down and folds her arms. "And it'll remain confidential."

"Thank you."

"I'd advise you to ease off on the nurses, though, because that's a dead giveaway. I'll tell you when she's out of theatre, and if you're in any fit state I'll get you in for a visit."

I'd kiss her, had I not already exceeded my quotient for inappropriate behaviour. "I would really appreciate that," I say.

"Not a problem. Do you need anything?"

"No, I'm okay."

"Hmm. You should get your head down for a bit. You look like crap, and it'll be a while before they're ready for you." She adjusts my bed and dims the cubicle lights. "Better?"

"Much." I shuffle down, my eyelids drooping. "You'll definitely come and get me?"

"Definitely," she says, and that's the last thing I hear for a while.

❖

I'm not sure whether it's the snow or whether Ansari has found something better to do, but he never turns up in A&E. Lewis ducks her head in to tell me that Pryce is stable and comfortable in the HDU, and I go down to theatre mid-morning with a smile on my face and the second flash drive tucked into my paper knickers.

"This shouldn't take long," the orthopaedic surgeon tells me. Brandishing my X-ray, he points out the pins I've knocked loose. "Tighten this, realign that, and you get a new cast for six weeks." He lowers the film and peers over his glasses at me. "And you won't be clobbering anyone with it, yes?"

I flash him a Scout's honour salute once the anaesthetist has stopped sticking needles in my other hand. "Absolutely, Doc."

"Excellent. I'll see you in there."

He's as good as his word, and I shake off the anaesthetic with coffee and buttered toast in a side ward guarded by a uniformed officer. MMP might have encouraged Jo's death to slip beneath the media radar, but the taking hostage and subsequent shooting of a detective sergeant is too big a story to put a lid on, and the North Wales police are keen to keep the press or other potentially malevolent parties away from me.

I lick the butter from my fingers, contemplating the door whilst concocting a number of progressively outlandish schemes whereby I distract my guard and the medical staff and totter over to the HDU. I'm about to put Plan Three into action when Ceinwen opens the door and crashes a wheelchair into the jamb.

"So much for a stealth mission," she mutters, striding over to smooch me on the cheek. "How's my favourite Mancunian?"

"All the better for seeing you."

"Likewise. You've got mad bed-head, kid."

I pat my hair. It's sticking out at wild angles and pancake-flat at the back. "Is it salvageable?"

She whips out a comb and dips it in my jug of water. "Hold still a sec."

Once I'm coiffured to her satisfaction, she drags the wheelchair across. "Dr. Lewis has gone home, so she asked me to do the honours." She holds out a zippered hoodie with "Ysbyty Gwynedd" embroidered on its top pocket. "Stick this on. It's chilly in the corridors."

I take the sweater gratefully. My clothes are stashed away in evidence bags, and I'm only wearing an arseless gown. Goose pimples cover my arms as I'm hit by a sudden flash of Pryce staggering through the snow barefoot, and Ceinwen steps in to zip my hoodie right to the top.

"She was hypothermic when she came to us," she says, perceptive as ever. "But she's snug under a warming blanket now, and she's got some colour back in her cheeks."

"Has she?" I ask quietly. I'm nervous about seeing her, for reasons too many to count.

"Yes. Just a dash, mind. She's mostly been asleep, but she smiled when I told her I was coming to fetch you."

"All right, then." I settle into the chair, and Ceinwen fusses like a mother hen, arranging a blanket over my legs.

"Thank you." I tilt my head so I can see her. She's all blurry, and she dabs my cheeks with a tissue.

"None of that, now," she tells me. "You're both going to be fine."

The HDU is pretty much the same as when I left it, with the exception of the police officer outside the fourth room and a frisson of excitement at the nurses' station. The officer stands as we approach, holding the door while Ceinwen manoeuvres the chair through. She parks me at the bedside.

"I'll check on you both in a bit." She drapes the call button across the pillow. "Press this if you need me any sooner."

As the door closes behind her, I chance my first look at Pryce. I don't expect her to be awake and looking at me, though it really shouldn't come as a surprise.

"Hiya," I say. I'm close enough to reach her hand, and I take it without thinking, threading my fingers through hers. "You should be asleep."

Her smile is drug-soaked and lazy and lovely. "So should you."

"Well, I was all ready for some shut-eye when Ceinwen came to cart me down here." I shrug, feigning nonchalance, but I can't keep my face straight, and she laughs. "How are you feeling?" I ask.

There's an IV dripping blood and fluid into the hand I'm holding, and a thin oxygen tube beneath her nose. I learned how to read the monitors during my previous stay here, so I know her heart rate is too fast and her blood pressure is too low.

"Lucky," she says. "They fixed almost everything. Might be left with a numb little finger, but I can live with that." She coughs, hoarse from the anaesthetic, and her pulse shoots up as the pain bites.

"Breathe," I tell her, feeling the pinch of a phantom chest tube. "It'll pass in a few seconds."

"Mmm." She's quiet until it eases, and her grip on my hand slowly relaxes. She licks her lips. "You break your arm again?"

"No, just buggered up a couple of the screws. Here, try this." I perch on the edge of the bed and offer her a spoonful of ice chips. She sucks them greedily, her tongue chasing the meltwater. I'm about to return to my chair when she catches my wrist and raises my hand, kissing the palm gently and then placing it against her bruised cheek.

"Stay," she whispers, as I'm busy relearning how to inhale. "Please?"

I can't remember her asking me for anything, certainly not like this, but someone could come in and see us, and they wouldn't even need to read between the lines, because it's all there in her eyes. Then I think, fuck it and fuck them, so I kiss her, and her lips are cold until they part and I feel the heat of her mouth. Neither of us is capable of finesse, and our teeth clack together as an alarm pings to warn us something's gone awry. No one outside seems to notice, though, and we pull away in our own sweet time, rumpled and flushed and still upsetting the monitors.

"Bloody hell," I say. I rub my sweaty cheek. "Bloody hellfire." With no sign of eloquence returning, I resite a little pad that's supposed to be on her chest and has ended up stuck to the bed rail, and the alarm stops wailing.

"Is that a good 'bloody hellfire' or a bad one?" she asks.

"It's a good one." I kiss her again, gentle and quick. A promise, nothing more.

"We'll have to be careful," she says, fighting to stay awake and sound sensible. "Till it's all finished."

"I know. We'll be careful. Don't worry."

She cracks an eye open. "Are you going to start calling me 'Bron'?"

I laugh. "Probably not."

"That's okay. I don't mind 'Pryce' when you say it." She winces as something pulls, but then her breathing steadies and slows.

I wait another minute, reluctant to move despite the ever-increasing risk. I've got one foot on the floor when she stirs and tugs urgently on my sleeve.

"The bullet's in my coat pocket," she says. "From the warehouse. They never found it. Didn't even look."

"Pryce," I lay her hand across her lap, "go to sleep."

"Might match mine," she murmurs.

"It might. I'll tell your boss to check. Now go to sleep."

She nods, satisfied that she's covered everything, and this time she settles properly. I resume my vigil from the wheelchair. If the medics want me back in my room, they'll have to drag me there.

❖

Deemed fit for discharge at morning rounds, I treat myself to a long, one-armed shower and then sit on my bed, swinging my bare legs and hoping some kind soul has retrieved the spare clothes from my car. Half of what I packed must have been cut off Pryce in A&E, but at least I'll have clean knickers and a pair of jeans. I'm aware of feeling weird: too cheerful, and bordering on flippant. I know the events of last night will hit me like a sledgehammer at some point, but for now I'm happy to be alive and in the clear, and even happier to have this as yet indefinable thing with Pryce.

One of the night shift nurses, her mind clearly warped by sleep deprivation, tells me someone will be here to pick me up in a couple of hours, though she can't remember who. She took the name down and promptly lost the piece of paper in a pile of notes.

"It was a man," she says. "Definitely a man…I think."

Whoever the "man" is, he'd better have ID and written authorisation to play my taxi driver, or I won't be going anywhere. I kick my heels against the bedrail, dreading the prospect of being stuck with Wallace or Ansari as a chauffeur. I'm too strung out for polite conversation, my thoughts still centred on HDU bed 4, where Pryce was cogent enough at dawn to send me back to my own room. I'm not sure when I'll next be able to visit her. If I'm whisked off to Manchester for an SMIU debrief, she'll be fully recovered and back at her desk before I see daylight again.

Bearing that in mind, I cadge a pair of slipper socks from an obliging auxiliary, tell my guard to turn a blind eye for twenty minutes, and follow the breakfast trolley out of the ward. After a brief detour to the cafe, I head for the HDU, where I find Pryce attempting to adjust the head of her bed with a recalcitrant remote. Something of an expert in these matters, I take it from her and keep the correct two buttons pressed in unison until she sighs with relief. She's been hooked up to her own morphine pump during the morning, but the beads of sweat on her forehead suggest she's gone cold turkey.

"Is that proper coffee?" she asks, her gaze fixed on my cup.

"It is, but aren't you nil by caffeine or something?"

"Not to my knowledge. They're quite keen to give me all sorts of drugs."

I smile and hold the cup for her, letting her take a sip.

"God, that's good," she whispers. She licks froth from her upper lip as I swallow a mouthful from the opposite side of the rim. The coffee is sweet and rich, and there's real comfort in the relative normality of this morning routine after the grim horror of the last two days.

"I've been discharged," I tell her. "I'm getting a lift home at ten-ish."

"Hopefully, I won't be too far behind you."

We both know that's very optimistic, and we finish the coffee without speaking. She's still subdued afterward, the healthy glow she acquired from the steam vanishing almost at once.

"Y'know, those drugs they're giving you don't work if you're not actually taking them," I say.

She makes no attempt to deny it. "They make me feel stupid and woozy."

"That's the point. You got shot, Pryce. You don't have to tough it out."

She shakes her head. "I'd rather be awake," she whispers, and she sounds so lost that I have to swallow past the grief that suddenly closes my throat.

"Are you having nightmares?" I manage to ask.

"No. Not that I can remember. It's just…they don't really tell me what they're doing, and I can't"—she lifts her hand, trailing wires and tubing—"I can't stop them."

She doesn't say anything else. She doesn't need to. I can see the abrasions from the duct tape and the trail of blistered burns on her arm.

"I'll have a word with Lewis," I say, which is about the best I can offer. We got away with it last night when the ordeal was fresh and raw, but I can't sit here indefinitely, as a bona fide girlfriend would. I can't bring her personal items from home or help her to shower or brush her teeth.

I bow my head, pissed off at being so utterly useless, and when I raise it again she's curled on her side, crying silently. The door is still shut, the blinds drawn at its small window, but I couldn't care less if someone does see us. I can't bear to leave her like this. I kiss her forehead and her cheek and use the sleeve of my hoodie to dry her tears. Her face is creased with pain, her hand tangled in the sheets and nowhere near the morphine pump. I know how the pump works and how long the dose will last. I can stay with her for that long.

"We've got till ten," I say. "Do you want me to press this for you?"

She nods slowly and lets me push the button, and I spend our last two hours together watching over her as she sleeps.

CHAPTER TWENTY-THREE

I return to my room a quarter of an hour early, intent on denying everything when my escort arrives, but the sight of DI Keelan standing by my window immediately puts paid to that notion. I keep my distance, letting him speak first.

"How is she?" he asks. There's no accusation or insinuation behind his question; he sounds exhausted and genuinely concerned. I sit on the corner of the bed closest to him. I'd rather he be here than anyone from MMP.

"She's in pain, and she's going to need a lot of support, even though she'll hate it," I tell him, because he's the one who'll need to provide this support now that I can't.

He nods, taking everything on board. "I'm going to see her this evening, and I've already spoken to a counsellor."

"You know what happened to her, then?"

"More or less. I read through your files, and Stephens volunteered for interview at the crack of dawn. He seems eager to avoid a lengthy sentence, particularly one with the Hamers as cellmates. He filled in a lot of the blanks." Keelan hands me a plastic bag full of neatly folded clothes. "I thought you'd appreciate these. Your DI is on his way to our HQ. We agreed it would be a sensible precaution for your debrief to take place at Colwyn Bay. If you're feeling up to it, that is."

"I am, and that's a very good idea," I say, delighted to have an independent observer accompanying me.

"Your DI was most amenable," he adds.

I don't laugh until I'm in the bathroom. I like Keelan a lot. He's got a fucking brilliant poker face.

We keep conversation to a minimum in the car. I have a ton of questions, but I want the full story, not snippets thrown out at red lights and stop signs. When we reach the HQ, he opens my door and lets me hang on to him as we negotiate several inches of slushy snow. Curious looks and whispers follow us up to the fourth floor, where he leads me to a pleasantly furnished interview room with its own brewing facilities and a window for natural light. He shows me where everything is and heads off to wait for Ansari.

I'm halfway through my first mug of coffee by the time he returns, showing Ansari into the room and then standing aside to admit my surprise guest, DS Granger. I attempt to stand on legs that feel like cotton wool, but Ansari waves me back into my seat. He helps himself to a brew, offering one to Granger as an afterthought. Keelan gets his own, topping up mine before he sits down.

"Detective Constable Clarke. You've certainly been busy, haven't you?" Ansari says. In deference to Keelan, he keeps his tone convivial, but he looks livid. I can't blame him for being angry. He's my immediate superior, but I went behind his back instead of trusting him to help me. It's a slight he's obviously not going to forgive in a hurry.

I say nothing. It's a tactic that proved effective the last time we met for drinks and conversation, and it does the trick on this occasion as well.

"Yes, right, then," he says as the seconds tick by on the clock behind his head. "Shall we get started?"

Granger places a handheld recorder onto the table and hits the red button.

"Two hours," Keelan states. He's watching the device, making sure he's on the record. "This interview will terminate no later than twelve fifty-three, for reasons pertaining to DC Clarke's recent surgery and her physical condition."

"Noted," Ansari says. He clears his throat, runs through the formalities—during which I decline the presence of a Fed rep—and consults the file on his lap.

"What's happened since you found us?" I ask, before he can begin. I'm not going to submit to an interrogation. They undoubtedly know more than I do at this point, and a trap would be easy to wander into.

He scowls, losing his focus, and it's Granger who steps uninvited into the breach. "DI Keelan uploaded your files to us while DS Pryce was in surgery. We knew we'd have to act fast before word got back to the Hamers, so we called in most of the MCT and worked through the night, analysing the information you'd collated. At approximately six thirty yesterday morning, we carried out a series of raids, making eighteen arrests across the Hamer family and business, including a number of their ancillary suppliers, purchasers, and distributors. The Ardwick factory has been sealed off, and drugs with a seven-figure street value were seized, along with half a dozen firearms." She nods her appreciation at me. "It was quite the haul."

"What about the Copthorne warehouse?" I ask. "Did you find Krzys's body?"

"No, we didn't," she says, and there's a hint of compassion in her voice, belying her stony demeanour. "It must have been moved prior to us searching the premises." She looks at Ansari. "Shall I start from the beginning, sir?"

He exchanges his notes for his coffee and settles back in his chair. "Go ahead," he tells her, and she turns to me, none too subtly dismissing him from the proceedings.

"I interviewed DC Stephens with DI Keelan this morning," she says. "He's angling for a deal, so he's been quite cooperative. Two years ago, as part of a wider investigation into forced prostitution, he received a tip relating to a business on Copthorne Road, but Donald Hamer Jnr.—the man you know as 'Dee'—paid him to bury the information and take no further action."

"Why would he agree to that?" I ask. I can't hide my dismay. Jez Stephens was a good bloke, one of my best friends on the force. It's hard to believe how close he came to murdering a fellow officer.

"He needed the money," she says bluntly, and then seems to recognise that won't suffice as an explanation. "He told a lengthy sob story about committing to a mortgage he couldn't afford and wanting to send his children to a public school, but it boiled down to him living beyond his means and getting into debt as a result. His marriage was in trouble, and he saw Dee's offer as a way to save it."

"He couldn't have asked a friend for help?" I say. I'd have helped him. I bet most of his immediate colleagues would have tried to do something if they'd known how desperate he was.

"Evidently not. Once his money worries eased, though, he started looking for an out, and he knew the Hamers were getting nervous about him. Dee asked him to go to Copthorne one night, where they forced Ms. Starek out at gunpoint and took her to the warehouse. Unbeknownst to Stephens, Mr. Janicki was already in the boot of the car. By implicating Stephens in Janicki's murder, the Hamers guaranteed his loyalty and dragged him even deeper into the business."

I push my coffee away. It's making me feel sick. "Did they wear masks or something that night?" I ask, and gulp the water Keelan puts in front of me. "Jo told me she'd never seen the faces of anyone from MMP."

"Balaclavas," Granger says. "We found a couple when we searched Dee's house. They're in the labs, along with a white transit van that the decomp dog showed a particular interest in. We suspect it was used to move Krzys's body after you and DS Pryce were seen at the warehouse."

I hold my glass to my forehead. The room is too hot, too crowded. "Can we open a window?"

Keelan shoves the pane up as far as it'll go, letting a frigid draught circulate. I'm tempted to stick my head out like a dog in a car— anything to help me think straight. I can't work the chronology out, and my questions are as slippery as eels, escaping within seconds of them occurring to me.

"Do you want to stop?" he asks.

I shake my head and then answer "no" for the tape. I go back to the beginning, walking through the case step by step. "Did Jez know I was UC at Hamer's?"

"Not until you took Ms. Starek to Wales," Granger says, "and by then he was up to his neck in it."

"He was in our car after we crashed. Did he tell you that? He and Dee ran us off the road, and they came down to us, and they left us for fucking dead. Did he tell you that when he gave you his life story?" I'm almost shouting, tears and snot flying everywhere, and Keelan pauses the tape and gives me a tissue. I blow my nose and then cover my face, humiliated by my outburst.

Unwilling to waste any more of his dwindling time, Ansari restarts the recorder with a stab of his finger. The sharp click of the button is like a slap to the face, and I turn back to Granger, crumpling the tissue and shoving it into my sleeve.

"You said Pryce and I were spotted at the warehouse. Were they already following us, or did they get lucky?"

"They'd been following you for days," she says. "Ever since you went to Ms. Starek's house."

"Jesus," I whisper. "How did they know?"

"The landlord contacted Donald Hamer Snr., as per a previous arrangement. Don Snr. tasked Dee to surveil the address, and that surveillance was heightened when you were identified at the house with DS Pryce. Shannon Millward added fuel to the fire by reporting her interview, but it was your search of the Copthorne warehouse that brought everything to a head. As soon as you found the body, they knew they had to act." Granger pauses to consult her notes, giving me time to digest what she's just told me.

"They meant to snatch us both, didn't they?" I say, thinking back to where I went and what I did after leaving Pryce's hotel room. "But they couldn't get me on my own, so they made do with Pryce at first."

"That about covers it. And then you found the flash drive, which provoked them into upping the ante."

"Don't remind me," I say, still riddled with guilt. "That's when they threatened her sister and her nieces."

"They're okay, by the way," Keelan interjects before I can ask. "DC Hughes checked on them, and they were unaware anything untoward had happened. Her sister is visiting her this afternoon."

I nod, thankful that Pryce will have someone other than her colleagues looking out for her. I rub the back of my neck. My arm's aching and making it difficult for me to concentrate as I grapple at yet another loose end. "Who was hacking my emails? Jo said there were two MMP officers on the books at Hamer's. Who was the second?"

There's an unspoken exchange between Granger and Ansari as they decide between themselves how much I'm allowed to know. They needn't be so cloak-and-dagger. I'm not interested in the culprit's name. I'm not about to mete out some kind of cack-handed vengeance on his arse. I just want confirmation that he's been arrested and that he'll pay for what he's done.

"He was a dispatcher in Comms," Ansari says, emphasising the past tense. "Once we knew he'd accessed your inbox, we were able to trace him through the server. He'd been in league with Hamer's for longer than Stephens, keeping his ear to the ground and passing on pertinent information. He was wasted in Comms; he could've found honest employment as a specialist tech, but the wage Hamer's offered was far more lucrative."

"How did he miss the UC assignment?" I ask. He can't have known about it, or I'd have been another body in the warehouse, rotting beside Krzys.

"We use a separate server for all UC work." Ansari states this as if it's obvious, but those of us at the sticky end of things aren't told much about the mechanisms keeping us safe. We're prepped on a need-to-know basis and expected to trust the rest to those higher up the food chain.

There's a pause as Granger goes to fill the kettle. She stands by the counter to wait, her arms folded. She looks as disgusted as I feel. "We've cast a wide net to identify other members of MMP who might have been employed by Hamer's," she says. "But so far, so good."

I'm unconvinced by her optimism. "They'll be lying low anyway."

"Quite possibly," she concedes. She flicks the switch as the water begins to boil and waits for absolute silence before she continues. "We found nothing to suggest you were involved in any way."

"I know. Jez told Pryce that when she asked him." I aim the comment at Ansari. This is the first matter he should have settled with me. He had no idea Pryce had already done his job for him. "Will you tell Jo's family the truth now so they can take her home?"

He squirms a little beneath the challenge. I doubt that's even crossed his mind, with all the swaggering he'll have been doing for the media since the raids.

"I'm sure that can be arranged," he says. "Now, in terms of your conduct—"

I raise a hand. Fuck him, I haven't finished. "There's a bullet in DS Pryce's coat pocket. She recovered it from the warehouse the night we found Krzys. It'll probably match the gun used to shoot her, which should tie Dee to the murder. She submitted a blood sample to the North Wales labs as well, taken from my apartment after someone tried to break in. She estimated four to six weeks for the results, but you might want to put a rush on it."

Keelan smirks and jots a note. "I'll speak to SOCO—they're still at her cottage—and I'll contact the lab."

"Cheers." I lean back in my chair. Granger has poured me a fresh mug of coffee, and it smells good. The wall clock reads twelve thirty-four, leaving Ansari nineteen minutes to read me the riot act. Much as he'll want to rant and rave, though, his hands are all but tied. MMP have scored a massive success with the infiltration and subsequent dismantling of a major drugs ring. They've solved two murders and apprehended two corrupt employees, and they can boast about all of it without needing to mention the lengths I went to to put a tick in their win column. Ansari might be an arsehole, but he's not stupid, and he'll be hard pushed to find real fault with what I did.

Granger stirs a sweetener into her tea, her spoon tinkling against the mug. "The SMIU will shortly be signing off on your case, DC Clarke," she says. I watch Ansari's dark skin redden, but he doesn't intervene.

"We'd like to thank you for your patience and your assistance. You will of course be asked to testify when the prosecutions go to trial."

"Of course," I say, matching the polite formality of her tone.

She checks the clock: fifteen minutes. "Counselling is available, should you require it, and I'm sure DI Ansari will be in touch as soon as Occupational Health has approved you for active duty."

"Thank you," I say. I truly am grateful to have her on my side, but I won't be returning to MMP. It doesn't matter what the outcome of the investigation proves; Jez was a popular officer, and some of my colleagues will always blame me for his downfall. I'll be the unstable, brain-injured detective whom no one trusts or wants to work with, the one who fucked off to cosy up with the Welsh police rather than confide in them.

I can't tell what Keelan sees in my expression, but he holds up his pen to prevent anyone else speaking.

"I think that's enough for now," he says, and turns off the tape.

EPILOGUE

L *landdwyn Island, 1-ish?* the text reads. *Up at the far end near the lighthouse. Make sure you time it right or you'll get your feet wet.*

Following the directions tagged onto the message, I park at the nature reserve and walk barefoot along the beach toward the small tidal island. It's a warm day for early June, the sun bright in cloud-free skies, with enough of a breeze to whitecap the waves. I tie my sweater around my waist and roll up my jeans, enjoying the sensation of damp sand between my toes. I haven't been to the seaside in years, and my scant childhood memories mainly evoke grey, miserable weekends spent shivering behind windbreaks and dropping pennies into slot machines that never paid out.

It's beautiful here, though. The sand is clean and dotted with shells, and the water is sparkling in the sunshine. Low tide makes the crossing easy, and I get my feet wet only because I paddle in the shallows on the way over. Back on dry land, I kneel to put my trainers on for the rough path to the lighthouse. The snub white building stands out on the horizon, marking our rendezvous spot, and I fumble with my laces despite having two fully functioning hands. I didn't expect to be so apprehensive. I've seen Pryce almost every week since her discharge from hospital, but snatched conversations outside a courtroom or sitting in the same briefing room don't constitute a date, and that's what today will be. Our first, honest to goodness, have a picnic and hold her hand if she'll let me, date.

The path gains height, passing the ruins of an ancient chapel, and I catch sight of her sitting on a tartan blanket. She's found an ideal spot on the far side of the lighthouse, a patch of grass sheltered from the main tourist route, with a view across to Snowdonia. You get the best of all worlds in this part of North Wales—beaches, lakes, and mountains—and even though I'm still more of a city girl, I'm rapidly falling in love with the place.

The wind catches her hair as I walk closer, and she rearranges it with her fingers. She tolerated a week of relying on other people to tie it back for her before she had it cut much shorter, and it suits her, no matter how self-conscious she is about the new style. She looks up as she hears my footsteps, raising her sunglasses and smiling at me.

"Gorgeous, isn't it?" she says. "I thought you might like to explore on your own for a while instead of meeting in the car park."

I sit beside her on the blanket and kick off my trainers again. "Were you giving me a fair chance to chicken out as well?"

"Maybe." She drops her glasses back down. "But I'm glad you didn't."

She leans against a tufted mound of grass, tugging at my belt until I join her and then taking my hand. She still has no sensation in her little finger, but it curls around mine with her other four.

"Have you unpacked anything yet?" she asks.

"Half my clothes. All my underwear," I say. Then, as an afterthought, "On Saturday."

I can't see her eyes, but I suspect she's rolling them. "Well, it's a start at least."

I've been in my new flat in Bangor for five weeks, and most of my stuff is still in boxes. As the first case against the Hamers went to trial, Keelan got wind of my pending resignation from MMP and head-hunted me for a newly formed offshoot of his own Major Crimes Team. He didn't need to ask me twice. The team deals exclusively with young offenders, and the workload has verged on overwhelming since the initiative launched. I'm enjoying the job, and I've been welcomed with open arms by my new colleagues, who credit me with saving the life of their DS. Everything seems a little too good to be true, and I don't want to jinx it by assuming I can stay and making myself at home.

I've obviously been quiet for a while, because she nudges her bare foot against mine. "How's the Welsh coming along?"

I groan. "It's not. Pendry's been teaching me the basics. Well, swearing mainly." I reconsider. "Actually, *just* swearing, because I'm terrible at the rest of it. I've no idea how Keelan managed to wangle the rules on that one for me."

"He works in mysterious ways. If you learn how to bake a nice bara brith, he won't give a damn what language you speak."

"Pencil that in for our second date," I tell her. "Be warned, though, if you think my Welsh is crap, wait till you see me in the kitchen."

She takes off her glasses so she can stare at me properly. "What the hell am I signing up for here?"

I shrug. "Anecdotal evidence suggests I'm good at football, and I may have other, as yet undiscovered talents."

"Now that does sound quite promising." She strokes her thumb against the underside of my wrist, the contact feather-light but enough to make my breath hitch, and I kiss her long and slow, tasting the sea salt on her lips and earning a volley of wolf whistles from a group of passing schoolkids.

"I brought lunch," she murmurs as we part.

I nod, evaluating our options. Some of the kids are less than ten feet away and still gawping. "I put my bed together last night," I say. "And I have a balcony with a sea view."

She kisses me again, her lips still touching mine as she asks, "Are you trying to seduce me, Alis Clarke?"

"Absolutely. Is it working?"

"Yes, very much so." She cups my cheek. "Okay, then. Picnic, bed, balcony, and undiscovered talents. Not necessarily in that order."

"*Definitely* not in that order," I say and then hesitate. "Unless… crap. Hang on. What if one of my talents is basket weaving?" I pause for effect. "Train spotting? Stamp collecting? Jesus. I might be a tap dancer!"

She mutters something very impolite in Welsh and starts to laugh. "Those aren't the kind of talents I had in mind."

I shrug, all innocence. "I wouldn't know what they are. They're undiscovered." I hold out my hand to her. "Shall we go and find out?"

About the Author

Cari Hunter lives in the northwest of England with her wife, their cat, and a field full of sheep. She works full-time as a paramedic and dreams up stories in her spare time.

Cari enjoys long, windswept, muddy walks in her beloved Peak District. In the summer she can usually be found sitting in the garden with her feet up, scribbling in her writing pad. Although she doesn't like to boast, she will admit that she makes a very fine Bakewell tart.

Her first novel, *Snowbound*, received an Alice B. Lavender Certificate for outstanding debut. *No Good Reason*, the first in the Dark Peak series, won a 2015 Rainbow Award for Best Mystery and was a finalist in the 2016 Lambda Literary Awards. Its sequel, *Cold to the Touch*, won a Goldie and a Rainbow Award for Best Mystery. *A Quiet Death*, the final book in the series, won the 2017 Rainbow Award for Best Mystery.

Cari can be contacted at carihunter@rocketmail.com.

Books Available From Bold Strokes Books

Alias by Cari Hunter. A car crash leaves a woman with no memory and no identity. Together with Detective Bronwen Pryce, she fights to uncover a truth that might just kill them both. (978-1-63555-221-8)

Death in Time by Robyn Nyx. Working in the past is hell on your future. (978-1-63555-053-5)

Hers to Protect by Nicole Disney. Ex–high school sweethearts Kaia and Adrienne will have to see past their differences and survive the vengeance of a brutal gang if they want to be together. (978-1-63555-229-4)

Perfect Little Worlds by Clifford Mae Henderson. Lucy can't hold the secret any longer. Twenty-six years ago, her sister did the unthinkable. (978-1-63555-164-8)

Room Service by Fiona Riley. Interior designer Olivia likes stability, but when work brings footloose Savannah into her world and into a new city every month, Olivia must decide if what makes her comfortable is what makes her happy. (978-1-63555-120-4)

Sparks Like Ours by Melissa Brayden. Professional surfers Gia Malone and Elle Britton can't deny their chemistry on and off the beach. But only one can win… (978-1-63555-016-0)

Take My Hand by Missouri Vaun. River Hemsworth arrives in Georgia intent on escaping quickly, but when she crashes her Mercedes into the Clip 'n Curl, sexy Clay Cahill ends up rescuing more than her car. (978-1-63555-104-4)

The Last Time I Saw Her by Kathleen Knowles. Lane Hudson only has twelve days to win back Alison's heart. That is, if she can gather the courage to try. (978-1-63555-067-2)

Wayworn Lovers by Gun Brooke. Will agoraphobic composer Giselle Bonnaire and Tierney Edwards, a wandering soul who can't remain in one place for long, trust in the passionate love destiny hands them? (978-1-62639-995-2)

Breakthrough by Kris Bryant. Falling for a sexy ranger is one thing, but is the possibility of love worth giving up the career Kennedy Wells has always dreamed of? (978-1-63555-179-2)

Certain Requirements by Elinor Zimmerman. Phoenix has always kept her love of kinky submission strictly behind the bedroom door and inside the bounds of romantic relationships, until she meets Kris Andersen. (978-1-63555-195-2)

Dark Euphoria by Ronica Black. When a high-profile case drops in Detective Maria Diaz's lap, she forges ahead only to discover this case, and her main suspect, aren't like any other. (978-1-63555-141-9)

Fore Play by Julie Cannon. Executive Leigh Marshall falls hard for Peyton Broader, her golf pro...and an ex-con. Will she risk sabotaging her career for love? (978-1-63555-102-0)

Love Came Calling by C. A. Popovich. Can a romantic looking for a long-term, committed relationship and a jaded cynic too busy for love conquer life's struggles and find their way to what matters most? (978-1-63555-205-8)

Outside the Law by Carsen Taite. Former sweethearts Tanner Cohen and Sydney Braswell must work together on a federal task force to see justice served, but will they choose to embrace their second chance at love? (978-1-63555-039-9)

The Princess Deception by Nell Stark. When journalist Missy Duke realizes Prince Sebastian is really his twin sister Viola in disguise, she plays along, but when sparks flare between them, will the double deception doom their fairy-tale romance? (978-1-62639-979-2)

The Smell of Rain by Cameron MacElvee. Reyha Arslan, a wise and elegant woman with a tragic past, shows Chrys that there's still beauty to embrace and reason to hope despite the world's cruelty. (978-1-63555-166-2)

The Talebearer by Sheri Lewis Wohl. Liz's visions show her the faces of the lost and the killers who took their lives. As one by one, the murdered are found, a stranger works to stop Liz before the serial killer is brought to justice. (978-1-63555-126-6)

White Wings Weeping by Lesley Davis. The world is full of discord and hatred, but how much of it is just human nature when an evil with sinister intent is invading people's hearts? (978-1-63555-191-4)

A Call Away by KC Richardson. Can a businesswoman from a big city find the answers she's looking for, and possibly love, on a small-town farm? (978-1-63555-025-2)

Berlin Hungers by Justine Saracen. Can the love between an RAF woman and the wife of a Luftwaffe pilot, former enemies, survive in besieged Berlin during the aftermath of World War II? (978-1-63555-116-7)

Blend by Georgia Beers. Lindsay and Piper are like night and day. Working together won't be easy, but not falling in love might prove the hardest job of all. (978-1-63555-189-1)

Hunger for You by Jenny Frame. Principe of an ancient vampire clan Byron Debrek must save her one true love from falling into the hands of her enemies and into the middle of a vampire war. (978-1-63555-168-6)

Mercy by Michelle Larkin. FBI Special Agent Mercy Parker and psychic ex-profiler Piper Vasey learn to love again as they race to stop a man with supernatural gifts who's bent on annihilating humankind. (978-1-63555-202-7)

Pride and Porters by Charlotte Greene. Will pride and prejudice prevent these modern-day lovers from living happily ever after? (978-1-63555-158-7)

Rocks and Stars by Sam Ledel. Kyle's struggle to own who she is and what she really wants may end up landing her on the bench and without the woman of her dreams. (978-1-63555-156-3)

The Boss of Her: Office Romance Novellas by Julie Cannon, Aurora Rey, and M. Ullrich. Going to work never felt so good. Three office romance novellas from talented writers Julie Cannon, Aurora Rey, and M. Ullrich. (978-1-63555-145-7)

The Deep End by Ellie Hart. When family ties become entangled in murder and deception, it's time to find a way out... (978-1-63555-288-1)

A Country Girl's Heart by Dena Blake. When Kat Jackson gets a second chance at love, following her heart will prove the hardest decision of all. (978-1-63555-134-1)

Dangerous Waters by Radclyffe. Life, death, and war on the home front. Two women join forces against a powerful opponent, nature itself. (978-1-63555-233-1)

Fury's Death by Brey Willows. When all we hold sacred fails, who will be there to save us? (978-1-63555-063-4)

It's Not a Date by Heather Blackmore. Kade's desire to keep things with Jen on a professional level is in Jen's best interest. Yet what's in Kade's best interest...is Jen. (978-1-63555-149-5)

Killer Winter by Kay Bigelow. Just when she thought things could get no worse, homicide Lieutenant Leah Samuels learns the woman she loves has betrayed her in devastating ways. (978-1-63555-177-8)

Score by MJ Williamz. Will an addiction to pain pills destroy Ronda's chance with the woman she loves, or will she come out on top and score a happily ever after? (978-1-62639-807-8)

Spring's Wake by Aurora Rey. When wanderer Willa Lange falls for Provincetown B&B owner Nora Calhoun, will past hurts and a fifteen-year age gap keep them from finding love? (978-1-63555-035-1)

The Northwoods by Jane Hoppen. When Evelyn Bauer, disguised as her dead husband, George, travels to a Northwoods logging camp to work, she and the camp cook Sarah Bell forge a friendship fraught with both tenderness and turmoil. (978-1-63555-143-3)

Truth or Dare by C. Spencer. For a group of six lesbian friends, life changes course after one long snow-filled weekend. (978-1-63555-148-8)

Children of the Healer by Barbara Ann Wright. Life becomes desperate for ex-soldier Cordelia Ross when the indigenous aliens of her planet are drawn into a civil war and old enemies linger in the shadows. Book Three of the Godfall Series. (978-1-63555-031-3)